Phoebe and Zoe

Also by Charles Whittlesey

The Islander: A Romance of the Future
Summer Solstice: Poems at the Halfway Point in Life

Phoebe and Zoe

Charles Whittlesey

Grey Partridge Press
2015

First Printing: November 2015

ISBN 978-0-578-17096-1

Grey Partridge Press
2844 Quentin Avenue
St. Louis Park, MN 55416
www.charleswhittlesey.com

For my family: Nancy, Elizabeth, and Claire

�

Part One
1984

1

Zoe Connor made a more beautiful bride than any model on the cover of any magazine in any bookstore in the world.

Jeremy was listening to his mother in the middle of the ballroom when he sensed her approach. *Sensed* was not really the right word. One didn't *sense* the arrival of a shooting star, a blazing bolt through a starlit sky. Every eye in the room, while feigning interest in someone else, was following *her* as she flitted from table to table and person to person, brightening every face she hovered over, as if the sun had abruptly broken through the clouds.

He no longer heard his mother harping about the long lines at the bar and gazed instead at the center of attention, an explosion of white among the drab colors around her; next to Zoe, every color, no matter how vivid, faded into gray. For Jeremy, the ballroom itself dimmed and disappeared, leaving only *her*, a mere ten feet away, chatting up a stranger with the air of a long-trusted friend.

A garland of white roses crowned Zoe's dark chestnut hair, braided and pinned above her neck, and a wispy veil floated on her white-marble shoulders. The bridal bodice emphasized the sway of her lower back and the swell below it that disappeared into a bubble skirt sweeping the floor like a tiny parade float.

The body imprisoned by the gown—imprisoned was the only word, for no fabric could restrain the spirit of its owner—was by no means perfect, with a boyish waist and the breasts of a young girl, but the same could not be said for the face now turning his way. The *em* of her upper lip arced into a smile, as though suppressing a private joke, and the licorice-brown eyes peering at him from a distant world locked him in a stare that he could no more escape than gravity.

She has to be smiling at someone else. She can't be crazy enough to marry me.

Then he caught the glint in Zoe's eye—some off-kilter wisecrack or mischievous prank brewing in that original mind.

"Jeremy," his mother said, "at least you could pretend to listen."

He turned and faced her. Tonight his mother looked younger than her fifty-four years, but only because her face was layered in makeup like an oil painting.

"How can you blame me?" he said. "Right now everyone in this room wants to be me."

"When you were a boy, you looked at me like that, and I'm jealous. She's taking you away from me. You don't know how final this night is for me—you'll never be my baby again. I'm happy for you, Jeremy, but you can't expect me to be glad about giving you up."

For a moment, he felt a pang of sympathy for his mother, but the ploy for his affection choked it off.

Then suddenly *she* was there, the tulle of her skirt rustling against his pants as she took his mother's hands, holding them like a pair of reins, and gazed imploringly into her eyes. "Everything is *so* beautiful, Maggie—beyond my wildest dreams. Jeremy and I will never forget this night. And it couldn't have happened without you and Bill. It's so incredibly kind of you, so perfect, so amazing—thank you, thank you, thank you. I want to say it a thousand times, but it's not enough to let you know how grateful I am."

Mrs. Edwards beamed, her envy washed away by the flow of gratitude gushing from her daughter-in-law. Jeremy was shocked to see his mother tearing up. Zoe took the cue and hugged her tightly, making some of the guests mistakenly think the bride was sharing a special moment with her own mother, instead of her mother-in-law.

Mrs. Edwards wiped away a tear. "Treat her well, Jeremy. If you don't, I'll disown you and adopt Zoe. Now forget about us old people, you two, and go have the night of your life. You only get one of these, you know."

His mother turned and swished away in her black-sequined gown.

Zoe clasped his hand. "Your mother kills me. She acts so tough, but underneath, she's a mush."

"And you bring it out better than anyone."

She ignored the remark and gave him the mischievous grin again. "I want to show you something."

"So show me."

"Not in here," she said mysteriously.

"You'd better be quick. The toasting will start."

She answered by towing him across the floor, parting the guests before them.

"Now we know who's wearing the pants," yelled Ben Nelson, his best man.

"Don't go far," said his older brother, a groomsmen. "We're ready to go."

Jeremy shrugged, grinning while his elfin bride pulled him between the tables topped with white anthuriums. Before he knew it, they were heading down a vacant hall toward a pair of swinging doors.

When Zoe pushed them open, the glare and the noise struck Jeremy in the face. The stainless-steel counters shone like mirrors, and the temperature jumped 20 degrees. Knives hammered on cutting boards, steaks sizzled, and plates banged dully on countertops. Laughter and four-letter words bounced off the tile walls—but the noise quickly died down as the squad of white-clad men noticed the two intruders.

"Zoe—what are we doing here?"

Her smile relieved the kitchen staff. The pantry chef clapped, and a busboy jammed his fingers into his mouth and whistled.

Zoe's grin widened, but she kept tugging Jeremy over the tiles. She seemed to know exactly where she was going. The applause grew louder. At the back wall, she flung open the door, pulled Jeremy through it, and let it swing shut behind them. He suddenly found himself on a concrete landing overlooking the parking lot.

He stared at the cigarette butts littering the concrete like flattened moths. "Is that it? If you have one, you'll be hooked again."

She leaned over the handrail and peered into the twilight. "I don't want a cigarette."

"Then what?"

But she was already tripping down the steps as fast as her white heels let her, one hand bunching up her skirt, the other hand skipping along the rail.

"Zoe!"

She touched down in the parking lot, darted between the cars, and stopped at the curb, checked by the grass. Two sharp scissor kicks, and off flew her spiked heels. She hiked up her dress again and bound barefoot over the lawn. She slowed once to gaze back at him, still waiting on the landing, trying to puzzle out her plan.

At last he understood. "You're crazy," he shouted.

By the time he started down, Zoe was already flying over the fairway. He took the steps in twos, dashed across the parking lot, and galloped over the grass, but Zoe had already pulled so far ahead he could barely make out her white dress bouncing in the shadows. He tried to put on speed, but his flat-soled shoes slipped on the grass while Zoe's bare feet let her scamper like a rabbit. Seconds later, he found himself alone in the dark under a canopy of elms.

Breathing hard, he glanced around. A crescent moon and a few bright stars peeked through the branches. To his right, a pair of headlights snaked up the hill, heading for the clubhouse. To his left, the trees thickened and snuffed out the light. Straight ahead, the fairway stretched into the deepening gloom with no trace of his bride. "Zoe," he called out quietly. "Where are you?"

"Over here."

He spun around. Behind the bell jar of a weeping willow with boughs hanging like saffron beads, a blurry but luminous shape appeared.

He parted the boughs. Moonbeams poured through the branches and painted Zoe's bare shoulders with amber light. Her bodice, sewn with silver thread, sparkled like a sunlit brook. She held the folds of her skirt bunched around her knees, and with each breath she took, it rose and fell like a net full of fireflies.

Moonlight washed her expectant face. She let out a faint sigh, helpless to control it.

As he came closer, her smile broadened. She crunched up the fabric of her skirt and raised it over her thighs and then above her bare hips.

By now, no fear of discovery could hold him back. Had the whole bridal party suddenly arrived, he would have taken her right in front of them.

While they kissed, Zoe deftly unzipped him, slipped a hand inside, and pulled him free. He grabbed her bare thighs, raised her off the ground, and backed her into the willow tree. As he fumbled to clear one last fold of fabric, she threw her arms around him and whispered in his ear, "I love you, Jeremy."

"I love you too, Zoe," he breathed back a second before he found her, and then words became impossible as every muscle in his body, every ounce of his blood, every synapse in his brain focused on one thing only—as her breath burned his neck, her fingers clutched his back, and the tulle rustled around his waist—to lose himself inside the woman he loved and had dreamed of marrying since the very first day he'd seen her.

2

Zoe and Jeremy scrambled back to the bridal table and took their place of honor. Behind them, 20-foot tall windows overlooked fairways flowing like rivers between lofty elms. In front of this panoramic view, Zoe had placed two Doric columns, rented from a local theater, and festooned them with blooming boughs—in imitation of *Daybreak*, her favorite painting by Maxfield Parrish—and she'd caught and set free dozens of butterflies in the airy ballroom, many of which lighted on the centerpieces, looking like part of the decor.

Sitting next to the bride and gazing nervously into a sea of bobbing heads was Zoe's fraternal twin, Phoebe. Unlike Zoe's softly rounded face, Phoebe's high cheekbones, thin lips, and narrow jaw gave her a proud, unapproachable air. Unlike Zoe's eyes, which opened up to let you in, Phoebe's narrowed to keep you out. And when you spoke to Phoebe, her sharply focused stare seemed to size you up and find you lacking, which meant that most strangers saw her at her worst, while most saw her sister at her best.

The strange division of the wedding guests in front of Phoebe put her on edge. On the groom's side, the men all looked alike in their dark, tailored suits and power ties. Their wives, many younger and fitter than their husbands, were dressed in tasteful gowns that somehow flattered their figures regardless of their shapes.

On Phoebe's side, many of the men wore suits and ties, but the stiff clothing and formal setting clearly threw them off. Standing out was a lime-green polyester suit, a camelhair coat, and a pair of checked pants. A few had shoulders so broad they stretched their jacket seams, and they gripped their low-ball drinks in their hands like toddler's cups. Their wives had curled and blow-dried their hair like cotton candy, and their gowns showed too much skin. They would have looked more at home playing the slots in Vegas than dining and dancing at a country club.

But Phoebe had no trouble getting beyond their dress and seeing her friends and family for what they really were: hardworking, humble, and honest people—and while the guests on the other side intrigued her, she didn't really trust them. Unlike her own family and friends, who used words like simple tools—to convey ideas or express their feelings—the others used words not only for practical means, but also for some ulterior reason—to prove their superiority, flatter the listener, or hide the truth instead of speak it. And because Phoebe was a frank young woman with a logical bent of mind, this aspect of their conversation both put her off and flustered her.

The sound of tinkling glasses rippled through the hall. The bride and groom responded with a long and sloppy kiss.

The young man beside Jeremy stood and seized the mic. "I'm Ben Nelson, but tonight I wish I were Jeremy. Tell me—have you ever seen a bride as beautiful as Zoe Edwards?"

When the applause died down, he told the story of their meeting. In seconds, Phoebe had tuned him out and was mentally reciting her own speech, but she'd only gotten halfway through it when Ben's voice suddenly rose.

"These two have not only found their perfect partners, but they have a perfect life rolled out before them like a red carpet. Zoe just finished her first year teaching at Emerson High. She's passionate about her job—just like all the boys in her class are passionate about her—and Jeremy is a rising star at the Herald, where I'm proud to work beside him. He's the best writer I've ever known, and management has already noticed. Maybe someday, he'll even run the paper.

"So we all should be happy for this lucky pair. Marriages like this don't happen often. At most weddings, it seems clear the bride and groom love each other, but they don't always seem well matched, and sometimes you wonder if they really know whom they're marrying. You get the feeling that once the glow fades, they'll embark on that lifelong futile quest of trying to change their partner into someone else. But I know that won't happen to Zoe and Jeremy. These two are soulmates, and they make each other happy just the way they are. That's why their marriage is so special and why all of us are so happy to see them together. Please join me and raise your glass to Jeremy and Zoe Edwards."

As two hundred glasses clinked together, the knot in Phoebe's stomach tightened. Now it was her turn.

She stood up, took the mic from Ben, and faced the hundreds of eyes boring into her.

She glanced at her written notes neatly penned on the back of her wedding program, and a wave of fear struck her. Suddenly everything about her speech looked wrong. Ben had talked glowingly about the bride, and she, in turn, should say something flattering about the groom, but her notes hardly mentioned him. Telling the guests what she really thought of Jeremy was out of bounds anyway, yet she wasn't going to lie and praise him in front of all these people. What she'd written down, though, was even worse. Her speech made her sound obsessed with her sister, focusing on their childhood past more than Zoe's marriage. It began with a stilted, academic phrase, *In Greek, Zoe means life*, and went on to list all her winning qualities, which sounded fine, except for the contrasts she kept drawing between the two of them, which made her sound insecure and jealous.

What could she do? She couldn't read the speech she'd written, but without the time to gather her thoughts, she couldn't think of anything else.

A silence spread across the room. By now the guests could tell that Phoebe had panicked, and they were starting to squirm. She knew that only she could ward off the coming disaster, but no matter how she tried, she couldn't wring out a single word. Heartbeats pounded in her brain, and her breaths came out in staccato bursts. Finally, her eyes welled up with tears.

Zoe rushed to her side and hugged her. A murmur rose from the guests, who found the moment touching, but Phoebe felt judged and only grew more embarrassed. As soon as Zoe took the mic, she sat down, breaking into a sweat and blushing.

"You'll have to excuse us," Zoe said. "We're both choked up tonight. I already knew what you were going to say, Phoebe, but you don't have to—not to me, at least. You've always been my best friend and, next to Jeremy, the most important person in my life. I'm so lucky you're my sister, and I'm so happy that you drove all this way to be my maid of honor. I wouldn't have gotten married without you standing right here beside me."

Phoebe forced a smile, and Zoe began telling her own story of her courtship. Throughout her speech, and the many that followed, Phoebe fixed her eyes on the flowers, trying not to look as if she wanted to crawl under the table, a feat that required all her self-control. And when the applause from the last speech faded, she pushed back her chair and made straight for the bar. Now that her official duties were over, it was time to do some serious drinking.

3

Phoebe neared the bar, noting the line with a frown. Before she could take her place at the back, four burly men cut her off like a herd of buffalo. She poked the nearest shoulder blade. "Excuse me, are you in line?"

Her poking had no more effect on the man than a fly lighting on his back. Of course they were all in line. Now it would take forever to get a drink. She glanced at the bar on the room's other side, where only two guests were standing.

She crossed the carpet and quickly got a glass of red wine, but as she turned, the DJ put on *Burning Down the House,* and a mob rushed out and packed the dance floor. Her route blocked, she turned into a maze of tables and chairs, holding her glass aloft. As she moved between them, an elderly woman rolled back her wheelchair and nearly crushed her toes. Blocked again, she turned around, but a couple suddenly rose in front of her, holding hands while their freckle-faced boy fumbled with his camera. Boxed in, Phoebe could only wait, tapping her feet.

Beside her, two middle-aged men were leaning inward and speaking in low voices. The heavier one had rolled up his white sleeves, and he cradled a caramel-colored lowball in his thick fingers. "She does make a pretty bride, but you know what they say . . . "

Phoebe cocked her head to listen.

"You can take the girl out of the trailer court, but you can't take the trailer court out of the girl."

Phoebe's cheeks blazed. The man had barely finished before she dumped her glass of wine down his back. He pitched forward as the red stain ran to his belt. Just as fast, he stood and wheeled around, ready for blows, if need be, with the guilty party, only to stop and gape at the maid of honor holding her empty goblet and glaring at him.

"Sorry. I'm such a klutz."

The friend rolled his eyes. "Here, Tom—use my napkin."

Neither he nor Tom, whose shirt made him look like a stabbing victim, bought her apology, but given the setting, they could only stare at her, dumbstruck.

"I'd help you clean up," Phoebe said, "but they need me back at the trailer court."

By now a path had cleared, and she made her escape. She set her goblet on a vacant table and joined the bridesmaids on the dance floor, where the heads were bobbing up and down like bubbles in boiling water. *To hell with everybody. I belong here too.* She swung her elbows, stomped her feet on the parquet floor, and lost herself in a frenzy of twists and turns, knowing how silly she looked in her sea-blue gown, but no longer caring what anyone else thought.

4

By eleven o'clock, Zoe and Jeremy were saying their goodbyes. Half the guests had already gone, leaving the linen tablecloths littered with crumbs, half-finished drinks, and a few discarded wedding programs.

Zoe steered between the tables, her arms akimbo as she cinched up her bodice. She grabbed a bar napkin, blotted her brow, and fixed her eyes on a short, stocky man in a white shirt. He was sitting by himself and cupping his drink with both hands, into which he was staring sadly. Deep lines etched his brow, and his lips clamped together, straining his jaw. His hands appeared too large for his frame. They looked carved from ancient wood, scorched by the sun, gouged by steel, riddled with knots, and strangely dark as though dirt had worked its way under the skin and dyed it brown.

This man was Martin Connor, Zoe's father.

She gazed at him fondly. So far, he hadn't seen her. A peep of a smile turned up her lips. She lifted her skirt above her ankles and scuttled toward him. When he looked up and saw her coming, his face transformed. His eyes, the mirror image of Zoe's, came to life, and a grin cracked his stony face. He set down his drink and tried standing up, but a halo of tulle enveloped him as Zoe plunked herself down on his lap like a little girl. She wrapped her arms around him and kissed him on the cheek. "Are you okay, Dad?"

He smiled gratefully, but said nothing. They gazed at each other without speaking, not needing any words, as both understood what the other was feeling.

"I'm okay," he finally said. "Kind of a bittersweet night."

She knew just what he wanted to hear. "Nobody will ever take your place, Dad."

"You always say the right thing."

"It's easy when you speak your heart. You taught me that."

"I did?"

"Of course you did."

"Then why can't I tell you what I want to now?"

"You don't have to."

"No, there's something I need to say. Something I never told you." He stopped and winced. "But now that you're here, and you look so happy, I don't think I will. Not on your wedding night."

A wrinkle marred Zoe's brow. "If it's that important, maybe you should."

"I'll tell you after your honeymoon."

"C'mon. You can't leave me hanging."

He paused for a long time, but finally forced out the words. "Did you know you saved my life, Zoe?"

"Me? How?"

"If it wasn't for you, I wouldn't be here."

At last, she understood. Tears filled her eyes. "Mom told me never to ask you about that."

"I'm glad you never did."

She laid her cheek on his shoulder and sighed. "A person can't take credit for being born."

"It was enough. And everything you did ever since. Every smile. Every hug. Every stupid joke you told." He struggled on. "Every night when I came home from work, I always knew that you and your sister would be there, lighting up the house like two Roman candles. Just watching you was enough—do you know what I'm saying?"

"I think so."

"It's quieter these days. A lot quieter."

She studied his face and frowned. "How much have you had to drink, Dad?"

"Not too much. I'm fine."

"I'm thinking about Mom."

"She'll be all right. Don't sound like her."

"But I want this to be a happy night for everybody."

"It is. I've said too much. You'd better go now. Your plane leaves early."

Zoe stayed put. "You know things won't change that much. We're never going to move. We both like our jobs. And we're still coming over for dinner every Sunday."

"I know. But it's not the same."

It was pointless to argue with him, so she hugged him instead. "I couldn't have asked for a better dad."

He hugged her back more tightly than she expected. "And I enjoyed spoiling you rotten."

"You did spoil me rotten. It wasn't good for me."

"Yes it was. And don't you worry. Life will unspoil you soon enough."

"Maybe it will, but every problem has an upside too, like a coin. You just have to flip it over, and there it is."

"That's what I love about you, Zoe. Nothing dents your smile for long. Stay that way—promise me?"

"Don't worry, Dad. I won't ever change."

5

At midnight, Mr. Edwards shut down the bars. The bride and groom had gone to their suite, and their friends made up most of the lingering guests. It then became the tiresome chore of the Edwards, the Connors, and the bridal party to clear out the drunken stragglers and close up the banquet hall. It took them an hour, but finally the bills were settled, the flowers boxed up, the dead butterflies swept away, and the wedding gifts loaded into the trunk of Mr. Connor's Mercury for the long drive back to the house where Phoebe and Zoe had grown up.

Phoebe said little during the trip, brooding in the back seat as her parents relived their favorite moments from the wedding. After a pause, her mother asked, "Are you okay, hon?"

"Just tired," she said, hoping her parents would leave her in peace. Her father and mother exchanged looks but didn't press her further.

At last they turned down a dark alley and pulled into a garage behind a modest Tudor house overshadowed by tall elms.

Phoebe and her father lugged the gifts through the back door while her mother arranged the flowers in the living room. Built in the thirties, the house had more charm than most: arches set off the common rooms, mahogany cupboards warmed the walls, and hardwood floors made the house feel open in spite of its small spaces. When Phoebe entered the living room, a rush of nostalgia overpowered her. Crickets were trilling through an open window, calling up those muggy summer nights when she and Zoe would camp on the porch, making a cozy nest with blankets and pillows. The minute their father began snoring, they would sneak out the front door, circle back to the alley, and scurry two blocks down to the creek. Hidden among the trees, they would run down the dewy slopes to the water's edge, strip to their underwear, and swim in the shallow, slow moving current, pushing themselves along the sandy bottom like mudskippers. When they were older, they skinny-dipped and spied on lovers spooning or making love on the grass.

She remembered, too, how Zoe, at 15, had woken her up one summer night to confess that down by the creek she'd lost her virginity to a boy at school, and how much she'd been awed as Zoe laughed and cried and said she didn't know whether she was happy or sad or bored about the whole thing.

Phoebe kicked off her heels and climbed the bare wooden steps leading to her old room. Her feet were hot and swollen from dancing, and the planks felt cool and smooth on her soles. Reaching the landing, she flicked on the light and stared through the open door. The neatness of the room struck her as odd. It reminded her that no one lived here anymore, having the feel of a bed-and-breakfast staged with mock belongings. Years ago, her mother had taken down The Who and Steely Dan posters from the sloping walls, but her track and cross-country ribbons and a handful of trophies remained proudly on her dresser. The mix of books in the shelves was eclectic enough to confuse or intimidate the few boys who made it up these stairs—the poetry of Pablo Neruda, *Death in Yellowstone,* and *Gödel, Escher, Bach.* The shelf near the window was filled with sci-fi novels, historical romances, and a good-sized collection of bodice-rippers.

She sat on her bed and stared at her chipped red toenails. A flood of memories came rushing through her: lying in bed reading *Anne of Green Gables* or sneaking into Zoe's room with a bag of marshmallows and a flashlight to read comic books under a quilt or talk about the places they'd visit when they grew up—Morocco, Paris, but mainly Greece, where Zoe said she would kiss the waiters, dance in the Parthenon, and skinny-dip in the Aegean Sea.

The memories of those countless hours spent on this cramped upper floor came back so vividly that Phoebe had to get up and pad across the landing into Zoe's room.

Zoe's room, the mirror image of her own, looked more lived-in. The floor was sprinkled with dirty socks and underwear, and a red fleece robe and pink pajama bottoms draped over a wooden chair. On the desk a stack of paperback novels tilted like the Tower of Pisa. Over the bed hung a print of Degas' blissful ballerina, *L'Étoile,* which Zoe said expressed the way she felt whenever she danced. The shelves above the desk were packed with novels, plays, and books of verse—*On the Road, The Diary of Anaïs Nin,* and the poetry of Keats cohabitating with *Fear of Flying* and *The Story of O.*

She pulled out a thick paperback, *The Shining,* by Stephen King. What a crazy quilt of contradictions her sister was. Zoe, for all her independence and daring—always the leader between them—had scared herself silly reading this book one night and had run into her room, begging to sleep with her. And she did, too, hugging Phoebe like a frightened kid every time the floor creaked. God, how she missed those carefree days growing up together in this tiny house, when the two of them could have fun doing nearly anything, playing *Scrabble*, dancing to their old, crackly LPs, or even washing the dishes and fighting with the suds.

Life was no longer that simple, and now it was duller too. Comparing the present to those happy childhood days rudely broke the spell of her reminiscing and reminded her that in two more days she'd be stuck back in the boondocks of Putnam, Minnesota, where she taught high-school algebra to bored and badly behaving students—living by herself with no love in her life, no real friends, no work for the long, hot summer, and few diversions to help the time pass by.

6

She creaked down the stairs, clutching her pack of cigarettes, tiptoed past her parent's bedroom, and nudged open the back door. Outside, the damp air had snuffed out the breeze, and it stuck to her skin like a wet coat of varnish. The neighbor's elm blocked the light from the alley, painting the yard in pitch. Still barefoot, she padded down the stoop and followed the walk to her mother's garden. Rows of bean and potato shoots had shoved their way through the dirt, with not a single weed in sight. *That's so like Mom,* she thought as she lit her cigarette. *Everything in perfect order.*

She stepped onto the wet grass, which nearly hissed on her feet, and leaned against the garage wall. As she took a puff, a shadow moved across the back door, and a second later, her mother trod lightly down the stoop.

Phoebe's blue letterman jacket hung like a poncho on her mother, its long white sleeves enveloping her hands. A ray of light crossed Rose's face, giving Phoebe the odd impression that her own double was nearing; she'd forgotten how much they looked alike in her mother's old pictures. Growing up, she'd used them to guess how she might look at later stages of her life. Sizing her mother up now, she saw that Rose had kept her figure better than most women her age and recalled that she'd reached her late forties before lines appeared at the corners of her eyes and creased her otherwise flawless skin.

"Can't sleep, hon?"

"Not trying to."

"Are you still upset about the wedding?"

"No ... yes."

Rose studied her as though weighing the purchase of a used car. Phoebe knew the look. Once her mother had picked up the scent of trouble, the truth was certain to come out, and she steeled herself for the baring of her soul that she knew would follow.

"Remember that phase when you were jealous of Zoe? Tonight you reminded me of that. I thought your behavior was passive-aggressive—forgetting your speech, dumping wine down that man's shirt—yes, I heard about that. Forget *passive*."

"You didn't hear what he said about Zoe."

"It doesn't matter. If I didn't know better, I'd say you tried to sabotage her wedding."

"That's not fair. I would never do that."

"All right, but something's going on. And I can't believe you don't know what."

She blew smoke out with her sigh. "I've been thinking about it all night, Mom."

"And?"

She choked out the words. "I miss her."

"Good God, we all miss her. You should see your father moping around the house. I can't believe she still has that much power over you."

"But she's my best friend, Mom."

"And you had her to yourself for eighteen years. You had the same friends, teachers, even the same birthday parties. I was glad you were close, but you're 24, Phoebe. You can't stay in her shadow forever. You need to get on with your life. That's what she's doing. You should be happy for her."

"It would be easier if I was happy myself."

"Ah, now you're making sense."

"It bugs me that everything that comes so hard for me comes so easy for her, like making friends and meeting guys."

"You're different, that's all."

"I don't want to be jealous, Mom, and I don't want to be like Zoe either— even if I could. I want to be myself." She bit her lip. "But I'm not sure who that is."

"So her wedding gave you an identity crisis."

"Well, why wouldn't it? Look at Zoe—she's happy. She likes who she is, she loves her job, and her students worship her. She's married to a guy—well, he doesn't do much for me—but Zoe adores him, and if she asked him to, he'd give up everything for her. They have fun together. They have a future. What do I have?"

"You don't have a future?"

Phoebe crushed out her cigarette. "I suck as a teacher. Ninth graders give me stage fright."

Her mother didn't reply, but even in the dark, Phoebe could read her disapproval.

She fought the urge to light another cigarette. The urge was alarmingly strong. "It's true. The kids hate me. Even the parents hate me."

"Phoebe, I've been in the field twenty years, and frankly, none of the first-year teachers are very good. Their expectations are way too high—for the students *and* for themselves. It takes time to make a good teacher. How can you know after only one year?"

"I have the evaluations to prove it."

"Well, kids can be cruel. And these days they're not very respectful."

"The cruel ones I can take. It's the nice ones that kill me—*I come in for help all the time, and I still don't get it.* Or what about this? *Ms. Connor has good ideas, but she can't explain them very well.* How's that for someone who explains things for a living? I can count the students who gave me good evaluations on one hand, but they're already the best students in the class—they don't even need me."

"They do need you. You're a role model. You're the only woman who teaches math in your district. Most are coaches."

"All the coaches are better than I am."

"But you'll improve. They won't. Don't forget—you've chosen a worthy calling. You're shaping people's lives, not just selling some useless widget. The world needs people like you, now more than ever. Our leaders don't care about anything but money anymore—not fairness or justice or future generations—and if ordinary folk don't stand up for the things that really matter, we'll lose them. Is that what you want? Do you want to live for material things or do you want to make a difference in the world?"

"Don't worry," Phoebe grumbled, hoping to avoid a lecture from her mother, a delegate for the local Democratic Party. "I'm not going over to the dark side."

"I didn't say you were, but you should be proud of your calling."

"I feel bad saying this," Phoebe said, avoiding her mother's eyes. "I know how much you and Dad scraped to put me through college, but the truth is, I think teaching was a big mistake."

She waited anxiously for her mother's response, which took its time in coming. At last, Rose sighed. Phoebe's words had hit their mark. "Well, I raised you to be an independent young woman. If teaching's not right for you, do something else. You're certainly smart enough. You could probably do whatever you wanted."

"I doubt that," Phoebe said, although hearing her mother say it encouraged her.

"Of course you could. Today, that is. When I was your age, I had three choices: nurse, secretary, or teacher."

Phoebe had also heard this speech before. "You forgot streetwalker."

Her mother chuckled. "Well, it pays the most."

Phoebe hung a cigarette from her lip and rocked her pelvis. "How would I look under a lamppost in Putnam?"

Rose shook her head. "Change if you have to, but don't do anything rash. Wait a year and see how it goes. A year from now you might see it differently."

"I guess you're right," she said, but she didn't feel it.

"And remember, you still have to pay off that loan."

"Don't remind me," she complained. "Tricks on the side?"

"Aren't there any good men in Putnam?"

"Ron from the septic service keeps calling."

"Never make fun of a working man, Phoebe. Your father's a working man."

"I know, I know. Dad's great, and I love him, but all the same, I'm looking for something different. I hope that doesn't offend you."

Her mother became pensive. "That's a topic for another night. I'd better go in and see how he's doing."

Before leaving, Rose gave Phoebe the kind of hug that only a mother can give, warm and comforting as a down quilt on a cold winter night, and even though Phoebe stood four inches taller than Rose, she felt like she was five years old again—but the warm feeling rapidly faded, and a second later, her mother turned and left her alone in the dark, itching for one last cigarette.

7

A week later, Phoebe threw her suitcase in her Ford Fiesta and merged onto Highway Ten, heading for Putnam. The early morning traffic was light, and before long, city and strip mall gave way to country. The scenery swept by in waves of greens and blues—rows of newly sprouted corn, puffy clouds mirrored in still lakes, shelterbelts enfolding barns, and rows of jack pine lining the road like soldiers on parade.

But the further north Phoebe traveled, the more deserted the road became, the more the woods closed around her, and the deeper her mood sank. She normally enjoyed these quiet drives in her new car, but today, with every small town she passed through, she felt a growing sense of dread.

A resort town of 2,000, Putnam lay among a crescent of lakes carved out by a prehistoric glacier. The surrounding hills were low and gentle, with elms and oaks in every vale, but never so dense they hemmed you in, and you couldn't go a quarter mile without running into a lake—clear, deep, and cool. Had Phoebe been happier, the humble beauty of the land might have lifted her spirits, but for unhappy people, beautiful places do the opposite, reminding them of what their lives are lacking, and so instead the scenery filled her with loneliness.

Shortly past noon, she pulled into a gravel drive beside an old white farmhouse. Phoebe had rented half the bottom floor from Mrs. Perkins, a widow, whom she sometimes helped with housework for a break in rent. Her quarters were cramped—a small bedroom, bath, and kitchen that doubled as a dining room—but she had a private entrance, allowing her to come and go as she pleased, and the high school was only four blocks away, an easy walk even in winter.

She lugged her suitcase into the bedroom, where the air was hot and stale as a pharaoh's tomb. Before she finished unpacking she'd sweat through her shirt. She was just leaving for the supermarket to pick up a six-pack of cold Pepsi, when a fellow teacher, Debbie Tucker, called and convinced her to come into Dupont Lakes for a day of sunning, swimming, and drinking on the beach.

Dupont Lakes, or *DL*, was the largest town in miles. During the summer it filled with families, high-school students, and swarms of singles looking to escape the dullness of the nearby towns and enjoy its beaches, bars, and restaurants. As a first-year teacher, Phoebe had yet to experience the tourist season, and all winter long had listened skeptically to stories of wild parties, drinking, and one-night stands told by her students and more than a few of her peers.

By midday, she and Debbie were leaning back in folding chairs and basting in tanning oil on the sandy shore of Big Dupont. Across the lake, popcorn clouds rose into a vast blue sky. The air was so humid that every time you glanced up the clouds seemed taller. Fishing boats, pontoons, and powerboats crisscrossed the lake's calm surface, and jet skis left behind fast-fading contrails as they cut the water in two.

Debbie had shocked Phoebe with her floss-like yellow bikini. Phoebe knew Debbie as a good natured, thickset blond with big eyes and a ready smile. Only now she couldn't help noting how much of Debbie's weight sat in her breasts and butt, making her strong hands and thick ankles all but invisible to the men passing by. Basking in their stares while pretending to ignore them, Debbie chatted briskly and drank from a Coke can spiked with Bacardi. "You gotta get a new suit, Phoebe. You'll never see any action in that one-piece."

"I tried on a few bikinis, but I looked like a stripper."

"And you're complaining?"

"It didn't feel right."

"C'mon. Men are like fish. You need the right kind of bait."

"I didn't know we were fishing."

Debbie laughed. "I don't know about you, but I always keep a line out. Need some more?"

She handed her Coke to Debbie, who topped it off with Bacardi.

"Watch it. I don't want to get wasted."

"Why not?"

"There might be kids around—or parents."

"Putnam is 20 miles away. No one's going to see you. And if they do, so what? It's summer. It's our time to have some fun."

"I'm not a prude, but I don't want a reputation, or a DUI—"

"Don't worry, we can take my car. Your reputation is your problem."

"Fair enough," Phoebe said with a smile. "Bottom's up."

8

After a swim, they slipped on their jelly shoes and cover-ups and packed their beach chairs in the trunk of Debbie's powder-blue Mustang convertible. They stopped at a public restroom to reapply their makeup and then cruised with the top down through the back streets of DL. *What's Love Got to Do with It* came on the radio, and Debbie cranked up the volume. Phoebe smiled as the wind blew back her hair and cooled her face and neck. The Bacardi had given her a buzz, and the wind teased her tanned skin. The music, sun, breeze, and the glide of the car combined to make her sharply aware of her own body. She glanced down at her bare thighs. True, she wasn't curvy like Debbie, but her legs were long and lean and her skin was taut. *Why don't guys like me? What the hell do I have to do—throw myself at them?* She laughed out loud. *I must be drunk.* "Having a nice little party over there?" Debbie asked.

"I was thinking about what you said—keeping a line out."

Debbie pulled into the parking lot of the Holiday Inn. "Sun and water always rev me up too. Gonna put yours out?"

"Depends on what swims by."

"Well, there's a whole damn school of fish in there."

The bar at the Holiday Inn overlooked the beach, although by happy hour, the boiling crowd blocked any view of the lake. Phoebe and Debbie sat on barstools and nibbled at the free hors d'oeuvres until a table cleared, then fell upon it like falcons in a power dive. Two margaritas later, they hit the dance floor. Within minutes, two men cut in and paired off with them. When the song ended, they invited them back to their table, but the women said *no,* and the men vanished. "They're too old for us," Phoebe complained.

"And too married."

"I didn't see any rings."

Debbie rolled her eyes. "Guys that age are always married. Or divorced—or they say they are."

"You seem to be an expert on married men."

"I'm not opposed to them, but I do have standards. At least they could be rich."

Phoebe laughed at the joke longer than it deserved.

On her way back from the restroom, she noticed two men at a nearby table watching her. She pointed them out to Debbie.

"Hey, that's Peter Lundberg. He teaches gym in Battle City."

"Who's the other guy?"

"Dunno. Let's find out."

Phoebe tried protesting, her main concern being that Peter's friend was too attractive for her, but Debbie was already halfway across the dance floor.

By the time she caught up, Debbie was flirting with Peter. Phoebe had no choice but to sit beside his friend, Jake, who peppered her with questions in a direct but friendly manner. Something about him opened her up, as she rarely did with strangers, and within an hour, he knew more about her than Debbie. Whenever his questions became too personal, he read her discomfort and steered the conversation back to himself.

He told her he worked construction in the Twin Cities, although he seemed more educated than any construction worker she'd met, and he'd driven up for the weekend to visit his cousin Peter and enjoy the lakes around DL.

It felt right to Phoebe when he asked her to dance. He smiled at her shuffling in place, and she, in turn, welcomed his stares. A bit lightheaded, she swung her arms and hips freely. She was surprised to find herself having a good time, dancing with someone who found her attractive and who seemed to be a decent guy, and as the night wore on, she began to wonder where it might lead. *Whatever happens, happens,* she thought, because no matter what did, it was nice to let her guard down and nice to be wanted, regardless of how the night ended.

Around midnight, Phoebe and Debbie stepped outside for a cigarette. Phoebe puffed away as Debbie leaned against a Malibu and talked about Peter, just her type, she said—a fun-loving, fit, and wisecracking guy.

"Are you going home with him?" Phoebe asked, which Debbie seemed to imply.

"Do you care?"

"I'll be okay."

"What about you? It's pretty clear he likes you."

"Maybe."

"What if he asks?"

"I was thinking more like a date."

"Looking for your one-and-only?"

"I'm not sure. I'm a little drunk, and I don't want to screw this up."

"Either way, we have to figure out the cars. If I take Peter home, you'll have to leave with Jake."

"That could be awkward."

"No, it's perfect. He can drive you back to your car—or anywhere you want."

"Hmm. Not a bad idea."

Debbie hugged her but quickly pulled away. "Shit! Put that out. He doesn't smoke."

Horrified, Phoebe crushed out her butt. She'd been so engrossed the whole night she hadn't even wanted a cigarette. And Debbie was right—Jake didn't smoke. She hoped it wasn't a big enough flaw for him to write her off, and if it was, the haze in the bar would cover any trace of her crime.

Back at their table, he didn't notice the smell, but when the music turned slow, he led her out to the dance floor. He circled her waist loosely, holding back at first, but feeling her melt into his arms, pulled her tight and buried his nose into her hair. A second later, he tipped back his head. "I didn't know you smoked."

She cringed. "I know, stupid habit."

"Then why don't you quit?"

"You sound like my mom."

"You should. My uncle was 31 when he died of lung cancer."

When their dance ended, he told her about his favorite uncle's death, which had left a deep scar on his childhood. Now she felt stupid not only for smoking but also for upsetting him, which made it hard for her to focus on his story. The four margaritas didn't help, and her reaction, she was certain, came off as uncaring or defensive.

Debbie and Peter flew back from the dance floor. Unaware of the flap, Peter asked Jake, "Do you mind if I get a ride with Debbie?"

"If Phoebe doesn't mind."

"I thought maybe you could take her back."

"I'd be happy to. Phoebe?"

"I guess so, thanks."

Peter winked at Jake. "And don't worry. I won't tell Susan."

"Who's Susan?" Phoebe asked.

Jake frowned and his face turned scarlet. "Susan's my girlfriend."

9

Phoebe escaped to the bar and did a slow burn. So Jake was nothing more than Peter's wingman. And he'd done his job expertly, she had to admit, charming her up to the last second when Peter had scored and it was safe for Jake to bail out. Instead of being the object of his desire, she thought with a blush, she was only the *ugly friend* who needed distracting. It had all seemed too nice, too good to be true, and it was.

She flagged down the bartender and ordered a margarita. "Can you make it strong?"

"For you, sure."

With no reason to hurry back, she planted her elbows on the counter and quaffed the whole drink. She considered bolting and walking the mile back to the beach alone, but in the end decided to face the music and ride with Jake. *Just get it over with. The sooner the better.*

The hot air in his Chevy truck made her woozy. As he pulled out of the lot, she rolled down the window and shoved her face into the wind.

"You're in no shape to drive. Where do you live?"

Phoebe answered as if her tongue had doubled in size. "I'm not leaving my car here."

"It won't go anywhere."

"I live twenty miles away."

"Coming back in the morning beats a DUI, or worse."

"First you save me from cancer, now a violent death. You're sure a great guy, Jake."

He smiled. "Just tell me the address."

She didn't answer. A minute later, he pulled into the beach lot beside her Ford Fiesta.

"Now look—I'm serious. You can't drive."

She stepped down from the cab. "Let me guess—your brother was killed by a drunk driver."

"That's not funny. If you want to kill yourself, that's your business, but you don't have the right to hurt anyone else."

"I'll walk it off. She left him sitting in the cab. *Jerk.* She wobbled across the road and into a park that fronted the beach.

The elm trees shrouded her in darkness. To her left, blinding headlights moved in slow motion up and down Main Street. To her right, the lights of the DL Pavilion burned against the pitch-black lake. Phoebe trundled through the abandoned park, aiming for a bench and trying not to bounce off the trees.

How many drinks did I have? In how many hours? She tried to figure out how long before she dared to drive, but couldn't do the simple math. *Great. Now the ground is spinning.*

She braced herself against a tree. *Oh, shit. Here it comes.* She fought heroically, but lost the battle. Her stomach jerked and the whole night's drinks and hors d'oeuvres gushed out.

She spat, trying to rid her mouth of the taste. *You're pathetic, Phoebe. Better sit.*

She sank into the grass and leaned against the tree trunk. She closed her eyes, but her head began to spin, forcing her eyes back open. "I just wanna sleep," she moaned.

"Not a good idea," came a nearby voice.

She stared up at his silhouette. "What the hell are you doing here? Can't you see I'm sick?"

"That's pretty plain. And this time I won't take *no* for an answer. I'm driving you home."

He pulled Phoebe up, wrapped her arm around his neck, and led her through the park like a wounded soldier.

In the glare of the street, her red cover-up, half unbuttoned and twisted around her waist, blazoned into view. Vomit speckled her suit, and strangely, her feet were bare. "Hey, where's my jellies?"

"You won't need them where you're going."

He's right. That's exactly where I'm going.

He opened the door to his truck and helped her in. She plopped into her seat, rested her elbow on the open window, and buried her cheek in her bicep. Her bangs draped across her eyes, blocking the light and hiding her face—both good things, from her point of view.

"What's the address?"

"Putnam."

He shook his head and eased into traffic. He drove through dark streets to avoid drawing attention to his semi-conscious passenger. Phoebe sat motionless, fighting to keep her stomach down. She nearly made it home, but when he missed a green light in Putnam and hit the brakes hard, her stomach kept moving. In the nick of time, she thrust her head out the window.

"Should I stop?"

"No—home."

Somehow, she directed him to her house and managed to drag herself out of the cab. He gripped her arm as she staggered to the door. He watched her stab at the lock with her key, missing it over and over again, until he finally grabbed it and unlocked the door himself. "Are you sure you're okay?"

"I'm great. How about a goodnight kiss?"

"You must be okay—you're still funny."

She held out her hand. He shook it carefully.

"Nice to meet you, Jake. Sorry about the truck."

"What?"

She stumbled into the dark hallway and shut the door.

Jake hurried back to his Chevy and found just what he feared. Phoebe had varnished the door panel with long, windblown streaks of vomit.

"Nice job, Phoebe," he muttered, shaking his head. "Are you ever going to hate yourself tomorrow."

10

Sunlight woke Phoebe up like an arrow fired though her skull. She squinted angrily into the glare and sat up in bed, but sitting made her feel as if she'd yanked the arrow out. She closed her eyes and waited for pain to ebb before pulling down the shade. She put her feet gently on the floor and stared at her bare thighs. She'd slept all night in her bathing suit.

The first memory that rushed back was that of hugging the toilet and throwing up again and again.

Next she recalled the ride home with Jake and, then rapidly, the whole evening—dancing with Debbie at the Holiday Inn, flirting with Jake, feeling like a fool after learning the truth, and finally downing that last damn margarita. The bartender must have poured her a triple. It had been a long time, maybe that stupid tequila party back in college, since she'd been that drunk. After that nightmare, it had taken her two full days to recover.

She forced herself out of bed. The smell in the bathroom made her queasy, but she steeled herself and wiped the toilet and tiles with a soapy rag. She wriggled out of her twisted one-piece, which left painful marks on her waist and hips, and took a long, hot shower. Knowing she couldn't eat for a long time, she put on her running clothes and took a walk.

She cut through the quiet town, heading to Big Boy Lake, a mile away, where cottonwoods and pines cooled the cottages hugging the shore. Walking down the shady road, her mind replayed the night's worst moments, dredging up every stupid thing she'd said and done and cringing with each new memory.

Recalling how she'd asked Jake for a goodnight kiss, she chuckled to herself. At lease he'd gotten the joke.

A quiet breeze came off the lake and teased loose the cobwebs in her mind. Overhead, the pine boughs swayed, the needles strumming the air, and slowly her mood began to shift. It was a magnificent day. The branches filtered out the hot sun, and barely a cloud drifted across the blue skies. From out of nowhere came the craving for a cigarette. She patted her running shorts, but the pockets were empty. *Damn. I left them at home.*

The thought of a long hike around the lake without a cigarette made the craving stronger, but also made her angry with herself for being so addicted to the dirty little stinkers. What's more, everything last night had started going downhill the second that Jake had smelled her smoky hair, and the unhappy memory awakened in Phoebe a sudden urge to quit. She'd been toying with the idea ever since coming to Putnam anyway—every time she crept outside her class for a furtive puff or two—and there was nothing like a night of excess to harden your resolve.

That's it. No more cigarettes. I'm done.

The resolution lifted her mood. More important, it broke the logjam in her mind and let in a fresh flow of thoughts. Looking back on her behavior at the wedding, she was struck by her own self-pity. The revelation dogged her all day, even while eating dinner at The Lakes Café. *Is my luck really that bad or am I my own worst enemy?*

She was still asking the question when she left. Halfway out the door, a poster on the glass stopped her cold.

Sign up for DL's biggest fitness event of the year! The Fourth of July Fun Run! 5K – 10K – Half marathon. Do it in DL!

She bit her lip. The last time she'd raced was back in college, three years ago. *You're out of shape, Phoebe. You're getting fat.* She fished a pen from her purse and scribbled down the date.

She spent the next two hours washing her clothes at the Laundromat, and by the time she'd folded and tucked them away, bed was calling. Before collapsing under the covers, she laid out her running gear, and for the first time in many months was looking forward to the next day, when she planned to rise at dawn, down a quick cup of coffee, lace up her Nikes, and jog around Big Boy Lake in the cool morning air.

11

On race day, Phoebe woke at six, threw on her running shorts and sports bra, tied her hair in a ponytail, and scarfed down a donut and a glass of orange juice. Throughout June, she'd trained rigorously, stepping up her daily runs to her goal of ten miles. She felt more energetic and fit than she had in years, but more importantly, running had kept her from smoking. She hadn't had a single puff since her wild night with Debbie at the Holiday Inn.

By seven o'clock, two thousand runners packed the roadbed and curbs of Main Street in DL. Betsy and Janice, both teachers at Putnam High, bumped into Phoebe as she left the registration tent. "You look like a serious runner," Janice said, staring at Phoebe's toned legs and arms.

"Used to be. Today I'm running for the bagels and beer."

"You'll earn 'em," Betsy said. "The high is 94."

Phoebe squinted at the sun climbing the cloudless sky. "The heat's okay. What kills you is the humidity."

"They're lining up. You'd better hurry."

She jogged to the race line, clogging Main Street for several blocks, and worked her way into the seven-minute milers, mostly young men with stern, warlike faces.

Squeezing into an open spot, she jostled a tall, clean-shaven man.

"Sure you're in the right place, sport?"

"Yeah, I'm sure. Are you?"

His friends laughed. "Some of these girls are pretty fast, Jim. I'll bet she kicks your butt."

"We'll see about that," he said sourly.

"I'll bring you a beer when you finish," Phoebe quipped. Spurred on by the men's laughter, she added, "*If* you finish."

She kept up the banter, feeling relaxed even though surrounded by strangers, but as the minutes ticked by, she realized the men around her now expected something from her, and she forgot her goal to merely finish the race and set her mind to beat as many as she could—or at the very least, the man who'd called her *sport*.

The starting gun cracked. She tried to surge ahead, but a wall of bibs held her back. "It will loosen up soon," said the man beside her.

She bit her lip and ran in place. Minutes later, it seemed, the runners began inching down the avenue like a giant snake. For the next half block, they foiled her every move—left, right, or straight ahead—and the tightly packed crowd made her itch to break out. Then without warning, runners were hurtling by her through holes in the pack. A few were nearly sprinting. In seconds, the whole field was breaking up and running briskly. Phoebe was swept up in the frenzy and found herself clipping along at a pace she knew she couldn't hold. *Get a good position. You can slow down when they do.*

For a mile, the course hugged the shore of Little Dupont and then turned sharply into the country. In the nearby ditches, red-winged blackbirds perched on cattails and peered at the endless herd thundering by. Phoebe had kept up the pace through the shaded town, but now on the treeless road, she began to waver. The hot, still air made her legs feel heavy and sapped her will. By now she'd lost track of the runners she'd started with, except for her rival, Jim, whose head was bobbing up and down a hundred feet in front of her. *This pace is crazy. I can't keep it up.* For a while she even thought she'd put herself in place with the six-minute milers instead of the seven.

Luckily, a mile later the road curved into a neighborhood, where elms and maples shaded the route and people lined the curbs, cheering the runners on. Phoebe clopped to a halt at the four-mile mark, chugged a glass of water, and jumped back into the race. *Only nine more miles to go.*

For the next few miles she hit her stride and ran for half an hour with hardly any effort—until she crossed a long, open bridge, around mile seven, and her body began to complain and fight her every step. By now it had reached the eighties, and the damp air held in her body heat like cling wrap. Sweat was pouring off her face and soaking through her sports bra. Her breaths were coming faster now, but still she couldn't draw in enough air. Even though her legs were begging her to stop, she knew from countless races the pain wouldn't kill her, and she grit her teeth and hammered on.

Her perseverance paid off. When she rounded the bend on the east shore of Big Dupont, she was blessed with every runner's dream, a second wind. Her breaths came more freely now, her feet tapped smartly on the pavement, and her knees rose and fell with fluid grace, her limbs driving her forward more like wings than arms and legs.

By now, the runners nearby had stretched into a long thin line, all men, and Phoebe started picking them off one by one. She set her sights on each new target, patiently closed in, and then took pleasure in the shocked turn of their heads as she, *a girl*, passed them by. Half a mile later, she made out the bobbing head of her rival, whom she'd lost at mile four, and quickened her pace.

The nine-mile mark was drawing close. The sun was baking the concrete and the damp air was clogging her lungs. Ignoring her pain, she put on a spurt, hoping to zoom past her rival so fast he'd lose the will to race her. Too tired to make a crack as she sped by, she forced a grin as he glanced up in despair and dropped out of sight.

On the last stretch of highway, the heat rose off the blacktop like a bed of coals. Sweat seeped through her brows and stung her eyes. Her shoes felt like wet boots, and she gulped in air like a fish out of water. But driven by the fear that her rival would catch her, she willed her body onward at the same breakneck speed.

She'd come to that point in every race that separates the serious runner from the pack, where the pain seems unbearable, but the runner calls on reserves from a deep inner well and chugs along like a trusty machine.

At last she spotted the ten-mile mark. *Three more miles of hell and you're done.*

The minutes wore on, and the town never seemed to come any closer. She felt like she was running through waist-deep water, and she cursed herself for signing up for the day's longest race. *What the hell was wrong with the 10K? Not tough enough for you?*

A gas station rolled by, then a grocery store. A southern breeze came off the lake. A block ahead, small groups of people lined the road, cheering the runners on. Two-story buildings rose up around her, forming a canyon, and the flocks of people grew dense and loud. Now the buildings were flying by, and then at last, *nirvana*—the placid blue waters of Little Dupont sparkled beyond the finish line. The crowd erupted. Phoebe tried to sprint, but nothing happened, and she could only hold her pace. *I must look like I'm dying. I feel like it, too.*

At last, it was over. She stumbled through the chute, gasping for air, so spent that had she been a cow going to slaughter and not a racer getting her number, she would have accepted her fate without a fight.

Janice and Betsy found her just beyond the chute. Phoebe tried to smile but couldn't raise the corners of her lips.

"Are you okay?" Betsy asked. "You're a tomato."

"Yeah, I gave a hundred percent."

"Here, take my water."

Phoebe sucked down half the bottle and poured the rest down her sports bra. "I could use a beer." She turned sharply and made a beeline for the tents.

By the time Janice and Betsy caught up with her, Phoebe had a beer in one hand and two bagels in the other. She tore off a wad of bagel with her teeth and ground away, but it was too dry to swallow. She took a swig of beer to wash it down, but most of the beer poured down her chin and bra. She glanced around, embarrassed, still chewing away, and then froze. Coming toward her through the crowd, and smiling directly at her, was Jake.

12

She turned around, hoping he'd walk by, and began chewing furiously—in case he didn't. But it was too late. A finger tapped her shoulder. When she didn't move, he circled round in front of her. She covered her mouth with one hand and raised her beer to shield her face. Her running clothes were soaked, sweat was dripping down her neck, and her scarlet cheeks made her look like a burning victim. She tried distracting him with a broad smile, but realized too late that a chunk of bagel was stuck between her teeth.

Her appearance did seem to startle him, but only for a second. "Phoebe— I saw you finish. You were amazing."

Her scarlet cheeks concealed her blush.

"So how've you been?" he asked.

"Well, I'm sober now."

"Oh, that—no big deal. We've all been there."

She paused and looked him over. In the light of day, he was not so hand-some as she remembered. In a crowd, he might not have caught her eye—fair skin and blond hair had never been her type. Although, she had to admit, his face had no obvious flaws, his eyes were kind, his smile warm. The hair was a bit overdone—thick and long in front, like James Dean in gym trunks, T-shirt, and sandals. The shirt's fit drew her gaze to his V-like torso, and his calm blue eyes stared into hers the same way they had at the Holiday Inn, which quickly rekindled in her the same feelings of attraction and loss from that humiliat-ing night.

"Not my finest hour."

"Forget it. You never told me you were such a good runner. How can you smoke and run so fast?"

"I quit."

"Hey, good for you."

"I'm trying to get back in shape."

"Trying? You already are. You look great."

Okay, what the hell is going on?

"Why are you in DL?"

"I came to see Peter. He's running the 10K. I thought Debbie told you."

"No," she said, disappointed, but cross with herself for being so. "I think it starts any minute," she added, hoping to end the conversation.

He didn't budge. "Would you like to have lunch after you rest up?"

"With Debbie and Peter?"

"No, they're driving to Fargo. I meant us."

She stared at him blankly. *You've got to be kidding.*

"I'll bet you're hungry."

That's it. I'm calling his bluff. I'll get to the bottom of this. "Are you buying?"

"Sure, my treat."

"Okay then. Give me half an hour."

She climbed into Jake's black Chevy and guided him to a supper club on the east side of Big Dupont.

"This place looks pretty nice," he said, noting the BMWs and Mercedes-Benzes in the parking lot.

"Not bad for DL." *The best place in town, in fact, or at least the most expensive.*

A hostess in a black dress led them to a table looking over the lake. Jake studied the clientele and frowned. His shorts and baggy shirt, to say nothing of Phoebe's running gear, made a mockery of the dress code.

He tried pulling out Phoebe's chair, but she beat him to it and plopped herself down.

He sat and stared at the menu. "Wow."

She felt a pang of guilt. He was trying so hard to be nice—although why, she couldn't say. "If you want, we can go Dutch."

"No, I said I'd pay, and I will."

I'll order a dinner salad and eat lots of bread.

Jake seemed uncertain how to behave in the formal setting, but his sudden shyness, instead of pleasing Phoebe, troubled her. Maybe she was laying the ice on a bit too thick. What if he really was a decent guy, just trying to be friendly, with no ulterior motives? It flitted through her mind that maybe it was her, and not him, who was making a fool of herself.

She ordered a $4 salad. He ordered a $10 cheeseburger.

"Do you like construction work?" she asked, trying to put him at ease.

"Summers, yes, but not winters. Ever been up on a roof in January?"

"Sounds cold."

"You have no idea. Actually, I'm looking for a new job."

"Doing what?"

"I have a buddy in waterproofing, but every day he takes a bath in xylene."

"What's that?"

"Kind of like radioactive turpentine."

"Not very good for your DNA."

"Or anything else. Anyway, he got a job with the manufacturer."

"That's pretty smart."

"I thought so too. Lots of companies are looking for guys who know their way around a jobsite. So I thought, why not? I hope to make a jump soon."

"And make other people bathe in xylene."

"I don't like that part. But I know there's better stuff around. If I worked for a company, I could help make the products safer. Maybe some of these places need an honest guy like me, a straight shooter."

His speech impressed but also puzzled her. If he really was a straight shooter, why hadn't he told her about Susan? Or had she vainly assumed from the start that his interest in her had always been romantic?

"Do you have any siblings?"

"Three brothers."

"Are you the youngest?"

"Why? Do I act spoiled?"

"I didn't mean it like that."

"You're kind of hard on me, you know."

Eager to confront the issue, Phoebe threw out the question she most wanted answered. "How long have you and Susan been dating?"

"About a year. She's really sweet. You'd like Susan—well, maybe you wouldn't."

"Why? Because I'm a bitch?"

"Phoebe, no." He shook his head. "The stuff you say."

"You're just not like her, that's all. She's more, I don't know, girly."

"And I'm not girly?"

"You're more like a tomboy."

Stung, she kept her poker face and pressed on. "A year. That's a long time. You must be in love."

"I am."

A mixture of hurt and anger welled inside her. "If you're in love with her, why are you here with me?"

He blushed. "She's in Des Moines, visiting her parents. I drove up to watch Peter. And I love it here."

"Are you looking for something on the side?" she asked pointedly. "Because if you are, you're wasting your time."

His blush deepened. "Phoebe, no, I promise. Look, I like talking with you. I think you're funny. I didn't know—"

At that moment, the waitress served Phoebe's salad and Jake's $10 cheeseburger. Jake stopped talking and slathered the bun with ketchup and mustard. Phoebe waited for him to finish his thought, but he showed no sign of doing so. Maybe there wasn't any point. Maybe he'd already said everything that needed saying.

Now Phoebe's face was burning. In her eagerness to unmask his motives, she'd not only given away her crush on him, but come off as catty, vain, and desperate all at once. *All right, calm down. He wants to be friends. Big deal. Be polite, finish your salad, and say goodbye.*

"I don't know any girls like you," he said thoughtfully. "Sometimes I don't understand girls. But you I get. You say just what you think, and I like that."

"You already have three brothers. Why do you need a fourth?"

"You see—that's funny. No girl I know would say that."

She stabbed at her salad greens. "Cool. After lunch we can shoot beers."

He grinned. "I'd shoot beers with you anytime, Phoebe."

"We already tried that," she said and steered the conversation back to safer topics. Jake seemed happy to let the current one die, and Phoebe listened halfheartedly as he told her stories about growing up in St. Clare. When the bill came, she let him pay for it all—with tax and tip it was $20. *His idea. His check.* But Jake didn't grumble. In fact, he seemed unfazed. He kept smiling and talking, unaware of the bruising he'd given her ego, and half an hour later, he dropped her off by her car, revved his black Chevy, and with a final wave from his cab, faded down the street.

13

Phoebe spent the next week licking her wounds. To keep herself busy, she lengthened her runs and got ready for her classes in the fall. But when Saturday came around, the boredom grew unbearable. Walking home from The Lakes Cafe, she passed by a greenhouse bursting with orange and red zinnias, and the lift it gave her mood inspired her to plant a garden. By midday, she'd bought a half-dozen flats of daisies, phlox, and black-eyed Susan's and was crawling on hands and knees in the dirt, attacking the baked ground with a hand spade and sweating like a wrestler. It was much too hot for this kind of work, but she kept going anyway. It felt good to sweat, to ram the spade through the crusty earth, bulldoze the dirt with her palms, and crumble the clods between her fingers. The planting absorbed her so completely—digging the holes, pulling apart the roots, and packing the dirt around them—that she failed to hear the car door slam and saw too late that somebody was standing above her.

Even before she saw his face, she knew it was him. Of course—her arms were caked with dirt, face dripping with sweat, hair blowsy as an old broom, so who else could it be?

She stood and with spade in hand wiped the sweat from her brow. There wasn't any point in trying to look decent. In her tied-up T-shirt and cutoff jeans, she looked like a hillbilly who'd crawled out of a ditch.

He stood before her, smiling stupidly. "Hey, Phoebe. Isn't it kind of hot for gardening?"

The question snapped the last thread of her patience. "No, I like the heat. When I'm finished digging, I'll slop the hogs."

He glanced around. "Hogs?"

"What are you doing here, Jake?"

"I came to see you."

"Really? Why do you waste your time?"

"Am I wasting my time?"

She stared at him, disbelieving. "I don't even know what to say anymore."

"How about, 'Hello, Jake. Nice to see you'?"

"Why did you drive all the way to Putnam, Minnesota, to see a teacher you barely know? Because you can't talk trucks and shoot beers with your girlfriend? Or because you think I'll fuck you, and I'm so far away, she'll never know?"

She threw down her spade. It stuck in the dirt. "Either way it doesn't matter. I don't want to be your buddy, Jake, and I'm sure as hell not fucking you."

She stopped, appalled by her tone and words. "Look," she said, calming down. "I'm sorry, but you should leave."

She pulled the spade from the dirt.

"Are you going to stab me with that?"

Strangely, her outburst hadn't bothered him, and the stupid smile lingered on his face.

"Hang around and I might."

"I wouldn't blame you. I owe you an apology."

She wrinkled her nose. "Why?"

"Ever since I met you, I wanted to ask you out. But I couldn't. Because of Susan."

Great. He's confused. "She's your girlfriend, Jake. Doesn't that mean anything to you?"

"It does, but we've been dating for over a year. She said I should know by now if I wanted to marry her. She said it was time for me to decide, or else—"

"Or else what?"

"Move on."

She eyed him uncertainly. *Was it the truth?* "And?"

"I told her—I'm sorry, I'm moving on."

"Why don't you want to marry her?"

He shoved his hands in his pockets. "I've been asking myself the same thing. Susan's a nice girl. All my friends like her. My parents like her. She's pretty. She's smart. She treats me well. I really don't have any reason to not marry her."

"There must be something."

He shrugged. "She's a little too pink for me, if you know what I mean."

Phoebe smiled. At last she understood. "I know exactly what you mean."

"And you're nowhere near pink."

"If that was a compliment, you'd better try again."

"All right. I said you weren't like any girl I knew, and I meant it. At first I thought I could be your friend—but it wasn't enough. I love being around you. You're funny. You never pull punches, and I respect that. Your eyes are amazing. I could stare at them for hours. In fact, I've been thinking about you ever since we met. That's why I drove up here—to tell you that—and to ask you out, today, or anytime you want."

Phoebe couldn't stop smiling. No man had ever spoken to her like this before, and his words washed away her doubts like a fresh spring rain. "Thank you, Jake, that's nice. And, yes, I'd love to."

14

Phoebe sponged off the dirt, brushed on her mascara, and changed into her new swimsuit, chosen with Debbie's help, a bright red bikini so skimpy that she hadn't yet summoned the courage to wear it. She threw on a knee-length cover-up to keep it hidden until the right moment.

They climbed into his Chevy, picked up a six-pack of beer and a bag of pretzels, and headed west of town. Phoebe guided him to a lake surrounded by waist-high cornfields. He parked on the shoulder, grabbed a Styrofoam cooler from the truck bed and followed Phoebe, who was toting her radio down a grassy trail to a narrow beach.

While Jake iced the cooler, Phoebe spread out her towel and casually slipped off her cover-up. She made a point of not looking up and promptly lay on her stomach. During the drive, they'd chirped like a pair of songbirds, but now that she was sprawled nearly naked on her towel, she began to worry. Jake too was suddenly quiet. *Either he likes what he sees or I have a big fat ass.*

When he sat beside her, her focus shifted. Jake had slipped off his T-shirt, and his bare muscles popped out like polished rocks, even the smaller ones around his ribs, flexing every time he moved. She turned her head away to keep from staring.

He offered her a beer. She popped the top, spraying the sand with foam. He tuned the radio to a rock station and leaned back on his towel. "You were right. This spot is perfect."

"It's great for tanning. There's never anyone here."

Jake was quiet again. The silence grew.

"I burn pretty easy. Can you put sunscreen on my back?"

He fumbled with the tube, but soon his warm hands were pressing firmly into her back. She closed her eyes and relaxed under his touch. After spreading the lotion, he lingered on her shoulders and arms, kneading them gently. She breathed out with each strong push of his hands. The radio was playing Deacon Blues, the sun was baking her bare skin from neck to toe, and already the beer was giving her a buzz.

He pushed a hand under her bikini string.

"Go ahead. Untie it."

He undid the knot, laid the strings carefully on the towel, and stroked the full length of her back.

She didn't speak. At this point, she didn't care where his hands went. He squeezed on more lotion, cool against her skin, but rapidly melting under his palms. After a while, he stopped and lay beside her on his stomach. She looked up and gave him a lazy, inviting smile, but its meaning escaped him.

"Mind returning the favor?" he asked.

"Fair enough."

He sat up and grabbed his knees. Feeling brazen, Phoebe pushed herself up and left her red top lying on the towel. Kneeling more or less naked behind him, she felt sexy, embarrassed, and silly all at once. While she stroked his back, the lotion slipped suggestively between her fingers, and when her nipple glanced his shoulder, she trembled. He flinched, but didn't move another muscle and kept gazing quietly across the lake. Disappointed, she lay down. Afraid she might be coming on too strong, she asked him about his hobbies. He seemed more relaxed now, even a touch relieved, telling her about hiking in Glacier Park and canoeing in the Boundary Waters.

The sun had climbed to its peak, and sweat was beading on Phoebe's back. She reached behind herself and retied her top. "I think I need a swim."

"Good idea."

The coolness of the lake shocked her. She inched along the sandy bottom, her toes sinking in, until the water lapped against her belly, and then she lunged forward. She breaststroked a while before Jake splashed by, chopping the water with his arms. He was aiming for a small island covered with trees. Phoebe admired his flexing back and shoulders and swam lazily in his wake.

He reached the shore long before she did. He stood on the sand, dripping and watching her glide toward him. "This is cool," he said. "Just like Huck Finn."

Who does that make me, Tom Sawyer?

He picked up a stone and skimmed it across the water. His behavior was confusing her, even while she decided to at least make him kiss her. The beer, the sun, the bracing swim, and the sight of his body combined with the pent-up desire from not being touched for over a year conquered her shyness. "Can you show me how to skip a stone?"

"That's easy. It just has to be flat."

She lobbed a few pebbles into the water. They all plopped once and disappeared. "I must be doing it wrong."

"It's your throw."

He stepped behind her, took her hand, and moved it through a sideways arc. "Try that."

Instead of trying, she faced him, but already he was stepping back. He sat down and clutched his knees again. "Go ahead. I'll watch."

After a couple of throws, she lost her patience. *I'll show him how to skip a fucking stone.* She picked up a perfect specimen and slung it with a sharp flick of her wrist. It bounced on the water like a rubber ball—seven, eight, nine times—before plunking into the water.

"Wow, Phoebe! That was great."

"Guess I found the right stone," she said and sat a few feet away, wondering if he'd really meant the words he'd said to her an hour ago or, now, having seen almost every square inch of her body, was having second thoughts.

15

By the time they left the beach, Phoebe had calmed down. She'd nursed another beer and accepted that Jake simply needed more time before getting physical. To Phoebe, it felt like a third date, but to him it was only a first. In truth, she had no good reason to be upset with him, and it was better to back off, she decided, than to be thought cheap.

Once she'd worked this out, the tension between them lifted. They drove along the highway as telephone poles cast shadows across the road. The fresh air poured through the open windows and cooled their faces. The country changed with every curve—wood, lake, and rolling hills. Both were high in spirits now and, after swimming, hungry. Four miles from Putnam, they stopped at a small resort, hid back in a corner booth, ordered burgers and fries, and shared a pitcher of beer.

The sun was setting when Jake parked his truck and walked Phoebe to her door. The two were quiet now, tired from hours of talking, yet Phoebe felt content basking in his gaze. As she walked, she could feel herself swaying. She unlocked the door and faced him. "Want a tour?"

He answered with a kiss. It took only one to rekindle her desire, and her fatigue vanished. Suddenly, they couldn't get enough contact between them; their bodies rubbed together and their fingers tangled in each other's hair. Jake circled her waist and backed her into the kitchen, leaving the outside door open. When he swept the cover-up off her shoulders, her bikini top came off with it. His shirt flew off as though it had a will of its own. As they caromed off the walls, his trunks fell to the floor. He tucked Phoebe's legs around his waist, carried her into the bedroom, and dropped her on the mattress. Her suit bottom came streaking off, a flash of red in the dim light, and in seconds their hips were locked together and their bodies moving together in a rapid beat. Phoebe held nothing back, meeting Jake blow for blow, even as it ran through her mind that in the morning she might regret it.

It was over in minutes. They lay beside each other, breathless, hearts beating madly. The window cast a pale light on their ruddy faces. "Sorry, I got carried away," he said. "Are you all right?"

"Yeah, but not sure about tomorrow."

"I couldn't' help myself." He kissed her on the lips.

The kiss, meant only to be tender, sent tingles up her spine, and soon their bodies were wrapped together again like two strands of rope, working to wring out every drop of pleasure. This time, when Jake was on the brink, she rolled him over and made him wait. Once he caught his breath, she climbed on top and, now in control, slowed the pace until they came together in a flurry of tender violence.

"That was even better," he groaned. "And I thought you were shy."

"Once I get to know a person, I'm pretty direct. That might take some getting used to."

"Not for me."

"You'll always know what I want," she said teasingly and took him in her hand.

"I think I need to wait some."

"We'll see about that."

Twenty minutes later, they finally rolled apart. "You're amazing, Phoebe. I don't deserve you."

"If I'm so amazing, what took you so long?"

"What do you mean?"

"On the beach. Didn't you like my suit?"

"What suit? You were basically naked. I nearly jumped you right there."

"Why do you think I picked that spot?"

He shook his head. "I guess I blew that one."

"Better keep your eyes open. Chances like that don't come along every day."

He smiled and kissed her neck. "Don't worry, Phoebe. It won't happen again."

16

Throughout the summer, Jake drove to Putnam every Friday night. Phoebe would meet him at the door in her robe, pop two beers, listen to his week, and then pull him into the bedroom. The week apart made their reunions intense and physical. They rarely ventured out of the apartment until Saturday morning.

The next two days were savored like fine chocolate. They slept till nine, had eggs and coffee at The Lakes café, and went into DL to shop or swim. On cloudy days, they drove around the countryside in Jake's truck, enjoying the placid lakes, the tree-crowned hills, and the scent of linden flowers rushing into the cab. Before dinner, they drove back for a nap, which always led to sex, as Phoebe was caught up in that early stage of romance when the only thing that mattered was to see her lover's face, hear his voice, and be hugged, kissed, or caressed every minute of the day.

Having Jake around made her cheerful and calm. At times she caught herself chatting with strangers, singing under her breath, or even smiling at bratty kids. She understood the silliness of her sudden change, but who cared? So what if she was falling in love, or whatever you called it. She was happy, and Jake seemed happy too, whether or not he loved her. For the time being, she wasn't going to spoil the present with questions about the future. The future would take care of itself, she thought, and she felt no reason to push it.

By September, she wanted her family to meet Jake, so she planned a dinner with Zoe and Jeremy and drove to the cities. On their way to a new restaurant in the warehouse district, a black rain was pelting the sidewalks, driving water down the alleys and swirling it around the sewers. A waitress with purple highlights and a pierced lip guided them to Zoe and Jeremy's table, where they waited drinking merlot. Zoe leaped up and hugged Phoebe while the two men shook hands and sized each other up. Jake had worn dress pants, a collared shirt, and tie, but finding Jeremy in jeans, a sport jacket, and T-shirt, he felt overdressed and underdressed at the same time.

A tidbit of local gossip distracted the women, leaving the two men briefly on their own.

"Why construction?" Jeremy asked.

"I fell into it after college. The money's good, and I didn't want to be chained to a desk."

"I hear it's dangerous. I read that two-thousand construction workers in the U.S. die every year."

Jake smiled as if the number were a badge of honor. "I could tell you some stories. One time, we had a guy walking a high beam with a bucket of bolts in each hand. He came to a crossbeam, set down a bucket, and the other one took him straight over the side."

"You're kidding. What happened to him?"

"He was paralyzed."

"Aren't you supposed to be tied up?"

"He took off his safety harness. He was in a hurry. Most of the time when people get killed, it's their own fault."

"Sounds like his boss should go to jail."

Zoe, who'd kept one ear on their conversation, could feel the coming quarrel and broke in, "Jake, I hear you're driving to Putnam every weekend. I love the lake country up there, don't you?"

It soon became clear to Zoe and Phoebe that both men would need constant help to keep the conversation flowing. Phoebe had thought that Jeremy might intimidate Jake, but she hadn't expected the opposite, that some quality of Jake's—maybe his physique or his frankness—would threaten Jeremy. He answered all of Jake's questions evasively, as if he felt cornered by their probing nature, and she and Zoe had to step in repeatedly to steer the conversation back to safer topics.

But the safer topics soon died out, and by the time their dinners came, Jeremy was discussing American foreign policy in the Middle East, leaving Jake entirely out of the conversation. By dessert, Jeremy had segued to local dining trends, drawing on his knowledge from the Herald, once again shutting Jake out. As the night wore on, he spoke less and less, picking at his bouillabaisse, which Zoe had recommended, but mostly stirring it with his spoon and sulking like a child sent to the corner.

"What do you like to read?" Jeremy asked.

"These days, not much. After work, I'm too tired. I watch TV and movies."

"What kind of films?"

"Mostly action movies. James Bond. Crime."

"You like romantic comedies," Phoebe threw out, but it was pointless trying to shore up his battered ego. He already seemed embarrassed by the constant lifelines that she'd been throwing to him the whole night long.

Shortly after dessert, Phoebe forced a yawn, complained about being tired, and proposed they call it a night.

Zoe saw through the excuse, but nodded eagerly. They split the check, the two men shook hands, the sisters hugged, and, mercifully, the dinner was over.

17

The ride back to the Connors' house was painfully quiet. The wipers flicked off the raindrops that drummed on the windshield, and the headlights bored a tunnel through the coal-black streets. Jake and Phoebe traded observations about Zoe and Jeremy, but neither one mentioned what really was on their minds.

After a pause, Jake finally said, "She's very pretty."

Phoebe hadn't gotten the idea that Zoe had bewitched him, but she wanted to be sure. "Guys always like Zoe better than me."

"*Pretty* is subjective."

"Zoe is prettier than me. You don't have to pretend."

"You're selling yourself short."

"I'm just honest."

"Okay, she's *beautiful*, but if I'd met her before you, I wouldn't have asked her out.

Phoebe was stung by the word beautiful. "Afraid she'd turn you down?"

"I'm sure she would—but no."

"Then what?"

"This might sound weird, but she reminded me of my mom's parakeet. It would peck open the door to its cage and fly around the house in a panic. We'd try to catch her, but she was too quick, and you'd have to be careful not to crush her wings. After a while, we'd give up and just leave the door open, and she'd fly back in by herself."

"You're wrong. Zoe might be small, but she's stronger than me. And more daring too."

"More daring, maybe, but not stronger. Daring and fragile is a bad combination."

"So let me get this right. You don't want me for my looks. You want me for my strength."

"I didn't say that." He threw up his hands. "I don't think I can win this one."

Phoebe didn't push him. The exchange only confirmed just how badly the night had gone. It didn't really matter what he'd meant or how they broke down the evening—it had knocked her off the stage of her Romeo-and-Juliet fantasy into the arms of a hissing crowd. She knew that no relationship could last for long without the blessing of the people who loved her, and knowing that Jake had already disappointed Zoe, whose opinion she valued above all others, she began to question the whole romance.

He pulled over and put the truck in park. "I'm sorry, Phoebe."

Christ, is he dumping me? She stared at him, panicky, forgetting all her doubts from seconds ago. "What do you mean, sorry?"

"I let you down. I made a bad impression."

Phoebe's heartbeat slowed. "No, it wasn't you, it was Jeremy. To be honest, I don't even like him. I only put up with him because of Zoe—but you can never let her know that."

"It still bothers me. I don't care what Jeremy thinks, but I do care what Zoe thinks."

"I won't know until we talk," she said unconvincingly.

The light ahead turned green. He put the truck back in gear. "There's something you should know about me. People always underestimate me. But if I want something badly enough, I get it. I never give up."

"Then what do you want?"

"I want you, Phoebe."

"In that case, I don't care what Zoe thinks. It only matters what I think."

He shook his head. "No, you're wrong. You shouldn't have to defend me. I've gotten lazy. You're a step up for me, and if I want you in my life, I'll have to try harder. And I will."

The compliment made her blush.

"I love you, Phoebe, and I'll do whatever I can to make you happy."

"I love you too, Jake," she said quietly, but only after saying the words did she know she really meant them.

18

Phoebe stared out her kitchen window as Jake's truck pulled into her drive. It was four o'clock, a Friday afternoon, sooner than he should be here. She'd just walked home from school, and she went outside to greet him in her gray sweater and black skirt, clasping her shoulders against the fall chill. Her first thought was that he'd been laid off. He'd warned her that winter construction work was hard to come by, and this year the ground had frozen early. "Everything okay?"

His smile put her at ease. He was still dressed in his work boots, jeans, and hooded jacket. He looked disheveled, but healthy and rugged.

He pecked her lips. "I'm good. We finished early, and they let me off."

As her worry faded, she felt like pulling him inside and peeling off his work clothes.

She kissed him slowly. "You could use a shower."

"Not before I try out my new toy."

"You didn't buy that damn Harley."

"If I had, I'd be driving it."

He reached into the bed of his truck and lifted out a metal detector.

Phoebe shook her head. "Do you know how stupid you look with that?"

"It was so cheap, I couldn't pass it up. It could be fun. People lose all kinds of stuff around here on the beaches."

"That's one step away from being a pickpocket."

"Come on. People never go back and find that stuff. So I might as well."

"When you drove up I was happy to see you, but a man with a metal detector is not very sexy."

"Who said it was? Let's try it."

"Suit yourself. I'm changing. Then you can show me your rusty nails."

Hoping that he'd quickly tire of his new toy, Phoebe slipped into a camisole, shaved her legs, and freshened her makeup. While she'd come to accept Jake's passion for gadgets, sometimes she worried that he was too much like her father. The longer they dated, the more the resemblance bothered her, as she had no intention of repeating her mother's life.

She peered out the window. A pair of headphones cupped Jake's ears, and he was grinning as he swept the black-metal disc over the grass. *He doesn't even know I'm waiting.*

She plopped on the couch, picked up a magazine, and flipped through it. A minute later, she slapped it down on the table. *This is pissing me off. Is that stupid little toy more exciting than me?*

She slipped on a pair of jeans, threw her coat over her camisole, and tracked him down. "Found the mother lode yet?"

"WHAT?"

She yanked the headphones off his ears. "DID YOU FIND THE FUCK-ING MOTHER LODE?"

He handed her a dirty coin. "No, but I did find a silver dollar."

"Cool. 1963. Know what that's worth?"

"Not really."

"One dollar."

"Phoebe—indulge me. You know I love this stuff. Give it a try. It's fun."

"Someone I know might see me."

He laughed. "They'll think it's for school."

"Yeah, the nerdy math teacher."

"What makes you think they care?"

"All right, give it here."

He cupped the phones over her ears and gave her the wand. "THE MORE IT CLICKS, THE CLOSER YOU ARE. THE LOUDER IT CLICKS, THE BIGGER THE FIND."

"THEY'RE PRETTY FAR APART."

"I FOUND THAT DOLLAR NEAR THE GARAGE."

She marched across the lawn, sweeping back and forth, knowing how silly she looked, but no longer caring. *What a girl does for love.*

"IT'S GETTING FASTER."

"WHEN IT'S STEADY, YOU FOUND SOMETHING."

"IT'S PRETTY STEADY NOW." *All right, this is kind of fun. Maybe I was being a little bitchy.*

When the clicks merged into a single tone, she pulled off the headset. Jake squatted and stabbed the turf with a garden spade. "It's an old tin."

He gripped the rusty edges and pulled it from the crumbly dirt.

"A coffee can," Phoebe said. "That could bring a fortune on the black market."

"Weird—it has a lid.

He brushed off the dirt. "You found it. You open it."

She stepped back. "Gross. I bet it's full of sow bugs."

He peeled back the lid and looked inside. "No bugs. Hmmm."

She grabbed the can. On the bottom sat a small velour box. "What the hell?"

She dipped her fingers in and palmed it, then glanced up at Jake.

His look gave him away. She didn't need to open the box. She already knew what hid inside. Her heart was beating rapidly now, but she kept the box closed and covered it with her palm.

His face dropped. "What's the matter?"

She tried to calm her racing heart and find the right words. "Jake—"

"Open it," he urged in a pleading tone. It moved her, and she wanted desperately to reassure him, but she couldn't.

"I know what this is, Jake, and I … I don't know."

Her response, or lack of one, crushed him.

"What I mean is, we've only known each other three months. It's so quick. I haven't had time to think about it."

"Then maybe you don't feel the way I do," he said bitterly. "Here, I'll take it back." He reached for the box, but Phoebe held it tightly. Her reluctance to let it go surprised her.

"Come on, Phoebe. You make everything so damn hard. Give it back to me and I'll forget it."

She stared at the box. "I want to know *why*."

"Why? That's a good question. I must be stupid, that's why."

"I'm serious, Jake. We don't act alike, we don't think alike, and we don't want the same things in life. Why in the world should two people like that get married?"

He shoved his hands into his pockets. "Because we love each other."

She let out a breath and tried slowing her thoughts. She had to be careful. His offer might be crazy, but she didn't want to lose him either. She thought for a second and then chose her words with as much tact as she could summon. "I'm sorry. That's not good enough. The world is full of people who get married because they fall in love, and ten years down the road, it goes to hell, because that was all they had. Love goes away. I know it does. And what's going to keep us together when that happens, Jake? I need to know." She took a deep breath. "And you'll have to convince me."

He studied her face, and his eyes came back to life. "You're not saying no?"

"I said you'll have to convince me." She paused and stared at the box again. Her knees began to weaken. "Here it is, Jake—what makes you think that you and I could be happy together, forever?"

His whole bearing changed. He straightened up, and his face got back its color. "I already know that."

She waited, hopeful, but doubtful.

"First of all, we *do* want the same things. You want a big house, and kids, right?"

"Someday, yes."

"So do I. And we're both willing to work hard to get them."

She nodded. "Okay, good point."

"Second, you need me."

"What?"

"No, I don't mean you *need* me, like you need a man. You're independent, and I love that. What I mean is—and don't be insulted—you have some traits that make life harder for you than it has to be."

"Like what?"

"You're shy. You're too caught up in your own head. And I help bring you out of that."

Like it or not, he was right. "Fair enough."

"At some point in your life you built a wall around yourself, maybe to protect yourself. Inside, you're a beautiful person—loyal, giving, kind—but not many people know that about you because you're defensive, and you push people away."

"So I'm a charity case."

"No, just the opposite. I feel lucky I know you. This will sound corny—I feel lucky you let me see who you really are. It tells me you trust me, and I know that doesn't come easy for you."

"I don't like to hear it, Jake, but you've got me pegged. I'm sorry."

"Don't be sorry. I'm not. I love that person stuck inside you, and I want the rest of the world to see her too."

"You're good for me, is that what you mean?"

"That's a better way of putting it."

"Okay, then—what is it, exactly, that I do for you?"

"That's easy. You might be shy, but you're more open-minded than me. You make me think about things I never have before, and I can talk to you about anything. I can tell you whatever comes into my head, even if it's dumb or crazy. You might laugh at me, but I know you won't judge me."

"I might laugh pretty hard."

He smiled. "I know that. You're not afraid to push me. I don't always like it, but I need it. You make me want to be smarter and stronger and more successful."

Her shoulders relaxed. At the same time, her stomach began to flutter.

"What else? You're smart. You're funny. You surprise me all the time, and you're never dull. You have beautiful brown eyes that I love staring at." He bit his lip. "And I have to say this, because I'm a guy—you have the best ass I've ever laid my eyes on, or my hands."

"That doesn't count—the ass, I mean."

He laughed and grabbed her wrists. "And the best part is, I'm not making this up. It's all true."

She gazed at him with glowing eyes.

"Say *yes*, Phoebe. Marry me."

She opened the box. The diamond wasn't large, but the size didn't matter. The tiny facets shone like the tip of the sun breaking over the horizon, filling the new day with hope and promise. It felt like a dream to hold it in her hand, a shining symbol of the life that he was asking her to share.

She plucked it from the cushion and slipped it on her finger. *Say it, stupid.*

"Yes, Jake, I'll marry you."

He lifted her off the ground and crushed her into his chest. She buried her face into his shoulder, and they clung to each other like two shipwrecked souls while tears streamed down Phoebe's cheeks.

He let out a long sigh. "For a minute there you had me scared."

"I'm sorry I put you through that. Forgive me."

"No, I'm glad you made me say it. You were right to."

She gazed into his eyes. *That's happiness I see. And he sees the same thing in mine.* "Now can we celebrate?"

"There's a cold bottle of champagne in the cab. I made a reservation for seven."

"You thought of everything."

"It's a nice place. We'd better change."

"First I need to clean you up." She took his hand and tugged him across the yard.

"Didn't you say something about a shower?"

"That's right, and I'm pretty damn good with a bar of soap."

"Now I know I asked the right woman."

"Yes, you did, you lucky bastard."

19

Jake parked his truck in front of the Connor's house. Martin was raking leaves, scratching the green lawn with short, forceful jabs. By the porch, Rose moved gracefully between leaf piles neater than Martin's, but smaller. Both seemed preoccupied with their work, unaware of the sun slanting through the clouds and lighting the trees with rusty-orange flames. Neither did they notice the brilliant pane of blue drifting in from the west—but Phoebe and Jake did, and they smiled at Rose and Martin doing their autumn chores, as unaware of their roles in the idyllic fall painting as the happy news they were about to hear.

Jake honked. Martin glanced up and grinned. He dropped his rake and crossed the lawn. He could tell that something out of the ordinary was happening.

Phoebe lighted on the grass and waited for Jake. When he came around, she clasped his hand and smiled at her father.

"What's this about?" he asked.

She paused, fighting to restrain herself as she waited for Rose, who was marching toward them, pulling off her gloves. Once her parents stood side by side, Phoebe said in a high-pitched voice, "We're getting married!"

"I knew it," Martin said." He pressed her into his barrel chest. "That's great news."

Rose looked startled, but the sight of Jake smiling tenderly as Phoebe and Martin hugged and teared up chased away her doubts. She grinned at Phoebe, who nearly jumped into her arms.

"I'm so happy, Mom. I really am."

"You look it. Congratulations, hon. I'm happy for you."

When she told her parents about his proposal, she didn't repeat all his words. She wanted to keep them to herself for a while, like the poems she'd written in high school, afraid of exposing them to the harsh light of the world.

As Phoebe and Rose discussed the wedding, Jake drove Martin to buy champagne. Jake had only spoken to Martin once before, and being alone with his future father-in-law made him anxious. At first Martin said little, guiding him through the leaf-cluttered streets, whether less excited about the engagement now that Phoebe was gone, or merely reflective, Jake couldn't tell. He glanced at the leather-faced man beside him, and his worry grew. Martin was chewing his lower lip and rubbing together his pawlike hands in a way that made Jake appreciate their power, and he felt sorry for any poor sap who found himself on their receiving end.

"This must be kind of sudden for you," Jake said, "but I want you to know, I think I'm the luckiest man in the world."

Martin came out of his trance. "I'm glad to hear it. Truth be told, she won't be easy. I know—I raised her. But I'd be surprised if you regret it."

It relieved him that Martin felt free to speak his mind with him. "I think I know her pretty well, and you're right, on both counts."

Martin fell silent and stared out the window. "Jake, I wanted you to come along so I could tell you something."

What now? A lecture? Advice? Some skeleton in the family closet? "Sure, go ahead."

"I like you Jake. I feel I can speak openly with you—is that okay?"

"Of course."

"Good." He paused briefly. "First of all, you know I love Phoebe. She's my own flesh and blood, so don't take what I'm saying wrong."

Jake's curiosity, along with his discomfort, grew.

Martin pursed his lips and frowned. "Rose is closer to Phoebe than me. I have to confess, I'm closer to Zoe. I know it isn't right—parents shouldn't have favorites. They should give all their kids the same amount of love. But I didn't do that. I had my reasons, but they don't matter. They don't make it right, and I know it hurt Phoebe growing up. I don't mean I was a bad parent. I didn't neglect her, but Zoe always got more of my attention."

Jake weighed his words. If Martin's intent was to make him love Phoebe more, it was working.

"That's funny. She's never said a bad thing about you."

"Maybe not, but I know it's there. I saw it in her eyes when she was a kid. And now I can't take it back."

He tried to find the right thing to say. "Can't you make it up to her?"

"I've tried, but for some reason, it's always harder with Phoebe." He pointed a thick finger at a faded beer sign over a liquor store. "Her sister was all smiles and giggles. She could be a little demon too—I'm not stupid. In high school, we lost plenty of hair over Zoe—but it was hard to stay mad at her. She was a charmer. Still is. And I needed that, especially when she was young."

Jake pulled into the parking lot. He put the Chevy in park but stayed in the cab. So did Martin.

"I don't get it. Why did that matter so much?"

"Well, here it is. When I was your age, I had big plans. I was a hard worker, a quick study. I could do just about anything with my hands. Rose was a pretty woman, sharp as a tack, and she had every right to expect something from the man she married."

Uh-oh, here it comes. My job.

"Then I went to Korea. I was a rifleman. I won't say much about it, except I saw and did things a person never wants to tell his wife and kids." He paused and gathered himself. "When I came back home, I couldn't get back to normal. I couldn't sleep. I had nightmares. I couldn't focus, and I was angry all the time. I took a job, any job, just to keep my hands busy—that calmed me down. And when I came home from work, I drank. A lot. That's how I got by for years. I forgot about my big plans. I didn't care anymore. They seemed pointless.

"I became a stone around my wife's neck. She tried to help me, but I pushed her away. I'm surprised she didn't leave me. I deserved it.

"After a while, I started to think about shooting myself. I thought about it all the time."

Jake swallowed. "What stopped you?"

"One day I found myself holding these two baby girls. They stared up at me with their big brown eyes, smiling and cooing. They didn't know about the holes I had in me—they didn't know what I'd done in Korea, and they weren't going to judge me. And I thought, if they can look at me with love in their eyes, then maybe I could start over. Maybe I could stand to look at myself in the mirror again.

"After that, I was okay. I was a good dad. Better than most. I came home every night and played with my kids. I read them books and told them bedtime stories. We had picnics by the creek. Vacations up north. We made them study and do their chores, and we brought them up to be good kids. They never had any shortage of love, although, like I said, I did favor Zoe—but now you know why. She wasn't so quiet and serious like Phoebe, and she always cheered me up. I love Phoebe just as much, but it's harder for me to show it.

"So here's where I'm going. I can tell Phoebe loves you. That's the most important thing, but it's not the only thing. She'll expect a lot from you. She'll challenge you. In fact, I know she won't be happy if her life isn't better than her father and mother's—do you understand me? I don't mean you have to make a lot of money to make her happy, but if you could give her more than I gave Rose, more than just a working man's life, I know that she'd be grateful, and so would I."

Jake nodded heavily. While many young men in his place would have felt insulted or bullied by Martin's request, he felt neither. Instead, he was moved that Martin had shared his past with him and knew that he'd spoken only out of love for his daughter. In fact, the same kind of thoughts about his future had been running through his own mind in the last few months.

"I already know that about her, Mr. Connor. And I want a good life for myself too. I'll do my best to make her happy."

"I know you will. Don't worry—you'll be fine. Let's go buy a good bottle of champagne. I could use a nice cigar. You smoke?"

"Sorry, no."

"Tonight you do, buster. It's on me."

20

Zoe ran into the kitchen, where Phoebe and Rose were doing dishes, and hugged her sister. All the right words came out—*I'm so happy for you, Phoebe, congratulations, I'm so excited, and she raved about her diamond* ring—but Phoebe could read the look in her eyes and saw it ran counter to her gushing words. Rattled by Zoe's behavior, she answered her questions halfheartedly, and the conversation soon became forced. Zoe rapidly picked up on Phoebe's mood, and without wasting time, grabbed her by the arm. "Let's go for a walk. You don't mind finishing up, do you, Mom?"

Phoebe put on a fall jacket and joined Zoe, waiting on the porch and smiling too hard. They clipped down the steps and marched along the dark sidewalks covered with fallen leaves, which their flats crunched or swept before them. The autumn chill flushed their cheeks, and both made fists of their hands and pushed them deep into their pockets.

"Okay, what's wrong?" Phoebe asked. "You think I'm making a mistake, don't you?"

Zoe glanced at her sheepishly. "No, not a mistake. It's just too fast."

"Maybe. It did happen fast." A tide of emotion rose inside her—but what that emotion was, she couldn't tell. "But it's *him*, Zoe. I know it's him."

"In three months? How can you?"

She wanted to recite Jake's proposal, line by line, convinced that once Zoe heard it, her doubts would vanish, and she would rave about Jake instead of question him, but for some reason she couldn't summon the words that she'd etched so deeply into her heart. Instead she kept quiet as a pot of ugly feelings stewed inside her—resentment, fear, jealousy, and strongest of all, an emotion that resembled grief. "You don't like him, do you?"

"I think he's a nice guy. But it doesn't matter what I think. What matters is whether or not he'll make you happy."

"Why wouldn't he?"

Zoe took a half a dozen steps before answering. "It comes down to this—you and I want different lives. A lot of people think I've charmed my way into this cushy life with Jeremy, but the truth is, money's not that important to me. What's really important is Jeremy and the family we're going to raise. The things we like don't cost money—books, movies, sex, friends. The rest is gravy. Now I'm not a fool, I won't turn the rest down, but I know I'd be happy if I married someone who *couldn't* give me those things. If I really loved him, it wouldn't matter, and I wouldn't care what other people thought of him either."

"That's just how I feel," Phoebe said with a trace of bitterness.

"But you're not like me. I would have been okay with someone like Dad, just raising a family, but I don't think you can."

"Christ, you don't think he's good enough for me."

"It's not that—it's whether or not he can give you the life you want. And don't be hurt, sis, but I don't think he can."

Phoebe simmered. There were too many daggers hidden in Zoe's words—the unflattering contrast between Jake and Jeremy, the doubting of her judgment, the insinuation that she was grasping, even while settling for less, and most of all, the blatant attack on Jake's ambition and brains.

"I can't believe it. I fall in love with a great guy, he asks me to marry him, I'm happy, and you run over and tell me to break it off before he ruins my life."

"That's not what I said."

"The hell it wasn't. You just called my fiancé a loser, not like *your Jeremy*, who's going to give you such a fucking cushy life while Jake and I raise our brats in a trailer court."

"Phoebe—calm down."

"What's so funny is I'm not even jealous. I can't stand Jeremy. I never could."

"You're angry. You don't mean that."

"Yes, I do. He's self-absorbed. He's dishonest. He never tells you what he really thinks."

"That's crazy. Jeremy tells me *everything*."

"No, he's quicksand, and someday he'll suck you down—that's what I thought when you got engaged, but I kept my mouth shut—if he made you happy, I thought I must be wrong—but now I wish I'd spoken up, because one day you'll see it, only by then it will be too late. You wait and see—Jake and I will have a better life than you and Jeremy. I'll put money on it."

Zoe stopped under the glare of a streetlamp. The look on her face finally ended Phoebe's tirade—the same look from their childhood fights, when Phoebe's temper reduced Zoe to tears. Now tears were streaming down Zoe's face as if she were ten years old again. "What a horrible thing to bet on. Don't ever say that again. I'm sorry, Phoebe, I thought I was doing the right thing. I love you, and I want you to be happy. That's all I want. Don't hate me for it. You're my only sister, and no matter what happens, we have to stick together."

Zoe's outburst startled Phoebe and brought her back to her senses. She saw just how close they'd come to charging off a cliff, and their quarrel left her shaken. She grabbed Zoe by the arms. "I'm sorry I said that. Forget it. You're my sister and my best friend and you always will be. No matter how things turn out, you can always count on me, okay?"

Zoe hugged her and sighed. "It doesn't matter who our husbands are. They're different, that's all, just like we're different. They won't be friends, we know that, but they can't ever come between us."

"Of course not."

Zoe wiped away her tears. "I get it now. He really is the one, or you wouldn't have been so mad. God, you were mad."

"He *is* the one, Zoe. I don't know how I know, but he is."

"I'm sorry I didn't believe you."

"I wish I hadn't said all that stuff. It was mean."

"Don't worry. I don't expect a perfect life. Nobody gets that. I can take whatever life dishes out to me and turn it into a casserole, but I can't go through life with you hating me."

"*You're* the casserole—inside you're all mush."

"So are you," Zoe said, laughing. "You just have a harder crust."

"Well, don't tell anyone."

Phoebe stared back down the block. Only now did she notice they both were shivering. "Your mascara's a mess. What should we tell Mom?"

"We had a good heart-to-heart. She doesn't need to know."

"She figures out more than you think."

"This should stay between you and me."

"All right, I won't say a thing."

They turned back, stepping more lightly now, eager to reach the warm, well-lit house.

"Do you care if I stay over?" Zoe asked.

"What about Jeremy?"

"He'll understand. There's a ton you haven't told me yet. All the good stuff, really. We'll put our jammies on, I'll bring in my pillows, and we'll curl up in bed like two cats."

"Like we did when you read those dumb horror books."

"We'll make chocolate-chip cookies with a whole stick of butter. We'll sleep in late. Tomorrow's Sunday. You can't turn me down. You know you can't."

"You're such a bad influence on me."

"Someone has to, or you'd never have any fun."

Phoebe smiled and hooked Zoe's arm. "Thanks for looking out for me, sis. Right now I can't think of a single thing I'd rather do."

21

The wedding took place in May. Jake's parents chipped in for the party, but with four boys, the youngest still in high school, they could only cover the beer and four-piece band. The Connors, whose means were equally modest, had spent much of their nest egg on Zoe's wedding, and because Phoebe's engagement had followed so quickly, they couldn't replenish their savings in time.

Phoebe nonetheless made a stunning bride in a backless white gown with her dark hair pinned up, showing off her shapely neck. The floor-length gown had such a slimming effect that Zoe teased her she looked like a birch tree.

The bridesmaids lined the dais in scarlet gowns, four red roses outshone by the white lily blooming before the altar. Jake grinned foolishly at Phoebe, while his three brothers, standing like marines in black tuxedos, looked like copies of himself at different ages. The ceremony was short and businesslike, the way Phoebe wanted. She kept a sober face until Jake recited his vows, when she beamed as if her face would break.

The shortcomings of the reception were harder to mask. The Connors had booked the Legion club, a gray, cinder-block building with a single window facing a busy street. But Phoebe was unfazed by the humble location. She and Jake had taken ballroom lessons before the wedding, and the bride's regal bearing, as Jake swept her over the dance floor, dusted with yellow powder, delighted the guests. Jake stared at Phoebe, entranced, as he spun her in circles to the tune of *Somewhere My Love.*

After the bridal dance, beer and wine began to flow, and rowdy voices filled the hall. Phoebe drank in the attention lavished on her by everybody— the staff, who granted her every wish, the older couples who told her tales of their own courtships, the friends who came from faraway cities, Jake's college friends, who gazed at her admiringly, and the little girls who laughed with glee as she held their hands and shook them up and down on the dance floor.

Years later, when she thought back to her wedding, it seemed that for a single day she'd become the person she'd always wanted to be, having shed the parts of herself she didn't like, and everybody there, that is, every person who cared about her, both saw and celebrated the change. The feeling affected her so deeply that she decided from this day forward to always give a louder voice to this bolder, more cheerful, and outgoing self.

Midway through the night, someone tapped her on the shoulder. She turned around to find Jeremy staring at her self-consciously. "May I dance with the bride?"

A slow waltz played. He lifted Phoebe's hand and pressed his right hand into her back. He was a good dancer, and he moved her effortlessly across the floor.

"There's something I have to say. It's touchy, but important. It's about the fight you and Zoe had after you got engaged."

For the first time that day, a frown marred Phoebe's face. "She told you about that?"

"She did. It really upset her."

"Everything?"

He studied her look. "I think so. Anyway, the part about Jake and me not being friends."

"I said a lot of mean things that night."

"I'm glad you worked it out. It's pretty clear that Jake and I don't have much in common—but I think you two are a good match, and that's what counts. He seems like a decent guy. I don't think we'll take vacations together—"

"Probably not."

"But I want you to promise me it will never push you and Zoe apart. No matter what you think of me, I know that Zoe loves you, and I don't want her to lose that. So can you promise me that Jake and I will never come between you?"

His plea touched her, and for the first time since meeting him, she wondered if she'd unfairly judged him. "I understand, Jeremy. That's very sweet of you. I promise."

Going back to the bridal table, they found Jake and Zoe, flush faced from dancing.

"Don't move," Jeremy said. He turned and hurried out the door.

"Now what?" Phoebe asked.

A minute later, he came back with four champagne flutes and a bottle of Moët & Chandon. He peeled off the foil, twisted off the wire cage, and popped the cork. Foam gushed over the neck and splattered on the floor. He filled all their flutes, straightened up, and looked directly at Phoebe and Jake. "I wish you every good thing that life has to offer—love, pleasure, prosperity, meaningful work, a beautiful home, good friends, happy children, and someday, grandchildren—the fulfillment of all your hopes and dreams."

"That's so kind of you, Jeremy," Phoebe said, her face glowing.

Jake raised his glass. "And we wish the same for you and Zoe."

They clinked their flutes together and tipped back their heads. Phoebe and Zoe hugged, and Jake and Jeremy shook hands and patted each other on the back.

For just a few seconds, the lights burned brighter, the room felt warmer, the music sounded finer, and the bride in her snowy gown looked even more beautiful. The memory of Jeremy's toast and the image of the future it painted in their minds would stay with each of them—although each for different reasons—to the final day of their lives.

Part Two
1990

22

Jeremy sat in the cafeteria across from Roberta Thompson, the national-news editor, and wrinkled his nose. This late in the day, the cafeteria provided a safe spot for a private conversation. Now and then two women in white aprons and hairnets appeared behind the stainless-steel counters, and the occasional editor shuffled through for a cup of coffee or a bag of pretzels, but otherwise the cafeteria, save for the buzz of the overhead lights, was eerily quiet.

Trouble was brewing at the Herald. According to the rumor mill, Jeremy's closest friend and the best man at his wedding, Ben Nelson, would soon be fired. A year ago, he'd been hired as the Herald's consumer affairs reporter and was given a green light by the paper to expose fraud and false advertising in local businesses. In the past year, Ben had scored several coups, including an exposé of a local bank and a health-club chain, but he'd overstepped his mandate when he wrote a story about a local car dealer who was selling a minivan that randomly accelerated, resulting in four crashes and a few broken bones. All the car dealers in the metro area had responded by joining forces and threatening to pull the plug on a million dollars worth of advertising—unless the Herald met their demands, which included firing Ben. And if the rumors were true, the Herald was already feeling the pinch and ready to cave in.

As soon as the rumor surfaced, Roberta began to muster the troops and lead the charge for Ben's cause. She'd pressured Jeremy into this covert meeting, not only to ask for his support, he assumed, but to draw out any information that he might be withholding.

Roberta had a sharp, over-caffeinated air and a quirky style of dress, combining tennis shoes with floral-patterned blouses and business jackets. She never styled her hair or bothered with make-up. If she had, Jeremy thought, she would have turned a lot of heads at the Herald, where she had the reputation of being too smart, too intense, and too overbearing to have a boyfriend. Speaking to Jeremy, she leaned into the table and glared at him with a prosecutorial zeal.

"Things are moving fast, Jeremy. Battle lines are being drawn. The villagers are taking up arms, and if they fire Ben, we'll storm the castle."

"That sounds heroic, but you might not like the result."

"You don't think we can win?"

"In this case, I don't think there is a win. None of the options look very good."

"For anyone who calls herself a journalist, there *is* only one option. Our advertisers have to know they can't cherry-pick the news, and our owners have to know they can't sell the truth to the highest bidder."

"I understand that, but to stick with your metaphor—what if you burn down the castle and the walls fall on top of you?"

"Meaning what?

"What happens when they start firing people?"

Instead of prompting Roberta to consider that a victory could backfire, his remark only fanned her outrage. "Let them fire me. Who wants to work for a paper that puts its quarterly profit before its obligation to report the truth?"

"You know I feel the same way. But you have to be realistic. You can't ignore the consequences."

Roberta shook her head like a bulldog. "How can you compromise on something like this? What's the point of anything we do, Jeremy—why bother coming to work if stories like this can't see the light of day? We're talking about little kids climbing into a death trap. That's a crime, and it's our job to let people know. That's what they pay us for. What the Herald is doing is wrong on so many levels, I can't even start. It's a knife in my gut, and whole staff feels the same way. How can you not be livid?"

"It sounds disturbing, yes, but so far they haven't done a thing."

"It's only a matter of time before Ansel fires Ben."

"I doubt he's making the call. I'm sure the pressure is coming from the owners."

"But they'll want his blessing. They know he can't do his job without his staff. That's why you have to talk him out of this. He's your boss, Jeremy, and it's our best chance to nip this in the bud. He respects you, and if you make clear the consequences of firing Ben, he might come around."

"I can do that, but it will only delay the crisis. How are we going to replace the lost revenue? A million dollars is nothing to scoff at. What happens when our owners hold Ansel accountable? What if they fire *him?* Have you thought of that? You're asking me to tell my boss to put his job on the line."

"Well, he *is* accountable. He signed off on the story."

"True," Jeremy grumbled.

Roberta leaned back, but her words belied her bearing. "It's not just about him, Jeremy. It's about you. A lot of people around here think you're Ansel's boy. I hate to give you the bad news, but sooner or later, you'll have to pick sides."

His cheeks burned. With an effort, he curbed his indignation and replied in a calm, measured voice. "That's where you and I part ways, Roberta. I don't see the problem as *us versus them.* It's our problem too. We need to solve it together."

Roberta snorted. "Listen to you. *Solve it together.* You sound like one of them. Next thing you'll say *there's no I in team.* Be careful, Jeremy. Some things really are black and white. You can lose your soul in shades of gray."

He stared at Roberta sullenly. Deep down, he knew that she was right, but he resented her for shoving her moral superiority down his throat, and her dismissal of the lost revenue profoundly disturbed him. "I see Ansel at four. I'll tell him what I think, but I doubt it will change his mind."

He stood abruptly and shoved in his chair. "Just leave my soul out of this."

23

Jeremy peered over his computer screen into the glass-walled office of the Herald's managing editor, Ansel Abrams. From 50 feet away, he could make out the tension in Ansel's face. His jaw was clamped shut like a baited dog, ready to bite the next person who strayed within the arc of his chain.

Ansel caught Jeremy's glance and waved him in. He steered between the scores of desks in the cavernous newsroom, unaffected by the chaos and noise that rivaled a stock exchange. No one stayed in any spot for long. Reporters flitted across the floor like sheets of paper driven by the wind. The openness of the room, built to foster communication among the staff, had always reassured him, forcing transparency on the paper's day-to-day operations, but now that his own movements and not someone else's were being watched, he felt like a target for hundreds of eyes.

He slipped through the glass door and sat without greeting his boss. Ansel glanced up over his tortoiseshell rims. His gunmetal gray suit was tailored to his tall, slim build, and silver locks curled behind his ears and brushed the collar of his white shirt. Every day he seemed to wear a new, more outrageous tie. Today his choice reminded Jeremy of a canvas strip torn from a Chagall.

He plucked the glasses from his nose and raised a cynical eyebrow. "This Ben Nelson thing is a nightmare."

"So I hear."

"I just met with management. They want me to fix it now. They won't interfere, which is damn clever of them—giving me just enough rope to hang myself. No matter what I do, it's my ass. If I fire Ben, the staff will go postal. If I buck the dealers and we can't make up the lost advertising, people will lose their jobs. Either way, I'm screwed."

Jeremy folded his hands. "I don't mean to sound callous, but you did hire Ben to do this job, and you did approve all his reports."

Ansel stared at him sharply. "You don't need to remind me. I'm not trying to shift the blame, and I don't regret my decision. That story needed telling. You know that."

"I do, but I'm surprised all the repercussions weren't thought through beforehand."

Ansel colored. "We did look at them. We discussed every possible outcome—or thought we had. But we got blindsided. We always knew we might lose the north metro dealers—they sell the damn minivan—and we were willing to risk that, but who thought the rest of them would join together and come after us? I still can't believe it. They hate each other."

"Apparently not as much as they hate us."

"I want your advice, Jeremy. You're in touch with the editorial staff. If you were in my position, what would you do?"

He screwed up his face.

"You can be frank. You and I have always been frank with each other."

"We have." Jeremy paused and thought for a while. "Well, it's not fair to punish Ben."

"Of course not. It would be a gross injustice."

"And I just talked with, um, a coworker."

"Roberta."

"All right, Roberta. If you let Ben go, the staff will mutiny. They already have a petition going around. She even talked about taking the story public."

"That's crazy. Would they rather lose their jobs?"

"As Roberta put it, who wants to work for a corrupt paper? And she thinks we can replace the lost advertising."

"*Journalists.* Easy for her to say. You can't make up that much revenue on short notice. They're already pulling their ads."

"How much time will management give us?"

"Three months. But that's not the biggest problem. People who know think we're going into a recession. Not the best environment for raising a million dollars."

"I'm not a businessman, so I can't tell you how to raise the money, but I can tell you what will happen if you fire Ben. You said the staff would go postal, and you're right. But I think there's more at stake here. Frankly, I'm surprised the Herald left the call entirely up to you. Not that I doubt your judgment—you know I respect it—but it tells me they don't really see the depth of the problem. If you make a mistake, not just you, but everybody who works here, including the owners, will lose their reputations. The paper might never recover. So I have to believe you start with the premise that Ben stays. If his piece was accurate, you have to stand behind him. Then it just becomes a practical matter of how to replace the advertising."

Ansel nodded. "You make a good case. It's very logical. But the fact is, the situation is *not* logical, so I disagree."

"Why is it not logical?"

He stood up and spread out his hands. "It's a power struggle, Jeremy—and we lost. The dealers have more power than we do. It's that simple."

Jeremy frowned. He'd picked journalism as a career because he saw it as a temple whose pillars of truth, civic virtue, and the supremacy of words stood impervious to the barbarian onslaught of money and power, yet here they were, ready to pound his pillars into rubble. "There must be a way to fight them," he muttered.

"What's to fight? It's their money. They can spend it wherever they want, and they won't spend it here unless we do what they say. If we don't, we'll have to fire people, and I don't want to be responsible for that."

"No offence, but some people say you already are."

Ansel met his gaze without flinching. "They're right. I *should* lose my job. If it makes you feel any better, I did offer myself in place of Ben. They turned me down."

"Who?"

"The dealers. I told them I approved the story, and that made me responsible, not Ben, and if anybody should go, it was me. But they want *Ben*."

"Why only him?"

"To the public, they're Ben's stories. Every time his byline shows up, they'll think of those crooked dealers who were selling mothers deathtraps for their kids. So Ben is the one who needs to go. My departure won't do them any good."

"That's so unfair, Ansel."

"I know. And that's why I can't fire him."

"But I thought you said—"

"I know what I said. What I meant was, I still have to appease the dealers."

"How can you?"

"By making sure his byline never appears in the paper again. I'm killing the consumer affairs column and moving Ben to the night side."

"The night side? Doing what?"

"I still haven't figured that out. But we always need reporters there."

"Because no one in his right mind wants to work it, especially if they have kids, like Ben."

"Well, at least he'll have a job."

"A job that ends his career." Jeremy shook his head. "And you're still letting the dealers control the news."

"Call it what you like. I can't think of a better solution. It boils down to numbers. It's one person's career against five or six others'. As much as I hate to punish Ben, it would be far worse to fire innocent people. Ben always knew the risks that came with the job, and he accepted them. Fair or not, he'll have to take the fall."

Jeremy turned away, stewing. "Ben was my best man at my wedding," he muttered.

"I know, Jeremy. I'm sorry, but I'm asking you to put aside your personal feelings. Assuming the dealers go for this, I'll need your help to persuade the staff there's no other course. They won't listen to me—but they might listen to you, if you explain my reasoning."

He rubbed the back of his neck. "I don't know, Ansel. How can I persuade them if I can't support it myself?"

"Things may seem clear to you now, but one day, you'll be a manager—you might even have my job—and your decisions will affect a lot of other people. Then you might see things differently."

"I hope you're wrong about that."

"I know it's a rotten deal. I wish there was some other way, but there isn't. Take some time and think about it, Jeremy. You have a good future ahead of you at the Herald. I respect your concerns, but I'm going to need your support to get through this one."

He frowned and cocked his head. "That almost sounded like a bribe."

"It's not. But someday I'll pick my replacement, and you can be sure that I won't pick anyone who hasn't stood behind me over the years, and right now I need your help like I never have before."

24

A blast of winter air chased Zoe into the foyer of Jake and Phoebe's new rambler. The wind tousled her cropped hair, and the cold splotched her cheeks with red. Her eyes still had the sparkle of a young girl's, only more tired now—the two reasons being the Santa-Claus-like belly that parted the waist of her navy-blue coat and the smaller copy of herself hiding behind her legs in a matching coat with enormous black buttons.

Phoebe held the door open for her niece, balking on the doorstep.

"Maddy—come inside," Zoe said. "You're letting in the cold."

"I don't mind," Phoebe said. "It feels good."

Not only did Phoebe's hair match Zoe's, but her face had the same fiery blush, and the half-orb of her belly stretched thin her cotton shirt. Otherwise, she looked unchanged, as if you could lift up the shirt, pull out a soccer ball, and have the old Phoebe back. "Do you have time for coffee?"

"No, I'm running late—Maddy, give me your coat."

Maddy, or Madison Edwards, let her coat be roughly pulled off while her eyes darted around the living room. Long, dark ringlets dangled on the shoulders of her velvet dress, fitted to her fine-boned frame. An impish light burned in her brown eyes, and her cherubic lips opened and closed as if savoring the feel of their own softness.

Released from her coat, she ran to Phoebe and hugged her legs. "Fee-wee! Pick me up!" she demanded.

Phoebe looked down and smiled. "Honey, I can't. You're too heavy for my baby."

Maddy stomped her feet and frowned at Phoebe's belly. She mulled it over angrily and then punched it.

"Ouch, Maddy!"

Zoe flew to her side. "Madison Edwards! Shame on you."

She knelt beside her daughter, grabbed her wrist, and stared at her woundedly. Maddy kept gazing at Phoebe's belly and wouldn't look at Zoe. "Bad baby," she pouted.

"No—good baby. Why did you hit Phoebe's baby?"

"It's okay," Phoebe offered. "I'm fine."

"It's not okay," Zoe said, wrinkling her brow at Maddy, who seemed to doubt that she'd done anything wrong. "Tell Phoebe you're sorry. Promise you'll never do it again."

"Sorry," Maddy said without looking very.

"Now get your toys and play in the dining room, where I can see you."

"I will, Mommy." Her face lit up, and acting like nothing had happened, she ran to her backpack and dug out her multi-colored ponies.

"Are you sure you're okay?" Zoe asked.

"I barely felt it. But it startled me."

"I don't know why she did that. You're Maddy's favorite. It's always Fee-wee this and Fee-wee that. She even tells people she has two mommies."

"That explains it."

"Of course—*bad baby.* She's jealous."

"I should be flattered."

"Are you sure you can handle her?"

"We'll be fine, Zoe. We always have fun together."

"All right," Zoe said, placing her hands on her belly. "I'd better go. I don't want to be late for this."

"Make sure you get some pictures. I want to see them too."

"Lift your shirt up, honey," the nurse said as though addressing a child, in spite of being the same age as Zoe.

Zoe lifted up her blouse and leaned back on the bed. The nurse wheeled over a cart supporting a console, keyboard, and charcoal screen salted around the edges with white numbers. She'd come to perform Zoe's 35-week ultrasound, ordered by her doctor to set the date of her caesarean.

"This will be cold."

She squirted out a blob of clear gel onto Zoe's swollen belly.

Zoe shivered. "Do they keep that stuff in the fridge?"

The nurse smiled. "Room temperature. But it's cold compared to your skin." Rather than spreading the blob with her hand, she dabbed it with the transducer and smeared it deftly in a circular pattern over Zoe's belly. A second later, a shifting, snowy image appeared on the screen. "Do you know the sex of your baby?"

"It's a boy—Oh my, I can see his face."

The nurse ignored her and focused on the morphing images matching the turns of her wrist. "He looks good. A bit on the small side. I'll take some measurements."

She dragged the mouse and plotted white lines along the baby's limbs. She marked down the numbers on a chart and began to measure the skull.

"He's on the low side, but in the normal range."

"Normal is good."

The nurse, intent on her work, swiveled her wrist and conjured up a new image. "There's his heart. You can see it beating."

Zoe pointed to the screen. "Are those holes?"

"No, they're blood vessels going through the heart wall. Except this one—it's a hole between the upper chambers, but it will close up after he's born and his lungs start working."

"Weird. All by itself?"

The nurse studied the image. "Hmm."

Zoe froze like a startled rabbit. "What's the matter?"

"Probably nothing." She popped a diskette into the drive and swirled the transducer.

"What are you doing?"

"Recording."

"What did you see?"

The nurse didn't answer. She quickly found her target and focused on the image. "Like I said—probably nothing."

Zoe stared darkly into the screen. If the grainy image of her child held any secret, it remained hidden from her.

The nurse pulled out the diskette. "You can pull down your shirt. I might be a minute." Without explaining further, she vanished through the door.

Zoe wiped her belly with a tissue, but she touched the skin more tenderly now. Suddenly it seemed risky, as if too much pressure might hurt her baby. A cold fear gripped her heart. *He has to be okay. Life can't be that cruel.* Now she wished that Jeremy had come along, the way they'd planned, before a crisis had kept him at the office.

Half an hour passed and the nurse didn't return. Zoe paged through every tabloid in the rack, but even the wildest stories couldn't keep her from dwelling on her worst fears, no matter how far-fetched they were, feeling as if her baby had already been given a death sentence.

She started pacing. *If this goes on much longer, I'll jump out of my skin.*

Finally, a middle-aged woman in a white coat stepped in, staring at a clipboard. She introduced herself as Dr. Zhang.

"Is there something wrong with my baby?" Zoe asked.

"We're not sure. Ultrasounds aren't very good at diagnosing heart defects—"

"Heart defects?"

"I'm afraid we have to check. We'd like to give you another test."

"What kind of test?"

"An echocardiogram. It's like an ultrasound, but we'll get a better picture of your baby's heart. Dr. Berndt will do the procedure. He's a pediatric cardiologist. Are you okay with that?"

Zoe went numb. It took her a while to answer. "Do I have a choice?"

"Of course, but you should have it done. If there's anything wrong with your baby, you'll want him to get all the care he needs, and the sooner the better."

25

When Jeremy walked in, Zoe leaped off the bed and gave him a long, anguished hug. She buried her face into his jacket as sobs shook her body.

"C'mon, Zoe. We don't know much yet."

"You're wrong. I already know."

"How can you?"

"I just do."

"Wait and see. They can't be much longer."

The last two hours had been the worst of her life. A nurse had helped her into a gown, put her in a wheelchair, and rolled her into a new room, where she sat for nearly an hour. A second nurse had finally wheeled in the echocardiograph, which looked the same as the ultrasound, and half an hour later, Dr. Berndt, a husky, bearded man, repeated the motions of her prior exam, only now Zoe lay on her back and moved her body into various poses. The whole time, Dr. Berndt kept the screen turned away from her, and each time he pursed his lips or narrowed his eyes, Zoe imagined that he'd found some fresh nightmare. Worse, he ignored her barrage of questions, calling the procedure *merely precautionary,* and constantly reminded her to lie still. He claimed not to be looking for anything specific, but only checking the functions of her child's heart to confirm that it was healthy.

Soon she found herself bargaining with God, begging forgiveness for every lie she'd told, every hurtful word she'd spoken, every drink or pill she'd taken, whether aspirin or quaaludes. It wasn't fair to punish her baby for things she'd done so many years ago, when young and foolish, and she promised God a hundred, desperate, crazy things, if only he'd forgive her past and let her child be healthy.

Something caught Dr. Berndt's eye. He swiveled the probe, squinted at the screen, and asked her to roll on her side. She could tell by his stiff face that he'd found something wrong. She wanted desperately to ask him what, but was too afraid, and convinced that he wouldn't tell her anyway, lay there trembling, succumbing to her worst fears and trying to hold back her sobs.

The door swung open. Dr. Berndt stepped in and shook Jeremy's hand. His lack of urgency told Zoe everything. In her experience, doctors never spent much time with you, and Dr. Berndt had come in with the air of someone who'd blocked out a long span of time to speak with his patient.

He sat on the stool. In one hand, he held a scaled model of a human heart. The sight of it crushed any remaining hope that her baby was healthy, and for a second, her mind went blank, but she quickly forced herself to refocus, knowing how critical the coming discussion would be.

Dr. Berndt smiled as if greeting them at church instead of pronouncing the fate of their child. "Your baby has a fairly common heart defect. It's called *atrial septal defect*, or ASD. In layman's terms, there's a hole between the upper chambers of his heart."

Hearing the word *hole*, she flinched. Her throat stopped up, making it hard to breathe.

Dr. Berndt snapped off the heart's outer wall, exposing four red and blue chambers. Using a pen, he pointed out the wall between the two upper atria. "It's right here, not very large, smaller than a pea. But that could change. It might grow. Then again it might not, and sometimes it closes all by itself and the problem goes away."

"What are the odds of that?" Jeremy asked.

"About 20 percent."

"What if it doesn't? What happens after he's born?"

"The chances are he'll lead a fairly normal life, assuming the hole doesn't grow. You'll have to restrict his activities, and he'll be prone to respiratory infections—but we have medications for those."

Zoe pinched the bridge of her nose and sighed. "Then it's not as bad as I thought. It can't kill him."

"Technically, it can. It's not common, but he could have blood clots or strokes. So if the hole doesn't resolve itself, or it gets any larger, we recommend that you repair it."

"You can fix it?" Jeremy asked.

Dr. Berndt paused. "With open-heart surgery."

"On a baby?" Zoe said.

"The timing would depend on the size of the hole and the severity of his problems."

"Are we talking about—" Jeremy glanced at Zoe. "Putting him on a breathing machine?"

"It would be traditional open-heart surgery. We stop the heart, connect him to a heart-lung machine, and then sew up the hole. If everything goes according to plan, from that point on, his heart will function normally."

"I can't imagine doing that," Zoe said with a shiver.

"He might not need it. But if he has trouble, I'd recommend it. If he were my child, I'd want it done as soon as possible. Then the problem's resolved."

"What's are the risks?" Jeremy asked.

"With surgery there's always a risk of complications, or death. But the odds are small. Our success rate is over 90 percent, and the mortality rate is somewhere between two and three percent."

"That's not so bad."

"That's terrible," Zoe snapped. "That's a three percent chance of dying."

Jeremy frowned. "Are there any alternatives?"

"I just heard about something new. They catheterize a vein in your thigh and move a small device up the vena cava. When it reaches the heart, they deploy it and plug the hole. Apart from the catheter, there's no incision, and the heart never stops beating. But it's all still experimental. It's years away from being perfected, let alone approved by the FDA."

"What if we do nothing?" Zoe asked. "You said he'd lead a fairly normal life. What does that mean?"

"The main thing is to keep him from taxing the heart. It would mean frequent doctor visits and tests. He might have to go on medications to strengthen the heart or to fight off infections. If blood flows back through the hole and into the right atrium, it could strain the heart and make it larger. Over time, that's not healthy. It would be one more reason to have the surgery."

"But if that doesn't happen, he might get by."

"He might. Then again, he might not. To be honest, we don't know right now. All we know is that he has a defect. We don't know how large it will be at birth or how it will affect him later on. But you need to be aware of the problems he could face and the treatments we can offer. And you need to think about them now—so when the time comes, you can make the right decision."

On the ride home, Jeremy went through the pros and cons of the medical treatments, but Zoe barely heard him. She slumped in her seat as the snow-draped yards and trees slipped by with never-ending sameness, focusing on her child and what she, not the doctors, could do for him. Unlike Jeremy, she'd already moved beyond the medical aspects of his illness. Unlike him, she was less concerned about the choice of treatments or the odds of one working better than another and was more concerned about the emotional health of her child. No matter how severe his illness, no matter what choices they made, he would be a fragile boy—one who would need constant watching, tireless care, and boundless love. And this she would give him without any bitterness or regret, even gladly, because his weakness justified any sacrifice that she had to make on his behalf, whether it be her own happiness, health, or even her life. She made this vow without any conscious effort. In a way, her child had made it for her, and she responded to his need in the only way she knew how, by devoting herself to him without reservation or limit. From this day forward, she knew beyond any doubt that he would be the focus of her energies, the object of her deepest love, and the source of all her joys and cares.

26

Jeremy shut Ansel's door and glanced furtively about the newsroom, but none of the staff had noticed him—or at least they pretended not to. He stared straight ahead and made his way back to his desk, capped with two monitors and cluttered with papers, black-and-white prints, and steno pads filled with hieroglyphic notes. Only after sitting behind his monitor did he permit himself a smile. Ansel had just told him that he was the top candidate to replace the Herald's deputy managing editor, who'd been hired away by a paper in Seattle. The competition for his job was fierce; a dozen applicants inside the paper were vying for the post—and many more outside it. Landing the job would not only raise Jeremy's salary by $5,000, a hefty sum for the industry, but almost guarantee that he become the Herald's next managing editor when Ansel retired.

The taste of victory lasted only seconds. He'd just started revising his piece on the state's proposed gas tax when Ben Nelson appeared before his desk. Ben's disheveled clothes conveyed the same downbeat mood as his face. Compared with his typically starched shirts and crisp khaki pants, his outfit today looked thrown on straight from the dryer, and his navy tie dangled around his neck like a noose.

"I saw you with Ansel. Anything I should know?"

The tension lifted from his face. At least he wouldn't have to lie. "It was about the job."

"A second interview?"

"Nothing that formal. Just a conversation."

"You've had quite a few of those."

"Keeping tabs on the competition?"

"I didn't mean to pry. I think you'll get it. You deserve it. Your judgment is good, and you don't waste time on the small stuff. That's what Ansel likes about you."

"Thanks, but I don't want to get too cocky."

"You'll get it, even though I might not be here to see it."

"Why do you say that?" he asked, appalled by the phony sound of his voice.

"They're sending me to the night side—haven't you heard?"

"I thought it was just a rumor."

"Why wouldn't they? I ruined the paper's balance sheet."

"You were doing your job, Ben."

"I know, but I feel responsible. The story was my idea. I pushed it through. I never thought it would get this out of hand."

"You couldn't predict that."

"Maybe, maybe not. Still, what they're doing is wrong. It makes a mockery of the free press."

His face tensed. He knew what Ben was leading up to. "It's a dilemma, that's for sure."

"Really? I'm surprised, Jeremy. Doesn't it bother you more? Don't you want to fight? Not for my sake—I wrote the damn story, and they can blame me if they want—I can live with that. What I can't live with is how they're caving in to keep the advertising. That's not about me. It affects the whole paper—anyone who writes a piece that might offend some powerful group— are you telling me we can't run those stories anymore? That's basically the end of journalism. I'm a little shocked it doesn't have you up in arms. You're more the crusader than I am."

"I'm as upset as anyone, but honestly, these days my head is barely at work. We just found out that our baby has a heart defect. Coping with that and meeting my deadlines is all I can handle right now."

Ben looked away. "I heard. I'm sorry. I know that's more important."

"It does change your outlook."

"Well, I don't expect you to lead the charge or anything, and I won't bring it up again, but do you know about the petition that's going around?"

"Roberta told me."

"Are you going to sign it?"

He felt like a hermit crab pulling into his shell. "Do you really think it will help?"

"I do. The petition is just a starting point. Roberta has Cohen and Jacobs on board, most of the section editors, and nearly all the reporters. They might even go public—give the story to the crosstown paper, the local radio, the street rags—anybody who'll listen. But we're hoping that management will back down before it goes that far."

"They might. Or they might fire the ringleaders."

Ben stiffened, as if the thought had never occurred to him. "They'd never fire Jacobs or Cohen.

"I hope you're right." He glanced around Ben. Across the newsroom, behind his glass wall, Ansel was eyeing him and looking unhappy.

He squirmed in his chair. In most situations, his course of action would have been clear. He knew where his duties lay—as a journalist, as a man, and, most of all, as a friend—yet it shocked him just how little Ben's scapegoating had angered him. In truth, he felt a bit peeved, even resentful, that Ben had run a story with such a predictable, negative outcome, even though he had less cause to be angry with Ben than with Ansel, who was dangling a job before him to keep him loyal. The trouble was that only Ansel could ease the burden of his sick child, and only Ansel could add to that burden by shelving his career—which not only made him more resentful of Ben than his boss, but also threw his deepest beliefs into confusion.

The glance hadn't escaped Ben. "He's watching, isn't he?"

"You're a good friend, Ben, so I don't know how to say this. But I need to ask you . . . not to ask me anymore. You know I'm on your side, but right now, I can't put my name on anyone's list—not yours or anyone else's, because if something happened to me—"

Ben held up his hand. "I get it. You don't have to explain. It's not your battle anyway—it's mine. Just give my love to Zoe. I hope the doctors are wrong, and your boy is perfectly healthy."

27

Jeremy filed his gas-tax story around seven, grabbed his briefcase, and clipped down the Herald's front steps. While he often worked late on deadlines, tonight, instead of going home, he tramped along Northstar Avenue into the snarling wind and bitter cold, feeling wounded by his conversation with Ben and debating whether or not to share it with Zoe.

A tangle of red neon lights guided him down the wind-swept sidewalk. On the ice-covered streets, cars mutely coasted by, wrapped in a white mist that dimmed their lights and blurred their shapes. Jeremy tucked his chin into his scarf and leaned into the wind, but the cold sliced through his coat as if it were made of crepe. Shivering, he stopped before The Trapper Bar & Grill, a brownstone building squeezed between a tobacco store and pawnshop, the sort of dive where he'd never be caught dead; but tonight, for some reason, the contrast with his everyday life drew him inside.

Abandon your cares ye who enter here read the sign above the door. As he opened it, a blast of volcanic heat struck his face. On the walls hung crooked neon signs, their cherry-red tubes glowing like a satanic glassworks. The long, dark room smelled of deep-fat fryers, grilling onions, and cigars. Cigarette butts and peanut shells covered the greasy floor. A haze of smoke sucked the air from his lungs and nearly hid the booths in the rear. A few lost souls huddled around tables, looking like people recently fired, evicted from their homes, or paralyzed by repeated bad luck and surviving by secret, underhanded means. There might be a small chance of running into a pressman here, Jeremy thought, but virtually no chance of running into any of his peers.

He approached the bar and pulled off his leather gloves. The bartender eyed them as if he'd laid a pistol on the counter.

"A very-dry vodka martini, straight-up—with two olives."

The bartender, a big-jowled troll with beady eyes, conjured up his martini. Despite the man's ugliness, Jeremy found him amusing. He commanded the space behind the bar with the air of a prison guard. His gorilla forearms, large as Jeremy's calves, seemed to rip open his rolled-up sleeves. He moved swiftly for a man his size, flinging bottles around with the ease of a practiced juggler. Ten to one he was a high-school linebacker or defensive end, 20 years ago, before he'd started packing on the pounds.

Jeremy put two dollars on the counter, and the man repaid him with a good stiff pour. Hoping to avoid any conversation, he slunk to the last booth, near the men's bathroom, and sat with his back to the street, making himself invisible to anyone who entered The Trapper.

He took a sip and savored the bite of glaciated vodka. It burned his tongue and felt like dry ice oozing down his throat. The rush cleared his head and numbed him to the nightmare unfolding at the Herald and the equally disturbing mood of martyrdom building at home. Either of the two, he could have managed, or one after the other, but work and home at the same time was more than he could bear.

He took a second, smaller sip. It was pointless to hide in The Trapper and pity himself. It wouldn't change a thing—even though it wasn't a crime to indulge himself for just one night. Just like other people, he needed a break now and then, an hour to escape from the stress that dogged him all day and recently had kept him from sleeping at night. The last few weeks at the office had passed in a fog, as he fought to complete the most urgent tasks while fresh deadlines boiled up around him. Deadlines were deadlines, no matter what his mood or energy level, but as fast as he knocked them off, others sprang up in their place. When he'd started at the Herald, the pressure hadn't bothered him much—he'd loved diving into a story, meeting the state's movers and shakers, touching the lives of thousands of people, while at the same time serving the public good. With the job had come a never-ending string of perks that made up for his modest salary—free meals, drinks, and tickets that PR firms and their clients were always pushing on the staff.

But over time the demands of the job had outpaced the perks. A single misstated fact could spread a rumor; destroy a career, a business, or even a life; or provoke a lawsuit and bankrupt the paper. There were always angry letters from people who felt misquoted, falsely accused, or somehow maligned by his stories. Equally troubling were the business owners and publicity hounds who tried to sway his stories for personal gain, and if they ever coaxed him to let down his guard, his reputation could be tarnished. On top of that were the long hours and the many evenings spent away from home. Zoe was a saint— she never complained about him working nights, not because she didn't mind, but only because she believed in his potential and the virtue of his calling.

Home, until recently, had always been a haven from the pressures at work. Zoe had not only remained the love of his life, but had proven to be a perfect mate, a loving mother, and a great household manager, skilled at juggling many roles. After seven years of marriage, he still preferred to spend time with her than anyone else. Neither age nor the humdrum of life had diminished her ideals, beauty, or sense of humor, and she still surprised him daily with her clever observations and witty remarks. More important, she seemed happy with her life, her career, and with him—and proud of him too, which in turn made him proud, being married to a woman who fascinated so many of his coworkers and friends.

But much had changed with this second pregnancy. As she had with her first, Zoe had turned inward, which seemed perfectly natural, given the radical changes that her body was undergoing. But this time around, Zoe had shown few signs of coming back. It wasn't only the unique bond that she and her child shared—that he understood. It was more that he couldn't reach *her*, almost as if she'd moved away or died, and he worried the change might last long after their son was born or maybe even for the rest of their lives.

He knew it was wrong to resent the child. Even so, a tinge of bitterness toward him did creep in now and then, at the same time his heart was bursting with compassion for him. As a man, he knew better the trials the boy would face, which Zoe, having grown up without brothers, couldn't guess. The odds were good he'd be forbidden from riding his bike, climbing trees, going to camps, or playing sports—the whole range of physical tests that defined a boy more than it did the average girl.

And that wouldn't be the worst part. He might be excluded, teased, or even bullied by his peers.

Beyond that, he would battle constant fatigue, spend hours in hospitals or doctor's offices, cope with chronic infections, require surgeries. God knows, he might even—

Jeremy stopped. Every time he imagined what the coming years would bring, his mind went numb. A fog clouded the future, and all he felt was panic. It was unlike him to react this way. He always liked to plan, to be prepared, but this time he couldn't set a proper course, because that would force him to accept the reality of his unlucky child as fact, and for some reason, he couldn't, even though he knew it beyond any doubt: there was a hole in the heart of his unborn son, and nothing he thought or said or did would make it go away.

28

Jeremy stomped the snow off his shoes and closed his front door, locking out the air so cold that breathing hurt his lungs. By contrast, the hardwood floors and stucco walls of the lit foyer, lined with Zoe and Maddy's winter coats, radiated warmth. He hung up his coat and tossed his cap on the shelf as Maddy pitter-pattered around the corner. Before he could leave the foyer, her tiny figure hugged him around the knees. "Daddy! Daddy!" she sang happily.

He gazed into her beaming face, admiring her big brown eyes, long dark lashes, and cherubic lips. After a day like today, nothing could be more welcome than his daughter's perfect smile.

"Where've you been, Daddy?"

"Working. Am I late for dinner?"

"Mommy's cooking a pizza."

Jeremy smiled. One of the few complaints he could level against Zoe was her dislike of cooking. "Are you helping her?"

"No, I'm playing with my Polly Pockets."

As quickly as she came, Maddy went back to her toys.

Zoe was standing in their kitchen with its black-and-white tiles, birch cabinets, and the 1930s radiator that hissed and clicked when the furnace ran. Swaddled in sweatpants and a cotton top, she was eyeing the oven door like a portly man who'd dropped his hat but couldn't bend over to pick it up. The sight of her standing there, so big and awkward, filled him with tenderness, but right on its heels came a feeling of dread. Her C-section was planned only two weeks from today.

"There you are," she said, coming toward him. "What's wrong?"

"It's Ben."

"They fired him?"

"No, but they might as well. They moved him to the night side."

She hugged him as best she could. "That's terrible news. I'm sorry, Jeremy."

"I'll tell you about it. But first I need a drink."

After eating pizza and watching *Pinocchio*, they tucked Maddy into her toddler bed and went to the living room. Jeremy poured himself a merlot, while Zoe stretched out on the sofa, propping her knees up with a pillow. "Okay—what happened?"

He cradled his goblet and sat beside her. "At five o'clock, Ansel called Ben into his office. Everybody could see them talking. It was a long time, but neither one looked upset. The next thing I know, Ben walks out, shakes my hand, and says goodbye."

"Just like that?"

"Just like that. The paper no longer has a consumer reporter. He starts the night shift on Monday. They put him on the crime beat."

Zoe's eyes flashed with helpless anger. "The crime beat? To make an example of him?"

"They want the dealers to think that."

"Ben's such a good guy. How can they do that?"

"To be honest, Zoe, I'm more worried about next week. Today the place was buzzing, and by Monday it's going to be a hornet's nest."

"Well, it should be."

"I know, but it puts me in a tough spot. I can't stay on the sidelines forever. Ansel is breathing down my neck and Roberta and her gang are hounding me too. No matter what I decide, I'm in trouble."

Zoe cast him a questioning glance. "Ben is your best friend. Doesn't that count for anything?"

"What am I supposed to do?" he said defensively. "Risk my career? Can we afford that now?"

"Wait a second—why would you risk your career?"

"This thing is polarizing the office. Everyone is taking sides. And my boss expects me to back him up."

"And you think he'll fire you if you don't?"

"No, but he could bring my career to a screeching halt."

Zoe stared at him sharply. "When did your career become so important to you, Jeremy? I mean, I'm proud of your work, but that doesn't mean you have to side with your boss when he's wrong. And he is wrong, isn't he?"

"It's not that simple."

"Maybe not. I don't know all the facts, but I hope you're not doing this for me. I didn't marry you for a paycheck. And don't do it for your son either. I think he'd rather respect his dad, even if he's poor."

Jeremy stared at the tangled maze of the Oriental rug. "It's not about money. It's about having a good life for our kids. I want them to have the same opportunities that I had."

"Honey, I know you're in a tough spot, and I know I haven't been here for you. I'm sorry, but you know why."

"Of course I do. And I don't want to cause you more stress."

"But I'm less stressed out than you. It's clouding your thinking. Just because we have this problem doesn't mean you have to sell your soul. If our baby were healthy, we wouldn't be discussing this. You'd be right there behind Ben, wouldn't you?"

"I guess so."

"Then you know what you need to do. You can't avoid it because there might be some unwanted side effect."

"That depends on the side effect."

"You can't predict that. And if you won't take a risk for what you believe, do you really believe it?"

"I don't know," he grumbled.

"Even if you had to quit, we'd get by. We'd still have my health insurance. That's the main thing."

"We couldn't pay our bills on one salary. And insurance won't cover all our medical costs. We don't even know what they'll be yet."

"If things get that bad, we could move in with your parents."

"Sure, and by the way, Mom and Dad, can you support our family?"

"C'mon, tell me you can't find another job."

"The Herald is the only paper in town, and you never wanted to move. Don't even bring up business. You know I'm not cut out for that."

"What about the crosstown paper?"

"They're not hiring now."

"What about TV or radio?"

"We're heading into a downturn, Zoe. No one's hiring. Even if they were, I wouldn't have the same future I do at the Herald."

"Is this promotion really that important to you?"

"No, but I think you're naïve about what it takes to make a living."

"I don't think so. My father and mother raised two kids on middle-class salaries."

"More power to them, but is that all you want? Don't you want our kids to have more than you and Phoebe?"

"Sure, I'd like it, but I wouldn't abandon my friend to get it. And I wouldn't let my job change who I was. Tell me who you want to be, Jeremy—that nice guy I married or someone else? Because I really liked that knight up there on the white horse, and if he fell off—well, that would put me somewhere I've never been before, and, frankly, it scares me. I don't think I'd like being married to someone who put his career before his family."

As Zoe spoke, he could feel her drifting away, like a ship heading out to sea. He fought back a feeling of panic. He had to do whatever he could to bring her back to shore. "All right, Zoe, I don't want that either. But I still don't know what I should do."

"Do the right thing."

"And what the hell is that?"

"Let them know you're supporting Ben. Whether you sign the petition or do something else, you have to make a stand. If people think you got this promotion by throwing your best friend under the bus—" Zoe shook her head. "They'll never look at you the same again."

He studied her face. In all their years together, he'd only seen that look a few times, and he knew exactly what it meant: no matter what he said, she wasn't going to bend.

He squeezed her hand. "Okay, Zoe. I'll do the right thing. I'll tell Ansel on Monday."

29

Monday morning, Ansel hunched over his desk, glaring at a stack of papers with the look of a man whose car had just been towed—disbelief mingled with rage.

He waved in Jeremy. He sat across from Ansel and pursed his lips. His boss reminded him of a circus tiger bowing its head to avoid the whip but waiting for the tamer to blink so he could tear him apart.

"Roberta just gave me a petition signed by 82 people. They're demanding I reinstate Ben as the consumer affairs reporter. If I refuse, they'll take the story to the national media."

"So I heard."

Ansel held up the stack of papers. "I didn't see your name on the list. Thank you, Jeremy."

He swallowed. Over the weekend, he'd devised a new strategy for solving the crisis—convincing Ansel that giving Ben his job back was the only practical, as well as ethical, solution. If it worked, he would no longer have to choose between two damning options. "What now? Are you going to meet their demands?"

Ansel looked up at him, annoyed. "It's too late for that," he grumbled.

"Are you certain? Sooner or later, I think it will come to that."

He scoffed. "I just demoted my star reporter. I can't turn around and tell my boss I made a mistake. Even if I could, the dealers already know that Ben is gone. They agreed to give us back the revenue—that was the deal we cut. If we break it now, we're back at square one, only the dealers will call me a liar and management will think I'm a fool."

"But the dealers don't get the backlash. That's your way out. If the story goes public, the Herald's reputation will be shattered. They have to know you can't permit that."

Ansel sighed. "I know you think there's a way around it, Jeremy, but there isn't. Sometimes you have to set a course and hold it, no matter how many hits you take. All we can do now is damage control."

"What do you mean by damage control?"

"We convince the staff that going public is suicide. We apply pressure internally. Failing there, we tap-dance, stonewall, delay. Eventually, readers will forget."

Jeremy squirmed. It was clear that Ansel had no intention of backing down, and he thought he knew why. In the middle of a desperate charge, retreat could spell disaster, and the only hope remaining was to press the attack.

Even as his plan fell apart, he struggled for the courage to play his last card. "I'm not sure I can support that. I've sat on the fence for a long time, but I'm getting lots of flak."

"Jeremy, you can't buckle now. I need you on my side. If I lose you, the floodgates will open."

"It seems they already have."

"Things can always get worse. If the lid comes off this mess, the paper will lose the million dollars *and* its reputation. We absolutely have to keep this thing inside—push back on the ringleaders, stop them from going public. I'm not asking you to help with that. I can be the bad guy, and management will back me up. All I'm asking is that you keep on the fence. Drag your feet. Do whatever you have to, but don't get involved. Somewhere down the road, you'll see it was your best choice."

There it was again, the veiled promise—stay on the fence and grab the prize. He wanted to ask his boss how losing the respect of his peers could be his best choice, but knew that Ansel couldn't answer without admitting the *quid pro quo*, which, of course, he would never do.

"So what's the verdict?"

He was quiet for a long time. It was one thing to sit on the couch with Zoe and discuss right and wrong like college students, but something very different to confront his boss and throw him to the dogs. It didn't help that he owed his career at the Herald to Ansel, or that he both liked and respected his boss, even though he disagreed with him on this one crucial matter.

The sound of his breathing filled the room. At last, he had to speak. "Tell you what. Give me a few more days. I'll think about it."

He thought Ansel would lose his temper, but instead he acted relieved. "I can live with that. A few more days means a few more days to maneuver. One day at a time, Jeremy. That's my mantra now. One day at a time."

30

He couldn't decide: should he or should he not have one more drink before going home? The troll was making them too damn strong, and the cheap vodka felt like battery acid burning through his gullet—even if the burn did provide a certain cathartic rush.

He'd broken his promise to himself and come back to The Trapper, where he'd found the same bartender, the same cast of lowlifes, and the same empty booth in the back, where'd he'd sat for the last hour, sipping martinis and brooding.

Inside, he was churning like a maelstrom, and foremost among his feelings was shame. Having put some time between his talk with Ansel, he now looked back on his behavior as cowardly and weak. Instead of holding his ground and defending his ideals, he'd sat there like a toady, asked a few timid questions, made a few bland remarks, and promptly made for the safe harbor of indecision.

And if he couldn't face himself, how could he face Zoe? How could he tell her he didn't have the courage to follow his convictions, that a promotion meant more to him than he ever imagined, that his lifelong friendship with Ben had proven weaker than his loyalty to his boss?

He made his way back to the bar. Maybe it was better not to say a thing. He could tell her that Ansel had been in meetings all day and they never got the chance to talk. But that would only delay the inevitable, and worse, it meant lying to Zoe—a path he didn't want to travel down. She would see it as a betrayal, and rightly so.

But he had to tell her something.

He ordered his third martini. The bartender gave him the usual look—a smile on the lips but a sneer in the eyes.

He left him a two-dollar tip and slunk back to his booth.

The first sip burned his throat and helped to loosen the kink in his neck. He found himself longing to be thrown a month into the future—because by then, one way or another, everything would be settled. Ben would either have his job back or be exiled for good, and their baby, healthy or not, would be at home. At least the waiting and not knowing would be over.

He glanced at his watch. *8:45? How did that happen? What am I doing? Why in the hell am I still here? Leaving my pregnant wife alone when I know what I should do—march into Ansel's office and tell him I won't stall anymore, that I'm signing the petition and supporting my friend, and not because it's my best option, but simply because it's right.*

All at once a yoke was lifted off his neck. He smiled for the first time in days. Just like that, he was free.

Tomorrow, he would do it. The doubt, the handwringing, the self-pity—it was over.

He took another sip and savored his plan. It would not only impress Zoe, but save his friendship with Ben, salvage his reputation at work, and reaffirm the principles he'd championed his entire life. As for Ansel and his promotion—if he thought he'd trade his soul for a raise, he could go to hell. He wasn't that sort of man. No, he was made of stronger stuff, and first thing tomorrow morning, Ansel would find that out.

His train of thought was wrenched off its tracks by a voice he never dreamed of hearing in The Trapper. *Could it really be him?*

He strained his ears.

"Kind of a bookish type. Tall, scruffy blond hair."

What the hell is he doing here?

Heart pounding, he jumped to his feet. A broad-shouldered man in a bomber jacket was standing at the bar, grilling the troll like a policeman. His sandy hair had receded since the wedding, but his face and physique hadn't changed.

"Jake, what are you doing here?"

He turned and gave him a look that lay bare the contempt he'd always thought that Jake felt for him. Then it struck him like a punch to the face. Only one thing would bring Jake to The Trapper, and he could see the chain of events with perfect clarity. The ceiling might as well have caved in on his head, and for a second he wished it would—to knock him out so he wouldn't have to bear the shame. *I'm a selfish, irresponsible bastard. No wonder he hates me.*

"I've been to half the bars in town looking for you."

"Is Zoe all right?"

"Her water broke two hours ago. Phoebe took her to the hospital. C'mon, let's get moving."

31

Jeremy leaned into the window at the maternity ward, eyeing the rows of white-bundled newborns in pink and blue caps. A few restless souls had batted theirs off to expose their bald, egg-shaped heads. Their ruddy faces, unlike the serene looks of their sleeping companions, gave the only hint of the trial they had just undergone. While these few clutched the air frantically or sucked at phantom nipples, nursing in their dreams, most displayed a sense of calm in their new surroundings they would seldom know again—certain that loving arms would lift them up and breasts magically appear the minute they awoke and hunger called.

Jeremy smiled. He remembered his first visit here, after Maddy was born, watching her fidget in her bassinet—his *little mermaid,* he'd called her—and being overcome by awe, as if he'd been granted passage to some hallowed, secret place—the temple of a goddess or the bedchamber of an angel. He'd felt unready for the challenges of fatherhood that lay ahead, but his fears were far outweighed by the feeling of being blessed by this beautiful creature in a tiny pink cap who was coming home with them for what, in that moment, seemed like forever.

With Marty, on the other hand, everything was different. Having missed the birth, he felt detached from his son, more like a spectator than his father. Maybe that shouldn't surprise him—he hadn't yet seen, let alone held Marty, while during Maddy's birth, he'd stayed with Zoe throughout the surgery and minutes after had cradled his newborn daughter in his arms, terrified that he would drop her, while she bleated like a baby lamb.

This time he'd sat by himself on a plastic chair in a sterile hall, berating himself for missing the birth as he waited for Zoe to recover, and he still didn't know when they would let him see her.

In spite of all that, the only thing that mattered now was the good news the nurse had given him—the delivery had gone well, Zoe was doing fine, and Marty appeared not to be in any danger. His heart was beating strongly and, in the main, he was a healthy, normal boy. They'd even let Zoe hold him briefly before whisking him away and placing him under observation in the neonatal intensive-care unit. Earlier, Dr. Berndt had told Jeremy that Marty had a small hole in the upper atrial wall, large enough to need watching, but not large enough to need surgery—although without it, he added, his growth would suffer and strenuous activities, like sports, were out of the question.

He felt relieved, but numb, and somewhat skeptical. He wanted proof that all was truly well in the form of Zoe's smiling face and his newborn son warm in his arms.

He stepped away from the glass. A nurse with broad shoulders, limp hair, and manlike hands was shuffling toward him in turquoise booties. He eyed her carefully, but nothing in her manner suggested any problem.

"Your wife is up, Mr. Edwards. She's asking for you."

The nurse led him down the hall and waved him through an open door. Zoe was sitting up in bed, supported by pillows and gazing pensively out the window. Without makeup, her face looked blood-drained and boyish, and her shoulders slumped like a marionette with severed strings, leaning against the headboard to keep from collapsing.

Her smile was faint, stripped of any beauty or desire to please, a look so helpless and naked, it pierced his heart. He hugged her as tightly as he dared. "Are you okay?"

"I've been worse."

He sat beside her, but his weight on the mattress made her wince.

"Sorry." He quickly stood.

"Just be slow."

He eased back down and took her hand. "Still hurts?"

"Just starting to."

"They told you everything?"

She nodded grimly, as if to stop him from repeating the prognosis. "Everything."

He watched her intently. She looked about to cry, but held it back. "You wouldn't know, except he's smaller."

"Like his mom."

"You'll see what I mean." She stared at him, eyes gleaming. "We can give him a good life, Jeremy."

"I know."

The nurse reappeared, cradling a white bundle so compact he barely knew it held a baby. The nurse gently passed the bundle to Zoe, who smiled and wrapped her arms around it.

She pulled the blanket back on a round, bald head. The face was perfectly formed, but the lidded eyes, button nose, and squiggly lips were so small they nearly touched.

The nurse loosened the knot behind Zoe's neck. Zoe dropped the corner of her gown and pressed the baby's mouth against her nipple. The tiny mouth twitched but failed to latch on. "Come on, Marty. You can do it."

Marty gummed away, to no effect. Soon his face wrinkled up and he began to wail.

"Rub your nipple on his cheek," said the nurse. "He'll open his mouth. Then be quick."

For a good minute, Marty ignored the nipple stroking his cheek and punished them all with a rising, angry scream. Then without warning, he turned his head and clamped on tight. His cheeks hollowed out while he sucked. "There," Zoe said proudly. "I knew you could do it."

Jeremy was thankful for the quiet. Screaming babies had always made his heart race, but the vision of his wife and son doing exactly what they should not only relieved him, but made him feel serene.

"That's a good sign, isn't it?" Zoe asked the nurse.

She nodded. "He'll need formula too, but I thought you should try first."

"Have you seen other baby's like him?" Jeremy asked.

"A few."

"How does he compare?"

"Well, he has plenty of color. Sometimes their skin is blue. That's not good."

Zoe stared at her sharply, upset by the conversation.

"It's not my place to say," the nurse said, "but I think he's doing fine. Doctors have to bring up everything that might go wrong—it's their job, but sometimes they're too negative."

"Can't we talk about that tomorrow?" Zoe asked.

"Of course. I'll give you some privacy. I'll come back in a while and check his oxygen levels. Nursing is hard work for a baby."

Although troubled by the thought of giving Marty up, even for a brief test, Zoe nodded. "If you have to."

After the nurse left, Jeremy leaned over and stroked Marty's smooth head. Zoe gazed up at him and smiled, imparting not only all the pain she'd undergone, but also the fierce devotion that she felt toward her child.

"We got a break, Zoe," he said, a shudder running up his spine. "I think he's going to be okay. I think we're all going to be okay."

32

The intrusion of doctors, nurses, and lab technicians into Jeremy's life kept him so busy during his week off that he barely thought about his last meeting with Ansel. But as he crossed the open savannah of the newsroom on Monday morning, the sense of impending doom returned—except that now he was the father of a basically healthy boy, whose arrival had made the promotion less important and strengthened his belief in the rightness of Ben's position and the wrongness of the Herald's. No matter how Ansel reacted, he would tell him in no uncertain terms that he planned to join the protest and sign the petition demanding that his friend be reinstated in his former job.

Luckily, Ansel was in a good mood, looking calm and dapper in a charcoal suit with a red-neon tie. He grinned at Jeremy and welcomed him back, showered him with questions, admired the photos of Marty, and listened patiently to Jeremy's explanation of his defect—almost going out of his way to please him. His behavior put Jeremy on edge. He wondered if Ansel wasn't being overly nice to make him feel guilty, but if he was, the ploy backfired. It only made him feel manipulated and steeled his resolve to follow through with his plan.

"By the way," he said. "We should talk about the petition."

Ansel waved him off. "No need to. While you were gone, everything got squared away."

His grip tightened on his pen. "Squared away?"

"I have some good news. On Friday we rehired Ben as our consumer reporter. We had to. Over two-hundred people signed that petition."

"Two hundred?" He was stunned. If this was good news, then why did he feel like he'd just been shoved out of a plane?

"They did me a favor, really. I showed the dealers the petition, looked them in the eye, and told them what would happen if we didn't rehire Ben. Their threat paled in comparison to our own staff's."

"And they accepted that?"

"They were angry, but what could they do? The threat wasn't idle. It took some work, but they finally came around."

"You got the advertising back?"

"We lost the north metro dealers, but we always thought we might. The others broke ranks and backed off—after we promised not to pursue the story."

Jeremy shook his head. "I guess I missed the boat. I was going to march in here and tell you I was signing the petition."

Ansel studied him gravely. "I'm sorry to hear that, Jeremy, but I can't say I blame you. I've been doing a lot of soul searching, and I think I was too quick to sacrifice Ben. I panicked, and I didn't weigh my options carefully enough. Let's just say we're lucky things turned out the way they did."

Jeremy pursed his lips. While the outcome might have been lucky for Ansel and the paper, he wondered if he could say the same for himself.

"I wouldn't worry," Ansel reassured him. "It was never your problem in the first place. We all know you had more important things going on."

"I guess I did," he said doubtfully.

"Besides, there's something else we have to discuss."

What now?

"While you were gone, I picked our new deputy managing editor."

"I see," he said, trying not to let his disappointment show. Apparently, he'd not only let down his peers, but lost the promotion too.

"And I picked you, Jeremy."

"You did?"

"Of course I did. Last week. But I wanted you back before I made it public."

"Ansel, you don't know how much that means to me."

"The bump in pay should come in handy. And you're the right man for the job. You're just what the paper needs."

But his boss's choice of words dampened his enthusiasm. Even if Ansel was right—that he was just what the paper needed—after the last few weeks, he wondered if he was still what the paper *wanted*.

Back at his desk, Jeremy stared blankly into his screen, recounting the crisis as it must have looked to his colleagues: when they rose up to save the Herald's reputation and stop the scapegoating of a star reporter, instead of joining the cause, he stalled and begged them off. At the same time, they knew he'd applied for a position that would be picked by the same person who'd demoted Ben. During his absence, they'd gotten Ben reinstated without his help, and when he came back, he was given that position. He shook his head. It didn't matter what they knew about his son or what kind of pressure it had put him under. It didn't matter that in the end he'd done the right thing—in the eyes of most people it was *quid pro quo*.

He picked up a paper and pretended to read. He would have to watch for any changes in his colleague's behavior—less eye contact, suspicious looks, or outright avoidance. They would tell the true story better than any words.

But finding out the truth was hard, as he soon learned a troubling fact about moving up the food chain—that once you have power over people, they treat you differently—you're no longer *one of us*, but *one of them*—someone who can make their lives better or worse, and consequently is often met with flattery, fear, or silence.

For a time, this new barrier between himself and his colleagues hid the truth, but after a month, he could no longer doubt it. While he still had his defenders, mainly old friends who felt sorry for him because of Marty, most of the staff no longer viewed him as a journalist but as a pawn of management—someone who valued the Herald's profits above its obligation to its readers, the public good, or the facts.

The realization came as a cruel blow to Jeremy, who'd always thought himself an altruistic man.

One Thursday night in March, he slunk back to The Trapper. Tucked in the rear booth under a heating vent that blasted out air so hot his face sweat, he brooded as he downed two martinis. When he sidled up to the bar for a third, the troll raised an eyebrow. "Rough day?"

"Rough month."

"They working you too hard?"

He stirred his olive pick. "Not really. But I've learned something important about myself."

"What's that?"

"I'm an asshole."

The troll grinned. "You're in good company, pal. This one's on me. "

33

Jake and his new boss, Tony Carlucci, leaned into the gray block walls of ConChem and stretched their calves. Carlucci ran during his lunch hours, and today, as the March sun was melting the snow and chasing it down the gutters, he'd invited Jake to come along. While Jake had never been a runner, he felt it wise to indulge his new boss, and right before lunch he'd driven home and changed into his teal-blue sweatsuit from college. He was pleased to find it still fit—until he stepped out of his car and found Carlucci in his black Gore-Tex pants and red-piped jacket strutting around the building like a professional boxer.

Jake had worked at ConChem, a producer of commercial waterproofing products, for three years, while Carlucci had worked there for only a month. The new VP of sales and marketing, Carlucci was handpicked by Heinrich Heinkel, ConChem's new CEO, or *Heinie,* as employees called him behind his back, owing to his thick German accent and Prussian style of management. ConChem's new German owners had charged Heinkel with transforming the company by any means required into a key player in the waterproofing market. With Heinkel in charge, everything at ConChem was rapidly changing—products, markets, reporting structure, workload, and, most visibly, people. *Weak performers* were getting pink slips and being replaced by *proven performers*, among them many of Heinkel's former reports, like Carlucci, who were being poached from other companies.

"At my old place, a bunch of us ran marathons," Carlucci said, twisting his waist from side to side. Tall, trim, and tan, he cut a dapper figure in his running gear. At 42, he still had a full head of black hair, perfectly combed and sparsely oiled. After meeting him, Phoebe had told Jake he reminded her of an Italian Sean Connery—not her type, she added, but certainly handsome. Carlucci's speech also impressed strangers with its polished, cocksure air. Jake admired the polish, but like many Minnesotans found the swagger annoying, and completely uncalled for, given Carlucci's long list of accomplishments.

"I can't imagine running that far," Jake said, shaking out his legs. "It hurts just to watch."

Carlucci smiled. "Don't you run with your wife?"

"I tried, but I can't keep up."

"She has a runner's build—you can see it even though she's pregnant. She'll get back in shape fast, I'll bet. Not many do."

"Knowing her, she will."

"Sometime she could run with us."

While he understood Carlucci's interest in a fellow runner, the comment galled him. There was something unseemly about the thought of his boss admiring his wife's shapely ass in a pair of running shorts. "A few more weeks, and she'll be spending all her lunches at daycare."

"I guess so. Ready?"

"Sure. I'll try not to slow you down."

Jake padded after Carlucci as he cut across the parking lot into the empty street. He found it fairly easy to match his pace. Keeping up with Phoebe the few times they'd run together had been harder. "Too fast?" Carlucci offered.

"I'm fine, for now."

"Good." They puffed along the office park in silence.

"So what do you think of all the changes?" Carlucci finally asked.

Jake paused at the loaded question. He felt obliged to answer honestly, but wondered if Carlucci would take it in the right spirit. There was something about the man that threw him off and made it hard for him to be himself around him. His previous boss had always welcomed his candor, but Carlucci gave him the impression that candor might be not only unwelcome, but dangerous.

"We need them," he said between breaths. "It's an old company, with old ways of doing things. If we're going to grow, we have to change. And it seems to be working—sales are up, we're gaining market share—but there's been a cost too."

"What do you mean? What kind of cost?"

"It's a lot of change in a short time."

"You don't strike me as someone who's afraid of change."

"I'm not, for the most part."

"Good. Because you're going to see a lot more."

"It's not the change that bothers me. It's the turmoil that comes with it."

"That can't be helped. Like Heinkel says—if you can't lead, follow. If you can't follow, get out of the way."

"That's what I mean. I think we're losing some good people."

Carlucci nodded grimly. "There's something else Heinkel says—nonperformers will not be tolerated, whether products, markets, or people."

Jake tried not to show how troubling he found the words. He ran beside Carlucci a dozen steps before responding. "Well, he's the CEO, and he can do whatever he wants, but I've lived in Minnesota all my life, and I don't think that management style will do well here."

"They'll fall in line. Trust me. I know Heinkel. They'll embrace the changes or they'll go. It's that simple."

He tried to think of a polite way of dropping the subject. Asking Carlucci to question the ethics of disrupting people's lives to increase profits for their new German owners would be not only pointless, but suicidal. And the way that Carlucci was clenching his jaw and glaring down the road made Jake wonder if he'd already gone too far.

"Being Heinkel's right-hand man isn't all it's cracked up to be," he said with a growl. "Sometimes you have to be the bad guy. When he wants something done, you'd better deliver. It doesn't always make you popular."

Watching his face, Jake felt a twinge of empathy for his boss. Although Heinkel often used him as a hatchet man, apparently he kept him on a short leash, and Jake had a hunch that he bullied him in private.

"So far he's pretty much ignored me. And to tell you the truth, I'm fine with that."

"That will change," Carlucci said, nicking him with his eyes. "He knows all there is to know about sealants, and he wants to expand your line aggressively."

Jake had been in business long enough to know the only fitting reply to the news—*Glad to hear it. What a great opportunity*—but instead the words forming in his mouth were *oh, shit.*

A few seconds ticked by before he grinned at Carlucci. "Then it sounds like my life will get pretty interesting."

Carlucci grinned back, feeling a sudden brotherhood with his new report. He slapped him on the shoulder. "You'll be fine, Jake, just fine. Because I'll be right there to help you out."

34

Jake hung up the phone and stared blankly out his office window, slender as an archer's port in a castle wall. Carlucci had just summoned him to the executive wing. After only a month of reporting to his new boss, Jake had already begun to dread his calls. Whenever they came, his neck and shoulders tightened, and his mood, normally buoyant, would sink. He found his reaction surprising. Outgoing and flexible, he was not easily thrown off balance—nor did he feel shy around people with unfamiliar backgrounds, even if they were older and more powerful. But no matter how he tried, he couldn't relax around Carlucci, and the thing that bothered him most was how it was getting worse as time passed, and not better.

When Carlucci had first come on board, he'd impressed Jake. In contrast with the khakis and Oxford shirts of his coworkers, he wore expensive, tailored suits, always black, and his mirror-polished Italian shoes cost more than many employees' suits. Quick and confident, Carlucci had an East Coast, cosmopolitan flair. He was unlike anyone that Jake had ever met, which made him eager to learn more about him. What's more, Carlucci seemed to like Jake and treated him as a confidante, as if the two were taking on the world together—although it did bother him to find this friendly manner absent in his conversations with many of their coworkers.

The tone that Carlucci used with the average employee was Jake's first clue that something unsavory was lurking beneath his polished veneer. Carlucci was patient around managers or anybody else he thought talented, but with the rank and file, his behavior bordered on the derisive. That not only offended Jake's sense of manners, but more importantly, his sense of justice. Having been raised to view modesty as a basic virtue, he could spot a bloated ego a mile away and would do his best to avoid the owner or, given the chance, knock him down a peg or two.

And Carlucci's high-handed air was doing more than putting people off—it was earning him enemies at ConChem. If that trend continued, Jake knew that somewhere down the line he'd have to make a no-win choice between his boss and his peers, most of whom he liked and respected.

He tapped his fingers on his desktop, stood up, and strode down the hall.

Carlucci stood waiting in the white atrium framed by the open doors of four vice presidents. On the other side of a closed door, Heinrich Heinkel was all but shouting in German, taking a call from their parent company in Munich.

Carlucci was staring at a desk where a row of sealant cartridges stood like artillery shells. The packaging was foreign to Jake, which made him uneasy. As product manager it was his job not only to know every brand of sealant in North America, but also to know their strengths and weaknesses.

Carlucci glanced up and smiled as if he'd just sunk a challenging pool shot.

Jake thought it best not to cover up his ignorance. "What's this?"

"*Our* new sealant line."

Carlucci kept smiling and waited for Jake's response.

"Our new sealant line?"

"That's right. We're breaking into the consumer market."

The news floored him. ConChem, or construction chemicals, had always made products for commercial use and thumbed its nose at the inferior sealants pedaled to homeowners, plumbers, and carpenters. "When did that happen?"

"Don't worry, it's not final. I want your opinion first."

He circled the table and studied the nearest cartridge. On a black foil wrapper, red letters blazed, *Premium Door and Window Sealant. Specially designed for exterior doors and windows.*

Carlucci picked up the cartridge. "Here's the angle. Most people don't know a damn thing about sealants. They want someone to tell them what to buy, and most of the time it's a kid at the hardware store. But guess what—he doesn't know a damn thing either. He picks up the tube and reads it back to them, like they were stupid."

Jake nodded. He'd seen it happen a dozen times.

"So we tell them—right in the name—*Door and Window Sealant*—not too sexy, but at least they know what they're getting. And the tip is brown, the most common color of trim."

"Actually, it's white."

"It doesn't matter. People see brown and think wood."

Carlucci picked up the black-tipped cartridge. "*Premium Roofing Sealant.* Now that one's plain as day. The best part is that people know even less about roofing than doors and windows. That makes *Roofing Sealant* a specialty product—meaning we can charge more for it.

"And here's the *coup de grâce*," he continued, holding a gray-tipped cartridge over his shoulder like a spear. "*Premium Concrete Sealant.* In this case, *premium* stands for price. People know absolutely nothing about concrete, so it costs twice as much as *Roofing Sealant.*"

"I don't get it," Jake said. "When did we develop all these new products?"

"We didn't."

"Are they German?"

Carlucci slapped him on the back. "Good guess, but we already make them. We just had them repackaged."

"Which products?"

"Your commercial sealants. We looked at selling them as private labels, but frankly, the profit margins sucked, so we made our own line."

"You mean—"

"CS-1—bronze, black, and concrete gray."

"You're kidding me."

"Why would I kid you?"

"It's the same product—just different colors."

"That's the beauty of it."

"That's . . ." He wanted to say *lying,* but he chose another word, "misleading."

Carlucci scoffed. "Who cares? Homeowners don't. What they care about is getting the right product: *Tell me what to buy. I don't care if it costs two bucks or five bucks—I'll toss a few in the cart and head for the checkout.* All we're doing is making life easier for them—and, sure, making a mint at the same time."

Jake was speechless. He had to admit the plan had a certain shrewd genius, but its bald dishonesty alarmed him. "Homeowners won't pay five dollars for a single tube."

"So we lower the price."

"What about my commercial clients? What if they find out they can buy our products cheaper at a hardware store?"

"How would they know? You can't tell a thing from the package."

"If word got out, we'd be in trouble."

Carlucci gave Jake the look he normally reserved for underlings. "We private label all the time. This won't be any different. Anyway, you don't have to worry about it—it won't be your line. Mitchell will sell it through the consumer division."

"And he's fine with it?"

Carlucci frowned. "I wanted you to know in case someone asked you—so you don't put your foot in your mouth." After a pause he added, "And I thought you might enjoy the marketing angle."

That angle's a bit too crooked for me, he thought, but held his tongue. "It sounds a bit risky," was all he dared to say.

"Well, like I said, it's not your problem. Commercial sealants are your problem. But you'll never get the kind of growth that Heinkel expects unless you add sales channels, and that means taking risks. You'll have to get more aggressive, Jake. Forewarned is forearmed." He glanced at his watch. "I have a three o'clock. I'll see you tomorrow."

Jake watched him swagger away, worried that he'd offended his boss not so much by pointing out the risks of his pet project, but worse, by failing to admire its cleverness. The knot in his stomach tightened. He no longer had any doubt that Carlucci, the man who had more power to make him miserable than anyone else he knew, was little better than a con man.

35

The words were still ringing in Jake's ears. *It's the worst product failure I've seen in 20 years.* Brad Zambrowski, the Ohio sales rep, had just told him that CS-2, a high-performance sealant used on an office tower in Cleveland, had completely failed. The viscous sealant, which should have skinned over in 24 hours, had melted into syrup and poured down the joints of an eight-story building. Rivers of brown slime were pooling on the sidewalks, running to the curbs, and dripping into the gutters.

The contractor was livid. He claimed the failure would ruin him. The building owner was already planning to sue him. Zambrowski had panicked and promised the owner—without Jake's approval—that ConChem would pay for the cleanup and give him a new batch of sealant that properly cured. Then he'd phoned Jake to verify the company would back up his pledge. Jake assured him they would—without consulting his boss—it was not only the right thing to do, but the smart thing. He was obliged to protect ConChem's reputation by standing behind its products, and this particular case wasn't even his greatest concern. What troubled him more was the fear that a whole batch of sealant had gone bad, and Zambrowski's call had only been the first in a coming rush of failures.

A disaster of this order would quickly reach Heinkel. Jake was expecting his call any minute. He squirmed as he wracked his brain to come up with answers—answers that he couldn't know until he'd interviewed a long list of people—the applicators on the jobsite, the plant manager where the batch had been made, the warehousemen who stored it, the driver who delivered it, and the chemist, on the off chance the formulation was bad. There were so many ways for something to fail—defective raw materials, contamination at the plant, freezing temperatures while trucking, or use of a wrong primer in the joint face—that he couldn't begin to guess the cause, let alone reassure the CEO that other failures weren't already in the pipeline, waiting to break out.

When the call finally came, he grabbed his notepad and, with the air of a doomed prisoner, dragged his feet down the hall to the executive wing.

Heinkel's secretary, a smartly dressed brunette fluent in three languages, waved him in. Carlucci was facing Heinkel with his black suit jackknifed against the wall. He was scowling, and didn't greet Jake or even glance his way. Jake ignored the passive-aggressive body language. Anybody being addressed by Heinkel had to focus 100 percent of his energy on the exchange. Heinkel was loud, caustic, slap-shot quick in thought, and unforgiving as a crocodile with its jaws clamped onto your leg. In the last month, Jake had watched him bawl out two veteran managers, reducing both to tears.

He paced behind his massive desk, jamming the phone receiver into his ear like a mechanic torquing a wrench. His stomach bulged out between his lapels, exposing a pair of red suspenders, but the broad shoulders and beefy arms under the jacket hinted at explosive power. Heinkel's stony blue eyes peered up at Jake through a pair of thick glasses. He always found his face impossible to read. His eyes never gave away his mood, and his only expressions were a razor-sharp focus on the matter at hand and a dozen degrees of impatience, which Jake could always measure by the rising of his voice.

He slammed the receiver into the cradle. "Christ, Jake—where the fuck have you been?" With his thick accent and pursed-lip speech, he reminded Jake of a man spitting cherry pits.

Barely a minute had passed since Heinkel had called. "Is this about the job in Ohio?"

"No, Jake, it's about the fuckin' Timberwolves. Of course it's about fuckin' Ohio."

"I haven't had time yet to track down the leads."

Carlucci glanced at him sideways. "Don't bother. We already know what happened."

"You do?"

He didn't reply, but raised an accusing brow at Heinkel. His face had the look of an angry, pouting child.

Heinkel stared through Jake, focusing on a point a mile beyond his head, and rubbed his fingernails, one after another, under his thumbnail. Both Jake and Carlucci knew to keep quiet while he marshaled his thoughts. "It's the formulation," he said at last. "We got to rule out everything else, but we'll get there pretty damn quick. At the end of the day, it will be the formulation."

"How do you know that? Zambrowski just called me."

"This isn't the first time CS-2 has failed," Carlucci said.

"True, we've had some minor failures, but they were all traced to poor surface prep. CS-2 has been steady as they come for six years."

"Last week there was a failure in Denver," Heinkel said.

"What? No one told me."

Heinkel remained quiet. He kept staring past Jake and sliding his nails back and forth.

Carlucci grinned ironically. "Well, are you going to?"

Heinkel stood. "Sure I am. How can he get us out of this fuckin' mess if he doesn't know what happened."

He swept around the desk and stopped inches from Jake. "Here's the deal, Jake. As you know, in the last two years, all products are getting value analysis—"

"But not CS-2."

"No. Last quarter we did CS-2."

He stared at Heinkel in disbelief. Shortly after coming to ConChem, the CEO had introduced *value analysis,* a practice that broke down a product's raw materials and replaced the most expensive ingredients with cheaper ones, with the goal of boosting the profit margin without affecting the performance. But Jake had never believed the latter part of the equation was a top priority, and he'd fought attempts to subject his sealant line to the process, and up until now, or so he thought, he'd prevailed. "I don't get it. Why didn't you tell me?"

"Well, Jake, everybody knows you're such a big fuckin' fan of value analysis, so we gave the job to Webber."

Everything tumbled into place. Rather than fight him, Heinkel had gone around him and straight to Webber, the lead chemist for his sealant line. But somehow Webber had made a disastrous error.

"So *our* changes caused the failure," he said forcibly.

"No one can prove that," said Carlucci.

"Two failures in the same week? All we have to do is check the batch numbers."

"Bullshit!" Heinkel snorted. "I don't give a shit about the batch numbers. What do we do now, Jake? That's why I called you. It's your product line. What options do we got?"

He paused, trying to gather his thoughts. Apparently, Heinkel had already moved beyond the issue of blame. More than likely, he'd already dressed down Webber and with single-minded zeal was galloping forward like a charging lancer, heedless of the bodies falling around him.

Although Jake's back and neck had tensed up, his mind was clicking. Three years of selling to hard-nosed contractors had taught him to focus on the facts, regardless of the pressure. "If the formulation is bad, we're going to have a boatload of failures."

"Jake, you're a fuckin' marketing genius. Now I know why you got the job."

He ignored the barb. If Heinkel was true to form, he'd already decided their course of action—he only wanted to know if Jake agreed.

"So first, we stop all shipments of CS-2. Second, we track down the bad batches and recall them. Third, we go back to the old formula. And fourth, we make good on any failures—we replace the bad material and pay to have it reinstalled." He stopped and mulled over his plan. "This will be expensive."

Carlucci grinned wickedly. "No shit."

Heinkel sliced the air with his hand. "*No shit* is right. One, two, three—good. Four—*bullshit!* We're not going to pay a fuckin' dime. Denver is a piss-ant deal. We don't care about those clowns."

Heinkel paused and pursed his lips. "And the Ohio job is way too big."

"And too public," added Carlucci.

"That's right. If we pay them off, every turkey who doesn't know which end of the tube to stick up his ass will come looking for money."

Heinkel's response horrified Jake. He'd come to accept that moral argument held little sway over Heinkel and his only resort lay in arguing that ConChem couldn't afford the repercussions, except that financially, Heinkel was right—if they lied and blamed the contractor, they just might wiggle off the hook, while if they admitted the error and paid everybody who'd been harmed, or imagined themselves harmed, there was no telling where it would end. "They'll sue us," he mumbled. "Bright boy. Let them. You know as well as I do, Jake, a job can fail for all kinds of reasons—rain, cold, contamination, wrong primer, bad mixing, bad joint design—there's a long fuckin' list of ways to screw it up."

"You make it sound pretty hard to apply our products correctly."

He thought the remark would set Heinkel off, but instead he laughed. "For some people, it's impossible. Like these assholes in Ohio."

Jake bowed his head. If they were sued, as product manager, he would be subpoenaed, and if he followed Heinkel's orders, be forced to lie under oath.

He let out a sigh. Was that his only option? Wasn't there anyone in the company, any senior manager who dared confront Heinkel? Right away, he thought of Virginia Hart, the corporate attorney. "Does Virginia know about this?"

Carlucci scoffed.

Heinkel smirked at Jake. For a second he seemed to forget there was any problem at all. "Yes, Jake, but we don't listen to her. She's a dried up old cunt. "

36

Phoebe rose from the couch with a grunt and waddled down the hallway of her new 1950s rambler. While many of the rooms were still missing blinds, pictures, or even furniture, the baby's room lacked for nothing. A glider rocker stood empty by the window. Brightly colored books filled a shelf, their spines uncracked; model cars and trucks, many from Jake's childhood, parked on the dresser; a mobile turned lazily in the middle of the room, hung with stars, planets, and spaceships; and by the wall, where her gaze was drawn, a white crib waited quietly for its new owner.

Every time she passed this door, Phoebe stopped and stared. She often walked inside, browsed around in disbelief, studied the crib and the fleece blankets patterned with puppies, and wondered what kind of creature would soon be swaddled inside them.

But now the pressure on her bladder kept her moving. In the bathroom, she loosened the drawstring on her pants and lowered herself onto the seat. As her tinkling echoed around the tiled room, she lifted her T-shirt and stared at the taut flesh of her belly. She held it with both hands, like a seer gazing into a giant crystal ball, and tenderly stroked its sides. As she did, something stirred like a minnow flipping in a shallow pond. The feeling thrilled her, and a smile lit her face. Already she felt a love for her child unlike any she'd ever known. She couldn't compare it to her love for Jake, which, although it hadn't faded in the last four years, had been tempered by all the daily problems and petty arguments of married life. Her child, by contrast, lived in a heavenly cloud, having no flaws and promising only love and joy to a degree that Phoebe had never thought possible.

At moments like this, everything else in her life seemed trivial—not just her own worries and desire, but everyone else's too. They only mattered to the degree they might affect, for good or bad, the happiness of her child. In the same way, the lives of her friends with children had become fascinating, while the lives of her childless friends had become dull. And the world of books, food, and current events, so important in the past, now hardly mattered at all, orbiting around the sun of her child like Pluto in the cold wilderness of space.

With hands planted on her belly, she waited, hoping for one more flutter, but her baby refused to grant her wish. *It's daytime. He must be sleeping.*

The moment passed. She stood and tied her pants, stretched her T-shirt over her belly, and waddled into the kitchen, where Jake was cooking dinner.

He was bending over the stove in his khaki pants, penny loafers, and white shirt, frying an omelet. He'd run his fingers through and ruffled his receding hair, and dark circles rimmed his eyes. His face had the look of a tired traveler disembarking from a red-eye flight.

He flipped the omelet, sprinkled it with ham and shredded cheese, and tipped it onto a plate. He took a second omelet from the oven, buttered two pieces of toast, and set both plates on the table.

Phoebe sat and picked at her food while he told her about his meeting with Heinkel. At first, she didn't get the point, feeling preoccupied and a little bored, but she perked up when he mentioned lying under oath, and when he said he might resign, her heart began to race.

"How can you even think about that? Look at me. I'm big as a cow."

"I know it sounds crazy, but the truth is, we can do it. We've socked away a few thousand dollars, and we'll still have your health insurance."

"But we can't survive on my salary."

"It will only be for a while. We'll buy less, or buy smarter. We'll put off some things, like that new stroller."

"The thought of you not working terrifies me. That puts all the pressure on me. It's the last thing I need right now."

"I'll find something fast."

"The economy's terrible, and you said yourself there aren't other companies like yours in town—and I'm not moving, so don't even bring it up."

"We both want to raise our family here. We should stick to that."

"What if I lost my job? We'd lose our house. We'd be living on the street."

"Wells and Decker is doing fine."

"We are now, but the software industry is volatile. Things change so fast, my job could be gone in six months."

"Six months is all I need."

"Six months? Are you kidding?"

He shrugged. "It can take that long."

Phoebe rubbed her forehead. "Jake, you can't. You just can't. Isn't there some other way? Can't you fight them?"

He'd barely touched his omelet. He stared out the window, where a gray sky frowned on the dirty snow and tufts of brownish grass. He got up and went to the stove, clicked on the gas burner, studied the pulsing blue flame, and clicked it off again.

"They want me to lie in court. To blame everything on people who did nothing wrong. Can you think of anything more dishonest?"

"I know that. I just think you're rash to quit. Aren't there other people who'll take your side? What about the attorney—can't she help?"

"The dried-up old cunt?"

Phoebe pinched her nose. "God, why did you ever take this job?"

"I recall you were pretty glad when I did."

"All right—forget that. But there must be someone who'll stand up to him."

"Everyone at ConChem is scared of Heinkel. Anybody who bucked him has been demoted or fired. No one's going to risk his neck to save my ass."

"I'm due in weeks. Can't you stall? I'd like to know our baby is fine before you make such a big decision."

"Are you still worried about that?"

Phoebe stroked her belly. "Of course I am. What would Zoe have done if Jeremy had lost his job?"

"But they always knew that Marty had a problem. We don't have any reason to worry. The doctors say he's healthy."

"No—they said they haven't found any problems. That's not the same."

Jake frowned. He had to concede her point. Maybe he was being too rash to bolt. Maybe this was only the cold, hard reality of business. No company was perfect, and he was bound to face dilemmas no matter where he worked. Maybe he was being too idealistic, expecting the company to follow to his personal moral code, when he couldn't predict the result if they followed the course that he thought best.

Phoebe stayed quiet, stroking her belly. The image was far more powerful than any of her arguments, and one he couldn't refute with logic or words. Whether or not they were ready, their child would soon arrive, and from that day forward his well being would carry much more weight than either Phoebe's or his own.

Was this what parenthood would demand of him—that in the future he must sacrifice his own wants and needs for the good of his son, regardless of the outcome? The answer came back in a heartbeat, *yes.*

But just as quickly, the answer turned on its head as he realized that quitting his job was not a selfish act, not something done to save his own soul, but something he should do for the sake of his child. "Here's what it comes down to," he said firmly. "What kind of a man do you want me to be?"

"What do you mean?"

"I mean, do you like me the way I am, or do you want me to be someone else? Because if I keep working for these people, I'll have to do what they tell me to, and that means doing things I know are wrong—covering up, lying, blaming innocent people, and who knows where it will stop. Sooner or later, I'll be just like them. So look me in the eyes, Phoebe, and tell me what you want—a husband you're proud of or a husband you're ashamed of."

Phoebe stopped stroking her belly. There was a long, tense pause. At last she welled up with tears. "It's the last thing I want. I'd rather be poor. I'm sorry, Jake, I'm just scared."

He took her hand. "I know. The timing couldn't be worse. But I don't think there's any other way."

She gazed at him, her eyes full of fear, but also love, and he knew by her look that she wouldn't change her mind and blame him later—that no matter what barriers they faced, they would overcome them together, and whether he rose to the top or fell to the bottom, she would proudly stand beside him.

"When do you plan on quitting?" she asked.

"Tomorrow morning. First chance I get."

37

At eight o' clock, Jake called Heinkel's secretary and scheduled a meeting with the CEO. There was an open slot at 10:45, just 15 minutes—not a minute longer—she'd warned him, so he'd better come ready. The brief window should more than suffice, Jake thought with a feeling of dread. He still didn't know how to confront Heinkel, but deep down he felt it wouldn't matter. Based on his past experience, he assumed that he'd be fired on the spot.

He sat through a nine-o'clock meeting barely hearing a word of Webber's update on CS-2. At ten o'clock, he downloaded his personal files onto four diskettes, slipped his picture of Phoebe into his briefcase, along with his coffee mug, planner, and Cross pens. He stashed his sales trophies and clock radio in a grocery bag and carried it to his car. The English ivy and pothos he would leave behind.

For the next half hour, he felt like a trespasser in his own office. The palms of his hands were sweaty, his fingers were cold as icicles, and his stomach was turning like a cement mixer. All he could think of was getting it over with, keeping Heinkel's outburst as short as possible, and getting away to start the only thing that mattered now—his search for a new job.

Promptly at 10:45, he stood in Heinkel's door with his hands stuffed in his pockets. Heinkel didn't bother to glance up from his work, and half a minute passed before he waved Jake in, still without looking up. He grabbed a fresh stack of papers and thumbed through them as if they had a will he felt essential to crush. His aggressive air made Jake smile, in spite of his nervous stomach and sweaty palms. It not only provided a welcome distraction, but reinforced his conviction that he was doing the right thing. After another minute of being ignored, he finally said, "I understand we only have 15 minutes."

Heinkel looked up "What is it, Jake? Make it quick. I have an eleven o'clock."

He cleared his throat. "It's about CS-2."

The CEO's bearing suddenly changed. His shoulders inched higher, and his eyes locked onto Jake's like an antiaircraft battery. "What's going on? Tell me."

With the moment here and Heinkel's stare boring into this head, the tension nearly made Jake twitch. Was he really going through with it? He knew that his resignation would be a match tossed into a can of gas. The explosion was certain; it was only a matter of how much damage it caused.

Before he knew it, he was speaking. "I've been thinking about the court case, and the bottom line is—I won't blame our customer, who installed our product correctly, and I won't lie about the formulation. It's not only bad for business, it's wrong. If I have to testify, I'll answer every question honestly. I won't make any false statements under oath." He paused and took a breath. "And if that's not acceptable to you, then I'll resign."

Heinkel scowled. "What's the matter, Jake? Don't you got the balls to get up there—"

"It's not about balls. It's about right and wrong."

"Christ, Jake. You can go crazy thinking like that. What's right and what's not? I don't know, and you sure as shit don't either. It's all about staying in business. You want to stay in business, don't you? Hell, yes, you do. So it's got to be done—it's not easy, it's not pretty, but you got to bite the fuckin' bullet and do it."

"Even if that means hurting innocent people?"

"You don't think these guys would kick our ass if the shoe was on the other fuckin' foot?"

"I can't speak for them, but no—I don't think most people would."

Heinkel scoffed. "We sell chemicals, Jake—we're not saving babies. Everybody knows we're here to make money. That's why we do it. Everything else is *bullshit*. You got to testify. You're the fuckin' product manager. When they call you up, you got to say what's good for the company. Everybody depends on you."

While all of Jake's past managers believed in the supremacy of profits, he'd never heard anyone express it so baldly. "In the first place, I don't think it's good for the company. In fact, it could ruin the company."

"You have no fuckin' clue, Jake. This kind of shit happens all the time. You live in a fuckin' fantasy world. People do whatever they got to—to get the business and to keep the business. I've been selling chemicals for twenty-five years. What do you know? You don't know shit."

"I know the difference between right and wrong," he said, his face coloring.

Heinkel stood, scuttled around his desk, and backed him into the wall. His cologne enveloped Jake's head like a cloud of nerve gas. He was gearing up for a full tirade now, growing louder with every sentence. "Don't give me this pansy-ass shit about right and wrong. I know what you want—you want to bring the check home to your wife and have a nice little family, and you're happy as long as someone else does the dirty work—right? You don't want to testify, you don't want to fight, you just want the fuckin' check. You don't want to worry about how we get the business or how we keep it, you just want someone else to keep it coming, right?"

Jake bristled. "I think that's called marketing,"

"Yes, we get the business from marketing. And you better be damn good at marketing, Jake, or I'm chewing your ass. But we get the business any way we can. Whatever it takes. And once we get it, we don't let go. You have to think big, Jake, bigger than you did before, or you won't make it here."

Jake's brow creased like a Chinese fan. Heinkel's speech conjured up images of backdoor deals, price-fixing, cooking the books—a world of business he'd only seen in movies and which, he liked to think, didn't encroach on the average person's life. "If that's the way it works, then maybe I don't want to make it here."

"You're pretty hot shit, Jake, but I can replace you."

"Anybody can be replaced."

Heinkel lowered his voice to a normal level. "Jake, I like you, you know that, and what you have done with the sealant line is great, but I know people who can take your job tomorrow."

This is going nowhere. Get it over with. "Then you'd better start looking. I'm not lying under oath. If I get subpoenaed, I'll tell them everything I know."

Heinkel turned crimson. "Jake, I will fire your ass."

He met his stare. "I think we're done talking now."

"This is your last chance," he sputtered. "If you walk out, I will guarantee you never find a job again."

"Maybe not in this industry, but if it's like you say, that's fine with me."

He made a motion to leave, but Heinkel cut him off. He shouted directly into Jake's face, dredging up every error he'd made over the last two years, no matter how small, and in terrifying detail. Jake's heart began to pound. Soon the only words he could make out were obscene. Heinkel's breath, reeking of coffee, blasted his face, and drops of spittle struck his cheeks. Repulsed, he brushed past Heinkel and hurried out the door.

In the atrium, the secretaries kept their heads down, pretending to work. The director of human resources got up from his desk, but only stared at Jake with tightly pressed lip. One of the VPs got up from his desk and quietly shut his door.

As Jake fled the executive wing, Heinkel chased him like a dive-bombing Stuka. By now he could no longer hear what Heinkel was saying, but he didn't care either. He only wanted to leave the building as quickly as he could. Only later, driving home in his car, did he realize that Heinkel had been shouting at him the whole time in German.

He strode down the hall, expecting Heinkel to pursue him back to his office, but after a dozen more steps, an uncanny silence filled the air. Through the open doors, his fellow workers stared at him as he rushed by, but he didn't stop at one to explain. He went straight to his office, grabbed his briefcase, cast a quick look around for anything he'd forgotten, and marched to the end of the hall and out the side exit. The door swung shut as he stepped over the green lawn. A breeze came from nowhere and swept across it, cooling his face and clearing his mind.

In the parking lot, he glanced back to see his colleagues standing in their windows like department-store manikins, watching him go. More than a few he would dearly miss, and he fought back a surge of anger, knowing that Heinkel had driven him out of a job, and perhaps a career, that he'd otherwise found rewarding.

He tossed his briefcase into his Camry and grabbed the wheel. He drove sternly past the front doors, but when he sped out the driveway into the street, he smiled. The thing was done. The die was cast. He'd gotten out with his good name intact, and the future, although uncertain, was a clean white canvas on which he could paint whatever he chose.

38

Up till now, the interview had been going well. But things always went downhill as soon as they asked, "*Why did you leave your last position?*"

Jake stared at his legal pad and pen lying on the table. He looked freshly minted in his dark-gray suit and red-striped tie, as if he'd walked straight from his bedroom into the meeting room.

Across him sat two middle-aged men—the regional sales manager and the marketing director for PowerCam Industries, a distributor of high-horse-power engines. Both wore khaki pants and oxford shirts. Neither wore jacket or tie. Jake's first interview with human resources, two days ago, had been more formal, prompting him to overdress for this one, and now he worried they would think him stiff or snobby.

Why did you leave your last position?

His pause had already put them on guard. They eyed him carefully and waited.

He bit his lip. During interviews with two other companies, he'd refused to discuss his firing, or quitting, whatever you called it—leery of knocking his past employer and coming across as a malcontent—but the gaps in his story had forced his interviewers to guess the reasons for his leaving, and their doubts, he felt sure, had weighed against him and, for all he knew, had cost him both jobs.

Don't hold back, Phoebe had told him the night before. *It might impress them. You tried it twice the other way. What have you got to lose?*

He cleared his throat. "My employer asked me to do something unethical and I wouldn't," he said, being careful not to break eye contact. "One of my products failed. They wanted me to lie about it and blame the contractor, so they wouldn't have to pay for it."

The sales manager shook his head, disgusted, but the marketing director, a stern-looking man with short, white hair, was harder to read. "Can you tell us more about it?" he said, his eyes narrowing.

"They say you should never speak poorly of a past employer, but if I don't, I can't tell you the story. It may take a while."

"Take your time," said the director.

He first painted colorful pictures of Tony Carlucci and Heinrich Heinkel. At times he thought his portrayals seemed petty or too farfetched to believe, but as he recounted Heinkel ordering him to lie in court, the shocked looks made him feel justified for having drawn such unflattering pictures of his former employers.

He ended by describing Heinkel chasing him down the hallway, shouting in German. The story made the sales manager laugh so much that Jake worried he'd turned the whole episode into a farce.

The marketing director, on the other hand, still didn't react. He propped his chin on both thumbs and stared at Jake. "And what would you do if that happened at PowerCam?"

Jake paused. The man's body language suggested he thought him insub-ordinate, but his gut told him his mettle was being tested to see if he'd back down when pushed.

"I'd do the same thing."

The man nodded and kept staring at him. He seemed angry, but Jake couldn't tell why.

If that was the wrong answer, then I might as well get the pleasure of blowing them off.

"Frankly, if your company's like ConChem, I wouldn't want to work here."

The director nodded. "If we ran things like that, I wouldn't either."

He'd barely breathed a sigh of relief when a young woman in a navy skirt and white blouse stepped into the room. "I'm sorry to barge in. Are you Jake Anderson?"

He looked up. No one interrupted a job interview to give an applicant a message unless something was wrong.

She stared at him, eyes wide. "Your wife called. She's in the hospital. She says she needs you more than we do."

He gawked at her grinning face and then jumped out of his chair. He tried brushing his pad and pen into his briefcase, but missed and sent them flying across the room. When he stooped to pick them up, he nearly knocked heads with the woman, who'd bent down first.

"Thank you, but I have to go," he said, making for the door. Halfway through it, he grabbed the metal frame and pulled himself back in. "I'm having a boy—I mean, my wife is—never mind."

The woman giggled.

"Good luck," said the director. "We'll be in touch." But Jake never heard. He'd had already left the interview a light-year behind. The job no longer mattered—the only thing that did now was reaching Phoebe quickly enough to help her through what he thought at the time would be the most trying ordeal of her life.

39

Jake stopped in the doorway, breathless. At the end of a long room with a vinyl couch and flowered drapes, Phoebe was sitting up in bed, already gowned, her knees forming a pale-blue tent. Zoe stood beside her in T-shirt and jeans, flat-bellied by now, holding both her hands.

Suddenly, Phoebe's brow creased and her shoulders lurched toward her belly.

"Breathe in-two-three," Zoe commanded, "out-two-three-four."

He stayed in the doorway and winced. Phoebe looked as if she'd just slammed her toe into a bedpost.

She closed her eyes while Zoe counted, breathing out in a long, slow *whoosh.* The contraction lasted only a minute, but to Jake it seemed to never end. For the first time he understood not only what Phoebe would be going through, but how trying it would be to watch her suffer.

Zoe glanced over her shoulder. "Here comes the mailman."

Phoebe's laugh gave way to a look that said *Thank God you're here, Where the hell have you been?* and *Help me!* all at once.

"I got here as fast as I could."

"Kill anybody on the road?" Zoe asked.

He blushed, recalling the open stretch that he'd barreled down at 90 miles per hour. He rounded the bed and took Phoebe's hand.

"Your sweaty," she said, disgusted, and pulled away her hand.

"Sorry. Nervous, I guess."

"No—*you* are not nervous. *I* am nervous."

"How are you holding up?"

"The pain is getting worse. I feel like I'm birthing a whale."

"Relax," Zoe said, pressing her thumbs into Phoebe's brow. "You can't control it. Don't try."

"Easy for you to say," Phoebe snapped. "You were fucking unconscious for both of yours."

Zoe laughed guiltily. "It's still good advice."

Dr. Richards, a middle-aged man with thick blond hair breezed through the door as though arriving at a cocktail party. Phoebe gave him a grateful look.

"I see your team's here," he said, extending a hand to Jake. "First time, dad?"

"I guess it shows."

He smiled reassuringly, stretched on a pair of latex gloves, and squeezed some gel on his fingers. "She's doing fine. So far, all routine."

The idea that having a baby could be routine struck Jake as odd, until it dawned on him that for Dr. Richards it was a more common event than cutting the grass.

Without warning Phoebe, he lifted her gown and slipped in his hand. She winced. He moved his arm as though fishing for a lost quarter under a sofa cushion.

"You're at six, and progressing nicely."

"Good. Fast is good."

"Up to a point."

"How long do you think this will take?"

"Do you need to be somewhere?"

"Shut up," Phoebe said, smiling.

"I can't say. Every birth is different."

"Thanks for sticking your neck out, Doc."

"For a first-time mother, the average is roughly eight hours."

"Eight hours?" She glared at Jake. "You son of a bitch."

He glanced back sheepishly, wanting to remind her they'd planned this together, but he knew it would only trigger a stronger reaction.

"You're ahead of schedule," Dr. Richards said. "And when it's over, I'm sure you'll think it's worth it."

"Oh, shit, here comes another one." Phoebe grimaced and began to puff.

Instead of coaching her, as Jake expected, Dr. Richards made for the door. "I'll come back when you're ready to push," he said. A second later he was gone.

"Keep breathing," Zoe said. "Slow down."

Phoebe seized up as if an electric current was flowing through her body. She gripped Zoe's hands so tightly that her knuckles turned white. At the peak of her contraction, her face pinched together so badly he barely recognized her. When the contraction faded, her features smoothed again, but the after-effect troubled him too—a smoke in her eyes that told of a journey to a far-off place where he couldn't follow, no matter how he tried. *This could go on for hours. And the longer it goes, the harder it will get.*

"Better now," Phoebe said with a sigh. "That was a bad one."

A wave of pity swept over him. Phoebe had been right about the pain, and nothing he did could stop it from coming back every three or four minutes for the next eight hours.

When the next contraction came, he tried grabbing her hand, but she brushed him away. Zoe stepped in, clamped Phoebe's hands, gazed without flinching into her eyes, and breathed along with her as the contraction peaked.

He sat on the couch, feeling useless. He was not the kind of person to stand by and watch as events played out, but one to roll up his sleeves and help, whether asked to or not. At the same time, he couldn't leave or even distract himself with a book or a magazine. He was forced to sit here, powerless, and watch Phoebe suffer. Eight hours seemed like an impossibly long time to watch her writhe in pain, and he couldn't imagine how much worse it would be for her.

Over the next few hours, the contractions became sharper and closer together. The banter between the sisters fell off as they focused on getting Phoebe through each new peak. The closer they came together, surprisingly, the less she seemed afraid—working through each contraction as if it were a sprint at the end of a race—but in this race the sprinting went on and on, and the finish line never seemed to draw any nearer.

As he watched, he marveled at the way that Zoe handled Phoebe, counting her breaths, massaging her hands, encouraging and sometimes teasing her, and how Phoebe hung on her every word, giving him the impression that if Zoe left the room, even for a second, Phoebe would unhinge—surrender, panic, scream—and the ordeal would become unbearable for everybody.

It baffled him why no one on the floor seemed to care how much his wife suffered. Dr. Richards hadn't checked in for two full hours, although a full parade of nurses had marched in and out, timing Phoebe's contractions, checking her cervix, and adjusting her IV. Twice he'd gone searching for Dr. Richards himself, and twice he was told by nurses that Phoebe wasn't ready to push, and the doctor would return as soon as he was needed.

After an especially hard contraction, Phoebe let loose a string of curses that would have impressed a drill sergeant, using every four-letter word that Jake knew, and then some. The outburst was so loud that he got up and closed the door to keep it from scaring the other mothers arriving on the ward.

At least the noise caught the attention of Phoebe's nurse, who rushed in and checked her cervix. "You're fully effaced. Hang on. I'll get Doctor Richards."

Jake looked down the hall, tapping his fingers on the doorframe. A foot away stood a bassinet on wheels. Was it for their boy, he wondered, or the room next door?

"Jake," came Zoe's voice. "She wants you."

Zoe was gazing at him with a tired smile. "I'm done. It's your turn."

"You're leaving?"

"It's up to you now."

He stared at her blankly, doubting he could take her place.

"She'll be fine. She just needs to know you're here." Zoe threw her arms around him, squeezed him tightly, and walked out the door.

He went to the bed and took Phoebe's hand, afraid she might slap it away or swear at him, but instead she gripped it and gazed at him fiercely. Wet hair stuck to her forehead, beads of sweat spotted her upper lip, and her skin had the white sheen of a wax figure. "Get me through this, Jake, can't you?"

He searched her eyes. They were begging for relief, but also glowing with the awareness of the miracle that soon would follow.

"You're almost done. You're very brave, and I love you."

"I needed that," she said, wincing. "I can do the rest." She raised her hips and bore down with all her might. "Oh, God," she groaned. "Here he comes."

Part Three
1995

40

Zoe leaned back in Maddy's bed, propped up by a landslide of pillows. On her left and right, Maddy and Marty tucked themselves into her faded sweatshirt, peering into the open pages of *Stellaluna,* which Zoe held on her lap. Looking like Princess Jasmine in her gold and turquoise nightgown, Maddy was growing into a taller, thinner version of her mother. She studied the pictures warily with her large brown eyes and fidgeted with her silky sleeves. Marty gripped the edge of the book and gawked at the pictures, clearly concerned about the fate of the poor little fruit bat who'd lost his mother. Marty had Jeremy's long face, blue eyes, and blond hair, but Zoe's body—slender legs and arms and elfin hands and feet. He looked too young for Kindergarten, just four months away, and his pale skin and bony frame made him look fragile, like a delicate vase, pleasant to view but only handled with the greatest of care.

Zoe had cropped her hair short to speed up her toilet in her busy day. No wrinkles yet showed around the corners of her brown eyes or full lips. A slight tummy, seen only in profile, barely detracted from her nearly perfect figure. The greatest change in the last five years appeared in her eyes. In her twenties, they burned with a mischievous fire, whereas now they merely smoldered, the fire checked by age and the never-ending demands of work and parenthood.

As Zoe read, a door slammed somewhere downstairs. She stopped in mid-sentence.

"Daddy's home," said Maddy.

Zoe waited, listening.

"Read the ending, when the mommy comes back," Marty said.

Zoe began reading again, but the banging kept distracting her.

"You said *Nets,* Mommy, it's *nest,*" Maddy complained.

"*Nest.* Good job, honey." Of course it had to be Jeremy, but the sounds were too sporadic and loud, as if a raccoon had climbed in the kitchen window.

Something hit the floor and shattered.

Zoe set down the book and vaulted over Maddy. She stopped in the doorway and turned. "Okay, you two, brush your teeth and go to bed. I have to see Daddy."

"What about Stellaluna?" Marty pleaded.

"Maddy can read it, can't you, Maddy?"

She proudly picked up the book. "I can read better than Mommy."

"Someday you will," Zoe said absently.

"I do better voices too."

Maddy sidled next to Marty with a motherly air, flipped back to the first page, and began reading fluently.

Zoe hurried down the stairs and into the kitchen. Jeremy was kneeling on the tile, surrounded by shards of broken glass. He was scraping them into a pile with a postcard and seemed not to notice her standing behind him. She watched him silently as he gathered the pieces.

"What happened?"

He screwed his head around. "I dropped a glass."

She opened the pantry, took out a broom and dustbin, and started sweeping. "It's pretty late. Have you been working?"

"More or less." He stood up and banged his hip into the table. Zoe stopped sweeping and stared at him. His bangs covered one eye like a patch, and his sport coat was crumpled as a wad of paper. The dark circles under his eyes made him look ten years older than his thirty-seven years.

Then the smell hit her. "Christ, you're drunk."

"Not really."

"Who were you with?"

"Tom and his pals," he said blithely. "We went to that new Irish pub."

His behavior struck her as not only dishonest, but mockingly defiant. "You're doing this way too often, Jeremy. You're starting to worry me."

"Are you saying I have a problem?"

"Keep it up, and you will. Besides, we can't afford it. Bars are not cheap."

He scowled and crossed his arms. "Hey, I work hard. I have a right to go out now and then. You're blowing this way out of proportion."

She drew a deep breath. "It's not just tonight. It's two or three nights a week. You spend more time with your friends than you do at home. It's not the working late—that I get, it's your job. But afterward, at least you could have dinner with us, instead of those clowns at the office."

"They're not clowns—they're my friends."

"Well, maybe, but Tom *does* have a drinking problem."

He shook his head. "Tom just likes to have fun." He took a glass from the cupboard, filled it with water, and downed it with a single gulp.

Zoe studied him. His voice and thinking were clear, but his subtly slow movements gave him away. A stream of water trickled down his chin. He wiped it with his hand before setting down the glass, as if trying to hide his clumsiness. The simple motion sent a shock through Zoe. She watched him, horrified. She'd seen him move that way a hundred times before, but had never thought it more than fatigue—because he'd never failed to speak and reason clearly, unlike her father, who always slurred and rambled when he drank. But what if Jeremy hadn't been tired all those times—what if he'd really been drunk? Dozens of past episodes popped into her head, and suddenly she felt as if the ground was giving way beneath her.

"Tell me something—is there any night you don't drink?"

He slammed down the glass. "Is this the fucking Inquisition? Yes, I do have a drink every night. So what? So do you. The damn Surgeon General says it's good for you."

"So you're drinking for your health?"

"No. Sometimes I need a break, that's all. Don't you ever need a break? At work I get nothing but shit, and then I come home and all I hear is nag, nag, nag. *Did you pay the dental bill? When are you going to mow the lawn? Where have you been all night?* And now you think I'm a drunk."

"I didn't say you were a drunk. And you know I'm not a nag. I hate women who nag. But these are real problems, Jeremy. We can't ignore them. The house is falling apart. We have bills we can't pay. And Maddy is mouthing off to her teachers—I have girls like that in my classroom, and I know the kind of homes they come from. I'm worried that we're becoming one of them."

"That's what I'm talking about," he said, pointing to her chest. "According to you, our family is a train wreck. That's what drives me crazy. It's why I work late at night and why I go out with my friends—to get away from this place and squeeze a little joy out of life—because my friends have their feet on the ground. They know it won't crack open and swallow them up because their kid mouthed off to some prissy teacher."

As he spoke, his face twisted with anger. Never before had he looked at her with such venom. It not only frightened Zoe, but also made it clear that he'd been holding it back for months, maybe even years, and now was it pouring out with the fury of a broken dam. Yet what drove a dagger deep into her heart—more than his lying, his petty accusations, or his scoffing at her efforts to nurture their kids—was the admission that he couldn't stand coming home—that he stayed out late at night to get away from *her*. It confirmed her fear that he no longer desired or even loved her, that she'd ceased to be his soulmate, and now she was merely around to manage the house and raise their kids, and she'd better do it right and quit complaining.

It was more than she could stand. A shout rose up in her throat, but nothing came out, and the words that popped into her head were, *I hate you—get out of my house.*

"I'm sorry you don't love me anymore," she said, fighting back tears.

"God, don't be so dramatic. I never said that."

"Yes, you did. You said it clearly."

He rubbed his face. "All right, Zoe, I'm sorry. I didn't mean it."

"No, you're not sorry. And you did mean it." She backed away, but stopped in the door. "Go say goodnight to your kids. You can sleep on the couch."

"You've got to be kidding," he grumbled, but he could tell by the look in her eyes she wasn't.

"I'll get some bedding."

She marched down the hallway, grabbed the railing, and froze. At the top of the stairs, a pajama-clad princess was staring down at her. *Dammit.*

Maddy bolted for her room. Zoe scrambled up the stairs. She found Maddy sitting cross-legged on her bed, her face blank. It wasn't the fear of being caught spying that troubled her, Zoe could tell. It was the fight she'd overheard.

Zoe sat beside her and squeezed her hand. "I'm not angry, Maddy, I just need to explain something."

She stared at her, confused. "Why doesn't Daddy love you?"

"Of course he loves me, and I love him. We had an argument, that's all." She paused and thought carefully. She had to get this right. "Sometimes when grownups argue, they get mad and say things they don't mean. That's what you heard. Do you understand?"

Maddy nodded, calmed by the explanation, but at the same time Zoe's heart sank, because she doubted her own words.

"If Daddy still loves you, why are you crying?"

She wiped a tear from her cheek. "Sometimes Mommy overreacts. Now go to sleep, honey. Everything will be fine in the morning."

She knew that Maddy needed more comforting, but she also knew that if she stayed, she would keep on crying, so she kissed Maddy on the cheek, told her she loved her, and turned off the light.

After tucking Marty in, she gathered up an armful of bedding, and carried it down the stairs. Oddly, the kitchen was empty and the living room dark. Jeremy seemed to have vanished.

A guttural groan rose from the shadows. Zoe flipped on the light to find him collapsed on the couch, one foot on the floor, a dislocated arm blocking his eyes, and his mouth agape. She watched him for a long time, alarmed by the thoughts running through her head, and finally dropped the blankets on the coffee table, retreated into her bedroom, and shut the door.

41

It was a warm afternoon with a lazy blue sky, as if a perfect summer day had been pushed back to April. After her final class, Zoe was still working at her desk, distracted now and then by the yellow buds quivering beyond the window and the breeze sifting under the sill and brushing her face and neck.

At a desk nearby, a new teacher, two years out of college, peered into a computer screen—or at least Zoe thought. In fact, he'd long since given up his work to study a much more compelling subject—Zoe and the ever-changing moods that were shifting across her face.

The two were creating a lesson plan for a class they team-taught, combining English and history.

When Zoe had first met Steve Roberts, she thought he was a high-school senior. She'd even asked him where he planned on going to college. He laughed and gently corrected her. "You look like a student yourself," he said. "Can I take you to prom?"

She smiled, put on her professional face, and quizzed him about his background.

Zoe had taught high-school English for ten years, and many days she fought to keep afloat the enthusiasm that had come so naturally when she was younger. Not surprisingly, she soon grew to appreciate Steve's passion for teaching and his fresh approach—and his knack for connecting with students while still preserving order in the classroom. She also enjoyed their planning sessions together, which took place in the quiet of her classroom after school. Sometimes their talks became personal, which Zoe liked too, as Steve openly shared his past with her but never pressed her much about her own life.

Today, as she graded papers, Steve's gaze lingered on her face. Every now and then his brow wrinkled. "Is something bothering you?"

His question broke her concentration. "No, I'm just tired."

"You don't look tired."

"I didn't sleep well last night."

"You don't look sleepy. You look sad."

The comment shook her. For a second, their eyes met. It flattered Zoe that he'd read her mood. "Maybe a bit," she said, adding a semicolon to a student's paper.

"Anything I can do?"

"Wish you could. Sorry."

"Maybe you should tell someone about it."

"What makes you think I haven't?"

"Sorry," he said, coloring. "I shouldn't make assumptions."

She felt guilty for brushing him off. He seemed so young and naïve, and he couldn't know just how deep a well he was plumbing. "The truth is, I haven't told anyone. It's too personal."

But the words had no sooner slipped her tongue than she longed to spill out her troubles. She only stopped herself with the strongest of efforts.

"I understand. But let me know if you change your mind."

Zoe knew it was only a matter of time before she poured out her feelings to someone. And maybe it was safer to confide in a coworker than a friend or family member, either of whom might gossip.

"Before you get married," she began, "make sure you know the person you'll spend the rest of your life with. A lot of people get lazy when they fall in love. They don't give it much thought." She paused and frowned. "The hard part is, even if you know each other well, you change. Ten years later, your wife might not be the same person she was on your wedding night—or it could be you who changes. Think about that before you get married. Try to look ahead and see the person she'll become in ten years, or twenty or forty, because that's the person you're really marrying."

"That's a scary thought."

"It is. And most people don't even think about it."

The room grew still, making Steve's voice surprisingly loud. "If you don't mind my asking, which one of you has changed?"

"Being a mother has changed me, but inside I think I'm the same."

"So it's him."

She nodded. "That's what I'm trying to work out. Or get used to."

"If you still love him, maybe you'll learn, you know, to appreciate the person he's become."

She smiled sadly. It had been hard for him to get that out, she could tell. He was thinking of her even when it conflicted with his own interests. And she would have laughed at the irony of his advice if her problem hadn't already caused her so much pain. "I don't think that's possible."

"Well, maybe you could meet him halfway."

She let out a snort. "There's no such thing as half an alcoholic."

He winced. "I'm sorry."

"I don't mean to burden you," she said, shoring herself up. "I don't know why I said that. I don't believe in self-pity. It doesn't solve anything."

"It's not self-pity. You're in a hard situation."

"And I don't know what I should do."

"Will he go into treatment?"

"He doesn't think he has a problem."

"Do they ever?"

"Well, now you know. That's why I've been so preoccupied. And I guess you're right—sad."

"If there's anything I can do, and I mean anything, Zoe, tell me. If you need me to cover a class or just need to talk, I'm here, okay?"

The tremor in his voice reminded her of the intimate nature of their talk, and she forced shut the door she'd briefly opened—although not fast enough to keep him from seeing the raw state of her soul.

"That's very sweet of you, Steve. You're a nice guy, but I need to work this out for myself."

42

Jeremy fought to pay attention as the young man gave his sales pitch, smartly canned except for the occasional slip in grammar.

"We may not be the biggest gym, but we do have the best hours. We open at 5:00 a.m. and we close at midnight. You won't find another downtown club with hours like that."

He reminded Jeremy of a blond SS officer in Dockers and a polo shirt. His tiny white-walled office barely fit the desk and chairs they sat in.

Despite his boredom, Jeremy did care about the hours. He was hoping to burn off the stress from work by going to the gym, replacing his drinking with a harmless, even healthy pastime. The sales pitch was pointless—he'd already made up his mind—but the recruiter said it was mandatory. Jeremy nodded and muttered, "Right, right," in a futile effort to bring it to a rapid end.

"What do you like?" the man asked. "Racquet ball? Cardio? Weights?"

"Running mostly. Maybe some weights."

He could tell by the man's smirk he thought him a novice to weightlifting. *Just shut up, bud, and give me the contract.*

He followed his guide into a long, low room filled by the whir of stationary bikes, the clip-clop of tennies on treadmills, and the clanking of iron plates.

He'd made up his mind to join a club the day after Zoe had made him sleep on the sofa. He'd woken up that morning with a parched mouth and pounding temples. He'd slept all night in his sport coat, and his laced-up loafers had made his toes go numb. He stood groggily, plodded into the bathroom, gulped down a gallon of water, and slunk back to the sofa, where he lay for the next hour as sunlight inched across the floor, wondering what in the hell he was doing.

It was bad enough to get drunk on a weeknight, but worse to believe that Zoe would ignore it—or even think it was funny. He kept mulling over their argument, trying to recall every word, like a sailor steering back to port through a dense fog. She'd called him an alcoholic, of that he was sure, and the accusation still burned in his mind like a cattle brand. *Alcoholic?* He was no more an alcoholic than Zoe was. What had he done, aside from last night, to make her come to such a rash conclusion?

He tried being honest with himself. True, there was a bad vein in the bloodline. His uncle Lowell had more or less destroyed his family. He'd abandoned his wife and three boys a decade ago, but claimed the problem was his wife and not his drinking. He wasn't becoming his uncle Lowell, was he?

Let me count—I had two martinis on Wednesday. Three merlots at dinner on Thursday. Friday night, I went to the pub with Jack and had, well, shit, way too many. Saturday, Rick brought over those two Zinfandels, and I had maybe four, maybe five glasses—but, after all, it was Saturday night. Sunday I took a break. Monday I had two martinis after work, and Tuesday night was the blowout. He stopped and frowned. *No wonder Zoe was getting worried. It had been one hell of a week. Counting last night it made 34 drinks.*

He shook his head. *That's a lot of drinks for a week. But does it make me an alcoholic? Do the math, stupid—34 divided by seven—almost five drinks a day.*

While he doubted that number made him an alcoholic, it did put him on a troubling path, and if he kept marching down it, before long there would be no turning back. *Five stiff drinks a day. That's too damn much.* Somehow, he had to lower that number.

When had things gotten so far out of control? Like most of his friends, he'd always liked a good bender now and then, but that was in his younger, partying days, while in his late twenties, the carousing had leveled off and stayed subdued—that is, until his promotion at the Herald. After that, work had taken a downward turn. The raise in pay didn't make up for the added hours or stress, and there were times when he felt unfit for managing people. Someone on his staff was always melting down, playing politics, or charging off on a personal crusade. But the worst part was the way his coworkers had treated him once he'd become their boss. Most of his old friends had deserted him. After the episode with Ben, he'd become their enemy, a traitor who'd sold out his ideals for money and power. Every time he thought of it, he burned with shame. It was so unfair. Nobody understood how every day he fought to reconcile the conflicting roles of his job—to report the news but also to keep his owners happy. What's more, no one seemed to care. How could such broadminded people judge him so harshly? They were biting the hand that fed them—hypocrites who expected the owners to pay them for sitting on their duffs and pounding out their personal manifestos.

He was so fed up with the politics, he could vomit. *Some days I can't stand walking into the office,* he thought as the sun peeked over the sill and poked him in the eyes, reminding him that in two mere hours he'd be chained to his desk, fighting like a drowning man to stay awake.

He glanced at the clock on the wall. Already it was after six. How in the hell would he get through the next 10 hours? And what should he say to Zoe and the kids when they got out of bed?

Don't say anything. Get them up and going. Keep them busy. Apologize later. I'm sorry you don't love me anymore.

How could Zoe think that? Did she really believe it? She looked like she did—or was it just a bad night, and she'd come back to earth by morning?

Either way, it's a bad sign when your wife tells you that. And Zoe is more forgiving than most. I admit I've been a lousy husband lately—not because I don't love her anymore, but because ... He tried to finish the sentence, but couldn't, and a second later his stomach plunged like a runaway elevator. *Was he really on the verge of losing her? Could she really leave him? Throw him out of the house or else take the kids and move out herself? She wouldn't do anything that drastic, would she?*

The thought terrified him. He knew that despite her bohemian streak, Zoe was an idealist. He'd always admired her altruism, but sometimes the paradox baffled him, because her easygoing air could turn on a dime over some deeply held belief, and then she couldn't be argued with. So it was possible that one day she might wake up and decide he'd fallen too far to save and he was no longer fit to be her husband. The thought was so upsetting that he sat upright on the couch. *If that ever happened, I don't know what I'd do. I don't think I'd make it through a single day.*

Then and there, he got up, washed his face, brushed his teeth, and crept into the kitchen. It was 6:30. He still had time to cook eggs and bacon for Zoe and the kids before they drove off to school. Granted, it would be a small gesture, but he couldn't think of anything better, and maybe it would be a baby step, with many more to come, toward earning her forgiveness.

43

Zoe sat against a maple tree in a park near the school. Her crossed legs pinned down her lavender dress patterned with yellow daisies, and the breeze kissed her bare arms and nuzzled her neck while she nibbled a mozzarella and tomato sandwich. Steve Roberts sat beside her in cargo pants and a Hawaiian shirt. Now and then, the breeze lifted his blond curls and held them aloft. Softened by the shade, his skin had the flawless, firm radiance of youth, and his blue eyes shone whenever Zoe spoke. It was plain that he was basking not only in the beautiful weather but also in the glow of his captivating companion.

It was the kind of day that tempted teachers to bring their students outdoors and circle them under a tree, hoping that none would disappear during the trip. The air hovered in the high seventies, crisp as a freshly plucked apple, and the breeze sifted between the maple boughs and bobbed the leaves like a billion tiny fans. The cloudless sky, peeking through holes in the canopy, made you marvel at its blueness, drink in the pristine air, and forget about the dull routines that burdened your life.

Zoe was glad when Steve proposed they spend their lunch in the park. The summerlike weather, as well as the worries swarming around her like a cloud of gnats, had ruined her concentration, and she couldn't resist his offer to escape the crowded school and relax in a quiet, green spot.

He was telling her about his first teaching job in a small Wisconsin town when he stopped mid-sentence.

He seemed caught up in a trance, even though he was staring directly at her.

"What is it?" she asked.

He leaned into Zoe and kissed her.

She froze, partly out of shock. He pressed the kiss, and when her lips parted, he breathed in deeply through his nose. Then she felt it, his desire rolling across the desert of her heart like a fast-moving storm, prefaced by a misty wind and the smell of dirt, promising to wash away her unhappiness.

But Zoe was no longer an impulsive young girl. The thought of her kids, as well as the openness of the park, quickly brought her back to her senses.

She pulled away, and the feeling vanished.

Steve was blushing furiously.

She scanned the park and street. Luckily, both were empty. "Why did you do that?"

He stared at her, confused.

"Why did you do that?" she demanded.

"I think you know why."

"I don't, and you'd better tell me," she insisted, even though she knew the answer.

"I'm in love with you, Zoe."

"No, you're not," she said, fighting back a blush. "You're infatuated. It's not the same. Infatuations come and go. Not love."

"I've felt this way for a long time."

"That's my fault. We've been spending too much time together. It's not healthy for either one of us. You should be looking for someone your own age, and I'm not—"

She wanted to say *available*, but the word stopped in her throat. "A good choice," she finished.

"You're the most fascinating woman I've ever met. And the most beautiful."

She blushed. In spite of her protests, she couldn't say the words his behavior called for: *I don't love you. I want you to stop.* Because the truth was, she didn't want him to stop.

In her hesitation, he saw an opening. "It drives me crazy when I see you, Zoe. But it's worse if I don't. Sometime I walk by your room just to catch a glimpse of you. Our meetings after school thrill and torture me. I'm supposed to be working, but all I can think about is you. Are you happy? Are you sad? Do you think about me?"

"That's it. Look, I'm flattered, but this has gone far enough. I should have said something earlier. I'm sorry if I led you on." She glanced around. "And in broad daylight. A few blocks from school. Are you crazy?"

"We could go for a drive."

Her blush deepened. "That's not what I meant. Steve—think about it. I'm ten years older than you. We work together. I have two kids. For God's sake, I'm married."

"You're married to a man who doesn't love you, and you're only staying with him because of your kids."

"How dare you," she said, getting up. "My family is off limits. You have no right to bring them up."

"I'm sorry," he said, scrambling to his feet. "I know it's none of my business, but it kills me to see you so unhappy. I've been watching you all year, and it keeps getting worse. You don't know what it's like to see a person you love suffer and not be able to help."

Tears sprang to Zoe's eyes, but whether from sorrow or shame, she couldn't tell. She grabbed her lunch bag and water bottle. It was pointless to argue with him. Nothing she said would change the way he felt, and it was time for them to leave. "We're late," she said coolly and started across the lawn. "Please don't bring this up again."

44

"My name is Bill, and I'm an alcoholic.

The man said it casually—as if reading off baseball scores from the paper. He couldn't be more than thirty, Jeremy thought. His mousy brown hair was thinning, and his wire-frame glasses, just coming into style, rested on his nose like an English aristocrat's. But this man was something much more impressive—a phoenix who'd burned his career as a financial advisor down to the ashes, along with his marriage to a beautiful woman, and then risen from those same ashes to quit drinking, remarry, and launch a successful new business in the software industry.

He told his life story in the three standard minutes allowed for each member, recounting with calm acceptance his drunkenness at home, on the job, and behind the wheel; his many affairs; and the perverse thought process that he used to justify his conduct.

The harsh contrast between his present and past lives baffled Jeremy. How could someone sink so low and still find the courage to face his demons, make such dramatic changes to his life, and reverse it so fully and swiftly that his fiery descent filled only a chapter in his otherwise impressive bio?

Nine other men sat in the circle of folding chairs, listening carefully. They ranged from their early twenties to their late fifties, some in suits, some in workman's clothes and boots, some in T-shirts and jeans. They struck Jeremy as an ordinary group, without much in common—until they began spilling their guts and sharing their eerily similar stories.

He stared at each new speaker like a sniper drawing a bead on his target. As each one spoke, the same disturbing question kept running through his mind—should he be here as a participant instead of a reporter writing a story? Had he waded so far into the quicksand of addiction that he could no longer fight his way out? How far down into the ooze had he sunk? Was he up to his knees? His waist? His neck?

The men's stories were terrifying. One had spent 20 years in a mindless fog, beaten his wife, and hinted at having abused his daughter—before Christ had forgiven him and put him back on a righteous path. One had been forced into treatment by three separate employers, the last of which had just fired him, and now he was living in a cardboard box under a bridge. The next man had also made himself unemployable, but he finally sobered up and started his own business, staying on the wagon for 16 years, only to relapse and lose his wife, kids, house, savings—and having hit rock bottom again was making one last desperate attempt at sobriety.

Other stories were less dramatic, but told of talent and promise wasted, wives betrayed, children abandoned. There were DUIs and near-fatal crashes, fits of rage and violence, shocking behavior at birthdays, baptisms, and weddings, while in the breast of every speaker burned an unquenchable fire of shame, each one horrified by how much he was willing to surrender to consume the poison that whipped him more savagely than the cruelest master.

When they began to read from the Bible, Jeremy's attention drifted. He skimmed the brochures they'd handed out and soon pegged himself as a heavy drinker—someone whose habit was affecting his work and family, but hadn't yet spun his life out of control, as it clearly had for the men here.

Even so, he found his thought process and theirs much too similar, especially in the way he made excuses for himself after a binge: *Zoe's bent out of shape because she had a bad day ... Everybody has to blow the carbon out of the engine once in a while ... The kids can't smell the booze. Even if they could, they don't know how much I've drunk.*

How lucky to catch himself at this early stage, he thought as the readings droned on, when he still had his job, his house, and Zoe, who, even if she sometimes nagged him, had stood faithfully by his side. In fact, she'd even backed off lately, as if she'd sensed his need for space to work things out for himself. Yes, thank God for Zoe—she was practically a saint—although he had to admit these last few years he'd given her far less than she deserved. A woman like that deserved much more, and if she wanted to could easily find it elsewhere—so he'd better sort himself out fast, he suddenly thought, and find his way back to her before they drifted so far apart that he couldn't make things right again.

When the meeting was over, he spoke with a few of the men, but the one he most wanted to meet, the phoenix, hurried out the door and disappeared, making him wonder if there wasn't something fishy about his story—but then again, what could you really tell about a person from a three-minute speech?

The sudden exit, along with the string of startling confessions, made Jeremy wonder just how much he knew about his own family and friends or how much they really knew about him. Did Zoe even know him at his deepest level? Was she aware of the maelstrom turning inside him or how close to the point of no return he was nearing? Of course, she'd long complained about his drinking, but he doubted that she knew how desperate the struggle had become. And for Zoe to really see, he would have to tell her everything—in spite of how much it might upset her. If they ever hoped to be close again, she'd have to know him at his core, with all his defenses stripped away. A full confession, he realized with a sharp, painful stab, was compulsory, and that meant admitting not only the extent of his drinking, but also the extent of his lying.

Could he really go through with that? Did he have the guts to make a full confession? And how would Zoe take it? How would she react when she found herself married to a man she didn't know? Could she live with such a man? Could she forgive him? And what would happen if she couldn't?

He wasn't sure.

As he drove home, a fierce battle raged inside him. Should he tell her the truth or not? He would find the courage to charge ahead, but then fall back under a hail of arrows as the cost of telling the truth became clear. Time and again, the battle lines moved forward and back, but in the end it didn't seem to matter which side triumphed: he was damned if he lost, and equally damned if he won.

His kept thinking back to the men in the circle of folding chairs and the trail of wreckage they'd left behind. Basically, the choice boiled down to this: did he want his life to become a broken wreck like theirs? Surely, it wasn't too late. There had to be time to save himself. And if he did come clean with Zoe, wouldn't she want to help him, to be his rock as he rebuilt his life? In spite of her nagging, he felt certain that she still loved him, and maybe that love would give him the strength he needed to put his life back on course.

There was no way around it. He had to confess, and soon. It might be now or never, so he'd better do it the second he walked through the door tonight.

At the same time, a full confession would be easier after a moment of closeness. Before he poured out his darkest secrets, he wanted Zoe's body, soft and warm, against his skin, to feel the tenderness and trust that he always felt after sex. Then, as they lay in bed with arms and legs interwoven, and both their bodies and souls bared, he would tell her everything.

But when he got home, Zoe snapped at him for coming home late. She asked him where he'd been, which he didn't want to say just yet, and when he tried to calm her down and touch her, she pushed him away, and with that push his resolution caved in like a rotted board.

He went to bed stinging from her refusal, but as he lay in the dark with his eyes wide open, a foot away from Zoe, what he felt more than anything, was relief.

45

Zoe spent the next few days in a fog. She managed to stay focused at home, but getting through six hours of English classes was a different matter. On her worst days, she wound up giving her students time in class to finish their homework while she graded papers, but she proved little better at grading than teaching. Today, the open windows and mild breeze didn't help. Neither did the couple flirting in the back row. She looked up now and then to catch them whispering, holding hands, and giggling. Caught in the act, they glanced down guiltily, puzzled that she didn't pounce on them, and resumed their flirting the second she looked away. Zoe watched them as she might a young couple at a movie theater and not her students, and the main emotion they aroused in her was jealousy—over their untroubled smiles, perfect bodies, and their effortless power to live in the present. Where in her own life had all of that gone? When had she stopped being a carefree girl and turned into a middle-aged school-marm, taken for granted by her students and maybe even laughed at in the halls?

Without telling them why, she got up and walked out the door. She clipped past a gauntlet of lockers, turned into the girl's bathroom, and stopped before her reflection in the hazy mirror. A mousy, sad-eyed woman stared back at her. While no wrinkles betrayed her age, her skin looked stretched and pinched, and the dark circles under her eyes made her look haggard. Over the years, the body in the yellow dress had changed from an X to an H—even though she hadn't gained a pound. *How was that even possible?*

Or maybe she worried about things that other people didn't notice. Her eyes, large for her face, still sparkled when she smiled, and her lips were soft and plump. She could tell by the stares she got in stores that men still found her attractive. But that only meant an admiring glance and her grin in return, when she had so much more to offer a man, and she wanted desperately to make him, whoever he was, happy. Like a flower just past the peak of its bloom, yet still bursting with pollen, she yearned to share her petals before they faded, but instead was living alone in a dark, airless room, wilting into a shriveled, black weed.

The right and normal place to find that love was *home,* but Jeremy hadn't paid her much attention in years. He still wanted sex now and then, but that didn't count. When he wasn't working, he was out with his buddies drinking, jumping at any excuse to leave the house. It didn't help they were both putting in such long hours. Between their jobs and family chores, they rarely spent much time together, and even then, they focused on schedules, errands, over-due bills, problems with Maddy, and the ongoing debate about Marty's surgery. Jeremy was always pushing for it, and she was always opposing him, having pinned her hopes on a new device that promised to fix Marty's hole without stopping his heart, the thought of which terrified her.

And Jeremy's drinking was even more troubling—something he'd plainly hidden from her for a very long time. She felt naïve having been fooled for so many years and dismayed that he'd covered up his problem instead of asking her for help. How could Jeremy, who'd always been her soulmate, not only shut her out, but lie to her on a daily basis for the last five years?

She felt as if the man she'd married had taken off his mask to show his true, disfigured face. That had been the worst part—not that his problems had driven him to drink—but to go down that road by himself, to run away from her and the kids and to lie about it, that was the part she couldn't forgive. And after all that to throw the blame back on her, calling her a nag who sucked the joy from his life—that was too much. It was the crime that had torn her heart in two and made her see she was truly alone, that Jeremy was no longer her lover and partner, but more like a stranger who slept in the same house, mowed the lawn, drove the kids, and paid his portion of the bills.

Consequently, Steve's overture, something that in the past she would have quickly rebuffed, had grown more tempting as she'd gotten increasingly lonely and desperate for any kind of attention, desperate for—dare she say it—*love*.

But love was absurd. Any thought of happiness with Steve was a fool's dream. Although unhappy, she still had the clarity of mind to realize that. She wasn't going to ruin her life by giving in to the passions of a moonstruck boy, no matter how adoring and handsome he was. To even contemplate it was crazy. Given their different ages, their salaries, her kids—to say nothing of the condemnation by family and friends, they wouldn't stand a chance. No, heading down that path would only promise tragedy.

But as she fantasized about running off with Steve, a thought rose up with startling force and hovered in the air like a dragonfly, refusing to go away. Just thinking about it made her pulse quicken. Could she really go through with something like that? It was a short-term fix—really no fix at all—but one that might get her through the day, the week, the month, and after running its course, quietly disappear—if she handled it carefully—without leaving any bad karma.

At the same time, it could easily backfire and produce any number of unpredictable, ugly consequences.

Yet drinking had such a firm grip on Jeremy that she felt certain she could hide it, and she felt equally certain that she could lead Steve wherever she wanted—but more than likely, once he'd gotten what he wanted and saw the futility of pressing it further, he'd back off all by himself. So from a purely selfish point of view, a fling was possible. The only question, then, was did she really want to do it? How, after all, would it help her?

In the long-term, it would accomplish nothing. But it wasn't the long term that frightened her—tomorrow did, and the day after that, when getting out of bed and stumbling through her day required a superhuman effort. At least this diversion would lessen the pain and buy her some time until—until what? Until some other way turned up to escape her trap, because that was the hardest part of all—being forced to sit here, waiting and doing nothing while Jeremy destroyed their family. She could no longer stand to suffer in silence as the walls closed in and crushed the air from her lungs. One way or another, she had to breathe. There had to be more to life than emptiness and despair, and if sleeping with Steve could put some joy back into her days, even for a short time, then she would take her chances—and let the chips fall where they may.

46

She found him at his desk, staring out the window.

"Did you ride your bike today?" she asked.

"I did. Why?"

"It's 91. You could have a heat stroke."

"I'll be okay."

"We could put your bike in my hatchback."

A ripple of confusion crossed his face. "When are you leaving?"

"Right now."

He shut his book. "I'll get my stuff."

For the first few blocks, he gazed at the homes gliding by his open window as Zoe gripped the wheel and stared straight ahead, unable to think of a word to say. Finally, he fastened his stare on her. "This isn't about the heat, is it?"

"What do you mean?"

"It's about our lunch, right? You don't have to worry—I'm sorry, and I hope you'll forgive me."

He waited for her to answer, but she kept on driving.

"I was thinking about myself, and not you. I know I didn't help. Please don't hold it against me. I value our friendship, and I don't want to lose it."

He paused again, waiting, but his words ran so counter to Zoe's plans that she couldn't respond.

"You're a good guy, Steve," she finally said. "Don't worry about it."

"It won't happen again. I promise."

"Do we turn here?"

He pointed up a hill. Zoe steered up the steep drive and parked before a two-story brick building overlooking a stagnant pond bordered by willows. She walked around the Escort to help Steve unload his bike. He'd already lifted up the hatch and was tugging at the front tire, caught between the wheel well and the back seat.

She grabbed the tire, but instead of pulling, fell forward, threw her arms around his waist, and crushed her breasts into his back. She'd wanted to see what it felt like to hold him and made it look like an accident. "Sorry," she said, backing away.

He froze for a second and then freed the bike with a tug. "No, my fault."

He set the bike down and stared at her.

It was now or never. She glanced up at the building. "I'll bet you have a great view up there."

"I do. I'm on the second floor."

"Care to show me?"

"Now?"

"Sure. I'd like to see where you live."

"There's not much to see, but sure."

He shouldered his bike and led her up a hot, suffocating stairwell. A bead of sweat ran down her ribs. He apologized for the broken elevator, but Zoe barely heard him. Her heart was beating so fast that she didn't want to speak, afraid that her voice might crack. It was easy to make a plan, but much harder to carry it out, and as she climbed the stairs, her courage began to waver.

In spite of her nerves, she followed him through the exit door and down the hall like a windup toy, unable to stop.

It took him forever to find his key. He made a few awkward stabs before unlocking the door. At last, they stepped into a living room with low ceilings and a picture window overlooking the pond. The place had the Spartan bland-ness of a young man's first apartment—a couch but no chairs, an oak-veneer coffee table, no drapes or blinds, and posters on the walls instead of paintings. Pepsi cans and crusted plates covered the coffee table, but otherwise the place was tidy and clean.

She gazed at his poster of Mahatma Gandhi. "That reminds me of college."

"I haven't been here long."

She walked by him. "How's the bedroom?"

The door was ajar. Without waiting for him, she pushed it open.

"Sorry, it's pretty messy." He followed her in.

There were no windows in the narrow room. A futon barely fit against the wall, with a paisley quilt spilling onto the floor, cluttered with books and magazines, dirty socks, candy-bar wrappers, and more Pepsi cans. On the quilt lay the April issue of *Penthouse*. He must have been hoping to keep her outside until he could stash it away. The irony made her smile.

He apologized as he picked up the wrappers and dirty socks.

While his back was turned, she put her finger in her mouth, twisted off her wedding ring, and set it on his desk. Oblivious, he kept picking up and saying he was sorry. When she looked again, the copy of *Penthouse* had disappeared.

She closed the door with a click.

He stopped, straightened up, and faced her. She tried to look seductive, but some other emotion surfaced, and her eyes filled with tears. She couldn't tell what Steve saw, but whatever it was, it clearly moved him.

She reached behind, found her zipper, and pulled it down with a scratching noise that made him start.

She'd planned to let her dress fall to the floor, but she lost her courage, taking stock in her flaws—her small breasts, her tummy, and the scars from her two cesareans. After all the tortured doubt, what if he didn't like what he saw? What if he thought her a slut? What if he laughed?

It was too late to backpedal. She peeled down her straps, exposing her upper breasts and, after a pause, her nipples. That was enough. He snapped out of his trance and rushed at her like a man trying to beat a red light. He grabbed both her arms and kissed her lips as though devouring a ripe nectarine. With every kiss, Zoe's worries faded and her desire grew. She crushed her breasts and ground her hips against him. Electrified, he lifted her off the floor. When she wrapped her legs around him, her dress tumbled down and bunched around her waist.

It was too much for Steve. He set her on the floor, yanked off her dress, and swept her like a dancer to the bed. She crab-walked back to the pillows, wriggling out of her thong while Steve nearly took off his head with his T-shirt. As he worked to unbuckle his belt, she grabbed it like a handle and pulled him down. His bare chest brushed her nipples, his tongue parted her lips, and his breath filled her mouth, burned her neck, and bellowed in her ears.

She pried off his buckle and yanked down his pants. He quickly found his mark and drove her into the mattress. All she could feel was the softness of his body against her skin and the stabbing bursts of pleasure that blotted out not only her pain but any awareness of the outside world.

The rawness of the sex took her by surprise. Jeremy's body had grown soft and weak, and their lovemaking had fallen into a lazy routine, while Steve attacked her like a lion consuming its prey. His powerful arms, the firmness of his back and thighs, and the rough hands cupping her butt overcame her self-control, and she arched her back into each fresh mauling, whether from his mouth, fingers, or the frantic pounding between her legs.

With a flurry, he cried out and came. Zoe tried to match him, but it was over too quickly, and Steve collapsed like a deflated balloon. She sighed and stroked his back, trying to catch her breath. The sex had been all she'd hoped for, but just a minute too brief.

His dead weight made breathing hard. She tried to push him off, but he wouldn't budge. Inside her, he was still firm. Not only that, he was beginning to move again. Zoe coiled her thighs around him and grabbed his butt, and in seconds he was driving into her as if he'd never stopped.

Twenty minutes and three orgasms later, she sprawled across the bed, sweaty and panting. Steve wobbled into the bathroom, the muscles of his lower back and butt flexing with every step. *Why can't I keep him and my family too?*

The thought of her kids made her start. *Day care.* She glanced at the clock radio—*5:45. Damn—I'll never make it.*

She leaped out of bed and gathered up her dress, thong, and sandals. When Steve came out of the bathroom, his face fell.

She brushed past him and plunked herself down on the toilet. "I have to get my kids."

He watched her worshipfully.

"What?" she asked

"Shouldn't we talk?"

"I don't have time."

"Not even five minutes?"

"No," she said, blotting herself. "Not even one." But she had no idea what to tell him anyway, now or later, because the last hour had thrown her so off balance that she had no idea what happened next.

She slipped her dress over her shoulders.

"When?" he persisted.

"I don't know. Is my hair okay? How about my lipstick?"

"You look fine," he said gloomily. "Nobody will know."

She sat on the futon and buckled her sandals.

"I'm in love with you, Zoe, or I wouldn't have done this."

She jumped up and kissed him on the neck. "You were amazing. But not now."

A second later she was out the door.

47

The next day, he shuffled into her classroom and placed a balled-up dishrag on her desk. Zoe glanced up from grading her papers. Neither one spoke, but their eyes made it plain that something secret and shameful had recently passed between them.

She opened the rag and peeked inside. Her diamond ring gleamed up at her. *Thank God.* She'd spent half the night thinking that Jeremy would notice it missing and she'd have to dream up some crazy story about losing it.

She stuffed the ring in her purse. "I was hoping you found it. Thank you."

He shrugged. "I thought about flushing it down the toilet."

She stared at him sharply. "I might not know what I'm doing, Steve, but I won't leave my family, messed up as it is. So don't you dare hurt them." In the same breath, she thought that if he wanted to, she was helpless to stop him. She tried to think how she could blackmail him, but quickly checked her impulse. *No need to sink any lower than I already have.*

"I would never do that," he said glumly.

She studied the tragic look on his face. A blond lock curled over one eye. The sleeves of his T-shirt exposed the soft curve of his biceps. The cotton fabric stretched across his chest but hugged his waist, braided, she recalled, with muscles whose names she didn't know.

"So what now?" he asked.

"I can finish up by four."

He gave her a puzzled look.

"Do you need more time?"

"No," he said, perking up. "Four is good."

Zoe picked up her pen and resumed grading. "Perfect. I'll see you there."

And thus Zoe embarked on her second life. Outwardly, nothing changed—every morning she dressed for work, dropped her kids off at school, taught her classes, picked up the kids promptly at six, cooked dinner, read to Maddy and Marty and tucked them in, and escaped into a novel or TV show while Jeremy worked in the basement.

But every day at four o'clock, she filed away her papers and drove to Steve's apartment, clutching the wheel with cold, sweaty palms. She always found him waiting in the bedroom, undressed and under the sheets, painfully hard. He barely said hello before he stripped off her clothes and crawled on top of, under, or behind her and reduced her universe down to that one small, tender spot.

Their lovemaking had lost none of the heat of their first encounter—in fact, as they learned to read each other better—where to touch, how soft or firm, what position or pace the other preferred—any trace of awkwardness vanished, and their passion climbed to a level that Zoe found disturbing. She came to anticipate their daily trysts with butterflies in her stomach, trembling legs, and a degree of lust she'd never felt before. She didn't know if her craving was fueled by the forbidden nature of the sex, her unhappiness at home, or Steve's flawless body and the strength of his desire—so intense that sometimes their couplings seemed more like rape than making love, the only difference being her eagerness to let herself be taken. And the more that Steve wanted her, the more it made her want him, spiraling the lovers around each other like two updrafts in a firestorm.

By mid-May, she began to worry that Steve's neighbors had noticed her visits. Twice now, a retired woman across the hall had caught her leaving and stared at her much too pointedly. Zoe had never been one to hold back her passion, and she wondered if noise from their wilder bouts had spilled out into the hall. Nearly as bad, Steve's apartment was only nine blocks from school, and a few boys walking home from their track workouts had spotted her coming and going. After a while, she put on sunglasses and a baseball cap, but the disguise only reaffirmed the danger along with their need to vary their trysts if they hoped to keep from being discovered.

But there were few other places to go. Zoe's house was out of the question, as well as the empty rooms at school—even though they considered both—and in the end they took refuge in her car like two desperate teenagers, driving around and looking for hidden parking spots. One day, they ended up in the suburbs, ran out of time, and had a quickie in the corner of a church parking lot. The next day, Steve found a dead-end street behind a deserted warehouse, where they spent ten sweaty minutes with the seats down in the hatchback. Neither one found it satisfying, but it did take the edge off and, more important, stop them from taking an even greater risk.

The end of the school year presented a fresh challenge, with Maddy and Marty home for the summer, but Zoe solved the problem so quickly and cleverly that she could hardly believe her brazenness. Saturday morning at the breakfast table, while her kids were scarfing down scrambled eggs and waffles, she floated her plan to Jeremy as he read the comics to Marty.

"You know those education credits I need? I found a class at the community center on Tuesdays and Thursdays. Do you care?"

He glanced up from the paper. "What about the kids?"

"Mom said she'd watch them."

"I bet she'd like that."

"And there's a modern dance class the same day."

"How much?"

"Ninety-five dollars for three months. Less than your health club," she added, surprised the heat from her blush hadn't set his paper on fire.

He dove back into the comics. "You teachers have a good thing going," he muttered.

Jeremy's nod set in motion her schedule for the remainder of the summer. While she did attend some dance classes, every Tuesday and Thursday morning, she dropped off her kids with Rose, rented a movie, bought a basket of strawberries, and then drove to Steve's. Undercover in her baseball cap and dark glasses, she hurried up the stairs, unlocked his door with a spare key, and woke him up by massaging his back and popping strawberries into his mouth.

She savored the ritual of waking up and seducing him on these long summer mornings—his tousled hair, sleepy groans, and happy-dog smile as she rubbed his back. He always woke up hard, and in minutes they were having sex, now less feverishly than before, but the warmth of Steve's body and the softness of his sheet-buffed skin, giving off his familiar scent of sweat and musk, made up for any loss of carnal pleasure. Afterward, they cuddled and napped until Zoe got up to make them breakfast.

The rest of the morning, they watched movies, mostly romantic comedies, or sometimes artsy or tragic films, depending on whether Zoe felt the urge to laugh at life or to plunge herself into its darker dramas. She also rented the movies to limit the time they talked, as their conversations often came to focus on her kids or the dead-end nature of their affair, and she preferred to spend her time with Steve having sex or discussing their shared tastes in music, film, and books.

Most days, he ran out and brought back lunch, and they always made love one last time before Zoe left to get her kids. Parting was hard for both, but for different reasons. Steve knew that he wouldn't see Zoe for days, while Zoe had to make the harder leap from being Steve's lover to Jeremy's wife and the mother of two small children.

As the summer wore on, playing the conflicting roles of wife, mother, and mistress, to say nothing of the constant lying, was stretching Zoe's nerves, and by August, they were ready to snap. She found herself breaking down while standing in line at the supermarket or reading stories to the kids. It was getting harder and harder to focus on her work, her conversations with Jeremy, or, for that matter, anything else. There were times when she didn't feel safe driving her car. On some days she pulled into her garage without any clue as to how she'd gotten home.

No matter how she tried, she saw no way out of her trap. Her mornings with Steve were precious to her, and she refused to give them up. At the same time, nothing at home had changed. Jeremy was showing no signs of curbing his drinking and so far seemed oblivious about her affair. As long as she didn't bother him, he seemed to be content. But Jeremy's state of mind wasn't the issue. Zoe had reached the point where she could no longer ignore the damage she was doing—not only to her marriage, but to her mental health, her kids, her reputation at school, and, to be fair, to Steve himself. The lying, the guilt, and the inner turmoil were no longer sustainable. Given her course and speed, it was only a matter of time before she jumped the tracks, soared through the air, and woke up in the twisted wreckage of her life. How much longer before

Jeremy caught them? Or before she got so depressed she couldn't get out of bed? How could she keep on going from one day to the next without any relief in sight? She didn't know the answer, and so she lived from day to day, counting the hours before her trysts, regretting them later, and dreading what she feared was unavoidable—their humiliating public exposure.

48

Phoebe leaned back in her chair at Starbucks, cell phone pressed to her cheek, and listened to the empty rings. It was the fourth time she'd called Zoe, who should have arrived by ten, but was now thirty minutes late. Not that Zoe was always on time, but she would never be this late without calling unless there was some kind of crisis.

It didn't help that neither Zoe nor Jeremy had embraced the new technologies emerging in the nineties, preferring their albums to CDs and refusing to buy cell phones, a device that Jeremy claimed was more annoying than a swarm of deerflies. Phoebe could see how an English teacher might not need a cell phone, but she couldn't understand how Jeremy, a journalist, could make it through a single day without one.

Her brow furrowed as she poked the *end* button. While tension brought out the wrinkles in her forehead, in a calm mood, she barely seemed touched by age. Her jaw and cheeks had grown more angular—but the change suited her slender build, maintained by strict adherence to her running schedule, and leaning back in her navy blouse, fitted jeans, and strappy sandals, she drew the stares of middle-aged men waiting in line for their coffee.

She'd taken the day off, hoping to finish some errands while Nate was still in day care. She'd only set aside an hour for Zoe, and time was fading fast. But it wasn't just Zoe's lateness that bothered her. Over the summer, her sister's behavior had begun to alarm her. She often seemed quiet and withdrawn, disengaged from family and friends, all of which ran against her nature. A few nights ago, at Nate's soccer game, Phoebe had caught her staring into space with a sad, defeated look. When Phoebe asked her about it, Zoe had said that she simply needed more sleep. Phoebe guessed it had more to do with Marty, whose condition, although it hadn't worsened, still caused Zoe a great deal of worry. What's more, she wondered if Zoe and Jeremy were having financial problems. They seemed to be living from paycheck to paycheck and never had anything held in reserve for crises—the water heater going out, a broken window, or, more commonly, an unexpected doctor bill that insurance wouldn't cover.

Just minutes ago, Phoebe had called her mother, but Rose hadn't spoken to Zoe since eight this morning when she'd dropped off her kids. She'd also tried Zoe's office and let the phone ring a dozen times before giving up. She briefly thought of calling Jeremy, but a voice inside her held her back, on the off chance that Zoe was planning something that she didn't want him to know about.

At 10:45, she drained her coffee and climbed into her Camry. Zoe's house was ten minutes away, and she was hoping that she'd find her there, reading or napping, and she could put her mind at rest.

It was a cloudless summer day. As Phoebe drove under a vault of elms past the 1930s stucco homes, she thought how strange it was that Zoe had stayed in the city, so close to their parents, while she had ended up in the suburbs—when her thoughts were cut short by a faded-blue Jeep parked in the middle of Zoe's driveway.

She pulled in behind it, stepped out, and peeked in the back window. Candy-bar wrappers and Pepsi cans littered the floor. She frowned. *Only a guy's car would be that full of junk. And why would some guy be at Zoe's house at eleven o'clock?* She walked around the Jeep and peered in the garage window. Zoe's Escort was hiding among the shadows. *Whoever he is, Zoe's here too.* She bit her lip. *It must be a teacher or maybe a student.*

On the other hand, a teacher or student wouldn't make her miss their meeting by an hour, and something about the run-down jeep struck Phoebe as sinister. She recalled that during her twenties, Zoe had attracted more than her share of unwanted admirers, including a few of her students. At the very least, she felt obliged to ring the bell and make sure that Zoe had only forgotten their meeting, and nothing else was wrong.

She climbed the stoop and pressed her nose into the door pane. Zoe's car keys and purse were lying on the kitchen table, but there was no other sign of her.

She rang the doorbell. She waited for a long time, but no one answered. She rang it five more times before she remembered it hadn't worked in years. She glanced around the yard, hemmed in by half-dead honeysuckles and pockmarked with dandelions gone to seed. *The doorbell's not the only thing that doesn't work around here.*

She put her ear against the glass. Inside, a rock-and-roll beat throbbed in the walls—or was the beat too loud and the rhythm slightly off? *Could it be construction? Maybe the jeep belonged to a workman doing repairs. The place sure could use it.*

Don't be a twit, Phoebe—knock.

She knocked for nearly a minute, but no one came. The beat inside the house didn't stop.

At last she tried the door. It opened without a sound. She slipped her head through the crack. "Zoe?"

In the kitchen, the beat grew louder, but also more distant, as if someone in the basement were knocking down walls. Phoebe glanced around the kitchen and stopped cold. From somewhere in the house came Zoe's voice, crying out in short stabs of pain. Phoebe's heart took off like the wings of a startled dove. Time slowed and lost its normal feel, and the air around her grew hazy, like a cloud condensing around her fear.

Zoe was in trouble. Somebody was hurting her. But what could she do? *You're in over your head, Phoebe. Call for help.* She reached into her purse and dug for her cell phone, but her fingers had turned into blocks of wood. She thrashed around her wallet, keys, mascara, and God knows what else before she realized her phone was in the car. *Don't panic. Slow down. Think.* There was no point in calling anyway. The police wouldn't get there in time. They could only pick up the pieces after the fact. But *she* was here, and she had to do something, anything, to help Zoe, even if it was reckless or just plain crazy.

On the table, near a cantaloupe carved open like a human skull, lay a knife with a ten-inch blade. Without thinking, she grabbed the handle, raised it over her shoulder, and with the blade trembling in her hand, tiptoed through the kitchen.

She took a step into the hallway and froze, stunned, trying to comprehend the spectacle in front of her. There was Zoe, pinned against the wall by a man—a young, naked man, and her feet were bobbing up and down on his muscular butt. Zoe's eyes were closed, her arms were clutching his neck, and instead of fighting him off, she was spurring him on, crying out with every slap of their hips. The raw image of her sister caught in the act horrified but riveted Phoebe. She felt like shouting Zoe's name and running to the door, but her lips clamped shut and her feet refused to move.

Zoe's eyes opened. She stared at Phoebe as if she were a car barreling toward her. Surprise and shame lit up her face like a red traffic light. Her body went stiff, and she pounded on the man's back and cried in his ear, "STOP! STOP!"

He froze and searched her eyes. Instantly, he knew. "Oh, shit!" he blurted out. He screwed his head around and threw Phoebe a stabbing glance. "Do you mind?" he barked. "Who the hell are you?"

She didn't answer. She backed up and dropped the knife. It stuck with a twang in the hardwood floor.

"Put me down!" Zoe snapped.

She caught up to Phoebe at the kitchen door and grabbed both her arms. "Phoebe—don't go."

It felt grotesque being held by her sweaty, naked sister. "I shouldn't be here, Zoe."

"I need to explain," she said, breathless. She glanced over her back. "STEVE—GET OUT OF HERE.

"He'll go," she added quietly. "He'll do what I say."

When Zoe let go of her, she fought the urge to run. She'd already seen and heard enough. At the same time, she couldn't leave, as if nothing out of the ordinary had taken place. "All right. I'll wait."

Zoe ran back to the hall. Voices, arguing fast and low, faded into the bedroom where Phoebe couldn't hear them.

She sat down at the kitchen table and stared at the butchered cantaloupe, her mind going blank. A minute later, a blushing but handsome young man in T-shirt and jeans barged in. "Whatever she tells you, I'm in love with her," he said forcefully. "I'm not a bad person. I wouldn't be here if I didn't love Zoe."

She came in right behind him. A baggy T-shirt hung from her collarbones, but her legs and feet were bare. "Just go, Steve. Don't try to explain."

She nearly pushed him out the door. At the last second, he planted his feet and spun around. "Before I go—" Then his face went blank, and he couldn't finish. "I'm sorry. It was my fault."

"No, it wasn't. We'll talk later. Just GO."

He looked down in despair, guessing the likely outcome of their discovery.

"I love you, Zoe" he said quietly and plodded down the steps.

But the disaster wasn't quite over. Phoebe's Camry had blocked Steve's Jeep, and before he could go, she had to follow him down the driveway and back out her car.

As he sped down the street, Phoebe sighed. All that remained now was to hear Zoe out—even though something told her that Zoe's tale was probably going to trouble her more than anything she'd already seen.

49

Zoe slumped in a chair beside the butchered cantaloupe. She glanced up when Phoebe came in, but turned away, too embarrassed to look her in the eyes.

Phoebe sat across the table, wondering why Zoe had asked her to stay. Did she really think that anything she said could justify her behavior? Or did she only want to be sure that no one else found out? On the other hand, it occurred to Phoebe that she might simply want her advice.

It was hard to imagine a more awkward situation. Over the years, Phoebe and Zoe had shared most, if not all, of their secrets, but stumbling across her sister in the throes of an orgasm with her paramour was much too private, and she couldn't get the image out of her mind. She stared at Zoe in her rumpled

T-shirt, head hanging down, bangs draped over her flushed face, and couldn't think of a word to say.

When Zoe glanced up, she looked so wretched that Phoebe took pity on her. *Who am I to judge? Don't make assumptions. Just get the facts.*

"All right, who is this guy?"

"Steve—" She broke off. "Steve. He's a teacher."

"At the high school?"

Zoe nodded.

"And he's in love with you?"

She nodded again.

"Are you in love with him?"

"I don't know." She paused and took a breath. "He wants me to leave Jeremy."

"Are you going to?"

"Right—two kids, one of them sick. Trying to live on teacher's salaries." Phoebe shrugged. "People do it. Mom and Dad—"

"Don't bring them into this."

"I'm not saying you should leave Jeremy."

There was a long silence broken by the ticking of the clock. It took Phoebe some time to form the question that she most wanted answered. "Why did you do it, Zoe?"

Zoe bit her lip and plowed her fingers through the cantaloupe seeds. "Do you think Jeremy has a drinking problem?"

She thought about it, but only for a second. "Yes."

Zoe grimaced.

"Whenever I see him, he has a drink in his hand. Every time we get together, he overdoes it. I guess it's hard to know. You live with him. What do you think?"

"He's an alcoholic. I know it."

Phoebe swallowed. Zoe's bluntly stated fact was strangely harder to accept than her own judgment. "So that's the reason, then, for Steve?"

Zoe shrugged. "What do I have to look forward to? Thirty more years of Jeremy coming home drunk? Raising my kids alone? Making excuses for him, pretending there isn't a problem?"

Phoebe looked away. "You know, sometimes I wonder if Dad has a problem."

"So I married my father. Is that what you're saying?"

"No, but it might explain why you put up with it. Frankly, I'm surprised. It doesn't seem like you."

"Maybe you don't know me as well as you think."

"Why haven't you told anyone?"

"Somehow that would make it too real. And I was hoping I was wrong. I thought I'd wake up one day and find the old Jeremy back." She scooped up a handful of seeds and clenched them tightly. "If it weren't for the kids, I'd leave him, but I can't even think about it. I'm trapped."

Phoebe didn't know how to respond. She couldn't disagree.

"And Steve adores me. He's such a great guy—someone you would have killed to meet in your twenties." She took a deep breath. "I guess I was feeling sorry for myself, and I took a bite of that forbidden apple. All the chemistry was there, the whole damn atomic chart, and I caved in."

"Does Jeremy know?"

"I doubt it. He's too busy covering his own tracks. He's glad I'm not bothering him. It would be funny if it weren't so tragic. We're both too busy hiding our own secrets to notice each other's. I go to Steve's twice a week after I drop off the kids. I'm supposed to be in class, but I never go. I'm sure I'll flunk. Jeremy never asks, but I always have a story just in case."

The more Zoe talked, the more Phoebe's heart sank. It would have been easier to accept that Zoe had strayed simply for the thrill—but this was far worse, having a long-term affair to replace the love that had vanished from her life.

"Why were you *here?*" Phoebe asked. "That's pretty daring, don't you think, in your own house?"

"We always go to Steve's, but there's a teacher in his building who saw me. Yesterday, she stopped me in the hall, and I don't think she bought my lesson-planning story. If she talks, we could both lose our jobs, so we didn't meet today. But Steve said he couldn't wait and he showed up here. I wasn't happy about it, but he was so … persistent. And then—"

"And then me."

"That's pretty much it."

"It was one hell of a shock."

For the first time, Zoe smiled. "You should have seen the look on your face, coming around the corner with that knife. Did you think I was getting raped? Were you going to stab him?"

"I have no idea. I saw the jeep, your door was open, and then I heard the walls coming down—tell me, Zoe, do you always do it standing up?"

"Guys like to think like they're strong."

"If you say so. The knife freaked me out too. And you sounded like a dying rabbit."

Zoe couldn't help laughing, but it was followed by a sob and a storm of tears. "I don't know what I should do, Phoebe," she said miserably. "Tell me what I should do."

Her outburst pierced Phoebe's heart. She took Zoe's hand and squeezed it. Zoe laid a wet cheek on the table. "God, what a mess I've made of my life."

To Phoebe, Zoe's course was plain as day. "You already know what you have to do."

"I don't. Tell me."

"Break it off with Steve. Tell him you won't see him anymore."

She stared Phoebe like a felon who'd just been read a long sentence. "That won't be easy."

"You can make me the bad guy if you want to. Tell him I'll talk. Tell him Jeremy's having you followed. Exaggerate. Lie. Do whatever it takes—just end it."

"And do what? Go back to the way—"

"No. Jeremy needs help. Get him into treatment."

"He won't go. He doesn't think he has a problem."

"Then prove it to him. The rest of us can help."

"Who?"

"His parents, friends, our mom and dad, maybe even his boss."

"I know what you're saying, but I don't think I could do it."

"You have to. You're strong enough, Zoe. You're just down right now."

"I don't want anyone to pity me."

"They'd be glad to help."

"Do you think so?"

"I know they would. Sometimes it's better to air your dirty laundry than live with the smell."

She smiled weakly. "I'll think about it."

"If I were you, I wouldn't wait."

Zoe bit her lip and ran her fingers through the seeds.

"Why the cantaloupe?" Phoebe asked.

"He couldn't find strawberries."

"What?"

"I have a thing about fruit. It's an aphrodisiac."

Phoebe picked up a square of cantaloupe and popped it into her mouth. "You're wrong, Zoe—it's just food."

50

The encounter with Zoe ruined the rest of Phoebe's day. She finished her errands, but was so distracted while driving that she missed a couple of turns. At one point, she found herself looking for tomato paste in a bookstore.

Walking down aisles and ticking items off her list seemed of no importance compared with the life-altering problems that Zoe was facing.

She lingered in the bookstore, leafing through the tabloids. The Hollywood scandals on the covers seemed eerily similar to her sister's life—minus the glamour and the money. But even while Zoe's affair had deeply troubled her, it had also brought back a childhood emotion that she'd thought long dead: jealousy. *Zoe always got the hottest guys.* Not that she had wanted to trade places with Zoe, seeing how unhappy she was, but the image of Steve's taut back and butt slapping her into the wall kept flickering in her mind, and for a second, as she paged through *Cosmopolitan,* she imagined herself scooped off the floor as she reached behind to grab—she stopped, glanced around, and blushed as if the elderly couple beside her could read her thoughts.

Phoebe shelved the Cosmo and wandered over to the tables stacked with bestsellers. Steve's flawless body had reminded her of how much Jake had neglected his. He hadn't gone to the gym in years, had put on a good twenty pounds, and when he wasn't working seemed more focused on food and TV than her. Phoebe, on the contrary, still felt she had the energy and the sex drive of a much younger woman.

Although her marriage was hardly in trouble, neither was it ideal: money was tight, schedules were overbooked, tempers were sometimes short, and both she and Jake often took each other for granted, treating their better halves more like business partners than husband or wife. And if she thought Jeremy a Luddite for not buying a cell phone, Jake had the opposite problem—he was on the damn thing so often he might as well screw it into his head. He never turned his phone off, just like he never missed a meeting, declined a project, or begged off a business trip. She admired his ambition and liked the comforts it bought them, but surely there had to be more to life than ticking off boxes on your task list, day after day, year after year, without taking time to relax and enjoy the people you loved.

Just as troubling to Phoebe was the promise she'd made to Zoe right before she left—she'd sworn not to tell a single soul, not even Jake, about her affair. But keeping that promise meant breaking an unspoken vow in her marriage. She and Jake had always told each other everything—not just their own secrets, but everything that family, friends, and coworkers had confessed to them.

Well, not this time. Zoe's secret was too radioactive to share, and her vulnerability trumped Phoebe's vow to be candid with Jake—even if it meant that when he got home from work tonight and he asked her about her day, she would have to lie.

Phoebe rinsed the dinner plates and put them in the washer as Jake leaned against the counter, poring over messages on his cell phone. He'd taken off his tie and rolled up his sleeves, but still wore his work pants and penny loafers. In the last few years, his hairline had ebbed like a slow-moving tide, exposing a tall widow's peak. His chest and shoulders were still broad, but his paunch made him look stocky instead of strong, like so many older athletes who quit working out, travel too often, and dine in restaurants every day.

He glanced up from his phone and studied Phoebe. Her frown and frequent pauses had made him aware that something was wrong. He assumed that she was irked with him for sitting on his duff and checking his messages while she loaded the washer by herself. He knew he'd been neglecting his chores of late—in fact, he'd been away on business five of the last ten days, and a surge of guilt wrinkled his brow.

Not that he liked to be away from Phoebe and Nate. It was more that work had filtered into every corner of his life. With each passing year, his responsibilities grew. As the marketing manager for his company's flagship product, he fielded calls from customers and sales reps in all 50 states. Meetings, new initiatives, and presentations popped up like dandelions, barely giving him time to read his mail. And he made matters worse by never turning down requests, feeling grateful to his employer, PowerCam Technologies, after his hasty exit from ConChem. His current employer, unlike his old, was honest, fair, and not only civil to its workers, but supportive.

He walked behind Phoebe and massaged her back. Her shoulder blades and collarbones felt birdlike in his hands, and her muscles were stubbornly tight.

She winced and pulled away. "You're hurting me."

"You're pretty tense. Everything all right?"

She kept loading the dishes. "Just tired."

"After a day off I thought you'd be more relaxed."

"Running errands isn't a day off."

"You never said how your lunch with Zoe went."

"She was late, for starters."

"No surprise."

"She's okay. You know, busy. Her life is ... complicated."

Puzzled by her mood, he failed to note her choice of words. Instead, a tender feeling welled inside him, caused by what he couldn't say.

"I know I've been working a lot," he said out of nowhere. "But I always like being home—you know that, don't you?"

She stared at him coolly and began stuffing knives into the baskets. "I'm glad you feel that way, but it doesn't help if you're never here."

Stung, he tried not to be defensive. "*Never* is a pretty strong word, although I know it's too much. Hey—why don't we go out for dinner on Friday, just the two of us?"

"You're going to Chicago. Did you forget?"

He stared at the floor, embarrassed. "Sorry, I did. What about next weekend?"

"Next week I'm in New York."

"I thought you bailed out of that."

"I couldn't," she said, slotting the knives more gently now." I forgot to tell you."

He bit his lower lip. "Is David still going?"

"Yes. Why wouldn't he?"

So that explained her mood. She wasn't angry with him, but nervous about her trip to New York. And from his point of view, there was good reason for her to be nervous, as he felt certain that David, Phoebe's coworker at Wells and Decker, was in love with her.

He wanted to say that David would at least come in handy for senior discounts, but he suppressed the urge. Although it seemed like a trip perfectly tailored to tempt his wife, he lacked any real grounds to be suspicious. Just because David was smitten with Phoebe didn't mean that Phoebe was smitten with him, so instead of complaining he chewed his lip in silence as she queued the goblets in the washer rack. "It's pretty poor timing," he said, "with Nate just starting kindergarten."

"Well, things don't always work out the way you want."

What the hell did that mean? Was she referring to their marriage? Was she implying that he'd been a disappointment to her?

Wounded, he didn't respond, but suspicion coiled inside him like a rattlesnake. Although he'd never lost his temper with Phoebe, more than once he'd blurted out things he'd later regretted, and he knew the words forming on his tongue right now would only spark a bitter and pointless argument. *Better take a break. Think about what you say before you open your big mouth.*

"I guess not. If you need me, I'll be in the den."

He shoved his phone in his back pocket and skulked away.

For the next hour, he stayed in his chair, frowning into his laptop, waiting for her to walk in and explain her words, but the clock kept ticking and Phoebe never came.

51

In Jake's view, men often took moral holidays on business trips. At every tradeshow he'd gone to, someone in his group had gotten falling-down drunk, come on to a coworker, gambled away a wad of cash, or stuffed a car payment into a stripper's thong. And sometimes they'd taken their misbehavior further, acting as if the trip had temporarily freed them from their marital vows—and what began as harmless flirting ended up as a bona fide affair. Then, of course, there was always the cold-blooded professional job.

For some reason, the guilty parties always believed their antics would stay behind them in the host city. And while it was true that management overlooked all but the worst cases, what happened in Vegas never stayed in Vegas. One way or another, word got out—the offender often tripping himself up by his own bragging—and traveled like wildfire throughout the office.

Knowing this, Jake made a point of being on his best behavior whenever he traveled. Dining out, he never had more than two drinks, and he always went back to his room early—long before the heavy drinking and any chance for trouble started. In college, he'd learned the hard way the best approach for keeping out of trouble was to avoid the people who were looking for it and who, despite your good intentions, could drag you into it.

On his trip to Chicago, however, he broke both his rules and went out barhopping with three of PowerCam's sales reps. After a two-hour wait for a one-hour meal at a well-known bar and grill, the men stepped out into the chaos of Rush Street. At night, the businesslike mood of the city morphed into a gritty Midwestern version of Mardi Gras, albeit with smaller crowds. But the same electric charge, the same anything-can-happen air energized the packs of college kids and businessmen roaming the streets, feeling safe in numbers, but steering clear of the pitch-black alleys as they would a snarling dog. The rule of downtown after dark was to always keep in the light, but the knowledge that mere feet stood between you and a potentially fatal mugging added to the allure of the diesel-filled air, which some people found as thrilling as others found unnerving.

Jake and his group filed through a door with a black-painted window. They tromped down a flight of stairs and emerged in a room as long as a basketball court. Smoke curled up and clung to the ceiling, and the parquet floor shook from dozens of dancing feet. Beyond the mass of moving bodies, a wall of speakers blared out eighties tunes that made talking almost impossible. Jake shook his head and smiled. It reminded him of his college days, whose passing he didn't miss and whose folly he didn't plan on repeating tonight. He plunked himself into a chair by the wall to better see the antics that he knew would play out before him in the next few hours.

Mike and Todd, two silver-haired salesmen, followed his lead, while Brian, the youngest in the group, went looking for the bathroom. The rest ordered beers on tap and tried talking shop, but their voices soon grew hoarse from shouting, and before long they gave up and turned their chairs to watch the college girls bouncing on the dance floor.

Five minutes passed before it dawned on Jake that Brian hadn't come back. He tapped Mike on the shoulder. "I'd better go check on him."

Mike didn't reply. Instead he pointed to the parquet floor, where Brian was mocking the moves of Vanilla Ice, glowing behind him on a giant video wall, making the woman across him smile. At first, Jake laughed, but the more he watched, the less he liked what he saw. The two were clearly dancing together. Under the girl's eyebrow piercings and creepy Goth makeup hid a stunning face, and inside her vintage dress moved a jaw-dropping body, which Brian had apparently seen before anyone else.

He tapped Mike again. "What the hell is he doing?"

Mike shrugged. "Brian likes to dance."

"His wife doesn't care if he dances with strangers?"

"I don't think she'll be a stranger for long."

Jake watched the two moving closer together. "Are you kidding me?"

"I guess you've never been out with Brian."

"Are you saying what I think you are?"

"I'm saying that Brian's a decent guy and a good employee, but a jerk to his wife."

"Decent guys aren't jerks to their wives."

"I don't get it either."

Suddenly the wild behavior surrounding him no longer seemed amusing. He glanced around the room. A handful of patrons were clutching the bar like an overturned lifeboat. The bartenders should have cut them off hours ago, but they turned a blind eye to their slurred speech and wobbly gaits. The smoke burned Jake's eyes, the music hurt his ears, and too many of the words he caught were crude. But all that paled compared to watching the spectacle of his coworker going through the steps of cheating on his wife.

At the same time, he wondered why it troubled him so much. If Brian chose to screw up his life, that was his business. Who was he to judge a marriage he knew nothing about? He chewed his lip and tried being honest with himself. Maybe it had nothing to do with Brian at all. Maybe it had more to do with himself. Maybe it troubled him so much because next Monday Phoebe was flying to Manhattan, a place she'd always dreamed of visiting, with a man whose friendship with her, in his opinion, was already far too close.

His thoughts carried him away from his friends. After a minute, he tapped Mike's shoulder. "I think I'll get a cab. How about you guys?"

Both Todd and Mike turned him down.

"Better watch out," he said, putting on his coat. "Twenty bucks she has a girlfriend."

Todd grinned. "Then Brian will need a wingman."

Jake shook his head. "Just make sure you don't get sucked into the slipstream."

Mike and Todd laughed, but Jake had been deadly serious. "Meeting's at eight tomorrow. Don't be late," he barked and headed for the stairs.

52

On the flight home, Jake was happy to sit in the back of the plane, far away from Todd and Mike. The nozzle overhead hissed air into his face while he gazed at the croplands scrolling beneath him like a green-and-tan mosaic. The novel he was reading, a bestseller about a double agent in the cold war, failed to hold his interest. He stuffed the paperback into the seat pocket and leaned back, brooding.

The same questions kept running through his head. What was Brian thinking as he flew back to his wife in California? What would he tell her when she met him at the gate and asked him about his trip? How could he look her in the eye? And how could he go to work on Monday and smile at his colleagues, present at meetings, and make small talk in the office as if nothing had happened? Jake couldn't imagine himself doing any of that, and so he didn't see how Brian could either. That kind of behavior wasn't part of his DNA. He could no more have an affair and cover it up calmly than rob a bank or run down a dog crossing the street.

He'd learned from Mike, as they waited to board, that Brian had woken up to find the girl gone, along with two hundred dollars from his wallet. Serves him right, he thought, wondering how Brian would explain the missing cash to his wife. No doubt by telling her another lie.

He tapped his fingers on the armrest. *It's not my problem. So why can't I stop thinking about it?*

He pulled out the in-flight magazine and leafed through it without reading the pages. He jammed it back in the pocket. *You can't get Brian out of your head because you're worried about Phoebe. It's her you should be thinking about, not Brian.*

It was undeniable that Phoebe had changed in the last year. The shift had been gradual, but certain. She'd grown less patient with him, catered less to his needs, and while she always complained about his traveling, when he came home, she seemed indifferent to him. What's more, she'd lost weight, bought a new wardrobe, and layered her long hair, which softened her features. He was proud of her for taking such good care of herself. She looked great for her age—no, great for *any* age. His coworkers were always shocked when they met her, and many of his friends openly flirted with her. In the past, that kind of behavior had always put Phoebe off, but lately she not only took it in stride, but seemed to enjoy it.

Her friendship with David had made the changes even more troubling. She and David had worked together for seven years at Wells and Decker, where Phoebe managed employee benefits, and the two of them shared a long list of interests beyond their work. At 52, David still ran marathons. He liked history, literature, and poetry, and Jake suspected that Phoebe's newfound interest in opera had started with him. He'd also traveled widely, which clearly impressed Phoebe, and his older-and-wiser air made Jake feel like a kid fresh out of school. He often caught himself looking for signs of fakery in the older man, reluctant to accept that his wisdom might be real, but he never found it.

Until recently, it hadn't bothered him much. He considered David a good friend of Phoebe's, a nice guy, and a safe outlet for interests that he and Phoebe didn't share. But all that changed a year ago when David's wife had left him. In the divorce, he'd lost custody of his two kids, and he became so depressed that he could barely work. Phoebe, in Jake's view, had been far too eager to step in and play his therapist. David had spent countless hours crying on her shoulder and telling her more about his personal life than Jake felt proper, blurring the already porous boundaries of their friendship.

David had finally regained his stride, but Jake often wondered if he'd gotten over his ex-wife only by replacing her with a prettier and much younger passion—Phoebe.

Worst of all, he'd given him a perfect opening by traveling and working 24/7, leaving a void in Phoebe's life that David had been only too happy to exploit.

But how could he help it? Work gobbled up so many hours. Fires were always flaring up, and if he didn't put them out fast, they grew into infernos. His cell phone was always ringing—morning, noon, and night—and the evening calls were often the most important—discussions with managers and other key players at PowerCam who relied on his expertise.

At the same time, he had to admit the attention flattered him. It felt good to be needed, to know his colleagues valued his opinion and sometimes waited in line to see him. It gave him a sense of worth and power that he knew would be very hard to surrender.

Life at home was no less demanding. Taking care of their new house was nearly a full-time job. Apart from mowing the lawn, shoveling snow, and cleaning the gutters, there was always a piece of trim that needed replacing, a faucet sprouting a leak, or a fallen branch that had to be sawed up and hauled away. And while he was always ready to brag about their son Nate, the driving to and from day care, soccer matches, and baseball games never stopped. Even Jake's Sundays were crammed. He sang in the church choir and chaired the publicity committee, whose meetings ate up priceless hours on both weekends and weekday nights.

And the few hours he did spend with Phoebe dealt with schedules, chores, and finances, leaving precious little time for casual conversation, fun, and least of all, for sex.

The breakneck pace of his life was not only hurting his marriage, but also taking a toll on his health. It galled him that David, 15 years his senior, had a flat stomach, a full head of dark hair, and a healthy glow to his cheeks. *He looks as young as me—maybe younger.* He glanced down and grabbed the inner tube of fat floating on his belt. *That can't be much of a turn-on.*

But how could he change? He thought through his list of duties and found it hard to cut a single one, either at work or home, without making drastic changes in their lives—taking a lower-paying job or trading their new house for a condo—neither of which Phoebe would find acceptable.

It crossed his mind that he might be simply stuck in that demanding phase of life when bills and work turned a man into a beast of burden, and there wasn't much he could do about it. It hadn't been his choice to carry all this weight. It was piled on his back by other people, including his wife, who in spite of her complaining added to it every day, and maybe the best he could do was to quit feeling sorry for himself and keep moving forward, lifting one heavy foot after the other, until the job was done.

His frown deepened. That couldn't be the answer. Even if no solution came to mind, he couldn't ignore the problem. His marriage, his family, his whole life might be at stake. By no means did he want to end up like David, alone and looking for love at 52.

Again, he pulled out the in-flight magazine and flipped through the pages. Suddenly, he stopped, staring at a white-sand beach with a middle-aged man and his shapely wife strolling down it, holding hands. *That could be us,* he thought, and right away his mind began to churn out travel plans. Phoebe was always grousing about how rarely they traveled, and she'd often spoken long-ingly of the Caribbean. Maybe this was just what they needed—to spend a full week together on a tropical beach, swimming, sunning, and drinking margaritas with lunch. Already he was paring down his projects and adding up his vacation days. Seeing how things were going, he'd better book a trip soon—in fact, he was hoping that he hadn't already waited too long.

53

Phoebe and David looked so relaxed dining together that most people in the restaurant mistook them for a couple. David tore off chunks of freshly baked naan and dipped them in spiced dal as Phoebe picked at her plate of curried chicken and rice. In truth, she didn't love Indian food, but David's enthusiasm more than compensated for it, and she took vicarious pleasure in his lavish praise of his chicken *tikka masala.* She did, however, love the atmosphere of

the restaurant—the low tables with pillows for seats, the peacock-blue tapes-
tries, the stunning photos of the Taj Mahal, and the unfamiliar, bracing aromas
wafting out of the kitchen. It made her feel as if she'd found an island of calm
amid the hurry and stress of her daily life.

When David spoke, his eyes flashed as if to imply that life was a march
of follies that most people failed to notice, and its main pleasure came from
sharing its ironies with a select group of like-minded souls, of which Phoebe
was his most cherished member. His nimble hands were always moving, gathering up the air, stroking the stem of his wine glass, palming the silk tablecloth,
precisely but languidly, reveling in the shape and texture of everything he
touched. At times the fluid movement of his hands mesmerized her, like a
child watching a magic show. But the calming effect also lowered her guard,
and now and then she had to catch herself to keep from being drawn into
overly personal subjects.

It didn't help that David was a well-dressed man, handsome in a suit or
a pair of jeans and polo shirt, articulate and kind, who took an interest in the
smallest details of Phoebe's life.

Today, she'd given in and accepted his invitation to lunch. She'd even
ordered a glass of Chardonnay, and then a second. She felt like she deserved
a break. All week long she'd been keyed up—worried about Zoe, feeling guilty
for hiding the affair from Jake, but still angry with him for going to Chicago
and sticking her once again with all the driving, cooking, and cleaning. And
as people often do when they feel misused, she began to vent, complaining
about Jake's traveling, his slave-like devotion to his cell phone, his failure to
help around the house, and even his more recent habit of snoring, which
sometimes kept her up at night and made it hard to focus the next day at work.

Ten minutes later, she took a deep breath and a sip of Chardonnay. Her
ranting had done more than vent her anger—it had swept away the tension
that had built up over the months, and coupled with the slight buzz from the
wine, made her feel heady, and a touch impulsive. At the same time, she felt
remorseful, as if she'd betrayed something sacred in her marriage, almost as if
she and David had been holding hands or kissing. Suddenly, she was blushing.

"Don't be embarrassed," he said. "Sooner or later it happens in every marriage. Someone gets too busy and takes their spouse for granted. The important
thing is not to let it go too long. It's funny—we all need space now and then,
but if you get too much, you drift apart, and sometimes you can't find your
way back. That's what happened with Karen and me."

"That's what bothers me," Phoebe said, relieved that David hadn't used
her rant to criticize her marriage. "It's been going on for years, and it's getting
worse, not better."

"Well, he'd better wake up. You're a remarkable woman, Phoebe. If he doesn't figure that out, he'll lose you."

The compliment made her blush. By *remarkable* he'd meant beautiful. His eyes and voice had said it plainly. Her emotions got the better of her, and her blush deepened. A second later, she felt like crying.

He reached over and touched her wrist. "Are you okay?"

She let him cup her hand. It was less a come on than a gesture of concern. "It's been a really hard week," she confessed. "Someone I know has a terrible problem. It's really upset me, but I can't talk about it."

He pulled back his hand. "If it's that bad, then maybe you should."

Before she knew it, she was telling him about Zoe.

She couldn't help herself. It just came out—and in full detail. When she got to the part about walking in on Zoe and Steve, the image of his arching back and tensing butt flashed in her mind. As much as the image had shocked her, she couldn't help seeing herself in Zoe's place, pinned against the wall with Steve moving inside her. As Phoebe talked, she stared at David's fingers stroking the rim of his plate and wondered how they would feel brushing her nipples or cupping her cheeks and sliding down between her—*Come on, Phoebe, stop it.* She'd lost her train of thought and was blushing furiously.

He seemed unfazed by her tale. He listened quietly, without judging. "What did you tell her?"

The question brought back her focus. "I told her to break it off. And to get Jeremy into treatment."

"Are you sure that's the best thing for her?"

"Of course," she said, but his question made her wonder if her advice had been wrong. "What else could I say?"

"I don't know. It depends on whether or not he quits drinking. In my experience, most people don't."

She stared at her plate. Her appetite had vanished.

"I'm sorry. I don't mean to upset you, but I know this from my divorce. It was no fun at the time, but afterward I had a new life, without the baggage. Getting to that point was rough. You know what a mess I was. But I'm much better off now."

She winced. Although he was clearly referring to Zoe, it somehow felt like he was addressing her. Zoe's dilemma and her own briefly blended, to the point that she tried to picture what life might be like on her own—but the thought quickly faded. It was too unsettling to consider for more than a few seconds.

"I don't think Zoe wants that. She and Jeremy used to be good together. If he stops drinking, they can fix it."

"I hope so. If not for their sake, for their kids'. The parents might be better off after a divorce, but not the kids. They recover sooner or later, but it takes a toll."

"Life's never easy, is it?"

He smiled wistfully.

> They are not long, the weeping and the laughter,
> Love and desire and hate;
> I think they have no portion in us after
> We pass the gate.
>
> They are not long, the days of wine and roses,
> Out of a misty dream
> Our path emerges for a while, then closes
> Within a dream.

"That's beautiful. Is there more?"

"No, that's all."

"It's so short."

"So is life."

She nodded sadly. Yes, it was all passing by too quickly. There was never enough wine, and the roses were dropping their petals at a disconcerting rate. Maybe it was better to share the wine today, while you still could, like Zoe, with your senses sharp and the sap still flowing in your veins. Wouldn't that be the best of all worlds—to have a husband to pay the bills and tend the yard and a lover to worship her, recite her poetry, and give her mind-altering orgasms—like so many men with a doting wife at home and a mistress on the side?

She glanced shyly at David, as if he could read her mind, and by the way he gazed back at her, she felt he could.

After lunch, Phoebe closed her office door and stared at market reports as her mind wandered. She'd drunk too much, and the wine had oiled her tongue. But now as she sobered up, guilt was settling in. She'd had no right telling David about Zoe, especially when she hadn't told Jake. Of course, David had never met Zoe or anyone in her circle, so the lapse was likely not fatal—but still, she'd taken a careless risk and, worse, had broken Zoe's trust.

What am I doing, bitching about my husband? Indulging in fantasies? Thinking about divorce? Have I lost my mind? Why all of a sudden do I have these crazy feelings?

Phoebe's logical mind searched for answers. Were her fantasies merely a product of the times, when sex purred in every book, film, and TV show—or was it simply hormonal, the peaking of her sex drive, fed by her belief that she had a right to use her body however she chose? Or was it something in her genes, like her father's drinking, that was pulling her down this path? She even wondered if the urge might be Freudian—David being a father figure who, unlike her own dad, never stopped showering her with affection and praise.

She didn't know. The only thing she knew for certain was how confused and restless she felt—unable to endure the status quo, but longing for something that could tear her life apart.

Still, the longing persisted.

And the thought that scared her most was that next week it would come to a head when she spent three days in Manhattan with David, who knew all the sights and sounds of the city and couldn't wait to show her. In the pit of her stomach, she knew that she would decide then and there. Because no matter what she did, something had to change. With events both at home and work bringing her closer to David with each passing month, there had to be a reaction soon. Like two subatomic particles, they must either merge into a single, new atom, or fly apart, forcibly and forever.

54

"I still don't get it," Jake said. "Why not?" He leaned against the kitchen counter and folded his arms across this chest.

Phoebe was sitting at the table in her navy suit, meeting his stare, but her rigid pose resembled a fly caught in a web, frozen, to avoid wiggling the strands and waking the spider.

"I'd love St. John's, but the timing's bad. Nate's starting Kindergarten, and I'm swamped at work. Why can't we wait until Christmas?"

He tried not to scowl. He wouldn't admit his real motive for wanting to leave now, just as he felt that Phoebe wouldn't admit her real motive for putting him off. Instead, they were dancing around the issue and arguing over trivia. All the same, he couldn't bring himself to accuse her. It was the last thing he wanted to believe, and even if she was guilty, he didn't have a shred of proof. "Tell me again why Zoe can't take care of Nate. Are you saying she can't handle him?"

"I don't want to bother her now," Phoebe said, blushing. "She's too busy."

"We were pretty damn busy when they left Maddy and Marty here and went to San Francisco. What did they give us—two days notice? But, you know, the world didn't come to an end. I seem to recall it was fun."

She stared back, steely faced. "Forget about Zoe. We'd have to find someone else."

"Who? Your mother's teaching. And my parents can't stay the whole week."

"It's too much to ask, anyway."

"How tough could it be for Zoe to drop Nate off at school every morning? He could stay there all day if he had to. I don't see what the problem is. Is something wrong with Zoe? The last time I saw her, she didn't look very good."

"Starting the new year is hard on teachers. I know. I've been there. And teaching is more stressful these days."

"Are you kidding? She just had the whole summer off. What's stressful about that?"

Phoebe folded her arms and clammed up. He stared at her intently, but she wouldn't look back. *That's enough. I'm getting to the bottom of this.* "Phoebe," he said firmly, "is there something going on I should know about?"

"What do you mean?"

"Is there something going on with you and David?"

She met his stare defiantly. "No—there's nothing going on. Is that what you're worried about—the trip to New York?"

Now that he'd leveled the charge and Phoebe had denied it, he no longer dared to push her. "Not exactly. I know you have to go. I just think we're overdue. We haven't gone anywhere since Nate was born. Sometimes I worry, you know, that we're so caught up with our jobs we're— "He wanted to say *drifting apart,* but the words seemed too charged, as if saying them aloud would make them true.

"Don't say *we.* You're so caught up with your job you sleep with your damn cell phone. Where have you been the last two years? Suddenly you're all over me because I won't drop everything and go to the Caribbean—as if it never occurred to you I might want to go anywhere. Frankly, hearing it now pisses me off. You're pretty late, you know, pretty damn late."

Jake flushed. He knew he'd lost the argument. It didn't matter how sound his logic was. Phoebe was no longer moving in the world of logic—she was unloading on him out of frustration, and while on one level he knew he deserved it, on another level he felt misused, because all the warning signs were there, and she still hadn't explained her behavior, whether or not she had something to hide.

There was no point in pressing her further. He knew that once Phoebe lost her temper, he might as well quit. The most logical people, once they lost control, always became the least. He'd have to wait and bring it up later, after she'd cooled down.

"I know I am," he said crossly. "We can talk about it when you're in a better mood."

But as he walked past her into the den, he was chilled by the last emotion he read on her face—relief that he was going.

55

Phoebe and David strolled down the sweeping path at the south end of Central Park. Moving under a vault of leaves and boughs, they could have passed for a local Manhattan couple. David had told Phoebe to wear black—New Yorkers thought bright colors garish, he claimed, at least in clothing. Phoebe took his advice and wore a simple black dress that showed off just enough leg to turn an eye without being tasteless. With her black heels, silver necklace, and bangs glancing over one eye, she gave off a cosmopolitan air, the effect of which she found amusing. Here she was, a mechanic's daughter from the Midwest, who'd never traveled to either coast, and two New Yorkers had already stopped to ask her for directions.

David looked her peer with his silver-streak temples, black fitted jacket, and buffed sable shoes. In most other cites, people would have stared at them or smiled, but in New York, Phoebe observed, no one stared at you, let alone smiled.

Not that it bothered her. In fact, she liked the invisibility and the feeling of freedom that came along with it. A person might be anyone here—a foreign dignitary, famous writer, courtesan, or mafia wife, and nobody cared, so long as you didn't make a scene.

The fairy-tale forest in the heart of Manhattan delighted Phoebe. Going from crowded sidewalks to rolling greens and lofty elms in less than a block made her feel like she'd found a magic vale where fauns frolicked on the grass, gnomes peeked from behind trees, and fairies left stardust trails as they leaped between the flower tops.

David smiled as Phoebe drank it in, beaming like a schoolgirl as he gave her a brief history of the park. It was his favorite place in the world, he said. His idea of a perfect afternoon was sitting under a tree on a summer day, buried in a novel or book of poems, and watching the people strolling by.

When they reached the Bethesda fountain, where the bronze Angel floated above The Lake like a heavenly guard, Phoebe gasped. Water rained around the angel's feet into an upper bowl and then poured into a vast reflecting pond.

Beyond the fountain, rowboats wheeled on a placid lake, and a gondolier in a striped shirt punted a flat-bottomed boat. Sheltered by oaks on the lake's far side emerged the Loeb Boathouse.

"I didn't know about this," Phoebe gushed. "It's the most beautiful park in the world."

For some reason, David seemed eager to move her along. "There's more ahead."

Phoebe wasn't ready to leave. She didn't understand what could possibly hold more interest.

Their destination didn't sink in until David led her around the lake and through the double French doors of the Boathouse. They clipped down the steps and stopped by a maître d' stand. "We have a reservation for one o'clock," he told the hostess. "For Spencer."

"How did you get that?" Phoebe asked, walking past tables gleaming with polished silver and long-stemmed glasses.

"I made the reservation a month ago."

The hostess pulled out her chair. Their table stood between two white pillars at the water's edge. "This is perfect, David. The lake. The fountain. What a treat."

"I thought you'd like it. Some wine?"

"Of course." She picked up the list and scanned the prices. "Ouch."

"I'd love to buy you lunch, Phoebe, but I know you won't let me."

"You're right. We'll split the check. Taking me here is enough."

"The wine's on me. I insist."

"Okay. But don't mortgage your house."

For the rest of her life, Phoebe would cherish the memory of their lunch at the Boathouse—patches of blue sky peeking through the canopy of elms, the air warm but crisp, the breeze soft on her bare arms, the fine merlot on her lips and tongue, the angel rising above the lake, the lovers in boats, and David sitting across from her, eyes aglow, teasing her, asking her questions, and telling her about the city—its buildings, theater, food, art—while their words flowed as smoothly as the water at the angel's feet.

At two-thirty, Phoebe glanced at her watch. "We'd better get back. We'll miss the next speaker."

He gave her a mischievous glance.

"What?"

"I've heard him. He's boring. I can tell you everything he'll say in two minutes."

"You want to skip it?"

"Why not? It's a beautiful day. I still have a lot to show you."

Phoebe swallowed. Suddenly she knew. This was the moment of truth. "Like what?" she asked, trying to slow her breathing.

"The Met overlooks the park. You'd love the Impressionism exhibit. I know it's your favorite period."

A shiver ran up her back. David had planned the rest of the day with patience and care. With perfect clarity, it unfurled in front of her. "Sounds nice. After that?"

"For dinner, I found a great place in Tribeca."

"And you made reservations?"

He paused. "I did."

"And after that?"

He stopped, flustered.

"Maybe a drink in your room?"

A trace of doubt flickered in his eyes. "I'd like that, Phoebe, and I hope you would too."

"You planned the whole day—and night—didn't you?"

"I wish you wouldn't see it like that. I only planned the day, but if something happened, yes, I'd be more than pleased."

"I'd rather be up front about it."

"Of course you would." He brought his face closer. "I love you, Phoebe. I have for a long time."

Something stirred inside her, but she didn't know if it was desire or panic. With trembling hand, she took a sip of wine. She barely set down her glass without spilling.

"I know that. And I have to admit, I feel something for you too. We have a lot in common. We always have a great time, and you always try to make me happy."

"You're the happiest when you make the people you love happy. It's selfish, really."

She smiled. "No, it's not, and it's hard to walk away from."

"Then don't."

She stared into her empty plate. "I've been thinking about it for a long time. It hasn't been easy. The truth is, up till now, I didn't know what I would do—but now that we're here, the words you just said to me—I can't say them back."

His face fell. "You don't love me."

"I thought I did. Or maybe I do, but there's too much in the way. Maybe I love Jake more than I think, or maybe it's that damn vow I took, and I can't break it. Watching Zoe didn't help. I've seen what a wreck she is. And how would I explain it to Nate? Because that's where it would end, you know. It always does."

He stayed quiet for a long time, staring across the water. "It's been confusing for me too," he finally said. "I knew I was interfering with your life, but I couldn't help myself. I feel that strongly about you. And I thought you were unhappy and looking for a way out." He studied her with a pained look. "Are you sure you're not?"

"It doesn't matter. There's a wall in front of me, and I can't break it down. If I do, I might break myself. Does that make sense?"

He nodded. "I guess so." His face had gone blank.

"I'm sorry if I led you on, David. I didn't mean to. I let it go too far. I'm sorry if I hurt you. If it's any consolation, it hurts me too."

She spoke these last words neither from self-pity nor any wish to be forgiven, but only because she knew that right in front of her a dear friend was slipping away—someone she'd honestly grown to love in the last two years—and she felt certain that her refusal would tear them apart forever.

56

Phoebe set down her suitcase and froze, startled by the broad-shouldered man sitting at the kitchen table, reading a paperback. He looked strangely relaxed in his black trunks and gray T-shirt. His calves popped out of his white socks and running shoes, and the book appeared small in his strong hands. His head was neatly shaven. It wasn't until he turned around that she recognized her own husband.

"Jake—what happened to you?"

"While you were gone I got a little crazy."

She studied how the cut changed his features. Jake had reached that point in life when a man looks in the mirror and sees what others have known for years—that fighting to keep his thinning hair didn't make him look younger, but only foolish. Now that it was gone, his face had a rugged, virile look—maybe older, but to Phoebe, much better.

The shock faded. She patted his stubbly pate. "You look like a hedgehog."

He blushed.

"I'm kidding. I like it." She sat beside him and stared, biting her lip.

"For a hedgehog."

"No, you look great. What got into you?"

He shrugged. He seemed reluctant to say.

"What's that?" She grabbed the paperback. *Jane Eyre?*

"I've been meaning to read it."

"Have you been in the sun too long?"

"No, but I did join a health club."

At last, it sunk in. She cupped his hand. "Jake, I'm flattered. That's sweet, but there's no reason for you to be jealous."

She pulled back her hand, partly because it wasn't true.

He stared at her skeptically, but she stayed composed. "Nothing happened in New York—well, something did." She stopped and sighed. "I lost a good friend."

"David?"

"I asked him to back off, and he didn't take it well. But I guess that means I had to say it."

"I always thought he was in love with you."

"He was." She was keenly aware of placing all the blame on David and leaving out her own feelings—more than strong enough to warrant his jealousy. On the flight back, she'd made up her mind to confess—eventually—but right now his ego was too fragile and the wound too fresh, and being too frank with him might backfire.

"It will be awkward for a while, but I'm glad I told him. It's been gnawing at me."

"I'm glad you did too."

Her eyes welled up, and she changed the subject. "There's something else. I have to apologize. I've been keeping something from you."

His brow wrinkled.

"No, it's not about me, but it's been affecting me a lot."

"What?"

She rubbed her temple as if in pain. "It's Zoe. She's a mess. She's having an affair."

"Are you sure?"

"Couldn't be any surer. I caught her in the act."

She told him everything. It was painful to recount, but once she finished, a burden lifted off her shoulders, and she realized for the first time how stressful it had been for her to hide the truth from Jake.

"I don't understand those two, but I feel sorry for Zoe, even though I'm disappointed in her."

"Don't be too hard on her. I've never seen her so unhappy."

"It reminds me of the night that Marty was born. Remember where I found Jeremy? She was having their baby, and he was in a bar, getting drunk."

"I know, but she can't leave him. She's stuck."

"You gave her good advice. I wish we could do more."

Jake's cell phone rang. When he grabbed it, Phoebe cast him a jaundiced eye. He read her look and checked the caller ID. "It's Nate."

How are you, Champ? Hey, you'd better come home for supper. Someone here wants to see you."

He passed the phone to Phoebe, who listened avidly to Nate's rambling story about finding their neighbor's lost dog.

She gave the phone back to Jake. "He wants you again."

After a pause, he covered the mouthpiece. "Tommy's parents want to know if he can stay for dinner and go to a movie."

"I guess he knows who to ask."

Jake shrugged. "We could go out for dinner ourselves."

"No, I'm sick of restaurants."

"Then we can stay home. I'll grill a steak. Make a salad. Open a bottle of wine."

"Hmm. You're being awfully nice."

She could tell by his smile that he'd caught the purr in her voice.

"You're in luck, Nate. Call when the movie's done, okay?"

He set down the phone. Phoebe was leafing through *Jane Eyre*. "This is my favorite book, you know."

"Now I know why."

"Good, isn't it?"

"That's not what I meant. Someone I know reminds me of Jane."

Phoebe smiled. "You flatter me, Mr. Rochester."

He folded his hands and stared at her sternly. "Now, Jane, it's come to my attention that you've been neglecting your household duties."

Her smile broadened. "I'm sure I can make it up to you, Mr. Rochester, if only you'll tell me how."

"It's been a very long time since you polished the candlesticks."

"But we only have one."

"Then you'd better polish it thoroughly."

"I shall, Mr. Rochester—but not until you bathe. I despise a dirty man."

"You won't find a speck of dirt on me, I promise."

"I'll see to it myself. I'll find a fresh bar of soap and meet you in the shower."

57

Jeremy parked in the unlit drive and stepped out of his Camry. It was a perfect fall evening, the air still, dry, steeped with the scent of burning wood. Now and then a puff of wind trembled the leaves fanning the backyard shadows. Surrounded by darkness, their little house poured out light. The saffron panes cheered him. Walking through the neighborhood at night had always lifted his mood—spotting people through their windows—having supper, watching TV, or reading. From the sidewalk, the scene always looked peaceful, cozy, safe. *Home is where the heart is. Home sweet home. The place that matters most of all.* Home was—dare he use the word? *Sacred.* At least tonight he felt it was. What would ever become of him if he couldn't sail back to his haven at night, after a long day's work, with its warm, glowing windows and his loving wife and two adoring kids waiting inside?

He stopped on the landing and frowned. If he really felt that way, then why did he always get home so late? Why did the evenings slip by so fast? And why did he spend most in his basement den where no one bothered him? If home was a haven, his anchor and refuge, then why did he spend so little time here?

He knew the answer. He tried to smother it, but it leaped back up like a prairie fire. *Shame. You're ashamed to face them—that's why you're never home. It's not that you don't love them, it's not that anything else is more important—the truth is, you don't deserve them. They deserve someone much better than you.*

He wavered on the landing. At least he'd been coming home earlier the last few months. The modest changes he was making to his life were starting to pay off. He'd been working out three nights a week for most of the summer and was getting back in shape again. His mood was better, and he was drinking less. He kept a tally in a notebook, so he couldn't fool himself, and every week for the last month, the line of hatch marks had gotten smaller. His family, as if responding to the change, had made it easier for him to be at home. Maddy was acting out less, Marty was more talkative, with fewer headaches, and Zoe seemed more patient and warm, or at least she'd backed off from riding him about all their financial problems.

He opened the kitchen door. The room was empty and the house silent. "Zoe? Anybody home?"

He expected Maddy or Marty to fly around the corner, but neither did. He set his briefcase on the table, found a glass, and filled it with water. *Where is everybody? Are they watching a movie? It's too quiet for that. But people are here—I can feel them.*

Puzzled, he stepped into the hallway. *What?*

Why in the hell was his dad sitting on the living-room couch with his head hanging down? And his mother staring sadly out the window? The tempo of his heart sped as he scanned the room, filled with people, *his people,* and most eerily of all, nobody was speaking a word. His in-laws, Rose and Martin, stood by the front door, holding hands. And Derek and Josh from The Herald. *Jesus—Ansel? And Ben Nelson?* They'd barely spoken in five years. Phoebe was there too, pacing back and forth, avoiding his eyes. Behind her stood Zoe, her back facing him, her arms wrapped around her waist. *Everyone important in my life is here,* he thought with a jolt. *Everyone except—* A sense of helpless horror rose inside him. Could it be that no one dared to look at him because the worst thing he could ever imagine had happened? No—it couldn't be. God would never be that cruel—it wasn't possible. A cold sweat oozed from his skin, and the blood rushed to his face. He felt like screaming the words, but all that came out was a hoarse whisper, "Where is he? Where's Marty?"

Zoe turned and ran toward him. The look in her eyes told him everything. *Their son was dead.*

"MARTY!" he cried out and lunged for the stairs.

Zoe chased him and cut him off. She grabbed him by the arms with unnatural strength. "He's all right, Jeremy, Marty's fine."

He stared at Zoe, stunned, trying to comprehend. "He's fine?"

"Yes, he and Maddy are with Jake."

His heart was slowing down, but now his whole body was trembling. "Why are they with Jake? Is something wrong with them?"

"Nothing's wrong with them," she said pleadingly. "It's you, Jeremy. There's something wrong with you. That's why we're here."

He stared at her blankly. *Did they really know the truth? All of them?*

He studied his family and friends. One by one, they lifted their heads and met his gaze, but now it was harder for him to meet theirs. He could read their faces clearly now—it wasn't grief—but worry, pity, and in the eyes of some, especially his father, anger.

Then it leaped up at him—the evidence. On the coffee table gathered a small army of airplane bottles, at least fifty—*the ones too small to count.* Seeing them deployed against him like a phalanx, glaring at him accusingly, it was clear they not only counted, but also composed the greater portion of his drinking.

"Where did you get those?" he mumbled.

"Every night I dig them out of the garbage," Zoe said. "I've been doing it for months. I mark all the bottles in the cupboard. I smell your clothes when you come home. I check your receipts. I know all the liquor stores, all the bars you stop at. We all do."

There was silence in the room.

"You're an alcoholic, Jeremy. You need help. And we all want to help you."

He stared at her, his face flushing. His knees had never stopped quaking, and now he felt like collapsing. He tried to speak, to fight the accusations or make fresh promises—promises he knew he wouldn't keep—but nothing came out. There was no point in lying. They all knew his deepest, darkest secret. Everybody knew what a fool he was. A liar and a fake. A coward with no self-control. A failure as a husband and father. The game was up. He felt an overpowering urge to throw himself at Zoe's feet, to beg her forgiveness and weep like a child, but the fear of being pushed away held him back.

"We love you, Jeremy, and we want you to get better."

What the hell is wrong with her? How can she still love me?

Zoe hugged him and sobbed. Her tears stung his neck and stained his collar. He clung to her as tears streamed down his own face. He didn't sob or sniffle, but stared with eyes open as the tears rained down.

"I'll do whatever you say. If you want me to leave, I will. If you want me to go into treatment, I'll go. I love you, and I'll do whatever I need to keep you."

Zoe quit sobbing and shook her head. "I don't want you to leave, Jeremy. I want you here with us, at home. But you *have* to go into treatment."

"All right, Zoe. I won't fight you anymore. You know best. If you say I have to, I'll go."

Part Four
2000

58

There was nothing in the open spaces behind Maddy's drawers. Nothing in the lining of her coat. Nothing taped to the back of her picture frames. Zoe had skipped the obvious hiding places—closet, backpack, pockets—and zeroed in on the more ingenious spots. She knew exactly where to look, having used them herself when she was only 15. Back then, she'd pried off the base trim of her built-in shelves and hid all kinds of contraband from her mother—erotic books, cigarettes, condoms, and pot.

But Maddy was only 13, and Zoe hadn't expected trouble, if at all, for a few more years.

She felt certain that Maddy was using. She'd caught the telltale whiff on her clothes three times now. The first time, Maddy had blamed the crowd at the Green Day concert, and Zoe had bought it, recalling smoke so thick at concerts in the seventies that you could barely see the stage. The second time Maddy had slunk home after a sleepover, but she'd thrown Zoe off by claiming her friend had worn her coat while getting stoned in the park. *I bought that one too.* And the final straw had come just minutes ago, while Zoe was sorting the dirty laundry and the smell had wafted up from Maddy's basket. She sniffed each blouse and shirt like a bloodhound until she found the offending hoodie, reeking like a campfire. *She's getting careless, dumping her clothes in the laundry. That's more than experimenting—that's a habit.*

She'd slipped by Maddy, watching *Friends* in the living room, tiptoed upstairs, and started looking.

A week ago, Maddy had finished seventh-grade at Franklin Middle School, and Zoe knew that if Maddy stuck with her current group of friends, the disciplinary war, if not lost, could never be won. She'd spend the next five years fighting to pull Maddy away from peers with failing grades, adult sexual habits, and drug or drinking problems. She knew this directly from her own high-school years. In ninth grade, she'd fallen in with a wild group—girls who smoked pot, dated older boys, and moved quickly from kissing and petting to intercourse—until a boy from another school had wooed her away. He also encouraged her to keep up her dancing, which helped her stay out of trouble, but every time they had a fight, she ran back to her old friends and resumed her risky behaviors—which never failed to pull the boyfriend back into orbit.

She'd gotten away with murder, and even then she knew it. Only after college did she realize how lucky she'd been, how easily she could have fallen over the edge—gotten expelled, pregnant, addicted, or even killed while driving drunk or stoned. There were many nights, she thought with a shudder, that could have ended tragically, if luck hadn't gone her way.

She glanced at Maddy's unmade bed, the cluttered desk, the mounds of dirty clothes on the floor, including thongs, attire for strippers, she thought, not 13-year-old girls. Last of all, she studied the posters of Kurt Cobain and Tupac Shakur, which made her squirm in the same way that her posters of Jim Morrison and David Bowie had made her own mother squirm back in the seventies.

She tried convincing herself that her former rock heroes were cleaner versions of today's rappers and grunge bands, but she knew it wasn't that simple. Dealing with kids every day at school, she knew the importance of music in their lives. They used it not only for entertainment, but self-expression, release, and a mostly benign form of rebellion against the adult world, which most kids had to reject before they could embrace it.

What bothered her more was the escalation of the last two decades. Sex, Drugs, and Rock and Roll may have been the mantra of her generation, but the current one chanted the mantra at a higher pitch: the sex was earlier and riskier; the drugs were not only stronger, but kids were using them in junior high; and rock and roll had given way to hip-hop and rap, whose messages on women and sex were degrading, especially when you considered they were being listened to by legions of prepubescent girls.

As Zoe brooded, something about the molding near the closet caught her eye. The gap between two boards seemed too wide. Even a mediocre workman would have filled it with putty and painted it over.

She knelt down, forced a finger into the gap, and pulled, but she only chipped her nail. Next she tried a wooden ruler, but it bent too far and nearly broke. Finally, she tiptoed down to the basement and found a chisel. Armed with the right tool, she forced the tip into the gap, pried once, and a ten-inch piece of molding rattled onto the floor, strangely clean of cobwebs or dust.

She ran her fingers under the wall. On her third pass, something skittered out of reach. She probed more gently and discovered not just one, but four neatly rolled joints.

Something turned in the pit of her stomach. *Great—keeping a stash at 13. If Maddy's smoking, what else is she doing?*

She brushed her hand under the wall again, but this time only gathered up dust and bits of broken plaster. Convinced there was nothing more to find, she pounded in the molding with the base of her palm. *This is one conversation I hoped I would never have.*

59

"What are you doing?"

Maddy's voice came from the door. It had that disrespectful tone that made Zoe's blood simmer.

She got up slowly. Sitting on her ankles had locked her knees, and she winced as she stood. She was conscious of looking old and ungraceful in her daughter's eyes.

In contrast, Maddy's willowy figure reminded Zoe of a ballerina. She stood an inch taller than Zoe, with slender ankles and wrists, spidery arms, and dainty hands and feet. Her breasts had come in early and were large for her frame. She drew attention to them with tight-fitting tops that showed her belly button, while her jeans, stone washed and tattered, hugged her butt and skinny thighs.

Zoe's friends often remarked how Maddy's face resembled Zoe's when she was younger. Maddy had the same high cheekbones, plump lips, dark chestnut hair, and licorice-brown eyes—even if they lacked her spark, giving off instead her father's more logical air.

Maddy's beauty and budding sexuality not only reminded Zoe of what she'd lost, but also made her nervous. She knew the power that beauty like that held over men, having used it herself to get what she wanted from teachers, boys, and later, bosses—although she'd never had a body like Maddy's—and she worried that it might entice her into adult behaviors long before she was ready.

"I don't like to snoop," she said, holding out the four joints, "but maybe I should start."

Maddy's face colored. "Those aren't mine," she said, her eyes flashing. "I'm keeping them for a friend."

"I'm not stupid. Tell me you made this perfect hiding place for a friend."

She wriggled her nose but said nothing.

"How long have you been smoking?"

"I've tried it a few times. It's not a big deal."

"Maddy—you're 13. You're way too young."

"How old do I have to be?"

Zoe balked. *How old was I? Fifteen?*

"I'd prefer you never did," she said, feeling like a hypocrite, "but you should be at least 18."

"Didn't you try it when you were young?"

Maddy had asked the question merely to provoke her, because she already knew the answer. "I was lucky. Not everybody I knew was. I knew a girl, Tanya, who got hooked on coke. She stole from her parents, and they kicked her out. She ended up stripping, and worse, to support her habit. A year ago, I read her obituary in the paper. She was homeless."

Maddy stared at her as if to say, *try another one.*

"Sophomore year I went to prom with Ted Harmon. Later that summer, he rolled his car and broke his neck. He was drunk."

"That was stupid."

"When they're drunk, smart people do stupid things. That's my point."

"Mom, I can't even drive."

"It's not just your age, Maddy. Your father's an alcoholic. He's been through treatment twice. That doesn't mean it's in your blood, but you can't afford to risk it."

There it was, the adolescent eye roll.

"You have to be more careful than your friends, don't you see that?"

"Nobody gets hooked on weed."

"You're wrong. You can get hooked on anything. If you smoke weed, you might try coke. If you try coke, why not meth?"

"Or heroin."

"Maddy, don't make light of it. You don't know where it will end."

"Well, I don't think it's a big deal, once in a while. It won't hurt me."

Zoe's patience had run out. She couldn't take any more of Maddy's absurd replies. "Well, you're wrong, and I'm grounding you. You're not going out for a month. And don't think you can hide it from me. That stuff reeks."

Maddy scowled, cranked up her CD player, and buried her nose in *Cosmo Girl.*

Zoe glared at Maddy and fought to keep her self-control.

What the song say we murder motherfuckers daily. Black out, blow the crack out, My lyrics neva fail me. I inhale strong weed, then release the stress, Deliver the bomb shit from east to west.

Zoe marched to the nightstand, plucked out the CD, and snapped it in two. A few shards zipped across the room.

Instead of getting angry, Maddy glowered at her briefly and kept paging through *Cosmo Girl.* The look had clearly said, *fuck you.*

Zoe searched her face for the slightest hint of remorse or fear, but saw none. She didn't understand her daughter's steely defiance. Being confronted by her mother for using drugs would have mortified Zoe, but Maddy seemed more annoyed than worried, and her response told Zoe that she had no intention of quitting. At the same time, Zoe felt partly to blame, even though it wasn't fair, simply because she'd done the same things in high school and had come out okay—so what right did she have to frighten Maddy with horror stories about dead friends?

But surely as a parent she had every right—and every duty. Kids were so damn sure that nothing could hurt them or even come back to haunt them later in life. But Zoe knew better, and it was her job to teach her daughter she wasn't immortal. But how could she instill a healthy sense of fear in someone who was basically fearless? The truth was, she had no idea, although she knew she had to think of something, and soon. There was always a critical window, a point of no return, especially with teens, and Zoe could only pray that her daughter hadn't already passed it.

60

In the basement, Jeremy was looking for something too. He stood before a shelf, studying Zoe's scrapbooks. The years were penned in black marker on the spines, starting with 1974, when Zoe, at 15, had begun pasting her most cherished memories in these many binders—photos, vacation maps concert tickets, love letters, and, later, prints of her kids' hands and feet, watercolors, report cards, and teacher's notes—filling more than two-dozen volumes. Anytime she felt nostalgic or sad, she'd steal downstairs to the den and flip through the pages, smiling to herself. Now and then, she'd bring up a photo to show Jeremy or the kids, but most of the time, she didn't share her thoughts. Afterward, her mood would always lift, and she would climb up the stairs, cheerful again, and resume her busy life.

The basement mainly served as Jeremy's office. There were nights when he couldn't stand the chaos upstairs—often caused by Zoe and Maddy fighting, but not far down the list were quarrels with Zoe about money or the house. The way she talked, you'd think the ground was giving way beneath them, and any minute the house might break in two and tumble off a cliff like the House of Usher. He often wondered why they'd bought a house in the first place—two people who hated cleaning, cooking, and yard work. Add to that the staggering cost, and it began to resemble madness. He couldn't count the number of times he'd pressed her to sell the place and move into a townhome, but every time he did, Zoe insisted the kids have their own yard and friends close by, the way she and Phoebe did, and that always ended the discussion.

Tucked beneath the ground in his windowless room, Jeremy read books on American history, listened to classical music or jazz, or watched *Nova* and *Masterpiece Theater*. It soothed his nerves, sitting by himself, with everything quiet but the calming hum of the air conditioner. There was no phone to ring, and his family rarely interrupted him. Some nights he even fell asleep in the recliner, and Zoe had to wake him and drag him upstairs to bed.

Not that he was unhappy with his wife and kids. Sometimes he simply got tired of meeting their endless needs and felt he deserved a break after a long day's work.

His job was a different matter. As his passion for work had faded, so had his altruism. He'd stopped believing that what he did mattered very much to the average person. As far as he could tell, people no longer cared about the truth. It was too much trouble. Better to give them scandal, theater, the crisis of the hour—without addressing the cause—complex issues condensed to sound bites, and personal attacks instead of debate. And these days, everything revolved around money. The only remaining sin was doing something that might hurt the bottom line of some powerful person or group. Everything else was kosher—but do anything that threatened somebody's cash flow, and they unleashed the Furies on you.

Well, it was only a job, and if he didn't do it, someone else would—maybe better, maybe worse, but either way it wasn't going to change the world.

On the home front, at least, the last five years hadn't been so bad. He felt lucky having dodged a fate that someday might have killed him. He'd gone through rehab twice now. The first time he'd relapsed just two months later. Ansel had told him point-blank to go back—or lose his job—and made it perfectly clear it would be his last chance. Zoe had upped the stakes by threatening to leave and take the kids with her. Three strikes and you're out, she said. The second time in treatment he couldn't afford to fail, and so in the end, fear had achieved what medication and therapy could not.

Now the only trace of his addiction was the rare underground tremor that worked its way to the surface. On certain days, it came out of nowhere and left him sweating as if he were straddling a bottomless crevice. If he lost his concentration and forgot his past—and it would only take one sip—he would plunge into the depths, never to be seen again. This he knew with utter certainty.

Whenever that feeling hit, he found a meeting, any meeting, and got there as fast as he could. The fellowship, the reassurances, and the cruel reminders of the pain and degradation of relapse always did the trick.

Today was such a day. He'd woken up at four a.m., sweating from a disconcerting dream—so vivid and real that he couldn't fall back to sleep. Groggy all day at work, he couldn't force it out of his head. It was the third time he'd dreamed it now—since that day he'd overheard Zoe telling a friend that she'd flunked a class five years ago, right before his first stint in rehab. Although his memory of those days wasn't very clear, he felt certain that Zoe had bragged about earning an *A*. When he asked her about it, she insisted that he'd misunderstood and claimed that she'd told her friend the same thing, but Jeremy was sure he'd overheard her say *flunked*.

He should have tracked down a meeting right after work, but he came home instead to leaf through her scrapbooks, hoping to find a clue about the meaning of his dream—well, its meaning was plain—it was more that he wanted to see if the dream had unveiled a hidden truth or merely reflected an unconscious fear.

In the dream, he and Zoe were dancing in a banquet hall. Zoe was in her mid-thirties. She wore a lavender dress with yellow daisies and looked as bewitching as she ever had. As they danced, it somehow came to him that she'd worn the dress to please someone else. Furious, he bolted from the banquet hall with Zoe on his heels. He barged into an elevator, but she jumped in after him and grabbed his arms, pleading for him to stop as the numbers blinked past—but her behavior only convinced him that something was wrong and made him all the more determined to find out what.

When the doors opened, he rushed out and ran down a long hall. He found their room, turned his key in the lock, and pushed open the door. There on the bed a shape was barely moving under a blanket. Filled with rage, he yanked the covers off like a matador, and there below him, lying face down on the mattress—was a naked man with curly blond hair, baby-smooth skin, and a firm, muscular butt. The man groaned but didn't move. He was so drunk he didn't even know that Jeremy was standing over him.

At that instant, he'd woken up. But the image of the naked man had stayed in his head all day long, and right after work he'd come downstairs to look through Zoe's books with a sense of dread mingled with some other emotion—anger, jealousy, self-pity, or was it guilt? He couldn't define it clearly, but whatever you called it, it was a dark and dangerous mood.

Knowing his wife, he was betting that if she'd really been unfaithful, she would have kept some token of her lover—a card, letter, or lock of hair—that he could find in her books and not only confirm his hunch, but offer a clue about who the man was.

As he paged through the binder marked 1995, a pair of footsteps came tripping down the steps.

It was too late to hide the book. He stayed calm and kept leafing through it. *Just walking down memory lane—just like her.*

She walked in without knocking. Her face was pinched, and she was nearly breathless.

"What's wrong?"

She closed the door. "I found these in Maddy's room." She opened her palm and held out the four joints.

Jeremy closed his eyes. "Shit. Are you sure they're Maddy's?"

"She tried to blame her friend, but then she fessed up. I told her—I told her everything you should, but she didn't buy a word."

"It's sooner than I expected."

"You expected this?"

"Sooner or later, everybody tries it."

"I don't believe that."

"You certainly did."

"I was older."

"What, a year?"

"Two," she protested. "So you're saying, 'like mother, like daughter'?"

Maybe someday she'll cheat on her husband too.

"No, what I mean is—" The fact was, he'd been so focused on his search that Zoe's revelation had mostly annoyed him. After all, he was on the trail of something much larger. "It could be a little problem," he said, "or a big problem. It's hard to know."

"Are you kidding? With your past, Maddy can't afford to fool around with drugs."

He bristled. "And what about yours?"

"I'm not trying to blame anyone, Jeremy. I just want Maddy to see that she's playing with fire." Zoe paced in the doorway. "I don't know what to do with her anymore. She won't listen to me. When I talk, she acts like I'm not even there. And she doesn't give a damn how much I punish her—she still does exactly what she wants. We have to do something."

He sighed wearily. "I'll talk to her."

"I think she needs therapy."

Great. More time. More money. "Let's not jump to conclusions." *One crisis at a time is all I can handle.*

He closed the binder—which Zoe either hadn't noticed or hadn't thought important. "I'll go and see her right now."

61

Zoe parked her Escort in the empty drive and turned off the lights. As she stepped outside, the damp summer air enveloped her. Aside from the buzzing streetlamp and the frogs trilling somewhere in the dark, the neighborhood was silent, a cul-de-sac bordered by two- and three-story homes that made her feel small. With a sweeping glance she took in the stone and stucco facades on every side. While the trees were all saplings, the lawns were lush, dense, and perfectly trimmed like putting greens. Compared to her own neighborhood, Orchard Valley might as well have been a foreign country.

The front door opened with a spray of light. Phoebe appeared like a backlit angel and waved her in.

On the coffee table stood a bottle of pinot noir and two full glasses. "I already poured you one," Phoebe said.

Zoe picked up a glass and almost disappeared into a plush chair. "Thanks. I can use it."

Phoebe sat across from her on a cream sofa. Zoe watched her settle in, guessing that her glow came from her newfound confidence, for at this stage of life, Phoebe had every reason to feel secure. She had a high-paying job, a good marriage, a well-adjusted son, a beautiful house, a new car, money to travel, and time left over to stay in shape and even relax. More important, she seemed at home in her own skin, something that she'd never been while growing up. In Zoe's mind, Phoebe had always sold herself short, and seeing her now so happy and poised, especially when things were going so badly in her own house, she was overcome with pride and love.

She jumped out of her chair and hugged Phoebe.

"Hey, are you all right?"

Her eyes were brimming. "Do you know what day it is today?"

"No, you're kidding. I forgot."

"I forgot too. I woke up in the middle of the night, and I felt so depressed I could have jumped off a bridge. I was going to call you, but everything made sense when I saw it was June 12th."

Phoebe studied her. "You know, sometimes I think it's been harder on you than Mom."

She stared back reproachfully. She knew that Phoebe hadn't meant to hurt her feelings, but she had. "Calling me a Daddy's girl?"

"I'm sorry. Don't get mad, but we both know how much he adored you. He loved me, I never doubted that, but it wasn't the same. Every time you walked in the room, his face lit up."

Phoebe's words touched Zoe. It was perhaps the most positive spin that her sister could put on the subject. "I know he loved you just as much. Remember how happy he was at your wedding? How proud he was about your first job? And then you moved back here and did so well. He always bragged about you."

I guess we each made him happy in our own way."

"We were lucky we could do that, weren't we?"

"You're right. We were."

Zoe sighed. "I planned on leaving flowers at the cemetery, but I never did. I had the worst day."

"How come?"

She dug through her purse and pinched a joint between her lips. "Wanna get wasted?"

"Where did you get that?" Phoebe glanced nervously into the kitchen. "Better watch out. Nate's in there."

As if on cue, he rounded the corner.

Zoe stuffed the joint in her purse. "Nate! Come here and hug me."

A ten-year-old boy with Jake's blond hair and Phoebe's brown eyes ambled in. His bright-blue jersey and pinstriped pants hugged his limber frame. In his right hand, he gripped a boloney and cheese sandwich like a fastball.

"Hey, get rid of the spikes," Phoebe said, "and the sandwich."

"Sorry, Mom." A minute later, he came back in stocking feet.

Zoe squeezed him like a boa constrictor. "You are *so* cute. Can you come home with me?" Nate blushed, but made no effort to free himself.

"Will you stop molesting my son?" Phoebe said.

"He doesn't mind." Zoe let him go. Despite Nate's blush, she could tell he enjoyed the hug.

"Hey, Mom, did you hear about my double?"

"Your dad told me. Your second this week, right?"

"Two doubles and two singles." He swung an imaginary bat. "Kapow!"

"Nice job—but it's past your bedtime. Better hit the showers, Kirby Puckett."

"Okay, Mom. Goodnight." He pecked her on the cheek and ran upstairs.

"The girls will eat him alive," Zoe said.

"They've already started. But he's a good kid. He does his homework, helps around the house, and hardly ever complains."

"Then you've never found a joint in his room."

"Maddy's?"

Zoe recounted the whole night, from finding her daughter's stash to her talk with Jeremy.

"I don't envy you," Phoebe said. "You've got your hands full with Maddy."

"Now I know what I put Mom through."

"And there was a lot she didn't know."

"Part of me thinks I deserve it," Zoe said contritely. "Jeremy as much as said so. Maybe you think so too."

"I don't, but you never seemed to know you were skating on thin ice. While you were having such a good time, the rest of us were pretty worried."

"Well, Maddy is worse. At least I was afraid of getting caught. She isn't."

"Or maybe since you know the ropes, you're better off to deal with her."

Zoe gazed into her glass. "I don't know. Sometimes I think I'm still skating on thin ice."

Phoebe frowned. "Is Jeremy okay?"

She ran a finger round her glass rim. "I don't know. He's been acting funny. Tonight I walked into his den, and he gave me this look—it was a mean look. I've never seen it before. And he was going through my scrapbooks—1995."

"Is he on to something?"

"Maybe I'm just paranoid. I always thought I'd tell him after rehab. But he fell off the wagon so fast. After that, I thought it would make him start again."

Phoebe's eyes narrowed. Zoe knew that she wouldn't like what she was about to hear.

"If he's on to something, you better tell him. If you fess up, at least you'll get a chance to explain. If he finds out from someone else, it will be a lot worse. He'll not only feel betrayed, but lied to. He'll never trust you again."

The old, familiar weight settled onto her shoulders. "Sometimes I think you're right, but then I can't go through with it. I'm afraid it will be too much for him, no matter how he finds out. I can't risk it."

Phoebe stared at her, unconvinced.

"It was a terrible time for us both. I made a mistake, but that was how I coped with his drinking. I know it was wrong, but I did what I did, and I can't change it now. That's why I never told him. What good would it do? Some things are better kept secret. If he knew, it would cause more trouble."

"You could be right," Phoebe said gravely, "or you could be kidding yourself to avoid a painful conversation."

"I'm not afraid of that," Zoe said, bristling. "You should know me better."

"Fair enough. Sorry."

"It's hard, and I wonder all the time if I'm doing the right thing."

Phoebe cocked her head. "Is there any way he could find out?"

"I doubt it. Steve got married three years ago. He still teaches at Emerson, so I can't believe he told anyone. Other teachers knew he liked me, but we were pretty careful. I can't imagine how Jeremy would find out."

Phoebe raised an eyebrow. "You didn't keep any souvenirs? Nothing in your scrapbook that might tip him off?"

Zoe blushed. "Well, there is something, but it's harmless. It means something to me, but no one else."

Phoebe took a slow sip. "Well, I hope you're right, Zoe. Because if you're not, it could turn your whole world upside down."

62

Jeremy settled back into his chair, having done his duty, but doubting the medicine had gone down. At first, Maddy had tried turning the tables on him, portraying their home as a prison she had to escape. She quickly moved on to school, painting it as pointless and dull, and she finished by passing judgment on the whole adult world as phony, money-grubbing, and mean. Her daily activities annoyed her—classes, homework, and household chores—much as they'd annoyed Jeremy during his teens, but he'd done them nonetheless. Maddy, on the contrary, seemed determined to not raise a finger. And every spare minute was spent hanging out with friends, listening to music, shopping at the mall, flirting with boys, and now, apparently, getting stoned. And who could say what else she was doing, especially with boys, who were drawn to her like a bear to honey. *Sex at 13? Had she already gone that far?*

He'd cut her off and told her story after story about drunks who'd lost their jobs, homes, families, and every ounce of self-respect along the way, leaving a trail of wreckage so long and grisly it barely seemed possible. But even as Maddy listened, her look told him that a deeper eddy was turning under her placid face—a lurid pleasure in the undoing of other people's lives. *She's too young to make the connection between them and her.* For Maddy, the stories were just another movie or TV show—someone else's train wreck, which she could safely watch, mesmerized, from a hill above the tracks.

He tried to explain that most demons started off small, but if fed over time, they turned into life-consuming monsters. And the change was deceptively subtle. You told yourself you were under control, still calling the shots, until one day you found the balance of power had tipped, and the booze, the drugs, the gambling, or whatever your fix happened to be, was now in charge, and when it said *dance*, you danced, no matter how close to the brink you came— even if it piped you straight over the edge.

Zoe had been right. Maddy needed a therapist. They would need all the help they could get to guide her through her teenage years, and they would take it from any quarter that offered—friends, relatives, neighbors, teachers. He knew from his own past the more ropes in the safety net, the greater its strength, and if they all worked together, they could hold Maddy up and cushion the blows of her self-destructive urges until she outgrew them—for he saw, unlike Maddy, that her risk taking was in fact a flirtation with death. Some might call it curiosity or merely a desire to live more fully—but over time it led to habits that pushed you beyond your natural limits, eroding the ground beneath you, clump after clump, until the earth gave way and down you went. And once the process began, it was very hard to stop.

He opened the scrapbook. *Maddy's like Zoe when she was young.* It was eerie how Maddy and Zoe even looked alike at age 13.

Staring at Zoe's pictures, it crossed his mind that he might not know his wife as well as he thought—just as Zoe hadn't really known him until he'd gone through treatment. At some level, there were always secrets you never surrendered. Could it be that Zoe too was leading a secret life, one that he knew absolutely nothing about—or at least had at some point in her past?

His stomach tightened. Maybe he didn't want to know. What could be the point of rocking a boat that was sailing along smoothly, when more than likely there was nothing to find?

He set down the book and tried to watch a TV show on the Hoover Dam, but his mind kept turning back to Zoe. He got up and paced the room. Avoiding the issue was pointless. Even though it filled him with dread, he knew he couldn't focus on anything else until he'd put his doubts to rest.

He reopened the scrapbook. A collage of photos, keepsakes, and handwritten notes fought for his attention. What prompted his wife, someone who'd always lived in the present, to record the past with the care a medieval scribe? Were these scrapbooks holding secrets that she'd kept from him their whole marriage? He'd always marveled how Zoe could shine her light on anyone, even strangers, and make them feel like long-trusted friends. All these years had he simply been naïve, watching her with a doting grin while she flirted with men, foolishly thinking that she saved her love only for him?

He pulled out two more volumes and peeked into the gap. Nothing but dust lined the shelf—except a manila folder, which he pulled out and peered into. It was stuffed with paper slips—receipts for copies, art supplies, and candy, things that Zoe had bought for her students with her own money. She was always buying them things her school couldn't afford, as if *she* could. Muttering to himself, he thumbed through the receipts.

12/22/1996, Craft Warehouse, red foil ribbon: $3.22 . . . 3/17/1998, Kinko's Copies, 35 sets of 10: $21.56 . . . 6/13/1995, Clark's Market, produce: $3.59 . . . July 25, 1995, Clark's Market, produce: $3.59.

He frowned and leafed backward. That was odd. Why so many receipts for Clark's Market? And why such a small amount? You could barely buy a head of broccoli for $3.59. *June 13*—that was five years ago. School would have been out for weeks, and if the bills weren't for school, but for home, why bother to keep them? He shook his head and kept sorting through the pile.

It wasn't long before another caught his eye. *Bloomdale Market, produce: $3.15. Hmmm.* He flipped through the pile more rapidly now, scanning for the telltale *produce* line. He might not be a crime reporter, but he could track a paper trail when the clues were laid out so plainly before him.

A few minutes later, he'd gathered more than 20 receipts—most from Clark's Market, a half dozen from Bloomdale Market, and two from Central Foods. He arranged them by date: *June 6, 8, 15—there's a break for a week—no, there's June 13, then June 20 and 22. Nothing over the Fourth of July, but it starts again on July 11 and keeps on going till the end up summer.*

A peculiar pattern had emerged. At roughly the same hour on two days of every week in the summer of 1995, Zoe had gone to a supermarket and bought a small amount of vegetables—the price of which never exceeded $4.

He bit his lip, opened his web browser, and found a calendar from 1995. A quick glance confirmed his hunch. All the days were Tuesdays or Thursdays. What the hell was so special about those two days? The mystery was getting deeper.

Tuesdays and Thursdays. Wait a minute—those were the days of Zoe's class. He was sure of it. Was the timing just a coincidence or was there a link between the receipts and the class?

But what could they possibly have in common? Had she stopped for breakfast every morning on her way to her class? But veggies for breakfast didn't make any sense.

Produce. Of course. It could be fruit.

He blushed. What a jerk he'd been for being so mistrustful. Getting upset over an apple or a bunch of grapes for breakfast every morning before she dropped the kids off at her mother's.

But why keep the receipts in her scrapbook? His brow furrowed. He typed Clark's Market into the search bar and printed the result. He did the same for Bloomdale Market and Central Foods. Last of all, he printed out and plotted all three addresses on a single map. All were a half-dozen blocks from each other, but strangely, not one was near their house, his mother-in-law's house, or the school where Zoe had taken her class. Instead, they were all near the high school where Zoe taught English.

A troubling thought bored into his brain. After he'd gotten back from treatment, Zoe had mysteriously quit eating grapes, strawberries and many other fruits, claiming the acid upset her stomach, which seemed odd for a person who'd always loved fruit and had never been bothered by it before.

He smiled wistfully. In fact, Zoe even linked fruit with sex. On their honeymoon in Mazatlan, she'd put strawberries on her breasts for him to nibble off and wedged a bunch of grapes down between her ... He froze, horrified. All of a sudden everything made sense—mind-numbing, stomach-turning sense. Every Tuesday and Thursday morning throughout the summer of 1995, instead of going to class, Zoe had dropped off the kids at her mother's house, stopped at Clark's Market for strawberries, driven to a spot near the high school, and gorged herself not only on fruit, but on sex with another man.

63

He parked in the front lot of Emerson High and stared at the double-glass doors. It was two o'clock, a sunny day in the middle of June. He was hoping to find few, in any, teachers in the building. It was summer, after all, and they should be working second jobs or enjoying their time off. Judging by the near-empty lot and the quiet doors, he was in luck.

He climbed out of his Taurus and approached the school. *Calm down. There's no reason to be nervous. Pretend you're here on business.* His light-blue oxford and khaki pants fit the mold perfectly. He could easily pass for a teacher or a parent volunteer.

Here we go.

He pulled on the door handle. It was unlocked. *First hurdle cleared.* Ahead to his left, behind a glass wall, a middle-aged woman sat talking on the phone. She didn't look up. He smiled and kept on going. *Second hurdle cleared.*

The hallway ahead was empty. The terrazzo floor smelled like ammonia, freshly mopped. He padded down it like a ghost, trying to walk naturally while not making a sound. It wasn't easy, but so far, he was pulling it off.

"May I help you?"

He swallowed and turned around. The secretary was peering at him with a pleasant but curious face.

"Hi, I'm Zoe Edward's husband. She asked me to pick something up."

"Sorry, we're supposed to check everybody in."

"No, it's my fault."

"That's okay. As long as I know you're here."

"Thanks. I'm kind of in a hurry."

"Let me know if I can help," she said obligingly. "And tell Zoe that Nora said, *Hi.*"

"I will. Thanks." He turned and slunk away. *Damn. How are you going to explain that? Never mind. You'll think of something.*

He clipped down the hall and turned into a long, open room divided by two rows of cubicles. Despite the humming in the vents, the hot, stale air smelled like a bus depot. He walked down the center aisle. In the second cube, a man with bifocals and ruffled hair chugged away on an IBM Selectric. He didn't look up when Jeremy passed.

He found Zoe's cube, the last on the right, ducked inside, and eased into the chair. He was invisible now—unless the owner of the cube across the aisle appeared.

He scanned the shelves where Zoe's gradebooks stood in neat rows. He pulled one out. The cover was clearly marked: *English 220. American Lit. Fall, 1997.*

He shoved it back in and pulled out a second, *1995.*

Ah—there it is.

Inside the book, Zoe's fluid pen filled row after row with student's names and grades, and her scribbled notes purled around the margins. Despite the occasional smudge or crossed-out word, the books had an order and even a beauty that he admired. He knew that Zoe took her job seriously, but he rarely saw it firsthand, as he did now, noting how organized she was. *Good. Organized means easy to find.*

The Selectric stopped chugging and the typist coughed. Jeremy froze. After a few seconds, the chugging resumed.

He began to leaf gently through the gradebook. A dozen pages in, a title caught his eye, *Comparative Studies: Hist. Context of Early American Lit. Z. Edwards / S. Roberts.*

S would be for Steve. Jeremy had met Steve at Spirit Night four years ago and recalled Zoe saying that all the girls in her class had crushes on him. Lean, blond, sensitive—he fit Zoe's type. If he were a woman looking to fuck somebody in this crummy old building, he would have picked Steve Roberts too.

But the gradebook gave up no secrets—only students' names and columns of capital letters crowned with dashed-off pluses and minuses.

He reshelved the book and glanced around. He opened the folders lying on the desk, rifled through the papers, and skimmed the handouts. Nothing but the normal office clutter. And why shouldn't there be? If Zoe had kept something damning, she would have tucked it away where nobody would think to check.

He eased open a file drawer and read the tabs: Romantic Poetry, Naturalism, 25 Writing Tips. *Why 25? Why not 50 or 100? Nothing here.* He put his hand behind the bank of files and pulled it forward. The space in back was empty except for a pencil with a broken point.

He pulled out another drawer and flipped through the tabs. *There it was again—Hist. Context of Early American Lit.*

It held 20 or 30 sheets of paper. He set the folder on the desk and paged through them. Syllabi, assignments, bibliographies, a few notes in Zoe's hand—and some, apparently, in Steve's: *"Got your point." "Great source." "Try to include."* He ignored the print and focused on the notes. Could a person tell, he wondered, if a man was fucking his wife based on his penmanship?

He unfolded a Post-it note.

Four o'clock?

C U there.

His shoulders tensed. What did he mean by *C U there?* Could this be the smoking gun?

Not likely. It might only refer to a meeting they were both invited to.

Still, he folded the note and stuffed it in his shirt pocket.

A bottom drawer likewise turned up nothing. But even this lone discovery and the mere hint of deceit had rattled him. His heart was beating faster now, and sweat was pooling under his arms. He caught himself sighing loudly. It had just occurred to him that if Zoe had kept a file containing Steve's notes, then Steve must have a file containing Zoe's, and if he put the two of them together, he just might find what he was looking for.

It would be risky, but he knew he'd never rest until he learned the truth. There was no stopping now. He would need to dig through Steve's office too.

He picked up an empty folder. As a reporter, he'd often had to bluff his way past receptionists and security guards, and he'd learned the key was a vague but plausible story and a friendly smile, as if you had every right to be there.

He went back to the cube where the man with ruffled hair was typing. "Excuse me," he said, holding up the folder. "I have to leave something for Steve Roberts. Do you know where I can find his office?"

The man squinted at him over his bifocals. "Sure. Follow me."

"I didn't mean to interrupt. Do you know the room?"

He settled back in his chair. "It's 228. Take a left out the door and go straight down the hall."

The man paused, and Jeremy could feel the coming, fatal question, so he smiled and turned away. "Got it. Thanks."

The hall was clear. His heart was pounding, and a bead of sweat trickled down his ribs. He could explain his poking around in Zoe's office, but getting caught in Steve's would pose a much greater challenge.

Room 228 appeared on the left. He glanced over his shoulder. *No one there.* He opened the door into a dark room and flipped on the switch. The fluorescent tubes flickered and lit up a small room with four cubes, none of them marked. He stole by each one, scanning for names. On a shelf in the last cube stood a photo of Steve, shirtless, dressed in low-slung cargo pants, canoeing in the Boundary Waters, with the armor-plated build of a young, athletic man.

He sat down and thumbed through a stack of papers, each one sticking on his sweaty fingertips. He was careful to put them back in the exact same order. Next, he rummaged through the desk drawers, filled with pens, rubber bands, and paper clips. Failing there, he opened the file drawers, flipped back the folders one by one, drawer after drawer—and suddenly there it was: a tab marked *Hist + Eng.* in Steve's scrawling hand.

He laid the open folder on the desk. *The hell with the printouts. Look for notes—and fast. Somebody could barge in any second.* He turned over page after page of crowded type. Unlike Zoe, Steve hadn't written any notes in the margins.

Before long, he was staring at the final page. *Dead end. All this sneaking around for nothing. Will I ever look like a jerk if I get caught now.* He turned over the final page. Before him lay a small folded note. He picked it up gingerly. It was flattened, smudged, and fingerprinted, as if it had been opened and closed back up countless times.

He peeled back the folds and pressed it flat on the desk. Four handwritten lines, two in blue, two in black, screamed up at him, making it clear why Steve had come back to read the note time and again. It was a keepsake, just like Zoe's receipts for the fruit. The smoking gun. The damning, undeniable truth. The meaning behind his dream. A bead of sweat dripped off his brow and blotted the paper. The simple words broke his back and stopped his heart. They leered up at him like the barrel of a loaded gun, and staring back at them, he could almost hear the trigger click.

C U in 10?

2 long 4 me

C U in 5?

So wet 4 U

64

A crescent moon climbed over the lake and lit the water with a blinding white fire, as if a billion pearls were bouncing on the surface. At Zoe's feet, the waves beat softly on the sand, churning up foam from the pitch-black water. It reminded her of a cherished line from Keats's "Ode to a Nightingale," *Charmed magic casements, opening on the foam of perilous seas in faery lands forlorn.*

Sixteen years ago, she and Jeremy had walked this same beach while visiting Phoebe in Putnam. In all that time, it seemed that not a bush, tree, or inch of beach had changed. Now, just like then, it was impossible not to relax here. She drank in the green air, the dancing shadows, the lapping waves, and the twirling cottonwood leaves, feeling like a child who'd never seen the moon and stars before or marveled at the alien majesty of the night.

On this trip, she walked the beach not with Jeremy—who was up in Delmar covering a story—but with her 10-year-old son, Marty.

Although he moved gracefully, Marty's legs swam in his shorts like a pair of stilts, and his long puppet-like arms hung by his sides. He stood a head shorter than Zoe, with sandy bangs, large blue eyes, a turned-up nose, and a tiny mouth. To Zoe, this fragile boy was precious far beyond the normal motherly bond. Without a second's pause, she would have filled her pockets with stones and plunged to the bottom of the lake to rescue him or thrown herself before a speeding car, if she thought her sacrifice could save him.

Tonight, under cover of darkness, he let Zoe wrap her arm around his waist. The last year, he'd begun to avoid her touch, at least around his friends. So far, it really hadn't bothered her—his budding attempts at manhood, while tender and comic, made her proud, and she knew by his response at home that he still enjoyed her motherly hugs.

"How does it work?" he asked in his clear, high voice.

"It's pretty simple. They cut a vein and push a tube up into your heart. The plug—it looks like a little cocoon—goes up the tube, spreads its wings like a butterfly, and covers the hole. After a while, the muscle grows over the wings, and guess what? You're good as new."

"It stays in me?"

"It's made from a special metal that won't hurt your body. You won't even know it's there."

"What do you mean by *good as new?*"

"I mean *good as new*—like the hole was never there."

"You mean I can play soccer?"

Of course he meant competitive soccer, which she didn't know about, but right now, it didn't seem to matter. "I'll bet you could bend it like Beckham."

"Nate could teach me that."

"He could teach you a lot."

"Could I skateboard?"

"If you're careful."

"Play baseball? Swim? All that stuff?"

It was funny, Zoe thought, how we all longed for things we couldn't do and took for granted the things we could. Nate would have given his pitching arm to play the guitar or draw like Marty, while Marty, who couldn't climb the stairs without getting winded, only dreamed of being a popular jock like his cousin. "You could run a marathon if you wanted to."

"I can't believe it, Mom."

" I meant it when I said *good as new*."

"That would be a miracle."

"I've been waiting for a long time. But don't get too impatient—we might have to wait another year."

"Why so long?"

"It still needs to be approved. And other kids need it more than you. We'll have to wait for them.

He nodded slowly. "That's okay."

"There's a chance it won't work, Marty, but it's small, compared to the operation. And they'll still have to put you under."

"I'm not afraid, Mom," he said firmly. "I wasn't afraid of the operation."

"Well, I couldn't take that—stopping your heart and cutting—ugh, it makes me shiver just to think about it. I knew sooner or later that something better would come along, and now it has, so we don't have to risk it. I know a five percent chance of failure doesn't sound like much—"

"Dad said two."

"Two to five. What counts is what *failure* means. It means—" She couldn't say the word.

"It means dying."

"It could."

"I'm not gonna die, Mom."

She crushed him against her chest. "No, you're going to be strong and healthy, just like Nate." She sighed and wiped a tear. "We're lucky it happened now, before you had your growth spurt."

He pulled away. She'd overstepped her bounds. "Mom, don't get all emo on me."

"Okay," she said, smiling, "but your mom's kind of an emo chick."

"Mom—stop it."

A pair of amber lights swept across the beach. Zoe turned and her smile vanished. A strange car was creeping down the road toward their cabin. "All right. We'd better get back and see what Maddy's doing."

65

The lights went dark, but her daughter's voice, carried by the wind, helped Zoe see Maddy's silhouette standing beside the car. Earlier that day, two boys had talked with Maddy as she sunned on the beach in her blue bikini—skimpy enough, Zoe thought, to attract every male in sight who wasn't wheelchair-bound. She'd watched the boys guardedly from the cabin window. Both were much too old for Maddy. They stayed for half an hour, and she was glad when they left and didn't come back—but seeing the car by the cabin now, she guessed they had.

She crossed the gravel road and peered into the window of a red Lexus. The green glow of the dashboard lit the boys' faces. She pegged them as high-school juniors or seniors. They looked back at her warily, as though being sniffed by a German shepherd.

"Hi, guys, what's going on?"

"Just talkin'," said the driver.

"Did you want something, Mom?" Maddy cut in.

Zoe ignored her. "Do you live around here?"

"We live in Fargo," said the other boy.

"You drove down here from Fargo?"

"Everybody does. My parents have a cabin on Beaver Tail."

"Then you're down here with your parents?"

There was an awkward pause. The driver said *yes* at the same time his friend said *no*.

Zoe shook her head. "She's 13, guys. How old are you?"

"Really?" said the driver.

"And she's not going with you."

"Dammit, Mom!" Maddy spun around and stomped into the cabin.

"Good night, guys. Don't bother coming back."

The driver popped the car in reverse.

Zoe crossed her arms and watched the taillights float down the road and disappear through the trees.

In no time, her talk with Maddy turned into a shouting match. Maddy denied planning to leave with the boys and claimed that Zoe had embarrassed her in front of them. Zoe didn't believe her, but didn't want to accuse her of lying, so instead she lectured Maddy about getting into cars with strangers— they might be drunk and drive off the road or take her where she was defenseless. Maddy listened in stony silence and then stormed into her bedroom, slamming the door behind her. Seconds later, the music blasted under the door and shook the panels like subwoofers.

Zoe pushed open the door, and in seconds the shouting started.

Afraid of alarming the neighbors, Zoe left Maddy in her room and went outside. She'd let her blow off steam for a while, find Marty, who'd wandered off when the fighting began, and then go back and confiscate the CD player. Luckily, the bedroom door didn't have a lock.

Parenthood never gave you a minute's rest, she thought with a shake of her head. Any calm spots were few and far between—and broken without any warning, like a thunderbolt from a clear blue sky.

She rubbed the back of her neck and tried to relax. The night still breathed with beauty, but the shadows seemed less friendly now, the lake colder and deeper and more apt to pull a careless swimmer down under the waves. Before long, a bank of clouds would drift across and blot out the moon.

What bothered Zoe was not so much this night, but the long, hard road that lay ahead. If Maddy was already telling lies and trying to run off with older boys, what did the future have in store? She not only worried about Maddy, but how she would handle the chaos herself. She had a fairly good idea of what to expect from watching the troubled girls at her school, and she didn't like what she saw. She'd always felt sorry for the parents of those girls, and here she was, becoming one of them.

And if she didn't feel up to the task, what about Jeremy? How would he cope? It wouldn't make staying sober any easier, that was certain.

As she walked along the beach, she felt fragile. Tonight her entire family seemed fragile: Maddy was playing with drugs and maybe sex, Marty's health was still frail, and Jeremy, while soldiering on, could hardly be called happy. No matter how he tried, he couldn't relax, and his moods, even at their best, had a brittle feel, and she lived in fear that sooner or later some crisis would make him crack, and he'd fall off the wagon a second, and possibly final, time.

And if that ever happened, she had no idea what she would do.

She loved them all so dearly and wanted so badly to shield them from every danger in the world, including themselves, which often proved to be the worst danger of all. She would go to any length to help them, without tiring or complaining, even when she felt weak herself or unsure of how to press onward. She would lay down her life for them, if need be, as any good mother would, but as she wandered through the dark looking for Marty, she worried that even this sacrifice might not be enough, because tonight, for some strange reason, the outcomes of their lives no longer seemed to be, and maybe never had been, within her control.

66

Zoe popped the trunk and barked at Maddy and Marty, who were climbing the steps, empty handed, leaving all the unpacking to their mother.

"I won't unlock that door until this car is empty!"

Her voice cracked as she lectured her kids. Sitting in the car for the last three hours had cramped her legs and fogged her brain. Near the city, traffic had backed up, and Maddy and Marty had begun to squabble—something they almost never did. But all that paled in comparison to coming home and finding the house dark and Jeremy's car nowhere in sight. It was nine o'clock. Where in the hell was he? He could have run out to buy a pizza, she thought, but it worried her that she hadn't heard a peep from him since Friday. He'd neither answered his cell phone nor returned her four voicemails. True, he wasn't always the best at checking in, but he should have been here hours ago—with a ready explanation for the break in his calls.

She forced Maddy and Marty to clean up the Coke cans, chip bags, and candy wrappers in the car before bringing in their suitcases. Marty tried lugging them up the staircase himself, but quickly ran out of breath and sat puffing halfway up, at which point Maddy, until now unwilling to help, hauled up bags and scolded him like an overprotective mother.

In the meantime, Zoe went to her room and paged through her address book. She quickly found the number she wanted.

Ansel picked up on the ninth ring.

"I'm sorry to call so late, Ansel, but I'm worried about Jeremy. We just got home, and he's still not back. Has he called you?"

The line was silent.

"Didn't he finish up today?"

"I don't understand, Zoe. Why would he call me?"

"About the story. In Delmar."

There was a long pause. Ansel cleared his throat. "I don't know about a story in Delmar. Jeremy told me he was going to a cabin with you and the kids."

For a second, her breathing stopped. She clenched the receiver, paralyzed. She felt like hanging up the phone and crawling under the bed.

"Somebody else might have sent him. I don't know everything that happens in the newsroom, although I should."

"Can you check for me?"

If Ansel hadn't already guessed her fear, he could sense it in her voice. "Don't panic, Zoe. I'll call around. Have you tried the highway patrol?"

Why would I call the highway patrol when I know where he is? "No, I haven't."

"You'd better call them, just in case. I'll let you know what I find out. Don't jump to conclusions. Just sit tight, okay?"

She nodded her head but didn't reply.

"Are you still there?"

She hung up. What Ansel did no longer mattered. He couldn't help her.

She paced the floor, rapped furiously on the dresser, and rushed into the hall. "Don't unpack your bags!" she yelled up the stairs. "Bring them back down."

Maddy's voice floated down the steps. "Mom, are you crazy?"

"You'd better hope so," she answered.

Barreling down the freeway, she hardly spoke to her baffled kids, refusing to say where they were going, or why. When they took the exit to Orchard Valley, Maddy frowned and caught Zoe's eyes in the rearview mirror. "Mom, is Dad in trouble?"

She couldn't bring herself to answer, especially with Marty in the car. "We'll see. I'll be out late. Tonight you'll stay with Phoebe and Jake."

As they pulled into the driveway, the front door opened, and Phoebe walked out to greet them, followed by Nate in his long pajamas. He swept his blond hair off his tanned face and without even saying hello began telling Marty about his new video game.

Maddy rolled her eyes and sulked by the car.

"Nate, help them carry their bags," Phoebe said.

Eager to help, he lifted them both from the hatchback and carried them inside.

The two sisters waited as Marty and Maddy followed Nate in.

"I called the highway patrol," Phoebe said. "No accidents—unless he came down the Wisconsin side."

Zoe shook her head. "He never goes that way."

"What do you think he's up to?"

"I'm expecting the worst."

"Suppose you're right. What are you going to do?"

"I don't know. One step at a time."

"Do you want me to come along?"

"No, you're doing too much already."

"Not really. Nate loves having Marty over."

"I need some time to think. Wish me luck."

Phoebe tried to hug her, but Zoe backed away. She didn't want her to know that she was trembling.

The drive went by like a fever dream. Once Zoe passed the outer suburbs, the pines formed coal-black curtains on either side of the road. Above their black spires, a few stars flickered. It was after eleven, and both lanes of the interstate were empty. Now and then, a pair of lights blazed in her rear-view mirror and made her tip it down, but otherwise, the car seemed to drive itself. She tried to rein in her scattered thoughts, but as she drove, mile after mile, no decision, no plan emerged, only a mounting sense of dread, as if the engines on her plane had failed and she was gliding down through the rushing air, waiting for impact. Much later, when she thought about the trip, she couldn't recall a minute, not one billboard or town or even if she stopped along the way, as if the entire memory had been erased from her mind.

She reached the Harbor Lights Hotel at two a.m. A grid of streetlamps cast a sulfur glow on the parking lot. She circled the parked cars, found Jeremy's Taurus, and pulled in beside it. As she stepped into the hot, damp air, the streetlamps buzzed like cicadas, and somewhere in the sky, a nighthawk shrieked and boomed.

She crossed the lot, opened the glass door, and approached the front desk. Red exit lights shone in the dim, vacant lobby. Behind the counter, a man with silver hair gazed into a computer screen.

She folded her hands on the counter. "I'm sorry to bother you, but I forgot my key, and my husband is still out. Can I get a spare?"

The man looked her over and perked up. She smiled coyly.

"Not a problem. What's your room number?"

"You're going to think I'm stupid, but I can't remember." She reached into her purse, opened her wallet, and pulled out her license. "My husband booked the room, Jeremy Edwards."

He glanced at her license. "No need for that," he said, waving it off. "Give me one second."

He clicked through a few screens and tapped the keys. Zoe kept silent, afraid of tripping herself up.

"You're in 215."

"That's it. Thank you so much."

He typed some numbers into a console and swiped a fresh card.

"There you go, Ms. Edwards. Have a good night."

She trotted up the stairs to the second floor and followed the numbered arrows. When she found room 215, she paused and glanced up and down the hall, hoping that nobody would come around the corner and force her to open the door. The hall was brightly lit, the wallpaper patterned with climbing vines, the carpet plush and clean. It didn't strike her as the kind of place for a marriage to end. Well, what kind of place did—a roadside motel or a trailer court? It felt surreal standing here on one side of the door, knowing that what lay behind it could shatter her life. In this frozen minute, the universe was still well ordered, the present familiar and safe; but the second she crossed that threshold, the order and light of her world could go screaming into a black hole. And once she took that step, she could never go back. The weight of the moment held her there in front of the door, swaying, unable to make that one final step.

Around the corner came the jingle of keys and a woman's voice. That was it. She swiped the card. The red dot turned green. She pushed the door open into a dark tomb. With her heart pounding in her ears, she slipped inside and shut the door behind her. No sooner had it clicked than someone in the darkness stirred.

67

The smell of Vodka filled the room like a fuel-air bomb, ready for a match to blow it to a million pieces. The smell triggered scores of bad memories in Zoe's mind and flooded her stomach with acid. She didn't even need to see him. The smell told her everything. In spite of believing the worst the whole length of her drive, now that her nightmare was no longer a possibility, but a certainty, it seemed beyond belief.

"Is someone there?" said a raspy voice.

She fumbled for the light switch. The sudden glare made her squint, but the effect was stronger on Jeremy.

He lay in bed, naked, with a sheet coiled like a serpent around his waist. His body looked fit, but his face belonged to a corpse—white as chalk, puffy, cold, and his jaw hung slack as if broken. Worse to see were his eyes—bloodshot and dazed, then disbelieving, then panicking like a spooked horse, and finally, as he took in the meaning of her arrival, they went dead. He gazed at the floor dully as though cut loose from everything in the world that mattered to him, drifting without hope in the emptiness of space. "Fuck," was all he said.

She stepped into the room. Five bottles of vodka, three empty, one a few inches full, stood on the desk beside a pile of newspapers, copies of Playboy and Hustler, and an open pizza box with a few shriveled slices. His clothes were strewn across the floor, but otherwise the room was empty. Nothing was overturned or broken, and, at least for now, he was alone.

Not that it really mattered.

"What time is it?" he groaned.

She felt back in control now—not calm—inside she was trembling, her heart was breaking, and she wondered how she would find the courage to get through the months ahead, but she understood fully what the moment demanded of her. Seeing Jeremy half dead while being flooded with all the sad, disturbing memories of his drinking made her course of action clear. There was only one thing to be done. And now she only had to do it.

She sat on the bed. The hope in his eyes was painful to watch. She took his hand, kissed it tenderly, and let it drop.

"Jeremy, I'm sorry you're drinking again. I hope you can quit, for your sake, and for our kids' sake."

She wanted to say, 'I love you,' but thought it would give him false hope, and she pressed on. "There's no point in coming home. If you do, I'll take the kids and move out."

She could hardly believe her own words, even though she'd meant them. There was no ambiguity in her voice, and Jeremy could see the resolve in her eyes.

"Jesus—you can't mean that."

"I do mean it. I cannot, I *will not* go through this again. Twice was hard enough—it was hell, Jeremy, and I won't do it again, not at this point in my life. When I get home, I'm filing for divorce."

"That's crazy."

"No, *this* is crazy."

"I'll quit," he pleaded. "I quit before, and I can—"

"Good. Quit again. But this time you'll have to do it yourself."

"What about the kids?"

"Frankly, the kids are better off with no father than a drunken father."

Her words hit their mark like a well-cast harpoon. There was no argument he could summon against them. He could see that her mind was made up, and nothing he said or did would change it. His chest heaved, and he sobbed like a child. "I'm sorry," he said over and over.

His tears moved her. She fought back her own. "Why did you do it, Jeremy? We've had four good years, haven't we?"

Strangely, her question steeled him. His jaw stiffened, and his eyes shrank to leering points. The sudden change frightened her. In all their years together, she'd never felt any fear of him, but now she did.

He threw back the covers.

She jumped to her feet and backed away, but Jeremy strode past her, naked, and made for the desk. He rifled through the papers and swept them onto the floor. A few pages floated down like mangled parachutes. He froze, picked up a small slip, lunged at Zoe, and thrust it in front of her face.

She took it in with a flick of her eyes.

C U in 10?

2 long 4 me

C U in 5?

So wet 4 U

The idiot. He kept it. He couldn't throw it away.

Then she thought of the keepsakes she'd kept herself—his key, a faded T-shirt, the receipts. *Had he found those too?*

She stared at him, tears streaking her face, overcome with shame. He glared back with hurt, resentful eyes. In that moment, they saw each other perfectly, like pebbles at the bottom of a glacial lake. All the lies were stripped away, but what they saw was that both were guilty. Yet the epiphany changed nothing. They both also knew it was over.

"I'm sorry, Jeremy," she said through her tears. "I wish I hadn't done it, but I can't change it now. It was just because I was so incredibly lonely, and I felt trapped. You never knew how bad it was for me. It wasn't really about the sex—I needed someone to care about me when you couldn't, and I thought you never would again."

He seemed not to hear her words. "How many others were there?"

"No one else—I swear. Only him."

He grimaced. "I don't believe you."

She stared at the carpet, humiliated. "I can't blame you, but all the same, it's true."

"How do you pull it off?" he asked cynically. "Such a busy woman, a full-time teacher, a mother, a social butterfly."

"It was only *one* summer. And you were *never* there. Even when you were, you weren't there."

"I was never jealous," he shot back, "even when you flirted with other men. I always thought it didn't matter—you were always going home with me."

Zoe covered her eyes. "I'm sorry for what I did. I'm sorry I lied to you. I was afraid that if I told you, you'd start drinking again."

"Then why can't we change?" he begged her. "I'll stop drinking. I can forgive you, if you can forgive me this *one* weekend. We can start over again—together."

His promise and tearful plea made her waver. He made it sound so natural, so easy to wipe the slate clean, but it was the easy part that bothered her. It had been easier to put up with his drinking than leave, easier to have the affair than ask for help, easier to cover up the affair than confess, and so by now she'd grown wary of anything that smacked of *easy*. In fact, just the opposite was true—staying together would be incredibly hard. From this point on, everything they said or did would be tainted by the past, with accusations hiding under every breath. Each felt so betrayed by the other that trust was no longer possible, and without trust, any attempt to reconcile was doomed.

"It's too late," she said flatly. "I'm sorry, Jeremy. I wish you all the luck in the world. And you'd better wish me luck too. I'm going to need it."

Afraid that his begging would make her buckle, she turned, walked out the door, and closed it behind herself with a final, disconcerting click.

68

The divorce was straightforward and fast. Straightforward, because both Jeremy and Zoe felt guilty, which held back their urges to punish each other and helped them negotiate in a civilized way. Fast because both got what they wanted. Jeremy wanted just two things—his 401K and Zoe's promise that she wouldn't tell a soul about his drinking, especially Ansel, knowing that if he knew, he'd be fired on the spot. Zoe, for her part, wanted the house and custody of the kids. Jeremy conceded both, but insisted on open visitation rights and custody every other weekend. He also promised not to tell anyone about Zoe's affair, and in return, she kept her demands for child support reasonable. All in all, things were handled fairly and without much arguing or finger pointing.

Maddy and Marty, on the other hand, didn't find the break so clean. Outwardly, Maddy acted nonchalant, telling her friends the divorce hadn't surprised her, but inwardly it shocked and angered her. As the custodial parent, Zoe bore the brunt of that anger, mainly because she presented the most convenient target. Among the many accusations that Maddy leveled against Zoe was that of nagging her father into falling off the wagon.

Marty took the divorce even harder. For him, it had come without the slightest warning. When Zoe told him that his father was moving out, he thought she was joking. Just five years old when Jeremy had last gone through treatment, he could only remember him as a sober and responsible dad. She might as well have said that Jeremy had grown a tail and wings and begun to belch out fire—although his idealized image of his father quickly faded as he watched him drink himself into a stupor every other weekend. It didn't take long before he took refuge in his room, where he read graphic novels, played video games, or drew pictures of giant monsters crushing buildings beneath their feet.

Moreover, the financial fallout of his parents' divorce had ended all discussion of his surgery. Up until now, Marty's health had always been the family's top priority, but suddenly no one seemed to pay him much attention. Everybody was too busy dealing with a host of daunting new problems—driving schedules, battles over belongings, legal matters, and bills that neither parent could pay—which subtly but unmistakably signaled to Marty that his own health and happiness were no longer so important.

Most of all, Zoe worried about money. Keeping quiet about Jeremy's drinking was easy, as she lived in fear that sooner or later Ansel would figure it out for himself and fire Jeremy, and then where would they be? She simply had to have the child support from his salary. It was hard enough to pay the mortgage and keep everybody clothed and fed, and she didn't know how they'd survive on one salary alone. Near the end of summer, she applied for a new job at Huntington High, a suburban school with a stellar reputation and better pay, but she had to compete against hundreds of other teachers, so she wasn't holding out much hope.

Going back to Emerson High in the fall, she found that her confidence had plunged. It became much harder to engage her students. She made mistakes, got flustered or defensive, and on her worst days barely fumbled through her lesson plans. Her students saw her weakness and rather than feeling sorry for her, took advantage of it, and for the first time in her life she fought to control her classrooms. At night, she dragged herself home, exhausted, cooked a quick meal, drove Maddy and Marty to games or friends, and chipped away at the mountain of laundry, mail, and other chores piling up around the house. Some nights, she simply gave in and sat before the TV, watching movies and stuffing herself with corn chips, ice cream, or M&M's.

Phoebe watched her sister's behavior with growing concern. She offered what encouragement she could, hoping the passage of time would heal Zoe's wounds, but autumn was over, Thanksgiving was just around the corner, and Zoe was getting worse, not better. Hoping to pull Zoe out of her spiral, Phoebe invited her family to Thanksgiving dinner, and after dessert, as they loaded the dishwasher, unveiled her plan.

"You need a break, sis. A vacation would do you wonders."

Zoe wiped the serving platter with a dishtowel. "Like that will happen. I can barely afford to buy groceries."

"I know. That's why I'm taking you to Mexico."

Zoe stared at her, dumbstruck. "You are not."

"I am, and I'm paying for it too—hotel, plane tickets, meals, everything."

"No, no, no—you can't do that. God, Phoebe, what am I, a charity case?"

"Of course not, but you've been through so much, you deserve it. I already booked our flights. We go the day after Christmas—it's a quickie—four nights and five days. I was hoping for Greece, but I couldn't make it work. And Cancun will be great. We'll lie on the beach, drink margaritas, watch the college boys—"

Zoe shook her head. "I can't leave Maddy and Marty, not now."

"They can stay with Jake. He said he'd be happy to watch them."

Zoe winced. "I can't let you, Phoebe. It's incredibly kind, but no."

Phoebe took away the platter and set it on the counter. "I won't take no for an answer. I have tickets and reservations, and you're getting on that plane with me if I have to drag you by the hair."

Phoebe's persistence wore Zoe down, and one month later, on the day after Christmas, when the temperature in the Twin Cities dropped to minus 14, the two sisters touched down at Cancun International Airport. As they climbed down the boarding ramp, the tropical air sponged their bare arms and legs, and before they crossed the tarmac, their upper lips were sweating. Eager to hit the beach, they took a taxi down a never-ending isthmus where hotels brimmed with red cabanas, azure pools, palm trees tall as wind turbines, and planters bursting with agave, poinsettias, Mexican sunflowers, and dahlias.

An hour later, they were melting into lounge chairs and sipping margaritas while gazing at the patina-colored waters of the Caribbean. Observing her sister's starry-eyed grin, Phoebe remembered that Zoe could never be in a bad mood near water. And, in fact, as the tequila oozed into Zoe's brain and the tanning oil sizzled on her skin, her worries lifted, and for the first time in many, many months, she was able to relax and enjoy herself again.

While Cancun was not the vacation spot she would have chosen herself—it was too young, crowded, and geared toward drinking and hooking up—with each passing day she found herself sinking more deeply, as if sitting on a soft pillow, into the mañana mood around her. She and Phoebe swam, baked in the sun, read trashy novels, and ate or drank whatever they pleased. When they got tired of lying around, they snorkeled through the canyons of staghorn coral off Isla Mujeres and took a bus to the ruins of Chichen Itza and climbed the 91 steps of El Castillo. But the best moments of the trip were the heart-to-hearts they had over meals, on the beach, or back in their room, spending long hours talking and laughing on the same bed, as they had so many nights while growing up.

The night before their flight home, they dined on the rooftop of a two-story building. As the sun dropped through the flaming clouds and a crescent moon rose above them, they sipped piña coladas and talked for hours about growing up in their old house, their parents, their kids, the men they'd loved, their hopes and dreams, and the joys and letdowns of the last 40 years, basking in the knowledge that no matter where life took them, they would always share a common past with so many vivid memories that just the mention of a place or name could make them sigh out loud or break out laughing—and then retell an old, familiar story, just for the pleasure of hearing it again.

At the end of the night, Zoe thanked her sister for the trip and vowed to pay her back.

"No—you did *me* a favor," Phoebe said. "I had the best time. We should do this every year."

Zoe fell silent. As good as it sounded, she knew it would never happen.

Phoebe read her thoughts. "And someday we're going to Greece."

"If it was meant to be, I'd have gone by now. We planned to go on our honeymoon, but it fell through. Then we had Maddy, and then Marty with all his troubles. After that—" Zoe shook her head. "Now it's too late."

Phoebe squeezed her hand. "You'll make it there someday. Remember what you said? You'd dance in the Parthenon, skinny-dip in the sea, and sleep with the waiters—"

"I did not—I said *kiss.*"

"Well, you could sleep with them now, if you wanted to."

"Right. That guy I danced with last night dropped me like a bad pass."

"A year from now you'll be a different person. You'll see."

"Better or worse?"

"Jeez, you've gotten cynical. It's not like you."

"Strange, you saying that to me."

"You're right. We've switched."

Zoe smiled sadly. "Remember the fight we had after you got engaged? You bet me that you would be happier. Back then, I thought you were throwing your life away, but the truth was, I was throwing mine away. I think you won the bet, Phoebe."

"Don't ever say that again. Do you know how many times I've regretted that?"

"You were right to be angry. I was wrong about Jake, and you were right about Jeremy."

"No one can predict how a person will turn out. I took a chance on Jake too."

"Well, your chance paid off. Mine didn't."

"Will you stop it? You've hit a rough patch, that's all. You'll find someone new. And you'll get that new teaching job. Things will get better. I know they will."

Zoe smiled as if she agreed, but knowing that tomorrow she would board her plane and fly back to her broken family and the ice-covered streets of Minnesota, she felt nothing but dread. The next year would be hard, she knew, harder than any she'd faced before, and getting through it would call for every ounce of her courage and strength. The months and years to come, she felt in the pit of her stomach, far from getting easier, were going to give her the fight of her life.

On the flight home, while Phoebe dozed, she stared down at the snowy fields of Wisconsin and prayed: *Please, God, help me to keep my family in one piece. Help me to fight every day for my kids. Help me to keep my daughter safe. Maddy still needs me, even if she doesn't know it. Don't let her push me away. And help me lift Marty up. Help me stop his hurting, bring him out of his shell, and find a way to get his operation. Help me to land that new job. I need it so badly, and I know that I can do it well. There's no other way but forward. I won't make it treading water, just trying to keep afloat—it's the same as drowning, only slower. So help me to keep moving forward. Stay beside me and make me strong. Somewhere along the way, I've lost my strength, and I don't know how to get it back again. I'm tired, I'm lonely, and I'm scared for my children. Don't let me give up on them, never let me give up. I'm the only thing between them and the wolves at the door, and I can never let down my guard, not for a second, and leave them exposed.*

69

Phoebe's house, nearly twice the size of Zoe's, had ample room for all three kids. In the basement, Marty and Nate pulled out the sleeper and created a command center, surrounded by the widescreen TV, video-game consoles, and foosball and Ping Pong tables. The two boys spent hours blasting foosballs into the goalie's box and slamming Ping-Pong balls across the room. One day, two of Nate's friends dropped by, and they spent five hours blowing up zombies on the widescreen TV. Watching the rowdy gang, Jake had to smile. Marty seemed to love being one of the boys—something that he rarely, Jake assumed, got to be at home.

Maddy spent most of the time locked in her room, talking on her phone and coming down only for the meals that Jake made at regular hours. Phoebe, like Zoe, had never put much effort into cooking, ordering pizza and dining out whenever possible, and Maddy and Marty were shocked to see a brawny man like Jake cutting carrots, tossing salads, and grilling chicken satays with peanut sauce.

At dinner one night, Maddy dropped her fork and lit into Marty and Nate over the endless hours they spent "killing tiny blobs of color" on the computer screen. Jake chewed his pork chop and eyed her uncertainly as she raked over the boys. He was getting the idea that he'd gotten off too easy with Maddy. Zoe had warned him to expect trouble from her daughter, and he knew it was only a matter of time before she would test his authority.

A few hours later, as he mounted a sheet of pegboard in the heated garage, a pair of headlights flashed in the window. The lights flickered, came to a halt, and pulled back into the street. Drill in hand, he peered out the glass. In front of the house, a red Lexus idled beyond a snowbank. Assuming the car was simply turning around, he went back to work—until a slender figure in a short coat glided past the window and hurried toward the car.

He set down the drill, yanked open the door, and chased Maddy down the driveway, oblivious to the cold air biting his face. He caught her in the street. Grabbing her by the arm, he stopped her mid-stride.

"Ouch!" Maddy tried squirming free, but he tightened his grip and held her there. In his view, Maddy had ridden roughshod over both of her parents, and he'd made up his mind not to let her do the same to him. "Where are you going, Maddy?"

"Christ," she complained, her breath coming out in clouds. "We're getting coffee. Will you let me go?"

"You could have told me. It's ten o'clock."

As they argued, the door of the Lexus opened and a lanky boy in a bomber jacket strutted their way.

"What do you think you're doing?" he asked Jake as if he were a superhero coming to rescue Maddy. Jake released her and stared into the face of an older teen or a man in his early twenties. He matched Jake in height but weighed twenty pounds less. The sneer on his face spoiled his otherwise handsome features—clear brown eyes, strong jaw, and Cupid's-bow lips.

"Who are you?" Jake demanded.

The boy gave Maddy a questioning look.

She rubbed her arm and tucked herself into him, pouting.

"One last time. Who are you?"

The boy shrugged. "I'm Davis. Maddy and I are going out for coffee. C'mon Maddy."

He hooked her arm and led her to the car. As they walked away, they whispered to each other.

Jake did a slow burn. "I wasn't finished."

Davis glanced over his shoulder and smirked.

The snotty smile was too much. Jake strode after him, clamped a hand on the back of his neck, grabbed his belt, and all but raised him off the ground.

"What the hell!" Davis shouted. "What's wrong with you?"

He marched him to the car's open door. Maddy chased after him, pounding on his back. "Let him go, dammit!"

Jake forced him into the driver's seat like a cop hauling in a suspect.

"Now get out of here and don't come back."

He slammed the door shut and stepped back from the car.

"You asshole!" Maddy shouted.

The engine revved and the tires spun on the ice. When they hit dry pavement, they screamed, and the Lexus flew down the block and disappeared.

A bit shaky, he watched the red lights fade before spotting Maddy running to the front door. He sighed, told himself to calm down, and followed her in.

She was making for her room. As Jake plodded up the stairs, she raced to the door, meaning to slam it shut, but he leaped up the steps and beat her to it. He shoved his boot in the crack, and the door bounced off it.

Maddy backed away, terrified. The look on her face made him pause. He bit his lip and weighed his options.

"Sit down. We have to talk."

She plopped onto the bed and eyed him nervously. Having provoked a stronger reaction than she expected, she seemed less eager to challenge him now. The sight of Davis being stuffed into his car like a piece of luggage stuck in her mind.

He paced back and forth as he delivered his speech. It was not a bad one, as speeches went—not so much scolding Maddy as stressing the importance of following rules, which often seemed pointless, but if repeatedly broken only promised greater, not fewer, limits on your freedom. After a few minutes, however, it became clear that she'd tuned him out. Like most of Maddy's teachers, he assumed that she'd never heard these things at home, or if she had, that hearing them from him would magically make her understand. But now he saw that everything he'd said was not only a waste of breath, but counterproductive.

He pulled out the desk chair, sat down, and studied Maddy. Tears and mascara striped her cheeks, her ruby lips shone like oil paint, and her long, dark hair was perfectly ironed. Her strapless tank focused your eyes on her breasts, and her short skirt made her legs seem endless, but the Converse shoes gave away her age. Switch them out with heels, and she could have passed for a 20-year-old hooker. No wonder Davis, who was much too old for her, thought she was fair game.

"So tell me about your boyfriend," he began.

By gently prying, he learned that Davis was a junior at Lakota Lakes High, where he played lacrosse and took advanced-placement classes. His parents were pushing him to apply at Ivy League schools, but he wanted to go to school and ski in Colorado. Maddy made it clear that his parents were rich—that explained the Lexus—and they didn't seem to care how late he stayed out at night. Altogether, he was too old, spoiled, and unsupervised for Maddy, who would turn 14 in a few weeks. Jake could see that she'd already fallen under his spell, dazzled by his family's enormous house, luxury cars, ski trips to Vail, and summer parties at their lake home. As he listened, his heart sank. How could Zoe, a single mother with an older house, a beat-up car, and a teacher's salary, compete with the glamorous life that Davis was tempting her with? *Twenty bucks she's already slept with him. I'll bet that's where they were going tonight.*

"How did you meet him?"

"At a resort up north."

"The Whispering Oaks?"

"How did you know that?"

"I've been there. Phoebe and I met in Dupont Lakes." He told Maddy the story of their courtship, and for the first time during her stay, she perked up and listened.

"That's a cool story. My mom and dad met at a bar. Pretty lame."

"I think there's more to it than that."

"And then they ruined each other's lives."

"That's not really fair. They used to love each other very much. I'm sure they still do. Sometimes it's not enough."

"If they really loved each other, they'd still be together."

"I wish it was that simple. It's not."

She stared at him as if he were lecturing her again. *Time to count your winnings and walk away.*

He stood and said goodnight, content that Maddy had not only listened to him, but also given him a glimpse into her private life. He'd take that as a victory of sorts—although he couldn't overplay its importance. He knew the fire that burned in Maddy couldn't be tamped down for long. Any minute, the faintest breeze might stir the coals, and the flames would leap back up and burn them all again.

70

Early one morning in September, as Zoe got ready for class in her new office at Huntington High, she overheard on the radio that a private plane had crashed into the North Tower of the World Trade Center in Manhattan. Luckily, the damage to the tower was minor, and firemen were already on the scene putting out the blaze. But events soon took a disturbing twist as it became clear the plane was neither small nor private, but a commercial jet filled with passengers, and a large number of people, both in the plane and in the tower, had died.

When her first hour ended, Zoe hurried to the break room and saw that a second commercial jet had just slammed into the South Tower. The middle portion of the building was burning out of control, while the fire in the North Tower continued to billow out clouds of inky black smoke.

She didn't need to hear the talking heads on the TV to realize what had taken place. The odds of two commercial jets randomly striking the towers were too great to compute. Someone had carefully planned and executed the attacks—on a scale that only a well-funded group, like a foreign government, could orchestrate. She felt in her bones that not only was she watching the worst tragedy of her lifetime, but that very soon her country would be at war.

With a sick feeling, she backed the bulky TV stand out of the AV closet and wheeled it down the hall. When she pushed it through the door, her students fell silent, sensing by her rapid steps and grim face that something was wrong.

When the image of the burning towers flickered on the screen, they gasped, and for a second Zoe wondered if she'd done the right thing. But they were juniors, after all, old enough to handle this, and now that she'd turned the TV on, she couldn't turn it off. She could hardly teach her class, nor her students listen, with the crisis still unfolding.

She told them what she knew and cut off their questions, telling them to watch instead.

Five minutes later, black smoke puffed out around the burning edges of the South Tower and its upper stories began a slow-motion plunge, pancaking the floors beneath them. At first, the reporter didn't understand what he was seeing, thinking an explosion had rocked the tower and failing to notice the black smoke was no longer hiding the building but hovering in its place.

Zoe's mind fought to process the horror unfolding in front of her. Inside the tower, hundreds, perhaps even thousands, of people were dying.

Again she questioned the wisdom of bringing in the TV. A couple of boys swore and one girl sobbed, but most only stared in disbelief at the smoldering hole in the sky.

Zoe gave a tissue to the sobbing girl and put a hand on her shoulder. "You don't have to watch, Mary. You can go study in the commons."

Mary wiped her tears, but stayed in her desk.

Minutes later, they learned a third plane had struck the Pentagon. The western wall had collapsed, and the building was in flames.

In half an hour, the horror compounded as the North Tower collapsed, pancaking the floors below in the same sickening way. Zoe collapsed into an empty desk, covered her mouth, and cried in front of her students. Now it was Mary who brought Zoe a tissue and gently rubbed her shoulder.

But the day only got worse.

Before the hour was done, a fourth plane slammed into a field near Shanksville, Pennsylvania. Everybody on board was presumed dead.

Both the media and the government seemed to be in the dark. No one had any idea who had carried out the attacks. No one knew how many hijacked planes remained in the sky or what other attacks might still be planned, or in progress. No one knew where the President was or what he was doing. The Pentagon was still burning. Congress had been evacuated. All of Washington, it seemed, was being evacuated.

By now, parents were flooding the school with calls. A few showed up in the school office, asking to pick up their kids, but the staff persuaded most to go back to work, although a handful of mothers wouldn't be turned away and took their kids home with them.

At noon, Dr. Draper, the principal, came over the PA, reported the attacks, assured the students they had nothing to fear, as if he knew something that no one else did, and said the day would proceed as usual.

But *proceed as usual* was a poor choice of words, as no one got much done the rest of the day, and Zoe guessed the students had only been kept in school to prevent the chaos of an evacuation. They had to stay somewhere until more was known, and school, after all, was maybe the safest place for them to be.

She kept the TV on until the final bell rang. At 3:15, she dismissed her class and dashed to her car to pick up Maddy and Marty. As she sped across town to the middle school, she thought how small her own troubles seemed by comparison, but the reflection quickly gave way to a deeper worry—that Nine-eleven would not only cast a pall of uncertainty over the entire country, but, very soon, over her own family too.

71

Hear plus *t* spells heart.

When Marty snapped down the t on the board, Zoe felt vaguely accused.

They were sitting at the kitchen table, playing Scrabble. Zoe studied Marty's face, but it showed no bitterness. Already he was losing his childlike features—his nose was getting larger, his eyes smaller, and his voice deeper. Now and then it gave way in a falsetto crack.

A month had passed since Nine-eleven. It was Saturday night, and Zoe was glad that Marty had stayed at home with her. He'd wanted to go with his friends and watch *Zoolander*, but Zoe couldn't spare the money.

Maddy was out with Davis. When the school year began, she'd lied about her age and landed a job as a hostess in a trendy restaurant. She was making her own money now and spending it as she pleased.

Zoe stared at the tiles, which seemed to stare back at her accusingly. Of course, Marty hadn't played the *t* on purpose, but it had to be weighing on his mind.

"Do you feel okay, Marty?"

"Fine, Mom. Your turn."

She added a *y* after his *t*, making *hearty*. "Are you still upset about the operation?"

He glanced up and then scanned his tiles again. "I can wait."

"The timing's bad. The economy's terrible. People are losing their jobs."

"I said I can wait."

"Maybe next year."

He snapped down an *x* before *ray*, with the *x* on double points. "I'm kicking your butt, Mom."

She smiled, happy to lose to Marty. It seemed like one of the few things that she could do to lift his spirits. The worst part was that *next year* didn't promise to be any better. Over the summer, the FDA had approved the device, but her insurance wouldn't cover the operation until it had a proven track record, which could take a year or more. Even then, she'd have out-of-pocket costs, and they were already stretched way too thin. Far too often she found herself forced to choose between things that in the past she thought essential—makeup, softener salt, or well-made clothing—and food. And with the economy heading south and the country bracing for war, she had no idea when they could dare take on the added cost.

"Yep, I've got boot marks on my butt. We'd better quit. It's past your bedtime, and Maddy hasn't called."

An hour later, Zoe shelved *Harry Potter and the Goblet of Fire*, kissed Marty goodnight, and trotted down the stairs, wondering if Maddy would give her trouble tonight. It was quarter past eleven, making her not only late, but in violation of curfew.

She paced the living room, cell phone pressed to her ear, and waited for Maddy to pick up, but her calls kept rolling over to voicemail. Maddy evidently had no intention of answering. How many times during her own teenage years had she made herself unreachable, Zoe reflected, thinking for the umpteenth time how sorely she must have tried her mother. *What goes around comes around. I guess I deserve it.*

By midnight, she'd gone from being resentful to worried. Neither Maddy nor Davis would answer their phones, and all of Maddy's friends claimed not to know where she was. Desperate, she called the Reeds' house in Lakota Lakes, but there too the phone kept rolling over to voicemail.

At one o'clock, she called Jeremy. He was awake, but drunk. His garbled speech and lack of concern infuriated Zoe. "She'll come home sooner or later," he kept repeating. In the background, the TV was blaring. He seemed to be watching a movie and trying to get her off the line as quickly as he could. She hung up in disgust.

She nearly called her mother to ask for advice, but thought it rude to wake her up and, worse, it would only make her look more inept as a mother than her mother already thought her.

At two a.m., she went upstairs and shook Marty gently. "Marty, I have to go look for Maddy.

"Okay," he mumbled and rolled back to sleep.

She threw on her jacket, grabbed her keys, and jumped into her car. She started the Escort with too much gas, and it buzzed like a chain saw before quieting down. In a couple of weeks she'd have to replace the muffler. She couldn't believe at forty-one that she was still driving this piece of junk. It had racked up 160,000 miles, the fabric had rubbed off the seats, and rust had eaten through the wheel wells. Wouldn't she look the trashy mother of the troubled Maddy as she pulled into the Reeds' driveway in her beater car, rumbling like a Harley chopper?

Maybe I'll park down the block.

It took half an hour to find the Reeds' house among the winding roads and cul-de-sacs of Lakota Lakes. When at last she parked before the imposing stone and stucco facade, the clock on her dash read 2:30.

Do people still build three-story houses? She glanced down the block. Nearly every house in sight was just as large. Even in the dark, the Reed's house oozed of money: soigné flowerbeds, flagstone retaining walls, bay and vaulted windows, and half a dozen lofty gables. She stepped out of the Escort and stared into the dark windows. *Am I really going to wake them up at 2:30 in the morning?*

A second later, her spine stiffened. *Damn right I am. Their son is God knows where with Maddy, and they should be as worried as I am.*

She marched to the door and rang the bell. She tapped her fingers on her thigh as she waited, but no one came. *I'm sure they're asleep.*

She banged on the door with the base of her palm. A minute passed and still no one answered. Finally, she pounded with her fist. A dog started barking—not in the Reeds' house—but in the house next door.

She thought for a second and then followed the pavement to the garage. She stood on her toes and peered through the window. Inside, there were two cars. One of them was Davis's Lexus, meaning that Maddy was either inside the house or not with Davis at all—and if the latter were true, then Maddy might be in more serious trouble than Zoe had even imagined.

This new fear prompted her to cross the lawn to the neighbor's house. As she approached the door, a yard light, tripped by a sensor, blinked on and nearly blinded her, and the barking inside the house grew louder.

Before she could knock, a shadow filled the door. Beside the shadow, a German shepherd growled. Through the glass, the shadow watched her. Then it grabbed the dog by the collar and led him away.

Seconds later, a man opened the door. He stood stiffly in the doorframe in T-shirt and pajamas bottoms. While maybe in his forties, his tired faced and ruffled hair made him look much older.

"I'm sorry to wake you up," Zoe said, "but I'm looking for my daughter. She went out with the Reeds' son and never came home."

"Davis?"

"Yes, have you seen them? Maddy has long dark-hair. She's taller than me, thin, pretty."

"I haven't seen anyone, but the Reeds are in California."

Zoe wrinkled her nose. "That explains it."

He stared at her sympathetically. "They won't answer?"

"No, but Davis's car is here. They have to be inside."

"Nice trick." He shook his head. "Teenagers."

"Every mother's payback."

It took him a second to understand. "I'm sure the police could wake them up."

"No, I don't want that. I hate to ask, but could I borrow a flashlight? I need to know she's really there."

"I see what you mean. Hold on."

He came back with a light and followed Zoe to the Reeds' door. He shone the beam through the windowpane and flashed it back and forth, lighting up a rug, a pair of loafers, and a still life with red grapes and wine bottles.

"Wait. Can you move it back?"

He swiveled back the light, but nothing else appeared.

"Can I try?"

Zoe held the light at a sharp downward angle and pressed her cheek into the pane. On a coat rack alongside the door hung a jean jacket, and below it, on the rug, lay a purse. "Thank goodness. Those are Maddy's."

"At least you know where she is," the man said. "Sure you don't want to call the police?"

"No, I've bothered you enough already. I don't need to wake up the rest of the neighborhood. I'll deal with this tomorrow."

But as she drove back home, fuming and fighting with Maddy in her head, she wondered how she would make her listen, and the worst part was, given Maddy's lack of guilt or fear, she didn't know the answer.

72

At nine o'clock on Sunday morning, the whine of a car engine woke Zoe up. She jumped off the couch, where she'd spent a sleepless night, dashed into the kitchen, and caught Maddy coming in the side door. Maddy glanced at her, hung her coat on the hook, and brushed past her as if she were coming home from work and not an unsupervised night at her boyfriend's.

Her eyes were bloodshot—whether from lack of sleep or smoking pot, or both—Zoe couldn't tell. She didn't know what shocked her more, the shameless face or the hip-hugging jeans, spiked heels, and plunging top. Even in her bedraggled state, Maddy looked mature, seductive, aloof. Her beauty gave her a suit of armor that deflected any weapon, including the daggers in her mother's eyes.

When she passed Zoe, a familiar smell wafted from her clothes.

Zoe scoffed in disbelief. "Couldn't you at least try to cover it up?"

Maddy stared at her, puzzled.

"The smell."

"You know, Mom, I'm really tired. I need some sleep." She rounded the kitchen corner.

"That's it?" Zoe said, her voice rising. "No apology? Nothing to say?"

Maddy stopped and faced her. "I know I should have called. I was going to come home at midnight, but I fell asleep."

"You fell asleep because you were wasted."

"I wasn't *wasted*, Mom."

"Just pleasantly buzzed?"

Maddy smirked. "You would know, wouldn't you?"

"What does that mean?"

"Dad told me some stuff about you."

Zoe colored. So many angry words ran through her head it was hard to get a single one out. "Of course he would say that. He's not exactly pulling for me."

"Do you mean he's lying?"

"Whatever I did, I never dreamed of staying overnight with my boyfriend and coming home smelling like pot. You're right—I was no angel—but that means you can't fool me. I know what you're doing. I was at the Reeds at three this morning. If you didn't notice, that was me pounding on the door."

Maddy stared at her defiantly.

"A neighbor told me the Reeds are in California, so don't tell me you were sleeping. That's a lie. You planned this. The two of you were getting high and fucking all night. I bet you didn't sleep a wink."

Maddy brushed away a lock of hair and scowled at Zoe as if spelling out her offense was worse than committing it. "Davis and I don't *fuck*. He loves me."

"He's not old enough to love you. He loves your body."

"How would you know?"

"Are you even taking anything? I told you we'd go see a doctor if you're sexually active."

Maddy grimaced. "Mom, nobody talks that way."

"The words don't matter—what you're doing matters."

"I don't really think it's a big deal."

"You're wrong. Having sex at 14 *is* a big deal. So is getting high. So is staying out all night and lying to your mother. And flunking out of school. You're a smart girl, Maddy, but you have *three Fs*. Call it what you want—you're throwing your life away. You're getting caught up in things you can't handle. You're too young to know the risks, and I'm scared for you. I know you're trying things, the way a lot of girls do, the way I did, and maybe it seems like fun now, but you're taking it too far, and before long you'll be in so deep you can't climb out."

"I'm not doing anything other kids aren't."

"Your entire class is getting high and having sex?"

"You need to wake up, Mom. It's not like it was back in the day."

"Maddy, I know what it's like out there. I have plenty of problem girls in my classroom. I don't want you to be like them."

"How old were you when you got your V-card swiped?"

It took her a second to figure out what Maddy had said. To her chagrin, she hadn't waited much longer—she'd simply kept it secret. But that was exactly what bothered Zoe—Maddy's lack of concern, or even caution. At least she'd known that she was playing with fire and might get burned. Maddy, on the other hand, thought she was fireproof.

"I was too young," she said, "but it's none of your business. It's not about me. It's about having limits. I'm your mother, and it's my job to set your limits, because I know the dangers and you don't. You think you're grown up, but you're still a child, and you won't see where you're going until it's too late. You might get away with something now, but it will catch up with you fast, and one day you'll wake up fighting for air."

"What do you mean, *fighting for air?*"

"Addicted. Pregnant. Poor. Trapped."

"Like you?"

The blood rose in Zoe's face. She pointed a finger at Maddy like a pistol. "That's it. You and Davis are done. You can't see him anymore. He's not welcome here—not that he ever shows his face—and you're not going over there either."

Maddy's reply sent a chill through Zoe. Instead of becoming angry, she stared at her calmly. "You know you can't stop me."

Zoe was dumbstruck. She could do her best to make her daughter's life miserable—take away her phone; refuse to drive her; spy on, hound, and punish her, but in the end Maddy was right. She couldn't do it 24/7, and the second she turned her back, Maddy would do whatever she wanted. Desperate, she threw out her trump card, a lie, but she'd run out of ideas and she thought it might scare her.

"If you won't follow the rules in this house, you can't live here. You'll have to live with Phoebe and Jake."

If nothing else, the threat got her attention. She stepped forward, bristling. "You'd never do that."

"We already talked about it. They said they'd do it."

Maddy screwed up her eyes. Although trembling with anger, she was still thinking. It frightened Zoe to see her calculating so coolly in the heat of battle. "Good—fine. I'd love to dump this fucked-up place. I hate it here. It depresses me. *You* depress me. That's why I'm always gone. You and Dad are both pathetic—why would I want to live with either one of you? I'd rather live with Phoebe and Jake—at least they're not losers."

Zoe's anger was spent. Her daughter's words had crushed the fight in her. She tried to remind herself that Maddy was only a teen and, like most, could be selfish and cruel, but that didn't stop her words from wounding her deeply. She struggled to find a fitting response. "Jake won't put up with Davis. You know what happened last time you were there."

"Well, at least he *did* something. Can you imagine Dad trying that?"

Zoe couldn't. Even though Maddy didn't like Jake, she did respect him, while she had no respect at all for her own father and mother.

She turned away, defeated. She wondered how much Jeremy had told Maddy about her past. The pot. The speed. Her liberal outlook on sex. Maybe her affair. Conversely, she knew that she'd complained too much about Jeremy in front of Maddy. It hadn't helped either of them. By running each other down, all they'd done was discredit each other. Now both were fallen angels in Maddy's eyes, and she didn't respect their rules, even though it was clear that she was craving some kind of authority in her life—she simply refused to accept it from her parents.

Feeling routed, she couldn't find the will to argue further. "Go upstairs and get some sleep. We'll talk about it later." But deep inside, she doubted they would.

73

Zoe fought to keep from quaking as her flats echoed down the halls of Huntington High. The day's last class had let out, but clumps of students lingered in the halls, waiting for teachers, heading off for locker rooms, or hanging out with friends.

Outside, the first snow covered the dead grass, and a current of cold air funneled down the hall like an icy wind—or maybe it was the fear coursing through her veins that made Zoe's hands clammy and her shoulders feel bare, as if she were locked outdoors, where the chill cut through her clothes as if they were made of paper.

Dr. Draper, her principal, had stopped by her office many times before, but he'd never called her down to his, and she found the timing, a Friday, late in the day, ominous. Rumors of layoffs had been swirling around the school for weeks. Zoe had spent all of November focusing single-mindedly on her class, working like a woman possessed to show the school and her students they couldn't do without her—while inside she was trembling like a rabbit under the watchful eyes of a circling hawk.

She told herself that she was getting worked up over nothing. More than likely, Dr. Draper wanted her to join a committee or take a role in some dull initiative, or maybe it was only a problem with a student. It could be any number of harmless, ordinary things, and all of them a million miles away from the one thing she feared.

As she entered the main office, Karen, the school secretary, smiled and jabbed a pencil over her shoulder. "He's waiting," she said. When their eyes met, Zoe caught a fleeting look of panic.

She walked by her desk with a floating sensation.

Dr. Draper glanced up from his work and smiled disarmingly. She breathed a sigh of relief. *He couldn't smile like that if he was going to fire me.*

She stopped in the door. "Can I help you, Dr. Draper?" *You sound like a waitress, Zoe.*

He stood up and looked her over. Dr. Draper reminded Zoe of a middle-aged man watching a football game and not the principal of a prestigious high school. Most days he shuffled around the halls in loafers and baggy sweaters like a lost parent. His low-key manner disarmed the students, staff, and parents alike, but his voice was deep and soothing, and his calm, logical words seldom failed to impress or persuade his audience.

"Have a seat," he said. He walked behind Zoe and shut the door.

Not a good sign.

He came back slowly, sat behind his desk, and stared at her. The gaze revealed nothing out of the ordinary—neither guilt, nor worry, nor sadness. But it was a little too pointed, too studied, like a mechanic sizing up an engine; he knew exactly what had to be done, but didn't know where to begin.

The cool detachment of his stare made her stomach loop.

At last, he raised both his hands. "There's no good way to say it, Zoe. I won't keep you on pins and needles, so here it is. I'm deeply sorry, but we're cutting your position."

The color draining from her face stopped him. He winced, cleared his throat, and continued.

"I hope it's not a huge shock. You know we've been looking at cuts for quite a while. With the bad economy, we've had to make some painful decisions, and this, I regret to say, is one of them."

The news hit Zoe physically. She felt like someone had slapped her face, grabbed her hair, and thrown her into a locker. She'd never been fired from any job before, and felt like she'd done something disgraceful and had been singled out for punishment. Only this was much worse, because the ground giving way beneath her was not only pulling herself down, but her entire family. "I have two kids. I raise them by myself. How can I do that without a job?"

Dr. Draper frowned. "That's why I'm telling you now. Your contract ends in June. I wanted to give you ample time to find a new position."

"There are no new positions. They're firing teachers everywhere."

"I know it's a tough market, but we don't have a choice. We're already over budget, and our projections are bleak. If it helps, there's a long list of people I would have picked over you, but you're a new hire, you don't have tenure, and you're on the lowest rung. It has nothing to do with your performance. I hear good things about you all the time. You're committed to your work, and the students like you. That's why I'm so sorry to give you this bad news. You're an excellent teacher, Zoe, but that's the way the system works, and there's nothing I can do about it."

Zoe had always thought of herself as a resilient person, but as she left Dr. Draper's office, she felt like a gazelle pounced on by a lion, programmed by nature to quickly bleed out and die.

Karen met her in the waiting room, crying. She hugged Zoe and apologized for not telling her—she'd been warned not to—but the words floated right by her. She kept telling Zoe how much the staff and students liked her and how she'd find another job before she knew it, and while a voice inside of Zoe said the same thing—this was merely a setback, another bump in life's road that would soon be overcome—another voice also cried out, a persistent, chilling voice that she had to suppress, for if it ever got the upper hand, it would drag her down into a black, swampy pit from which she might never rise again.

74

Zoe and her kids spent Christmas Day at Phoebe's. The bright, airy rooms, the blazing tree, and the abundance of gifts, gadgets, and toys lifted their spirits. The smell of baking cherry and pumpkin pies filled the house all day, and for dinner, Phoebe roasted a 20-pound turkey and served it with stuffing, sweet potatoes crusted with butter and brown sugar, Brussels sprouts, wild rice, pillowy popovers, and cranberry sauce. She uncorked her best bottle of Chenin blanc, and by dinnertime, she and Zoe had polished the whole thing off.

Yet after the meal, Zoe's mood sank. While Phoebe had done her best to make the day fun and carefree, treating the Connors to things they couldn't afford, she'd overdone it. The sumptuous meal, the twenty-dollar bottle of wine, and the perfectly-chosen gifts were too much for Zoe, reminding her of what Phoebe had that her own family lacked, and humbled by the contrast, she grew pensive and withdrawn.

Once the table was cleared, the boys ran off to play video games, Jake lay down in the den for a nap, and Zoe and Phoebe left the dishes on the kitchen counter and took advantage of the quiet to have a talk. Phoebe unbuttoned her jeans and propped up her feet on a footstool, while Zoe sunk into the cushions of the matching couch and pulled her knees into her chest like a curled-up hedgehog.

Her behavior was alarming Phoebe. She'd been hoping for a chance to speak with Zoe by herself, and finally getting her window, she wasted no time. "How are you doing, Zoe? You seem kind of depressed."

"Really? Why should I be depressed?"

"You haven't been drawing the best cards lately."

"I can't even get my hands on the deck."

Phoebe sipped her wine and thought. "The kids seem all right."

"Marty's my little trooper. He keeps me from feeling sorry for myself. Maddy hasn't changed. She's completely self-centered."

"Pretty typical for a teenager."

"Worse than most."

"Can I do anything?"

"Know any principals I can blow?"

"That's not funny."

"Well, that's what I need. I need a job."

"Are you paying your bills?"

"I'm treading water, for now. Sometimes I have to borrow."

"Not with credit cards, I hope."

"I do what I have to."

Phoebe frowned. "I know you'd never ask me, but maybe I could help."

"C'mon, Phoebe. You can't start paying my bills."

She stared at Zoe sternly.

"Dammit, I know that look. What are you planning now?"

"Don't get mad. I just want to help."

"Stop beating around the bush. You're scaring me."

"No—you're scaring *me*. You're not just down, Zoe, you're in a depression, or going into one."

"I've never been depressed. I'm just—" She couldn't finish, but waved off the accusation.

"You've never been in this situation before."

"I know." Zoe bit her lip and looked up sheepishly, "Okay, sis, better give it to me straight."

Still ballsy, even when she's down.

As much as it pained her, Phoebe knew she had to be blunt or Zoe wouldn't listen. "All right, here's what I see. You're not *you* anymore. You're too quiet. You move around like you're sleepwalking, and the light's gone out from your eyes. You act like you don't give a damn. You're cynical and pessimistic—no, I take that back—you're *fatalistic*. Like it's too much trouble to fight. And all those are classic signs of depression."

Zoe let the words sink in. "You think I need drugs."

"Why not, if they get you through it? You wouldn't believe how many people take them. I know. I see the bills at work. Sometimes I think more people take antidepressants than don't."

"Even if you're right, I can't afford them, or the shrink."

"You still have insurance."

"It only covers so much. And I have co-pays."

"I'll cover whatever it doesn't, until you find a new job."

Zoe drew back in thought. Phoebe could tell her pride was fighting with her fears and Phoebe's stark appraisal of her condition.

"Zoe, please. I can't think of all the times you've helped me out. I owe it to you."

Zoe's eyes welled up. "You don't owe me anything. You paid for Cancun, and now you want to pay my doctor bills. What's next? Where's it going to end?"

Phoebe reached over and clasped her hands. "It will end when you get a job. Then things will get back to normal. But right now, you need help."

Zoe let out a long, shaky sigh. "I suppose you're right."

"Call a psychiatrist Monday morning. If you want, I'll go in with you. I'll get you some names, okay? Promise?"

"Okay, Phoebe," Zoe said, gazing at the carpet. "I guess I've been kidding myself. I really do need some help."

75

In March, Jeremy lost his job at the Herald. Pushed to the limit by endless sick days and missed deadlines, Ansel could no longer protect him, and he was forced to break their 19-year bond and fire him. It didn't surprise Zoe, even though she'd lived in fear of it for months, as it virtually ended her child-support payments. After giving her the bad news, Jeremy quit answering her calls, and a week later, when she drove to his apartment, she found neither him nor any of his belongings, with no forwarding address left behind. Even his parents didn't know where he was living or how he was getting by.

With her own job ending in 10 weeks, Zoe's search became increasingly frantic. In April, she was asked to interview at a private school to fill in for a teacher going on maternity leave. Dr. Draper had recommended her, and because the job was short-term, the school was only considering a handful of applicants. Still more promising, Zoe learned that after having her baby the teacher might not return, possibly giving Zoe a shot at landing a full-time job without undergoing the typical and more competitive hiring process.

She felt on edge waiting in the office for Dr. Morton, the principal. Greeting her, he smiled a bit too broadly—but never mind—she would use whatever means she could, fair or not, to land this job. A bald, portly man in his fifties, Dr. Morton responded warmly to her smile, his oval head beaming like a light bulb. Walking down the hall to his office, they engaged in banter that bordered on flirting. The first few critical minutes had gone perfectly, Zoe thought as she sat facing his desk—but now it was time to get serious.

She described her previous job with poise, but when Dr. Morton turned to more abstract matters, she began to bog down. Somehow, the subject of semiotics came up, and Dr. Morton asked her to explain her views on the obscure field dealing with signs and symbols. While familiar with the basic concepts, Zoe struggled to put her knowledge into words. Like a cart plowing through mud, she struggled for traction, but every turn of the wheels demanded superhuman effort. In the middle of a long, complex answer, she got so mixed up that she had to stop. Blushing, she asked Dr. Morton to repeat the question.

He did, mildly concerned, but looked relieved when Zoe picked up where she left off. She managed to eke out a few more sentences before she faltered and stopped again.

In the middle of her thought, her mind had gone suddenly blank. Now Dr. Morton was squinting at her, waiting for her to finish, but no matter how she tried, she couldn't pick up the lost reins of her thought. The vacuum in her head was absolute and terrifying.

He asked her a question, but for some reason, the meaning of his words vanished in the air. She asked him to repeat his question, blushing, knowing how confused she had to sound. At the same time, her heart began to race, a lump formed in her throat, and breathing became hard.

She watched Dr. Morton speak, bewildered by the sounds coming out of his mouth, knowing how important it was that she not only understand him but respond to him properly, but God knows why she couldn't do either.

The realization made her heart race faster. It was pounding in her ears like a circus drum. The room began to swim and everything around her, including Dr. Morton, looked like a flat paper cutout plastered on canvas. Her stomach knotted. A cold bead of sweat ran down her ribs and nearly made her start. The longer Dr. Morton spoke, the less she understood. And when at last it dawned on her that she couldn't make out a single word—that he might as well be talking gibberish—a wordless horror crawled up her spine. She tried over and over to pull herself back into the conversation, but to no effect. Her mind had lost its anchor, and she was sliding down a muddy shoal into a deep ocean trench.

Get out of here, Zoe. Say anything you have to, but you need to go now.

"I'm sorry," she said, her voice sounding far away. "I don't feel very well. I'd better leave."

She leapt to her feet and fled the office.

In the safety of her own bedroom, she called Phoebe and recounted the disaster. "What's wrong with me, Phoebe?" she said through her tears. "Am I losing my mind?"

"You're not," Phoebe told her. "It sounds like a panic attack."

"It was more than panic. It was terror."

"I hear they're pretty bad."

"I won't stay like this, will I?"

"It will go away, but if you don't do something about it, it will come back."

"I don't think I could stand more of these."

"Stay where you are. I'll come over and we'll find someone who can see you now. They have medications for this. And no more dragging your feet, all right? I've been bugging you about this for months."

They found a doctor who put her on Zoloft. The medication ended the panic attacks and helped her depression, but Zoe soon came to despise the pills, which fogged her brain, added pounds to her hips, and woke her up in the middle of the night, sweating like a boxer. What's more, they flattened her feelings—something that Zoe had always considered a vital part of her life.

But they did work. They got her out of bed every morning. They let her face her class with confidence and finish her lessons every day. They gave her the energy to cook for her kids and help them with their homework, and on good nights, enough left over to write a few cover letters or submit an online application before collapsing into bed.

What her medication couldn't do was keep the school year from coming to an end. Her last day at Huntington High arrived with breathtaking speed. She could hardly believe it when she walked out the door on May 26th, a Tuesday afternoon, with her briefcase full of cards and letters from her farewell party. In the parking lot, she turned and looked back at the sprawling campus. It seemed like only a week ago, she'd stepped out of her car on the first day of school, anxious, but eager to start her new job.

Everyone at the party had been overly kind. There were hugs, smiles, pats on the back, promises of coffee dates and lunches, and many had pledged to give her name to their contacts at other schools. But she held out little hope of finding a new teaching job. She'd spent the last four months applying all over the city, even in the small towns, but nobody was hiring. In fact, most schools were laying teachers off. And with summer already here, the odds of finding a full-time job by September went from small to infinitesimal.

With her mailbox overflowing with bills, she had no option but to look for lower-paying jobs, the kind she'd worked in college—receptionist, waitress, sales clerk—but here, too, no matter where she applied, the result never varied, and most days she felt like she'd have as much luck tossing her resumes out the open window of a speeding car.

76

In mid-July, Zoe got a break. She landed a full-time job as a sales clerk in a clothing boutique. To get the job, she lied about her fashion knowledge, flirted with the owner, and told him that after dealing with the parents at Huntington High, working with the store's upscale clients would be a cinch. On the down side, even after commissions, the job paid much less than teaching and failed to give her the one thing she needed most—health insurance.

She took it anyway. She could always leave if something better came along. Meanwhile, it would buy her time to figure out whether or not to stay in teaching or switch careers entirely—because the last year had proven to Zoe that paying the mortgage, keeping up the house, and raising two kids on a teacher's salary was impossible.

Another problem was the hours. Zoe often had to work on weekends, and her weekday shifts ended at nine, which meant not only missing dinner with the kids, but leaving them unsupervised for most of the night. Maddy fully exploited her absence, to the point that Zoe rarely knew where her daughter was. Every now and then she wouldn't come home till morning, and her return always led to shouting, threats, and tears, which sent Marty running off to his room, where he stayed until the fighting stopped.

Her shifts at the boutique at least distracted Zoe from her problems. Her beauty, faded but far from gone, helped her sell the store's upscale clothing line to its wealthy patrons. She bought new outfits, dabbed on more makeup, and tried a shorter hairstyle. Her customers were always changing, and she liked the challenge of winning them over and making a sale, and while they admired themselves in the mirror, she observed their quirks or tried to guess their professions.

One Friday night, a man in his twenties came in, looking for a business shirt. His broad shoulders and tapered waist, which she couldn't ignore as he tried on shirts, coupled with his carefree manner and easy smile, stirred something inside her.

He paced back and forth in a blue, fitted Geoffrey Beene and studied himself in the mirror. "Now that's I'm looking for."

"You look great in that," Zoe said, "but you're all crumpled up in back. You could use an iron."

"Can you press it for me?"

She smiled coyly. "Our tailor's gone for the night … but I have an iron at my place."

Her line threw him off, but only for a second. He smiled back. "What time do you get off, Zoe?"

He followed her home in his rented car. Marty was spending the night with Nate, and Maddy was doing one of her vanishing acts, and even if she did come home and find a strange man in their house, so what? Why at this point in her life couldn't she bring someone home to chase away her loneliness, at least for a night? Drew was a hunk, but more than anything, she wanted a warm, soft body lying beside her till morning. She wouldn't ask too much, only that he treat her kindly, and in return she would do whatever he wanted.

She poured two stiff vodka gimlets. They drank them on the couch, and before they polished them off, they were kissing. Soon their clothes began to drop, and they stumbled, half naked, into the bedroom. Zoe dimmed the light, threw herself onto the bed in her bra and thong, and bent her legs seductively as Drew whisked off his pants. Naked, he looked even better than she imagined, cut like a marble statue from his shoulders to his calves. He leaped onto the bed like a lion, crushed his lips into hers, and wasted no time cupping his hand between her legs.

Zoe arched her back into him, which he took as a signal to end the foreplay. He clambered over her, grabbed her by the hips, and plowed into her with abandon. His weight on her breasts, his smooth skin, and the rush of being taken gave her the release she craved, but after a few minutes, he strangely eased up, and she got the impression that he was fighting to keep erect. She drove back, spurring him on for a while, but she couldn't shake the feeling the sex was becoming work. Drew grabbed her shoulders and pulled her down into himself, but as he toiled away, sweat began to cover his body. Now Zoe panicked. All she could think of was her fleshy belly, the give in her butt and thighs, and Drew's erection swimming inside her, shrinking fast.

Desperate, she fell back on her voice. She urged him on with groans, coos, and grunts. Her cries quickly rekindled his lust, and a minute later he let out a long groan and collapsed on her chest.

As he washed in the bathroom, Zoe stood before the full-length mirror and studied herself. No wonder he'd lost interest—why in the hell would a man like Drew want an old, out-of-shape body like hers? Once the thrill of the chase was gone, he could barely finish the job.

She felt humiliated. While rarely afraid to admit her flaws, she'd never considered being a bad lay among them.

He came out of the bathroom and began dressing. *Classic. Wham, bam, thank you, ma'am.*

"Can't you stay for a while?" she said, hating herself for asking.

"Thanks, that was great," he said, buttoning up his new shirt, which he'd never gotten the chance to iron, "but I have a flight tomorrow morning."

"We could get up early. I'll make you breakfast."

"That's a nice offer, but I have a presentation to give. I need a good night's sleep."

"It's only ten o'clock."

He gathered up his shoes. He sat on the mattress, bent down, and knotted the laces. In a few more seconds, he would be gone.

Zoe felt herself sinking. She fought to keep silent and preserve a shred of dignity, but she couldn't help herself. "What can I do to make you stay?"

He looked up, irked by her persistence, and stared at her coldly. "Have a little self-respect. I think we both know I never meant to stay."

77

Zoe climbed the back steps, locked the kitchen door, and gazed at the ring of keys spread in her palm like the hands of a clock. It was the last day of September, a breathtakingly beautiful day. A gentle wind stirred the warm, dry air and fanned the curling maple leaves trimmed with orange, while the slanting rays of the sun cast shadows of elms on the still-green lawn. A day so perfect it was painful to behold. Its splendor stabbed Zoe like a spear and made her think it would keep her from ever enjoying a fall day like this again.

Jake and Phoebe watched her from the driveway. Phoebe drew close and whispered in Jake's ear. He nodded, shoved his hands into his pockets, and set off down the sidewalk.

Zoe dropped the key ring into her purse and shuffled down the back steps. Her jeans, cinched up by her belt, bagged around her hips, and her shapeless blouse could have belonged to a scarecrow. From afar, the weight loss flattered her figure, but face-to-face, she looked gaunt. Her cheekbones rode unnaturally high, and her jaw stuck out like the prow of a ship, disturbing her friends and family—but not so much as the look in her eyes, gazing out of their dark sockets without a glimmer of light.

Phoebe met her halfway down the driveway. They stared at each other awkwardly. A trace of resentment flickered on Zoe's face, but it soon gave way to a deeper emotion that Phoebe couldn't fathom, and, finally, it turned hard, like molten lead plunged into water. Of all three looks, the hardened was the worst—one that Phoebe had never seen on her sister's face before.

"Where's Jake?"

"He went for a walk."

Zoe's eyes followed him. "I see," she mumbled.

"What now, Zoe?"

She glanced around searchingly. "I want to sit on the front steps."

Neither spoke as they shuffled down the driveway. They came back up the stone path and sat on the landing. There was barely enough room for both of them to sit.

Oak branches threw shadows like barbwire on the freshly cut lawn. A solitary robin patrolled the grass. To Zoe, its clear, curling cry sounded like a dirge. Somewhere down the block, the cries of boys fighting, then laughing, hovered in the air. Across the street, sunlight spilled around the homes and hid their flaws, making the facades look freshly painted and the yards perfectly groomed. Like Zoe, Phoebe felt the sacred beauty of the neighborhood. But it was too pure, too idyllic—better to walk away from a hovel in winter than her quaint little home in a flawless fall masterpiece. Somehow that would have made it more bearable to leave it all behind.

"When the kids were small," Zoe said, "I'd sit here and watch them play. Sometimes the other moms would bring down their kids, and we'd have a drink and watch them play together. Once in a while you'd get a day like this—one you could sell for a million dollars."

"I came over once and saw you here, drinking margaritas. Your lawn was like a day care."

Zoe nodded absently. "Someday I'll buy this house back. I'll get my realtor's license and make a pile of money. I don't think I'll ever teach again. I loved teaching, but it wasn't very practical. I never did want to make a lot of money, you know—enough for my kids, that's all. You had a better idea, Phoebe. Make a lot of money and then you're free. It's funny. I spent my whole life trying to be free, and now here I am, with no freedom at all."

"You talk about your life as if it were over."

"It is over," she said flatly. "The rest is just waiting."

"Don't say that. I know it's a terrible loss, Zoe, but you have to keep trying."

"I do? Why? I've lost everything I ever wanted. My teaching career is over. Even if I found a job again, I wouldn't have the courage to stand up in front of a class. I have no idea where Jeremy is. He might as well be dead. Maybe soon he will be dead. I hardly see Maddy, and when I do, she treats me like an old broom. I still have Marty, but the only thing he really needs, I can't give him. And now our house is gone. We don't even have a decent apartment. Tell me, Phoebe, just what should I be living for?"

"You still have your kids. And they need you. You have to pull yourself together, if not for yourself, for them."

"Do you know how much money we put into this house? How much work? And for what? We don't have a penny to show for it."

"I know you don't want to hear this, but it could be worse. You still have a roof over your head. Okay, it's not your own house, but you're safe and dry. And you still have a job—maybe not your first choice—but you can pay the rent and put food on the table. And you have two kids who love you. And I love you, Zoe, and so does Mom, and we'll do whatever we can to help."

Phoebe had spoken with uncharacteristic emotion, and she expected Zoe's response to be equally heartfelt, but instead she only stared at her sarcastically. "What's the matter? Afraid I might kill myself?"

The idea startled Phoebe, although it did relieve her to hear Zoe make light of it. "I know you'd never do that. Your kids mean too much to you."

"I'd do anything for them," she said, her voice quivering.

"You're still taking your meds, right?"

She paused. "I am, but my panic attacks are back."

"You should up the dosage. Or change it. You can't fool around, Zoe. You have to see your doctor again."

"I hate those damn pills."

"Are you really taking them? You look so thin. You said they made you fat."

"Not if you don't eat."

Phoebe didn't know what to say. There was so much they should talk about—but right now she was afraid it would only make things harder for Zoe. Maybe it was better, at least for the present, to let her grieve without anyone pestering her about the future.

"You had a lot of good times here," she said, trying to sound upbeat.

"Too many to count." Zoe sighed loudly. "I can't believe I can never go back. I'll never sit on this porch again. They might as well have cut out my heart. I lived here for 17 years. I raised my kids here. This is *my home*. How can they take it away from me?"

Phoebe put her arm around her. "I feel so bad. I wish I could fix it."

Zoe leaned against her like a rag doll "You've already done so much for us. You found the apartment, helped us move, paid the first month's rent. I don't know what I would have done without you."

"I wish I could do more."

"You and Jake have your own family. I can't ruin your life too."

"We're fine, but let's not talk about it. Let's just sit here and watch the sunset."

Zoe looked up at the horizon, a blending watercolor of blues, reds, and purples. "Red sky at night, sailor's delight. Remember how Dad always said that?"

Phoebe smiled. "I forgot."

"No matter what they do, they can't take away my sunsets, can they, Phoebe?"

"No, Zoe, you'll always have those."

"All the same, I hope I never have to watch a sunset like this one again."

78

It was long past midnight. It might have been two or three. Zoe couldn't tell, but she knew she would need a coat—it was late October, and a winter chill was in the air. She stood before the closet in a faded T-shirt and jeans, her short hair tousled and wild. She'd washed off her makeup, leaving her face pale, and her feet were bare.

Behind her, the sofa and two armchairs filled the living room like a storage compartment. Two candles guttered on the coffee table, the room's only source of light, while on the CD player, turned down low to keep Marty from waking, Mimi poured out her heart in *La Bohème*.

She slipped her jean jacket off a hanger. Shoving a hand into a sleeve, she knocked it to the floor. She picked up the jacket and fumbled for the armhole, but she put her hand through the wrong one. She yanked out her am and tried again, but she dropped the coat a second time. She stared at the heap of denim lying on the floor, puzzled, and after a minute, gave up and went back to the couch.

On the coffee table lay a shot glass, an orchard of sucked-out lemon slices, a shaker of salt, and a half-empty fifth of tequila. Flecks of salt had found their way into her open scrapbook, grating on the pages when she flipped them over.

She was staring at a photo of a young, happy bride dancing with a tall blond man in a black tuxedo. Zoe had a hard time believing the bride was her. She looked just like Maddy, and for a second, she wondered if she was looking at the wrong picture, but, of course, it made no sense, Maddy wearing a wedding gown.

She gripped the bottle and filled the shot glass. She pressed her fist into the scattered salt, licked it like a cat, closed her eyes, and tossed back the tequila. Wincing, she jammed a lemon slice into her mouth and bit down. Her mouth exploded. Her tongue burned, her cheeks puckered, her eyes watered. But the pain felt good. It reminded her that she wasn't dead, that life could still hold a rush or two.

> *O for a beaker full of the warm South!*
> *Full of the true, the blushful Hippocrene,*
> *With beaded bubbles winking at the brim,*
> *And purple-stainèd mouth;*
> *That I might drink, and leave the world unseen,*
> *And with thee fade away into the forest dim:*

She clunked down the glass and breathed in, light-headed. *Where was I going? That's right. The park.*

She stood and stumbled to the door. Halfway there, she stopped, thinking deeply.

She frowned, turned, and crept back to Marty's room. With great care, she quietly opened the door and peered inside. It was black as a bottomless well. She went back to the coffee table, lifted the candle from its sconce, and cupping the flame, retraced her steps. The candle threw an arc of light on

Marty's walls and striped his blanket with shadows like a tiger's fur. She tiptoed into the silent room. She thought it wise to keep her distance from the bed—the last thing she wanted now was to wake him up—but she couldn't keep herself from drawing closer and soon found herself standing beside him.

His head was nestled in his pillow. He slept on his shoulder with a bare arm outside the covers, breathing gently, his face serene, angelic, pure. His collarbone struck her as a work of art, fragile and bowed like the wing of a wounded dove. Tears sprang to her eyes. She reached down and with trembling hand pulled the blanket over his shoulder. When she did, candle wax dripped down and blotted the sheet. The light flickered on Marty's face, and he frowned. In a panic, Zoe blew out the candle and froze in the dark, barely breathing for a long time, but Marty didn't stir again. When she felt it was safe, she tiptoed out the door and shut it softly behind her.

I should check on Maddy. But then she remembered that Maddy hadn't come home, and since it was Friday night, probably wouldn't. *Her choice,* she thought with a sad shake of her head. *Her choice.*

She opened the apartment door, glanced back as if she'd forgotten something, but didn't know what, and stepped into the hallway. The dirty shag carpet and the sulfuric glow of the lights jarred on her eyes, and the smell of mildew nearly gagged her. Hell, if there was such a place, was an empty hall with soiled carpets, water-stained ceilings, and rows of locked doors. She had to get out of here right away and blot the image of this hated place out of her mind, and in her rush to leave, she closed the door and padded down the hall, leaving her keys behind on the kitchen table.

She stepped out the back door, and the night rose up like a living thing. The brisk air quickened her blood. It poured into her lungs and cleared the fog in her brain, sharpening every color and shape around her. The golden boughs of elms waved above her, and the stars winked down between them, as if promising a better life—one last glimmer of magic in this sordid world where the only surprises left were unwelcome.

> *Here, where men sit and hear each other groan;*
> *Where palsy shakes a few, sad, last gray hairs,*
> *Where youth grows pale, and spectre-thin, and dies;*
> *Where but to think is to be full of sorrow*
> *And leaden-eyed despairs;*
> *Where beauty cannot keep her lustrous eyes,*
> *Or new Love pine at them beyond to-morrow.*

The leaves rose and fell in the moving air, and the cold grass prickled her toes, but it wasn't painful, it was liberating, bracing. It made her body feel light as a young girl's, the way it felt when she and Phoebe used to run across their neighbors' lawns, sneaking down to the creek on summer nights over 30 years ago.

She stayed on the grass near the sidewalk. The glimmering path would serve as her guide, a river whose banks she could trace to the chosen spot, the place she'd picked out days ago, which on a night like this would be the most beautiful place for miles around.

I cannot see what flowers are at my feet,
Nor what soft incense hangs upon the boughs,
But, in embalmed darkness, guess each sweet
Wherewith the seasonable month endows
The grass, the thicket, and the fruit-tree wild;

A few cars hugged the curbs of the quiet streets. The sidewalks were empty, and shadows hid the grass between the streetlights. As she neared each one, a globe of rusted orange and red leaves burst into view and then faded into gray and, finally, as she passed by, into black. The leaves overhead whispered like a million disembodied voices, mingling with the babbling of a brook hidden somewhere in the trees—no, that wasn't right—the brook was flowing here where the sidewalk had been, and the moonlight sparkled on its surface like a bed filled with broken glass. High over the cottonwoods, in the coal-black dome of the sky, the stars blinked down, bewildering in their brightness, formidable in their cold beauty, distant beyond measure, and yet so close you could reach up, grab a cluster in your hand, and shove it in your pocket. What would that be like, she wondered, going home, turning out your pocket, and casting forth the splendor of the universe across your kitchen table?

She tried to guess how many blocks she'd come, but couldn't. The portion of her mind that counted no longer functioned—or had simply been overwhelmed by the portion that perceived.

As she neared the park, specters floated among the bushes and voices drifted past, soft at first, but growing louder. She stopped and listened. Somewhere in the shadows, people were moving. Who were they and what were they doing here in the middle of the night? Judging by the few words she caught, they seemed to be heading for a party.

Suddenly, black shapes above her wheeled, swerved, and dipped like swallows. *Were they bats?* A steady stream, almost a flock, was flowing overhead.

At the next light, she looked up and grinned—they were neither bats nor swallows, but luna moths, sailing on sea-foam wings, studded with big brown eyes gazing at her like the eyes of cows.

Something high above them called out shrilly. *Nighthawks.*

The cries conjured up a bitter memory, transporting her back to that parking lot in Delmar, heading for the front desk of that wretched hotel where her life began its downward spiral. At the same time, the memory stirred a painful longing, a yearning so intense it tugged on her ribs as if it would break them. Just one last time, she ached to see Jeremy again and tease him into a smile. It had always been so easy, and it never failed to make her feel happy too. If only he'd let her, she could have spent the rest of her life making him smile and loving him, and been satisfied.

She might have lingered in this morbid vein, had the trees not disappeared and the grass rolled down a hill into a vast lawn. Zoe's mouth formed an *O. There it is. The place I've been looking for. And it's even more beautiful than I hoped.*

Above the fringe of black trees, the moon was a gold coin floating in a pond. It spilled its amber light across the field, burnishing every blade of grass quivering in the cool autumn air. The blades were so clear that if she'd had the time, she could have counted every one.

And haply the Queen-Moon is on her throne,
Cluster'd around by all her starry Fays;
But here there is no light,
Save what from heaven is with the breezes blown
Through verdurous glooms and winding mossy ways.

Incredibly, a lavish party was taking place in the park. Skirted tables covered the lawn, and Chinese lanterns, strung in rows, bobbed in low branches. At the base of the hill, a garland braided with roses hung between two pillars, forming a gate. I*t's a wedding reception,* Zoe thought with a start, and she ran forward, nearly tripping head over heels as she trotted down the slope.

On the lawn, men stood in black coats and ties and women in ballroom gowns. Behind Zoe, still more people were pouring down the slope and heading for the tables, where guests drank champagne, laughed, and gossiped. Finally it struck her. This was not some stranger's wedding, but her own. Her heart leapt as she looked around and realized that all the guests had come to see *her.* They'd all been waiting for the bride to appear—but no one knew that she was here because like a twit she'd forgotten to wear her wedding gown. *How stupid of me. I came to my own wedding in a T-shirt and a pair of jeans.* She laughed out loud at the irony. She wanted to shout, *It's me! I'm here!* but knew they wouldn't listen. A bride has to look like a bride, and without her sparkling, silver gown, she might as well be a wedding crasher.

She weaved among the tables as a waltz began to play. All the guests smiled as she glided by. She grinned back and saw that now they all knew her—or else they wouldn't be smiling—and when she glanced down, the arc of her bubble skirt came into view, rustling over the grass and bouncing with every step. At last she was wearing her wedding gown with the pearled bodice that bared her shoulders and hugged her waist. Gone were the flaws of age and back again was the glow of youth. She didn't need a mirror to know she'd lost the lines of care that in recent years had cut so cruelly into her face.

But none of that mattered now. She glided from table to table, giddy with joy. The champagne had gone to her head. How many glasses had she drunk? Was it good to be so drunk on your wedding night? She'd better watch herself. At this rate, she might not make it to the bridal suite.

But where is the groom? The love of her life, the man who God made just for her? It was his night too. Why wasn't he anywhere in sight?

All of a sudden, there he was, striding down the hill in his black tuxedo. Tall. Happy. Proud.

She grinned, raised her skirt, and ran after him, her bare feet flying over the grass.

But instead of rushing to meet her, he turned away from the party and strode off toward a stand of elms.

How could he not see her, dressed in white like no one else? He must have seen her, she thought, slowing down—but then why hadn't he run over and embraced her?

Of course. He wanted her to follow him. He was guiding her to a private spot where they could be alone, hidden from all the guests. Tonight, just like on their wedding night, he wanted her all to himself.

"Jeremy," she cried out. "Wait!"

He ignored her cry and strode even faster.

She could tell where he was going. It stood by the forest edge, timeless and familiar, its boughs swaying, a curtain of golden beads with fireflies blinking beyond them—the willow tree from their wedding night, inviting her into a magical world where everything was calm, carefree, and safe.

Jeremy stopped to part the boughs, turned, and then at last, he smiled. It was a beautiful smile, burning with the fire of youth, bright-eyed, full-lipped, his brow unbent by worry, his eyes untroubled by sorrow. She ran to him, aching to feel his arms around her, to kiss those tender lips, and let his passion fill her up, just the way it had been under the willow boughs almost twenty years ago.

He vanished beyond the curtain. Afraid of losing him, she rushed to the spot where he vanished, her heart beating wildly, and reached out to part the boughs. Only a second more, and she would kiss him—the Jeremy she loved, the man she married, and not the man he became. He would lift her off the ground, hold her in the air, and all would be as it was in the past, perfect in every way.

But there on the curtain's other side only the rough bark of the willow stared back at her. Jeremy was nowhere in sight.

She stood alone, imprisoned by the boughs, glancing to and fro, wanting to make sure that Jeremy hadn't escaped into the woods nearby. But in her heart of hearts, she knew that he was gone. Not only gone, she thought with a sickening plunge in her stomach, but had never been here at all. The whole time she'd been chasing a phantom. Just like the wedding party and all the guests, he was only a dream conjured up by her mind.

She looked down at her bare feet. The wedding dress had disappeared. Her toes were numb and turning blue. The park behind the willow was empty and dark, and the only sound was the cry of the nighthawk circling above her, an ugly, mocking shriek. Oh, how she hated that sound and hoped she would never hear it again.

Drained, she sat and slumped against the tree. It felt good to relax, to give up the fight, even though a thousand pins were pricking her toes. They tingled in pain. She wiggled them gently, but that only made it worse.

I kept some for that, just in case. She dug her fingers into her front pocket and painstakingly worked out a handful of tiny pills. She stared at the mound in her palm for a long time.

Finally, she grimaced, cupped them into her mouth, and began to chew. *Bitter pills. That's where it comes from—life is a bitter pill to swallow.*

Darkling I listen; and, for many a time
I have been half in love with easeful Death,
Call'd him soft names in many a musèd rhyme,
To take into the air my quiet breath;
Now more than ever seems it rich to die,
To cease upon the midnight with no pain

She coughed and sputtered, swallowing over and over, trying to choke down the last of the chalky powder.

Done at last, she leaned back into the bark and closed her eyes. *God, I'm tired. I've never, ever, been this tired.* It wasn't possible to get up again. No matter what happened now, here she would stay, rooted to this spot as firmly as the willow tree itself. Getting up wouldn't change a thing anyway. By now there was no escape. Already something heavy and black was sifting down toward her through the branches—a shroud too heavy to weigh, too black to comprehend. There was no point in looking up to watch it fall. She knew it well—she'd faced and fought it back a hundred times before, but this time, nothing would stop it. And by now she was so tired, it no longer frightened her. It carried with it not so much fear as relief. It paused above her for a few, final seconds, patient and still, then wrapped around her body like the wings of a dark angel, bent its black pinions, and folded her inside.

Part Five
2002

79

Jake leaned into Phoebe, who sat beside him in the front pew, and said quietly, "You don't have to do this. I can read it for you."

She stared at him uncertainly. It was clear he thought she couldn't do it. She doubted herself if she could do it. She'd spent the whole day crying, the last three days, in fact, crying. But her state of mind didn't matter. It had to be done, and no one else could do it for her.

"I let Zoe down once before, on her wedding day. This time I can't."

He nodded glumly. "All right. Then hold your head up." He pecked her on the cheek. "I love you."

She rose from her seat. The church was still as a tomb. Every eye followed her as she marched to the lectern in her black dress.

Nearing the casket, she wavered. The hulking black box made her stomach loop. It seemed to send out an invisible force, pushing her away.

She fought off the feeling and mounted the dais. The minister stepped back, and Phoebe took his place. She unfolded her written notes on the lectern, gripped the edges, and peered into the crowd.

Hundreds of mourners packed the church. Front and center, next to Jake, sat Rose, small and shriveled in a flowered dress. Beside her sat Jeremy, whose hollowed eyes no longer seemed anchored to the world, then Marty, clinging to his father's arm with tearstained cheeks, and then Maddy, looking bitter, defiant, and ten years older than her 15 years. In the next row were Jeremy's parents, Maggie and Bill, his brother Tom, sister-in-law Paige, and their three teenage boys. Filling the next two rows were Jake's parents, his three brothers and their wives, and all their kids. Then came the faces of countless friends, neighbors, relatives, and by the entrance, dozens of Zoe's students, some of whom went back a decade or more. The church, by no means small, couldn't fit them all in, and they stood in rows two-deep behind the last pew.

Ordinarily the watching eyes would have flustered her, but gazing into the faces of so many people who'd known and loved her sister gave her strength. Their silent presence cleared her mind and calmed her trembling hands. At last she ended her pause and began to speak in a clear, loud voice.

"If my sister had thought about this day, which I doubt, she wouldn't want us to be sad, but to laugh and tell stories and have a good time. Zoe would have wanted a party."

A few people in the crowd smiled.

"But I can't do that," Phoebe said, struggling for a second. "This is the hardest day of my life, and no matter how I try, I can't do the one thing she would have wanted. And when I look at all of you, I can tell you don't feel like having a party either."

She waited for her words to settle. "But what I can do for Zoe is celebrate her life. That part's easy, because in Greek, Zoe means *life*, and my sister had more life in her little finger than any person I've ever met.

"Some of you know our mother loved Greek mythology, and she gave us these funny names back in the sixties, when no other kids had them. I was self-conscious about mine, but Zoe loved being different. Whenever someone said, 'I've never heard that name before,' she always told them proudly what it meant.

"But I don't think her name made Zoe who she was. She was born full of life. It was part of her, like her smile and her brown big eyes—big enough, I like to think, to take in the entire world.

"I know that some of you feel sorry for Zoe. I have myself, the last few years. It's been hard not to. But I think our pity is a mistake. For most of her life, Zoe was happy. And even when times were hard, she was still more alive than most of us. The truth is, a lot of people go through life half dead. Good things happen to them, and they don't feel joy. Bad things happen to them, and they don't feel pain. They just do their best to get through the day, to get it done with. But Zoe found something to love in every person she met, something remarkable in every tree and flower, every song she listened to, every poem she read. She got more joy spotting a hummingbird in her garden than a kid going down a waterslide. If I live to be a hundred, I won't know half the joy that Zoe squeezed out of life in her 42 years.

"Take dancing. Zoe loved to dance more than anything else. And I hope I won't be struck by lightning if I say she wasn't the best dancer in any of her troupes. But she stole the show anyway, because the other dancers looked so serious, and she looked happy just to be out there, moving her body—so your pleasure came less from watching her dance than watching the pleasure that dancing gave her.

"No one here needs to be reminded that Zoe was beautiful. It wasn't just her looks—it was something inside. Wherever Zoe went, people noticed her. When she walked into a room, the conversation picked up. People started laughing and telling jokes, as if they were trying to draw her in. I won't lie to you—Zoe knew this about herself. But even though she enjoyed it, she wasn't vain. Most of the time, she used it to make other people happy. She never held a part of herself back. Zoe shared her true self with every person she met, no matter who they were—young or old, rich or poor, friend or stranger. When you were with her, you got every ounce of her, as if the sun were shining only on you, and the rest of the world was covered in clouds.

"Unlike so many people, Zoe always followed her own heart. She was proud to call herself a nonconformist. In college, when everybody was going to discos, she grew her hair down her back and dressed like a hippy. She had fun in college, but she loved her classes too, and it was there she found her calling. She could have been successful in any field, but she became a teacher because she believed that nothing was more important than opening up the minds of young people and giving them the tools to lead a deeper life. She tried new teaching methods, paid for movies and books with her own money, and brought her own life experience into her classrooms, becoming a friend and confidante to many of her students.

"It warms my heart to see so many of you here. Your presence would have made Zoe happy. She would rightly see it as an affirmation of her life's work.

"Apart from teaching, the only thing that mattered more to Zoe was her family. She was fiercely devoted to Maddy and Marty, and she put two-hundred percent of her love and energy into raising them. Nothing gave her greater pleasure than telling you about them. Her face would light up whenever she did. Even later, when her life was falling apart, she always put them first, and she gave up things for herself so they could have the same things that other children had.

"It was Zoe's nature to give, and she gave freely to everyone she knew. She never expected much in return. A smile. A laugh. Some little sign that she was appreciated.

"These are just a few of the good things I hope you remember about my sister—not the last two years, when luck abandoned her, but the bulk of her life—a happy life lived by a happy person—who brought joy into the world every day, and whose passing means a lot less joy for all of us who loved her."

Phoebe stopped and listened to the silence. As it often happens with eulogies, she kept her poise until she spoke her final words, and then, as their meaning sank in, her face crumpled and she fled the dais in a storm of tears.

80

As the pews emptied, Phoebe gathered her family in the lobby, waiting for Jeremy and his kids to join them. Before long, he came drifting down the aisle with downcast eyes. In the last decade, Phoebe had gone through a range of emotions about him, most recently believing that he'd not only ruined Zoe's life, but also caused her death. As he drew closer, however, a wave of sympathy for him overcame her. Despite his flaws, Phoebe was certain that he'd always loved Zoe, even after the divorce, and her death had plainly crushed what little joy remained in his life. When their eyes met, it only reinforced the observation. Two dark sockets gazed back at her, expressing nothing. His hair was flat and greasy, his shirt and coat wrinkled, and his tie crooked. Twice during the service, Phoebe had caught a whiff of vodka in the air. It had made her so mad that she wanted to climb over Jake and light into Jeremy, but she held back the urge. Attacking him now would accomplish nothing except to make things even more painful for everybody there.

More important, she still had one crucial matter to settle with him before the day was over.

He stopped and faced her. Maddy and Marty huddled behind him, using his body as a shield. Maddy wrapped a protective arm around Marty, who was still crying, and fed him tissues from her purse.

"I'm sorry," Jeremy said, "but I can't go out there."

"Out where?"

"To the cemetery. I couldn't stand it. Watching the casket, you know, all of that."

The image of Zoe's casket being lowered into the ground rattled Phoebe too. But she felt she had to see it—all of them did, especially Maddy and Marty, to help them accept their mother's death, and grieve.

"None of us wants to go, but we have to."

"Then do what you have to."

His reply set her off. "What's your plan, Jeremy? Take the kids and run away—like you ran away from everything else in your life? This time you can't. Maddy and Marty need to be there when their mother—"

He threw up his hand as if to ward her off. "Phoebe, don't."

"Do you want them to run away from life and wind up just like you?"

Jake put a hand on her shoulder. "I don't think he means the kids."

"The kids will go," Jeremy said, "I can't."

Phoebe paused and let her anger fade. "I see. Well, if that's what you want, fine. We'll see you afterward."

"I don't think so."

"You're not coming to the reception?"

"I don't think anybody wants me there."

The intensely private conversation was making Phoebe nervous. By now people were filling the lobby and swirling around them. Most held back politely, waiting for them to finish, but they wouldn't much longer. Coming down the aisle were Jeremy's parents, whom Phoebe hoped to avoid. She was still livid with them for blaming the divorce on Zoe and treating her affair as a long-standing pattern, even running her down in front of Maddy and Marty. The last thing she wanted now was to hear their two-faced apology. She was afraid of what she might say in return.

"She was your wife, Jeremy. Your children's mother. You *have* to go."

"Look, I know emotions are running high," he said sharply, even though on the verge of crying, "but let me finish." He paused and pulled himself up. "I talked with my parents about your plan. They won't give you any trouble. They don't like the idea, but they won't fight it."

Phoebe's throat caught. "Jeremy, not here—"

"This won't take long," he said, waving her off. "It was Zoe's last wish, and that's enough for me. The kids are okay with it. They know I can't give them a decent home. I can barely keep my own head above water. All I ask is that you let me see them whenever I want."

Maddy pulled Marty into her chest. Her bitter, defiant look intensified, but now it was tempered by a touch of fear.

Phoebe sighed in relief. Jeremy had just given her the one thing she wanted, and for which she would have fought without mercy or rest. Having won it, she was happy to concede his wish. "Of course. You're their father."

After a pause, she added, "but when you visit you have to be sober."

He struggled with her stipulation before nodding. "That's only fair."

"Not only are you welcome, but I expect you, often. They need you, Jeremy."

"I know." Then without explaining more, he turned and hugged Maddy and Marty. Marty clung to him fiercely, but as the mourners closed around him, he peeled himself away and fled out the front door.

Jake and Phoebe traded glances, begged off their in-laws and friends, and eager to escape the Edwards, steered their suddenly larger family through the crowd and into the waiting limousine.

81

It was after eight when the last guest went home. Many had stayed to help clean up, just as earlier that week they'd dropped off casseroles, pork sandwiches, potato chips, and brownies, letting the family concentrate on the draining ordeal of arranging their loved one's last farewell. Naturally, the lion's share of the burden had fallen on Phoebe and Jake. Zoe had named Phoebe her executor, and Jeremy had more or less vanished since picking up Maddy and Marty on the day of Zoe's death, which made Phoebe the de facto planner of the funeral. She and Jake spoke with the minister, helped him with his eulogy, chose the music, flowers, and the photos on the memory board, picked out the casket, wrote the obituary, and took care of countless other details, to say nothing of calling dozens of friends and relatives and informing them of Zoe's death. And after all that, Phoebe hosted the reception at her house in Orchard Valley and dealt with all the planning, chaos, and mess that came along with it.

When the house at last was quiet, she sat on her bed, slipped off her heels, and rubbed her sore feet. Every muscle in her body ached and begged for rest, but her heart was overflowing and her mind was humming, and she knew that neither would let her sleep for many hours to come.

She thought back on how they'd reached a strange turning point late in the reception, when everybody forgot the reason for their gathering and began to enjoy themselves, unaware they were celebrating Zoe's life simply by taking pleasure in each other's company. Phoebe had welcomed the change, and for several hours it made her world seem normal again—but now that all the guests had gone and she was alone again, the weight of the day and all its sorrow came back with added force.

She stared at her dresser, stood up, and opened the top drawer.

Before she faced Maddy and Marty again, she wanted to read it one more time—the letter she'd found resting against a flower vase on Zoe's kitchen table, right where Zoe had promised in her last voicemail.

She sat back down on the bed, unfolded the page of handwritten lines, and began to read the now-familiar words:

Phoebe—my best friend, my sister, my savior,

> *If you're reading this, it means I've done it, and now I'm nothing more than a memory. For some reason, being a memory doesn't bother me, as long as I left behind more good ones than bad. Most of all, Phoebe, I hope that as the years go by, the good memories will wash away the bad ones you must have of me today.*

I'm sorry for what I've done. Forgive me if you can. I know I'm leaving behind a horrible mess. In spite of how guilty I feel, the truth is, I don't see any other way out. I don't have the courage to face another day. My heart is broken in a hundred pieces, and the thought of picking them back up and going on is unbearable—like most of my days for the last two years. But I won't talk about things you already know.

I find it strange coming to a point in my life when I'm worth more dead than alive. What I mean is this: after I divorced Jeremy, I kept up payments on my life insurance policy. I knew that if anything happened to me, our kids couldn't rely on him, and the insurance might be the only thing they had to fall back on. It's $250,000—enough, I hope, to get them through college. Yes, you already know what I'm asking. No—I'm not asking, I'm begging, Phoebe. Please take them into your house and raise them as you would your own. I know that's a terrible thing to ask, but there's no other place for them to go. Jeremy can't raise them. It's sad to say, but drinking is more important to him now than his own kids. On the plus side, I doubt he'll give you much trouble. Show him this letter if you have to—and don't back down.

A couple of things about my kids. Number one, make sure you fix Marty's heart. There's a folder in my desk with all the information you'll need. After you become his guardian, you can cover the cost with your health insurance.

Marty's a lot like you. He acts tough on the outside, but he's soft on the inside, and he needs a lot of love and encouragement. Try not to be stingy with either.

Maddy is a good kid at heart, but she's had some rocky years. Think of me at 15 but with an absent father and a depressed mother. She needs a bucketful of love and a barrel full of discipline. You were always better at discipline than I was, but give her lots of both if you can.

It might help you to know that Maddy and Marty think the world of you and Jake. Try to remember that—no matter how they behave. They'll test you, but be as patient as you can. They'll come around eventually, I know they will.

One last thing—I'd like them to think this was an accident for as long as possible. They're not ready for the truth yet, especially not Marty. I'll trust you to pick the right time to tell them. The same thing goes for everybody else. I don't want people to gossip. It will only make things harder for my kids.

There's so much more I want to say, but time is up, and there's no point in dragging you through all the dark places I've been in my heart.

I've always felt blessed, Phoebe, to have you as my sister. You've been my anchor and best pal since birth. I could always tell you anything, and I knew you wouldn't judge me, even when you had reason to. At the same time, it never kept you from telling me the truth. It's a rare thing to get both love and honesty from the same person, but I always did from you— whether or not I deserved it.

It's made me proud to see you get stronger and wiser with each passing year. What you've done with your life is a marvel—your marriage, family, career, your determination, courage, and wisdom. I admire you, Phoebe. And I love you. In many ways you were the best part of my life, and I can't believe I'm saying goodbye for the last time. I hope that you stay happy, and what I've done won't cause you too much pain. It might help to know that most of my life was not so unhappy. On the whole, it was a great life, and if I could do it over again, I don't think I'd change a lot, except that God would have made me stronger or given me better luck, but I guess that neither of those was meant to be.

Love, forever,
Zoe

82

Later that night, Phoebe held a family meeting. They all sat around the kitchen table, looking haggard. Jake was barely able to keep his eyes open. Nate looked resentful of his new siblings, but also guilty about his feelings. Maddy sat stiffly in her rumpled dress, giving off the same antisocial vibe she'd sent out to the world since middle school. Marty's face was the most painful to see. Always brave in coping with his weak heart, tonight he reminded Phoebe of a two-year-old kid lost in a department store.

Everybody stared at Phoebe. She knew what she had to say, but was so tired and scatterbrained she couldn't find the words. After a few awkward seconds, she brought up the first subject that came to mind.

"I hate to bring it up, but we have a lot of practical things to work out, and the sooner we do the better. First of all, bedrooms. Nate, I'm sorry, but from now on, you'll sleep in the basement."

He drew back in shock. "I have to leave my room?"

"I want you and Marty together. You'll be sharing a lot."

"Sharing?"

"Yes, all of you will to have to share more. You'd better get used to it."

Nate cast his mother a wounded glance, but could tell by her look he'd better not complain.

"What about me?" Maddy said. "Where do I sleep?"

"You'll be in Nate's old room, upstairs," Phoebe said curtly. She didn't mention her reason—that every time Maddy left her room she'd have to pass by Phoebe and Jake's. But she didn't have to say it. Maddy knew immediately and glared back at her. "That's stupid. Why can't I be with Marty?"

She balked, not wanting to say why. At last, she said, "Because we're not two different families now. I don't want you and Marty down there all by yourselves."

Jake broke in to back her up. "Your mother asked us to raise you like our own kids, and that's what we'll do. We won't treat you any differently than Nate. We'll pay for your food and clothes, drive you where you have to go, and when the time comes, we'll pay for your college. From now on, our house will be your home. I know we can't replace your mother and father, but we'll give you all the love and support we can."

Phoebe blushed, embarrassed that Jake, and not she, had spoken what Maddy and Marty had most needed to hear. But Zoe's plea to discipline her kids was fresh in Phoebe's mind, and so she pushed ahead in the same vein. "But you'll have to follow our rules, and they'll be stricter than what you had before."

"What about school?" Maddy asked. "I don't want to change mine."

"If you want to, you can finish up at Lincoln. Marty, you can stay at Dewey or switch to Orchard Valley. It's your choice."

Marty's doubtful glance sent a pang through Phoebe. He seemed not to believe her.

"By the way, did your dad call your schools?"

Maddy shrugged. "I doubt it."

"I'll call them tomorrow. I'm taking the week off. We're going to rearrange the house. Both of you can help. After we set up your rooms, we'll bring your things over from the apartment."

Phoebe was conscious of sounding like an office manager, but what else could she do? Every topic she'd brought up had to be addressed, and life wasn't going to stop while they sat around and discussed their options.

"Is there anything you want to ask Jake and me?"

Neither child would look her in the eye.

"Okay, let's get some rest. We all need it." After a pause, she added, "I think we can all sleep late tomorrow."

Marty, who'd barely spoken a word the whole night, blurted out, "I want to sleep with Maddy."

Maddy nodded defiantly.

Phoebe turned to Jake. He shrugged.

"Okay, for a couple of nights—but that's all."

Marty was still pouting, but the panic left his face.

"All right. Let's put on some clean bedding."

She stood, eager to finish the day's final duty before collapsing into bed, but as she pulled a stack of blankets from the hallway closet, she had the sinking feeling that by following Zoe's wish and giving her kids a dose of much-needed discipline that she'd fumbled this critical first encounter, and when the sun rose tomorrow, she'd have a steep hill to climb just to get back to the starting point.

83

Phoebe's week off passed in a blur. Sorting through everything in Zoe's apartment and carting much of it to Orchard Valley consumed two whole days. After Maddy and Marty cleared out their belongings, they wouldn't go back, which left Phoebe and Jake to finish the job alone. What they couldn't keep or give away, they boxed up and hauled to a storage locker.

It took another day to arrange the new bedrooms. Both of Zoe's children seemed eager to have their own space, and each spent hours shelving books, hanging posters, folding underwear and socks, and organizing their desk drawers. It helped them feel secure, Phoebe thought, treating their worldly goods with such loving care. She encouraged the endeavor but largely kept out of their way.

Nate remained in school all week and kept up his normal schedule, but on Saturday morning, he missed a big soccer game. When his team lost, they blamed their star player for not showing up. Nate moped around the house for hours until Phoebe caught him in his room and scolded him.

"But, Mom, they're all mad at me. How am I supposed to act?"

"You don't need to act happy, but stop looking so put out. Think about it. What if I died, and you had to live with Zoe and Jeremy? Would you want to feel like you were messing up their lives?"

"But they *are* messing up our lives."

"No—it's not *their lives* and *our lives*. We're one family now," she insisted, but it didn't feel right when she said it, because she didn't feel it herself.

He dropped his chin and pouted.

"They need your help, Nate. *I* need your help. Some days I feel like I'm falling apart. Please don't make this any harder for me. I was hoping you'd make it easier."

He looked at her in a way he never had before. The pout vanished, and he ran into her arms.

She squeezed him tightly. "We'll be okay, Nate, but you'll have to be patient."

"I'll try harder, Mom. I will."

Throughout the week, there were funeral bills to pay, a hundred thank-you notes to write, papers to read and sign, and as the executor of Zoe's will, Phoebe had to settle a host of financial and legal matters. It didn't surprise her to learn that Zoe was $40,000 in debt, which she paid off with her life insurance policy. The funeral cost $6,000 dollars, which still left her with over $200,000, the majority of which she invested in corporate bonds and blue-chip stocks. Adept with numbers and investments, she carried out these tasks without much trouble and was relieved to find that financially, at least, they would be all right—better off, in fact, she thought with a twinge of guilt. And Zoe's kids would no longer lack for basic needs, like decent clothes and healthy food, and perhaps more important, opportunities like after-school lessons, tutors, and college.

She kept her emotions in check around the kids, but underneath, they built up steam like a powerful geyser. One morning, while the kids were in school, she came around a corner and banged her head into an open cabinet door. When the pain subsided, she screamed and cursed like a crazy person, threw books against the wall, breaking a glass picture frame, and threw herself on her bed, in turn hating Zoe for being such a coward and recalling tender moments spent with her, which made her cry.

She simply couldn't believe that Zoe was gone. She felt hounded by a pack of wolves, and the wounds had cut so deep they would never heal. What, after all, could replace 42 years of a shared life—the heart-to-hearts, inside jokes, familiar looks and phrases, all the joys and sorrows of growing up together: family meals, vacations, weddings, the birth of their kids and all their games, plays, and concerts? Even the last two painful years were precious to her now. By comparison, every other friendship in her life seemed empty or shallow.

Meanwhile, time refused to slow down. With the house rearranged and the kids back in school, the weeks that followed finally put some rhythm back into Phoebe's life. Every morning, Jake drove Nate to school in Orchard Valley and Phoebe drove Maddy and Marty to their schools in the city. After work, they switched kids, and Jake took the longer route.

Marty agreed to see a therapist twice a week, but Maddy refused to see anyone. She persisted in her self-imposed exile, although when home was neither rude nor disrespectful to Phoebe and Jake. They rarely knew where she went after dinner, presumably out with Davis, now a freshman at the University, but she always came home by 10, rolled out of bed by seven each morning, and was earning passing grades in school. For the time being, that was enough, Phoebe thought, even though it troubled her that Maddy barely spoke with her. She longed for a deeper bond with her niece, hoping to find in her some of the closeness that she'd lost with Zoe. Maddy, however, hid her feelings like a cat, preferring to stay a stranger not only to Phoebe, but also to everyone else in the house.

With Marty, on the other hand, she saw a better chance. He seemed to find comfort in her constant mothering—the meals she cooked, the school lunches she packed each day, the shopping trips to buy him clothes, the washing, ironing, and folding of his laundry. Her unflagging interest in his schoolwork, hobbies, friends, and health—even checking on him in the middle of the night—grounded and calmed him.

Still, Phoebe hadn't seen him smile once since Zoe's death. He rarely spoke unless spoken to, and almost never mentioned his father or mother. Phoebe tried to respect his need for space, even though she knew that he was longing for love. He was simply too wounded to let anyone into his heart for now, and so for the time being she focused on the small things that didn't stir the waters of his delicate psyche, but made him feel more secure in his new surroundings.

One November night, she woke up at two a.m., slipped on her bathrobe, and crept down the basement stairs.

She took three steps across the carpet and froze. The lower level had sliding glass doors that opened onto the back yard. Close to the glass, lit by the pale moon, Marty sat with crossed legs in his T-shirt and underwear. His spindly arms were too long for his body and his feet stuck out under his knees like broken rudders. Outside, the snow-draped junipers were silent and still, and the moon painted the trees with silver borders. The scene could have been a black and white photo in an art museum. Phoebe stood without speaking and studied Marty, who didn't know he was being watched. He was gazing at the moon as though speaking to it and not moving a muscle.

She felt a tug at her heart. "Marty?" she said softly.

He looked up for a second and turned back to the window.

She crossed the carpet sat down beside him. "Are you okay?"

He kept staring out the glass.

She wanted to ask him why he was up, but worried her prodding might shut him down. "Can I get you anything? Some warm milk with honey?"

Still he didn't speak.

"Did you want to talk?"

He turned and pierced her with his gaze. "Did my mom kill herself?"

Phoebe tensed. The way that he was looking at her, it seemed foolish to lie. Still, she had to think for a while before she answered. "She didn't want you to know that, Marty."

"I thought so."

"How did you figure it out?"

"My dad said she mixed up her pills, but no one else would talk about it."

"She didn't want you to know how unhappy she was. She didn't want you to think …"

She stopped and struggled for the right thing to say, not knowing if being honest would help or hurt Marty. In either case, it was too late to backtrack. He'd brought up the question himself, and they were already discussing the matter like two adults.

"… that leaving was her decision."

The look on his face made her doubt her frankness, so she quickly added, "But you have to know, Marty, it really wasn't her choice. Depressed people can't make decisions like the rest of us. Their feelings overwhelm them, and they can't think clearly. It's like drowning. They panic, and they can't grab the lifesavers that people throw at them. They slip right through their hands."

He nodded slowly. "That sounds like her."

"If she was healthy, she never would have done it. I know that. I know how much she loved you, Marty. She would have died for you."

"Did she?"

The question stunned her. "What do you mean?"

"I mean—did she kill herself so we could get that money and live with you?"

Phoebe stared into the snow. There was no point in deceiving Marty. He'd already assumed the worst. Still, she'd have to frame her words carefully. They had the power to either console him or cause him lasting harm. "I don't think so, but maybe it was easier knowing that I would take care of you. If it meant leaving you and Maddy alone—it never would have crossed her mind."

He nodded, deep in thought.

"We always had this agreement. If either one of us died, we'd take care of each other's kids. It's called being a guardian. Your mother made Jake and me your guardians. Maybe that makes you wish I wasn't around, but I'm sorry, I can't change that, Marty."

He turned and gave her the look she'd been longing for since he moved in. "I'm really glad you're my guardian, Phoebe."

His words poured over her like a wave, and all the sorrow of the last month came out in sobs. Marty broke down too, and Phoebe held him and rocked him back and forth, stroking the back of his head. "It's okay, Marty. You're going to be okay."

A minute passed before either one could speak. "I miss her too," Phoebe said. "She was my best friend. I'll never be that close to anyone else." She sighed deeply. "But life goes on. We all have to keep going. Your mother would have wanted that."

He straightened up and wiped his nose. "You don't have to worry," he said stoically. "My heart might not be strong, but the rest of me is."

She brushed away her tears and smiled. "When you grow up, Marty, you're going to be a strong man. I know you will. And that heart of yours, we're going to fix."

84

Phoebe stood over Marty as he lay on a bed in the cardiac catheterization lab. Above Marty hung a block of monitors for showing different views of his heart during his operation. On a counter, out of sight, were a pile of clear, sterilized packets holding the dilator, catheter, and titanium-mesh device that would soon be inserted into his heart.

A blue apron covered his legs and hips but left his chest exposed. As he breathed, his rib cage rose and fell like a bellows. His right inner thigh, where the catheter would enter his femoral vein, was painted with yellow-brown iodine. Marty kept lifting his head off the pillow and staring at the black X on his thigh. He seemed not to care that Phoebe could see him half-naked, and when she held his hand, he made no effort to pull it back. His cold, damp palm and darting eyes gave away the effort his front of courage required, even though Dr. Esse, his surgeon, had told him that he'd performed this operation 32 times without a single complication.

Those were the kinds of odds that Phoebe liked—although sitting by Marty now, she understood for the first time Zoe's misgivings about open-heart surgery. The rate of failure had always seemed incredibly small to Phoebe, until you considered that any mishap, regardless of the odds, could maim or kill Marty.

"A couple of hours, and you'll be a new boy," she said, squeezing his hand.

"I want it to be over."

"Waiting is the hardest part, and that's almost done. In a couple of minutes you'll be asleep."

He nodded gravely. She could guess the fears tumbling through his mind. "You're a brave kid, Marty. Don't worry. You'll be fine."

"Will you pray for me?"

She fought back her tears. That last thing she wanted now was for him to see her cry. "Of course I will. The whole time."

Dr. Esse sat on the stool beside him. In his ice-blue scrubs and surgical bonnet, he looked like a giant Smurf. "We're all set to go. Any questions?"

"What do you say, Marty? Are you ready?"

He nodded doubtfully.

The anesthetist cupped a mask over his nose and mouth. "Just breathe normally," he said over the hum of forced air.

As Marty breathed, his eyes widened in panic, but mercifully, seconds later, they shut, and his face relaxed.

Dr. Esse nodded to Phoebe, and the surgical team gathered around Marty. She stood with a feeling of dread, gave his calm face one last glance, and pushed open the swinging doors, handing over the life of her adopted son to a room full of strangers.

In the waiting room, Nate quietly read a comic book, but Maddy was pacing back and forth like an expectant father. As soon as Phoebe came through the doors, Maddy pounced on her.

"What did they say? Did they start?"

Her eyes had the same panicky look she'd seen in Marty's. And given the recent events in her life, Phoebe understood. If anything went wrong, God forbid, her entire family would be wiped out.

She put a hand on Maddy's shoulder. "Yes, they started. Everything's fine."

Maddy covered her mouth.

"Try to calm down. We could be here for hours."

Her report was either too curt or spoken too casually. Maddy's face colored and she fled down the hall.

Jake shrugged. "It doesn't matter what you say. She's been like that all morning."

"I can't blame her. Marty's all she has left."

"I guess she must see it that way."

"But the odds are in our favor."

"Yes, all we need now is the absence of bad luck."

Phoebe sat next to him and leaned on his shoulder. "I should take my own advice and calm down. The waiting will be awful."

It was. She picked at her fingernails, paced, and twisted her hair. She tried reading People magazine, but nothing sunk into her scattered mind. Talking with Nate or Jake required too much effort, and she missed half of what they said anyway. After a while, they all stopped talking. Nate paged through sports magazines with a weary air and finally walked down to the lunchroom. Half an hour later, Maddy reappeared, but she couldn't stay in her chair and left to pace the halls again. At the same time, she couldn't stand to be away for long, in case Dr. Esse came out with news, so she kept going and coming back. Now and then, Jake tried distracting her with questions, but she acted like he wasn't there, not saying a word and staring miserably at the floor.

Although moving in slow motion, the hands on the clock marched steadily forward, and Phoebe could hardly believe her eyes when Dr. Esse, still in scrubs, barged through the double swinging doors. She jumped to her feet and froze. Spotting her, he smiled and gave her a thumbs-up. After that, she barely heard a word he said, but it didn't really matter. The flick of his thumb had told her everything.

Half an hour later, they joined Marty in the recovery room. An IV was taped to his wrist, but his face was a healthy pink, and he was breathing evenly. When Phoebe sat beside him, his eyes half opened, but still under the grip of the anesthetic, he nodded off again without speaking.

Maddy smiled and kissed both his cheeks. She squeezed his hand over and over. As they gathered around Marty, Phoebe felt, if for only a minute, they were all brought closer together by the happy realization of this common, heartfelt wish.

Dr. Esse came by and went over the post-op instructions. Marty would spend the next 24 hours under observation. He would have an ultrasound in the morning to confirm the device hadn't shifted. If everything looked fine, as he expected it would, Marty could leave by noon. For a month, he would take antibiotics and a daily aspirin to prevent clotting, but after that could engage in any physical activity he chose—without any restrictions.

Marty soon emerged from his anesthetic fog. When Phoebe told him the operation had gone as planned, his grin cracked his face in two. "This spring I'm going out for 10 sports," he bragged.

"Okay, Superman, but you'd better start slow. Your body won't be used to it."

"You'll be amazed, Phoebe—you won't believe it."

She nodded and tried to keep the tears from coming. For a split second, she thought of picking up the phone and telling Zoe the good news, only to be stung by the folly of her wish. What a shame, Phoebe thought, that Zoe couldn't be here to see this day. How happy it would have made her. And how happy Marty would have been with his mother smiling down at him and covering him in kisses. Every time she imagined the scene, the tears welled up, and so she tried to block it from her mind. Because today should be a happy day, a day that looked forward into the future and not backward into the past. She didn't want Marty to cry over his mother, but to find joy in his newfound health and to bathe in the loving glow of the people around him, who, for the rest of his life, would be his only family.

85

After the operation, Phoebe kept up her habit of waking up at night, tiptoeing down the stairs, and checking on Marty. It never failed to comfort her to find him sleeping quietly in his bed. Many nights, she pulled up his blankets and covered his cold arms, and sometimes she stood beside him in the feeble light and watched him breathe.

Bringing these two children into her home hadn't been easy, but watching Marty while his chest rose and fell in the stillness of his room, she felt a bond with him that transcended her duty to her sister, and with every passing month he felt less like the nephew she'd been forced to raise and more like her own son.

After her late-night visits, she always slept soundly. And a good night's sleep was something that Phoebe needed badly. While the pain of losing Zoe had lessened, the demands of raising her children continued without relief. Every spare minute she was buying groceries, packing lunches, driving, filling out forms, checking with teachers, and hardest of all, trying to cope with the emotional ups and downs of three developing teenage minds.

While Marty was gradually adapting to his new life and Nate was getting used to sharing his mom and dad, Maddy continued to worry Phoebe. Although she got up each morning and went to school, she rarely spoke to anyone and hid for hours in her room, listening to her iPod, texting, and doing God-knows-what. She came down briefly for dinner, ignored every question they asked her, and after picking at her food with a scowl on her face, went back upstairs.

Phoebe learned from Maddy's teachers that Maddy had quit hanging out with her old circle of friends. When Phoebe asked her if she felt depressed, she denied being unhappy or in need of help, including medication, saying that even if she was depressed she would never take the same drugs that her mother had used to kill herself.

Phoebe had to admit that although Maddy seemed withdrawn, she never complained. In the morning, she always dressed promptly, ate her breakfast, and piled into the car without holding anyone up. She was getting *B*s and *C*s in school in spite of never studying. Her teachers had told Phoebe that Maddy was vastly underperforming—no surprise, given her situation—but they also said that she'd established that pattern long before her mother had died.

Late in March, Phoebe learned the true reason behind Maddy's puzzling behavior. She'd just finished her midnight check on Marty and, going back to bed, cracked open the door to Maddy's room. Maddy was lying motionless under her blankets, but tonight, for some reason, Phoebe tiptoed inside. As she neared the bed, the shape of the blankets made her freeze. She ran back to the door, switched on the light, and stared in disbelief at Maddy's pillow, where Marty's football was sporting a long black wig. She yanked the covers off to find a pair of pajamas stuffed with towels, matching the shape of Maddy's body.

Phoebe had fallen for the oldest trick in the book—the same trick that she and Zoe had used on their midnight romps down to the creek. In a flash, it became clear that Maddy had been pulling this stunt for months, which not only explained her fatigue, but also her getting up and trudging off to school without complaining. She didn't want them to know that she was up all night and paying off her sleep debt every day after school behind the locked door of her room.

"Jake, get up."

He squinted, half asleep. "What's the matter?"

"Maddy's gone."

"Shit." He threw back the covers and planted his feet on the carpet. "Did she run away?"

"I don't think so. But she's been sneaking out for weeks."

"Davis."

Phoebe nodded. "That explains why she never talks about him. I thought they'd broken up, but I guess not."

"Let's hope she's with him."

Phoebe slipped her feet into a pair of dirty jeans. "He must pick her up and bring her back in the morning."

Jake flicked on the light and rummaged through his clothes drawer. "That's pretty damn devious. Did you call her cell?"

"She won't answer. But I know that Davis lives in a house near the U."

"There are dozens of those."

"His car's a dead giveaway."

"You're right. I'd better tell the boys we're going."

He opened Marty's door, beaming a cone of light into his room. To his surprise, Marty was already sitting up in bed.

"Are you okay, Marty?"

"I heard the noise."

"Phoebe and I have to go look for Maddy. She snuck out."

Marty stared at him quietly. His rigid pose told him that he already knew. Jake sat on the bed and peered into his face, covered by shadows. "Do you know where she is?"

"I promised I wouldn't tell."

"Maddy shouldn't be out this late. It's not safe."

"I know. I should have said."

"What's going on?"

"When you fall asleep, she comes down and wakes me up. She goes out the patio door. After she leaves, I lock it up. She gives me her cell phone and calls me when she comes back, so I can let her in."

"How long has she been doing this?"

"Since we came here. I'm sorry, but she said if she couldn't go she'd kill herself."

Jake rubbed the back of his neck and thought. "It's not your fault, Marty. I understand why you did it, but you know you're not helping her."

Marty gave him a guilty look. "I guess not. I promise I won't do it again."

"Don't worry. Go back to sleep. But first give me her cell phone. It might help us find her."

86

They found Davis's number on Maddy's cell. Jake booted up his laptop, ran a reverse phone search, and located the address.

It was two a.m. when they parked by a decrepit Queen-Anne house on the east bank of the university. All the lights were out except for one—an upstairs window with a drawn curtain. Phoebe and Jake stepped into the cold, damp air and waddled around the house like penguins on a poorly shoveled path. Before banging on anybody's door at this hour, they had to be sure it was the right place. In the backyard, Jake waded through knee-deep snow and peered into the garage window. Amid the shadows, he made out Davis's red Lexus. "It's here," he called back to Phoebe.

They retraced their steps and rang the front bell. When no one came, they knocked on the door. The house remained dark. They kept on knocking for nearly a minute.

Finally, a light flicked on and the door swept back. Davis stood behind the screen, fully dressed, but alone.

Phoebe tried to keep her voice level. "Davis—is Maddy here?"

He shot Jake a nervous glance. Since Maddy had moved in, he hadn't stopped by the Andersons once. Apparently, his first and only visit had made a lasting impression on him. "No, she isn't."

"You're lying," Jake said.

Phoebe gave him a look that said, *Let me do the talking.*

"Do you know where she is?"

"She was here a minute ago. When she saw you, she ran out the back door. I was just going to find her."

"Can we come in and talk with you?"

Davis balked.

"We know Maddy's been coming here. Look, Davis, you know what she's been through. We're very worried about her. I'm not blaming you, but we need some answers. If you really care about her, you'll help us out."

He stared at their feet. "Yeah, I'm worried too. C'mon."

They followed him into the living room. He dragged his feet to a shabby chair and plopped himself down. Jake and Phoebe took in the beer cans and pizza boxes on the TV and coffee table, the woodwork fattened by countless coats of paint, the heavy-metal posters, the car and men's magazines, the hookah in the corner, and the incense oozing from the curtains and walls.

Jake took a pizza box off the couch so he and Phoebe could sit.

Davis glanced nervously around the room. His dark bangs covered one eye like a patch, and he clutched his knees with his hands. He looked different since Jake had last seen him—anxious and unsure. The arrogance was gone, although now and then his eyes still flickered with anger.

"I won't harp on this," Phoebe said in a businesslike tone, "but for starters, Maddy is 16, and a minor. You're, what—20? If you're having sex with Maddy, that's statutory rape. If you're buying her alcohol, you're corrupting a minor. The pot I can smell, and that could mean prison time. But I won't dwell on that, because Maddy's problems go much deeper. I think she's depressed, and she comes here looking for something she lost when her mother died. But let's face it, Davis, you're a kid yourself, and Maddy's problems are far too big for you to handle.

"So you have to stop. Maddy can't come here anymore. If you love her and you have to see her, fine. I won't interfere. I know she cares about you, and I would never take that away from her.

"But for better or worse, Jake and I are her parents now, and that means we have to know where she is and what she's doing. Maddy's very fragile, and to tell you the truth, I'm scared—" Phoebe stopped. She didn't dare express her greatest fear.

Davis brushed back his bangs and spoke softly. "After her mom died, she changed. She's always sad, and when she's not, she's angry. Sometimes she takes it out on me. After we fight, she gets drunk—really drunk."

Phoebe's stomach twisted. "You know her dad's an alcoholic."

"I always thought she was too young for that. I mean, how young can you be?"

"Davis, please be honest. Does she drink every night?"

"Most nights, yeah."

"Does she get drunk every night?"

"I try and distract her." He paused awkwardly. "That normally works."

Phoebe could easily guess the nature of the distracting. "Great—drowning her grief in alcohol and sex. How are we supposed to help her with that going on?"

He shrugged.

"You have to give her back, Davis. You're only making her worse. If you want to see her, come to our house. Visit whenever you want."

He stared coldly at Jake. "I was told I wasn't welcome there."

"Things are different now," Jake said. "As long as you don't sneak out with her, you can come over anytime."

He crossed his arms. "I'll think about it."

"If you want to see Maddy," Phoebe said, "you don't have a choice. I don't want to make this a legal matter. I'd rather have you on our side. What do you say?"

He thought for a second, weighing the threat behind the plea, then nodded. "All right. But she might not listen to me either."

Eyeing Davis, Phoebe got the idea that his relationship with Maddy had grown much more complicated than he'd ever planned.

"All you can do is try," she said. "Now let's go out and find her."

87

For the next hour, they searched the icy streets and alleys around the house, only to frighten a stray cat and make a few dogs bark. By now it was three a.m. Phoebe walked like a zombie, and her mind was just as blank. Jake was crabby; in just five hours, he had to give a presentation. Davis too was getting surly. Finally, he convinced Phoebe and Jake that Maddy wasn't far away—they even thought he knew where—and would reappear the minute they left, but he promised to drive her home as soon as she did. Convinced they were only keeping Maddy out in the cold, they climbed into their Explorer and headed back to Orchard Valley. They felt apprehensive leaving Maddy behind, but didn't know what else they could do.

The green glow of the dashboard lit Phoebe's face as the snowbanks glided by her window. "What are we going to do with her, Jake?"

"I'll be damned if I know."

"How do you keep someone that young from ruining her life? I feel like I'm talking to a block of wood. She's completely shut me out."

"I don't really get this girl thing. My brothers and I didn't always obey the rules, but we weren't that sneaky. If we got caught, we fessed up and took our lumps. Maddy lies and then runs off and does whatever she wants, even when she gets caught."

"She needs help, but how can we if she won't even talk to us?"

"I don't mean to sound cold, but we can't solve all her problems. We can give her a good home, but she's the only person who can put her life together."

Phoebe shook her head. "She can't do it by herself. She lost her mother. She has a drunken, deadbeat father, a family history of alcoholism, and she's living with—I hate to say it, Jake, but we're strangers. Look at what happened to Zoe. She came from a good family with lots of love and discipline. Maddy hasn't had any of that."

"She could end up in treatment before long."

Phoebe's face grew dark. "That's not my biggest fear. Some days I think she might not stick around."

"You mean run away?"

"No, I mean end up like Zoe."

Jake winced. He turned the wheel and steered down the exit ramp. "I hadn't thought of that."

"I don't know if I could survive it."

He reached over and pressed her hand. "Have some faith. We can wear her down. She's stubborn, but we can be stubborn too. We just have to get her through these next few years."

"Maybe you're right." Phoebe sighed. "I'm sorry I got you messed up in all this. I know it wasn't the life you signed up for."

"For better or worse—that's what I said."

"But you didn't know how worse it would be."

"To tell the truth, things were getting too quiet for me. Except for Maddy's problems, I like all the activity, and I really enjoy Marty. Nate likes him too."

Phoebe's heart swelled. "You've been so good to me, Jake. You always have. I couldn't do it without you. You know that, don't you?"

He smiled. "When I proposed, I said we'd be good for each other. And I was right—even though you didn't believe me."

"I was such a dummy. I wanted proof you could make me happy. It's funny now, because I thought it was me taking such a big risk, when really it was you."

"Everybody takes the same chance. I got lucky. In 20 years, I haven't met anyone who could have made me happier."

She wanted to tell him the same thing, but the words caught in her throat, and she could only gaze back at him, her eyes welling up, and nod.

Back at home, Jake tramped upstairs to catch a few hours of sleep before his presentation. Phoebe lay on the living room couch and covered herself with a quilt.

The sunlight pouring through the window woke her up. The second she opened her eyes, the memory of last night rushed in. She threw off the quilt and trotted up the stairs to check Maddy's room.

The door was ajar. She eased it open. Inside, as if she'd never left, Maddy lay under the covers, sleeping.

Phoebe stood over her for almost a minute, wondering what to do. Finally, she grabbed Maddy's arm and shook it.

Maddy opened her eyes and looked up at her. Her expression was tired but calm. Her eyes held no trace of guilt or fear. Phoebe kept staring at her.

"What?"

"It's 7:30. You're late for school."

She frowned at her alarm clock. "I don't feel good. Maybe I should stay home."

"If you don't feel well, that's your fault." Phoebe tugged open the blinds. A burst of sunlight filled the room. Maddy covered her eyes. "What the hell?"

She flipped on the overhead light. "Get up and get ready for school. And next time, we'll call the police." Not waiting for Maddy's response, she crossed the hall into her room, where Jake was already dressing. They both had long days ahead of them and had agreed to save the confrontation for after work.

Phoebe dropped Maddy and Marty off at school, picked up a latte at Caribou and sipped it as she sped down the highway. Without any warning, the traffic in front of her came to a dead halt. Deep in thought, she kept her foot on the gas for a second too long, and the backed-up line of cars came racing toward her windshield. In a panic, she slammed on the brakes, fishtailed her car, and screeched to a halt inches away from a black SUV. Her eyes jumped to the rearview mirror, but the van behind her braked aggressively and stopped a few feet back. She sighed in relief. *Get me through this day, God, that's all I ask. And then get me through tomorrow too.*

The traffic didn't move for a long time, and then it began to crawl. *No point in staying here.* She cranked the wheel, took the first exit ramp, and began winding through the city streets. It might add five or ten minutes to her commute, but it beat sitting on the freeway, fighting to keep awake.

At a red light, the back of a Ryder truck blocked her view. She tapped on the wheel and glanced left, where a mountain of snow took up half a parking lot. On her right, a strip mall hid behind a ridge of dirty snow. *March has to be the ugliest month of the year. I'd love to skip the whole damn thing.* Then a blue and white awning caught her eye, and her hands nearly flew off the wheel. There in the shop window, in red vinyl letters, cried out a column of foreign words: *moussaka, souvlaki, spanakopita, gyros, baklava. That's it,* she thought, as her trip to Mexico with Zoe leaped back into her mind. How stupid of her to not think of it sooner—for her own mental health, for Zoe, and for the sake of her troubled children, they would all go to Greece.

88

Getting to Greece in two short months proved a challenge. Neither Phoebe nor Jake had traveled abroad, and they barely knew where to begin. Their main concern was passports, which after Nine-eleven were taking months to get, but Phoebe crawled the Web and found a service to expedite their applications. Next were plane tickets with a complex schedule of flights to New York, Amsterdam, and finally, Athens. They bought CDs and travel books to pick hotels and places to visit, but their daily lives were so busy they had little time to study them. In the long run, friends and coworkers who'd been to Greece proved the most helpful, and after a flurry of transatlantic calls and lots of guesswork, they pieced together a 10-day plan.

On June 4, they lifted off the tarmac in the Twin Cites and landed at JFK just before midnight. Rechecking their bags and going through customs took longer than they expected, and they barely made their next flight; the agent closed the door behind them as they trundled down the jetway. At two a.m., their 747 climbed high above the Atlantic Ocean for its seven-hour journey. The children, although exhausted, couldn't fall asleep, unnerved by the vast, empty stretches of water, and near the end, they ran into storms. Every dip and bump terrified Maddy, and when the plane dropped without warning, she screamed. Phoebe did her best to calm her down. "Planes are built to handle this," she said. But she'd no sooner convinced Maddy that everything was fine when the pilot's voice crackled that bad weather was forcing them down in Shannon, Ireland, for an unplanned refueling, before they flew on to Amsterdam.

The sun was rising as they touched down in Shannon. Stuck inside the plane, they waited on the tarmac for two hours, trying but failing to fall asleep. They took off again at nine a.m., and five hours later, they lumbered off the jetway into Schiphol—hungry, groggy, cranky, thoroughly sick of airports and planes, and discouraged to know that a four-hour flight still remained between them and Athens. If this was vacation, Maddy grumbled, she'd rather be at home doing algebra.

When at last their 727 was poised over Athens, the city was dark. From the air, it looked like any other city, a checkerboard of black squares crisscrossed by roads that twinkled like Christmas lights.

Phoebe sighed in relief as the big engines roared to a halt and the plane taxied off the runway. They claimed their bags, stacked everything on a wobbly cart, and wheeled it out to the rental lot. Their red Fiat was so small that after stuffing the trunk and back seat with their bags, there was barely room for the Andersons. Marty had to sit on Maddy's lap, and Maddy and Nate were pressed so tightly together that neither one dared move, lest someone brush against a forbidden body part.

Finding their hotel among the tangled streets of Athens, filled with impatient drivers scornful of traffic laws, took an hour. On their route, they had two near misses, as Jake called them, or as Phoebe called them, near-death encounters. Jake seemed unfazed by the frantic pace of driving, but he did worry about the morning traffic when the number of cars would double or triple.

Twenty-four hours after leaving home, they checked into a family hotel a mile from the Acropolis. Famished, they dropped their bags in their rooms, walked a few blocks, and found a taverna. Phoebe ordered pork souvlaki, while Jake and the kids, leery of the strange-sounding dishes, ordered cheeseburgers. After the food was served, hardly anyone spoke. They ate like cattle chewing their cud, and all they could think of was going to sleep.

After dinner, they tromped back to their rooms and unpacked their bags. Phoebe and Maddy, who were sharing a room, ironed their clothes, while Jake and the boys went straight to bed. Phoebe threw on a camisole and crawled blissfully under the covers, while Maddy, happy to find she had phone service, began texting feverishly. Phoebe warned her not to stay up too late, rolled onto her side, clamped a pillow over her ears, and in minutes, was sleeping like a bear in the bowels of a cave.

Morning brought the sun, and with it, new energy, a thirst for adventure, and the promise of the Parthenon. Phoebe dressed quickly and dragged her family back to their taverna, but this time coaxed Jake and the kids into trying a few Greek foods, like *milopita* and oranges with honey, which, to her delight, they gobbled down as greedily as their waffles and bacon.

By ten o'clock, they parked at the foot of the Acropolis—Jake having found his way there without killing any Vespa drivers using the center stripe as a traffic lane—and as the sun gleamed off the limestone cliffs, they began their climb. Phoebe felt a thrill as she marched up the stone-cut steps leading to the flat-topped summit where the Parthenon and a score of smaller ruins towered over the city. Nate and Marty raced past the tourists, trying to be first to reach the top, while Maddy lagged behind, grumbling about the lack of elevators.

As they neared the summit, Phoebe stared into the cloudless sky, and her jaw dropped in disbelief. Ugly black scaffoldings covered the Propylaea and, beyond it, marred the majestic lines of the world's most impressive Wonder. The chalk-covered boards and rusted pipes not only spoiled the grandeur of the Parthenon, but made her feel like she was visiting a construction site. And the closer they got, the more it let her down. Many of the temple's columns had been dismantled, their segments scattered over the ground like paving blocks, while in the center, where the gold statue of Athena had once proudly stood, a tower crane rose up and desecrated the sky.

Jake could read her dismay. "It's a nice view up here," he said, staring down at the jumble of white buildings nearly blending with the rock below.

"But *this* should be the view," Phoebe said, pointing to a truncated pillar.

"Good grief," Jake grumbled. "Look at that."

Phoebe turned and stared in shock as a horde of tourists began pouring through the Propylaea. To her it seemed like Xerxes and the entire Persian army were charging up the steps to storm, loot, and burn the Parthenon a second time. "Where did they come from?"

"Over there," Jake said, pointing to four massive ferries floating in the harbor like alien spaceships.

Phoebe leaned against a pillar and shook her head. She might have known better. Jake had told her to not expect too much from this trip, but she hadn't listened. She couldn't help it. She'd even planned on doing the same things in Greece that Zoe had wanted to, but now that she was here, dancing in the Parthenon, half dismantled and swarming with tourists, seemed a farce, let alone flirting with men in front of her kids, and even more absurd, skinny dipping on a crowded public beach.

Her disappointment stuck with her the rest of the day. Little of what she saw—the ancient ruins, the white, armless statues, the grand museums—impressed her much. They passed by like dull prairie seen from a bus window. The sun was setting by the time they got back to their rooms, tired, sweaty, sunburned—and dining at their now familiar taverna, Phoebe needed two full glasses Chardonnay before she could be civil to her family again.

89

The next morning, they checked out of their hotel and drove for two hours down the west coast of Attica. The route cut through rocky hills dramatically dropping into sparkling blue and green inlets and bays. Orange and red poppies flowed like waterfalls down the hills, and high on the peaks, villas nestled amid lush gardens, olive groves, and tall, waving palms. Phoebe sighed as they escaped the noise and gridlock of Athens, and as they wound through the hills, her mood picked up. *At last, here's the real Greece. This is the beauty we came to see.*

Their destination was the village of Sounion, where the Temple of Poseidon stood high on a cliff overlooking the Aegean Sea. Phoebe had planned a hike from Sounion to the place where King Aegeus, thinking his son Theseus had been slain by the Minotaur, had thrown himself from the cliff into the steely blue water.

She also hoped to find the marble column where the poet Lord Byron had carved his name, something that Zoe had often talked about.

While the pilgrimage to Sounion meant something to Phoebe, it failed to impress her children. When they finally stood sweating on the sunbaked plain before the ruins, Nate grumbled, "We drove all this way for *that?*" Maddy stared at the crumbling white columns, sparse and crooked as an old woman's teeth, and complained, "Is that it? A bunch of crappy pillars?"

Phoebe wanted to let her know what seeing these crappy pillars would have meant to her mother, but knew that she couldn't without getting angry. And when she tried explaining the temple's storied past, Maddy repaid her with a sullen, bored stare.

Finding the Lord Byron carving briefly cheered Phoebe up, but for the rest of the family, the plainly cut letters could have spelled *boring*.

The plunge from the cliff down to the Sea held their interest longer, but only for a minute, and after hiking back to Sounion for a snack, they agreed to drive straight to Vouliagmeni, check into their new hotel, and spend the rest of the day relaxing on the beach.

They found their hotel perched high on a hill, overlooking a chain of islands in a vast blue Gulf. They wasted no time in putting on their suits, drove down a twisting road, and parked in a beachside lot. To the north unspooled a long ribbon of white sand, dotted by blue umbrellas and lapped by the bejeweled waters of the Aegean.

The beach was not very crowded. Jake, Marty, and Nate charged straight into the water and swam to a rocky tidal pool on a nearby point. Phoebe scouted out a seaside bar, ordered a margarita spiked with ouzo, and plopped herself into a beach chair. She hoped that Maddy would sit with her and let her explain why this trip would have meant so much to her mother, but Maddy had other ideas. Instead, she slipped off her cover-up, threw it over a chair, and strutted across the sand like a runway model.

Phoebe scrunched up her nose and watched Maddy glide. The second she'd bared her long legs and supple curves, covered only by the patches of her red bikini, a gunshot could have echoed down the beach. Phoebe could almost hear the necks cracking as every male in sight—young, middle-aged, old—turned their heads to stare at her.

She didn't get a hundred feet before the first man approached—dark skinned, handsome, and ten years her senior—smiling and talking without pause. Maddy smiled back, listened for a minute, and then moved on. The man smirked in defeat and melted back among his friends.

She'd no sooner sent him packing than a much older man took his place, paunchy and bald, with a gold chain around his neck. Phoebe could hardly keep herself from jumping up and scolding the man for trying to pick up a teenage girl, but she grit her teeth and stayed in her chair. Maybe he only wanted to make small talk with Maddy, or tell her she was pretty. *Then again, maybe not.*

On the other hand, it wasn't fair to entirely blame the men. Maddy could have easily passed for 21, and she carried herself with a confident, even worldly, air. *Better get used to it, Phoebe. It's going to happen on every beach you go to.*

She finished her first margarita as a parade of men hit on Maddy. She counted five in 20 minutes. Thankfully, Maddy dismissed them all quickly. *That damn Davis is finally coming in handy for something.*

Reassured by Maddy's aloofness, she went back to the bar and got a second margarita. She'd just sat down when a fresh suitor, a swarthy young man, swaggered up to Maddy, staring at her like a cat stalking a sparrow. At this rate, Phoebe thought, she wouldn't make it a hundred yards before they left for dinner.

The second margarita soon went to her head. With Maddy still close, and the boys exploring the tidal pool, Phoebe leaned back, soaked in the blue-green sea, and savored the hot sun on her skin and the breeze that carried it away. The view, the air, the ouzo tingling her tongue—in that moment everything was perfect, and she wondered, with a trace of guilt, if what she really needed wasn't more time spent with her family, but more time spent away from them.

Having slept poorly the night before, she closed her eyes and let the sun bake her lids, no longer caring, for a few blissful seconds, what Maddy or the boys or anyone else on the beach was doing ...

The next thing she knew, Jake was poking her arm. "Phoebe—where's Maddy?"

She sat up sleepily. "Over there."

But when she scanned the beach, Maddy was nowhere in sight.

"Did she go swimming?" Phoebe asked, squinting at the bobbing heads in the water.

"I would have seen her."

By now Phoebe was standing. "Her cover-up's gone. *Damn.* She left with that guy."

"What guy?"

"The guy she was talking to. Half the beach was trying to pick her up."

"What does he look like?"

A familiar feeling of dread gripped Phoebe's heart. "Jake, I have no idea who he is. She could be in trouble. For God's sake, we're in a foreign country."

"Don't panic. We'll ask around. Someone had to see them."

The beachgoers, however, gave them conflicting stories. The bartender claimed that Maddy had driven off with a man in a yellow Lamborghini. But the man with the gold chain swore that Maddy and a boy had strolled down the beach to a rocky wall. And they couldn't tell which account was true, because the Lamborghini had vanished from the lot and the beach near the rocky wall looked empty.

"We'd better split up," Phoebe said. "You take the car and look for that Lamborghini."

"I'm supposed to catch it with a Fiat?"

"Whatever you do, don't speed. I'll look around here. Someone said there's another beach beyond the rocks."

"Hidden from the prying eyes of world?"

"Or the parents, at least. Keep your cell phone out."

"What about the boys?"

"They'd better stay here, in case she comes back." She gave Marty and Nate a menacing look. "Don't you move an inch from this spot. Do you hear me? And keep your eyes peeled for Maddy."

"Can we swim?" Nate asked.

"If you want to be grounded for life."

He shook his head in disgust. "Girls," he muttered.

As Jake made for the parking lot, Phoebe threw on her cover-up, bent down and buckled her sandals, and started off for the rocky wall. *Here we go again. I can't believe that girl. Is it ever going to stop?*

90

Maddy walked the narrow trail beyond the hidden beach where Fotis had left her. She had no idea where it led, and, truthfully, she didn't care.

She had to admit the red bikini was a bad idea. She'd used the same trick to attract Davis, three years ago, at a resort near Putnam, and thought it would have the same effect on the right boy here, but things hadn't gone the way she hoped.

It had been a long time since she'd bared her body in public. Davis complained every time she wore tight-fitting clothes, worried about the way it affected other guys—meaning the same way it affected him. She'd never liked how men reacted to her body. It seemed to transform nice, thoughtful guys into cold-hearted creeps. And here, where the men were so pushy, the change had been scary.

At first she'd felt a thrill, basking in the freedom of her bare hips and thighs, the hot sand pushing between her toes, the sun baking her neck, and the breeze sweeping her locks across her back. But it didn't take long for the eyes to zero in. Most were friendly, but a few were alarming. Instead of admiring her, they seemed intent on taking something from her, and they didn't care if they hurt her in the process. Before long, she felt less like a swimsuit model and more like an antelope surrounded by lions.

The first man to approach her wasn't too bad. He was handsome and friendly, but his swagger gave away his self-doubt, and nothing he said could overcome it, because more than anyone else she'd always doubted herself, and so her boyfriends had to have self-confidence to balance her own lack of it.

He'd read her lack of interest, made his move too fast, knowing it would fail, and soon rejoined his friends.

The next man was too old, much too old. Middle-aged men were the worst. Did they really think she'd sleep with them because they had nice clothes, money, and cars? The faith they put in their money was sad, but all the same, men like that worried her. Money was power, including the power to cause you trouble. Luckily, most of the time she only had to hint that she wasn't impressed and they folded up like an empty wallet and left her alone.

The next man both angered and frightened her. *That's one nice piece of ass,* he muttered as he walked by. She felt relieved when he didn't stop. Crude language had never upset her, but it sounded more sinister coming from a forty-year old man instead of her peers. She held up her chin and tried to shrug off the remark, but it rolled around in her brain as she walked past the staring men. By now she felt sure they were all thinking the same thing, and her courage began to fail.

Just then, Fotis had come along. His friendly eyes had no trace of doubt, his smile seemed genuine, and her clumsy answers to his questions didn't confuse him or put him off. Guessing that she was too shy to talk about herself, he began telling her about growing up in Athens. She assumed that he was wealthy, but he didn't brag about his money, although he did seem overly proud of his *Lambor-whatsi,* which he kept wanting to show her. After she turned him down, he said they should climb the rocks to another beach where scores of red starfish roamed in the shallow waters. Wanting to escape Phoebe's stare as much as see the starfish, Maddy agreed.

They strolled along in the lapping waves until they reached a dirt path snaking up the rocks. They climbed it quickly and dropped down to a narrow strip of sand surrounded on three sides by stony bluffs. There was no one in sight, and Maddy felt nervous in a secluded spot with Fotis, who was staring at her now like the other men on the beach. There was no trace of the promised red starfish, and not a minute passed before he started pawing her. He gripped her hands and told her in a low voice how pretty she was. When he first spied her, he'd sworn that Aphrodite was coming out of the sea and walking toward him. Before Maddy knew it, his hands were tangled in her hair. He whispered something into her ear, but his English failed, and he fell back on his Greek. Then without warning he kissed her—not a soft, gentle kiss, but hard, wet, and greedy. Before she could pull back, he brushed his hands up her ribs and cupped her breasts.

She pushed him away.

"Maddy—no," he begged, grabbing her arms.

Something inside her broke, and she lashed out and clawed his arms like a frightened cat. She scratched deep and hard, leaving long streaks of blood.

He jumped back. "Are you crazy?" he shouted, staring in shock at his shredded arms. I should hit you, bitch!"

"Don't," she begged. "Leave me alone, please. That's all I want—just go away."

He shook his head, enraged. "I can't believe you. You're a crazy fucking bitch."

Maddy's heart beat like a galloping horse, but Fotis didn't strike her. In fact, he didn't speak another word. He turned around, strode across the sand, clambered up the trail, muttering to himself, and disappeared over the rocks.

She kept her eye on the trail for a long time, but he didn't return.

Alone, she gazed at the sea and wondered what to do. The last thing she wanted now was to go back the way she came. She couldn't stand to walk through that gauntlet of eyes again. And her aunt and uncle waiting beyond it were just as bad—pretending to be her mother and father—as if they had a right to. They couldn't come within a million miles. They could never, ever, be a shadow of her real mother and father. And worse, unforgivably, they'd taken Marty away from her, the only person left in the world who loved her. They'd won him over with their money and the operation for his heart, and now he no longer needed her. Just like everyone else in her life, he'd abandoned her the minute that something better had come along. No, she couldn't go back and face them again. That would be unbearable.

Battered by her feeling, she glanced around. Where the beach ended, a narrow path rose out the rocks and angled up a cliff. Without knowing why, she began to climb. As the path grew steeper, her mind teemed with troubling thoughts. She didn't know where the path would take her or what she would do when she got there.

It soon leveled off to a narrow sandy ledge. Below her, a cliff dropped thirty feet into the surf, studded with rocks jagged and sharp as a gator's teeth. She inched her way to the edge and stared down into the maw. The rocks leaped up at her, and a loud rushing noise filled her ears. Maddy's heart hammered. The shoreline spun. She tried to hold her ground, to steel herself, and look the monster in the eye, but it was too much, and she backed away.

What in God's name was she doing? Why had she crept so close to the edge? She broke into a sweat as she found the words for the impulse that had nearly overpowered her. How easy it would have been, if not to jump, to sway in the breeze or slip on the wet stone and vanish forever in the field of rocks below?

Fotis was right. You're a crazy fucking bitch.

But what other choice did she have? Stone walls hemmed her in, below her rose the siren call of the sea, and taking the trail, back to *those people*, and, finally, her tattered life back in Minnesota, was unthinkable. Even if Davis still loved her, which she doubted, he was helpless in the face of her pain. Her mother was dead, her father as good as dead, and Marty no longer needed her. Her aunt and uncle were always in her face, nagging, judging, punishing her. School was just as bad, maybe worse, with boys hounding her for dates while snickering about her breasts behind her back. *That's one nice piece of ass.* She couldn't trust her friends, the few she had, and her teachers either hated her or threw up their hands in despair, failing to see that she couldn't focus on the crap they put on the board because at this point in her life learning seemed so unimportant compared with the daily struggle of fighting back the urge that just seconds ago had driven her, trembling, to the edge of the abyss.

Was there really no way out? She was trapped by rocks, the sea below, and a trail that led back to hell. The impasse was a perfect symbol of her life—there was no place to go, no escape from her despair, and the odds for a happy ending were nonexistent. This had to be what her mother had felt before she'd taken those pills—that life had raised its daggers and driven them repeatedly into her heart. How could she blame her, now that she saw how lonely and pointless life could be—a thing only to be endured until some merciful blow ended the pain?

And if that was true, why wait? Sooner or later, the end would come—only once it did, she would be old, used up, and broken, just like her mother. Why suffer through all of that? Why march down that hellish trail when the final result would only be the same?

Would anybody even care? Probably not. No one loved her. No one needed her. In fact, the opposite was true. She'd become a burden to everyone around her. Maybe they'd all sigh in relief if she was gone, just one less problem for them to worry about.

She took a deep breath, clenched her fists until her knuckles turned white, and stepped back to the ledge. As she peered down into the rocks, her head began to float. She had the odd sensation of rising out of her body and staring down at herself teetering on the brink. She barely knew the face of the girl there, frozen in a mask of fear and grief—a face barely human, the face of a girl who'd lost her mind. *You're a crazy fucking bitch.* Nothing about herself, not her own body, not even her thoughts, seemed anchored in reality. Everything was slipping away into a murky, panic-filled chaos, a nightmare that she couldn't stand a second longer, and the only way to stop it was by taking that one final step off the cliff and forever slamming shut the door on the demons who without mercy or rest were tearing apart her soul.

91

Phoebe discovered the hidden beach without much trouble. The sandy trail, marked with two sets of footprints, guided her over the rocks, but on the other side, the tracks intermixed, as though dancing. The pattern made little sense, except that finally one set of prints went back the way it came. She was trying to figure out what that meant when the smaller set of prints appeared to head off toward a bluff. She followed them, and just when Phoebe thought she'd reached a dead end, a narrow path angled up a wall. She began to climb, gripping the chiseled rocks with her hands to pull herself up.

As she neared the top, breathing hard, Maddy's back and long dark hair came into view. She sighed in relief, clambered over the last rock, and stepped onto the sandy ledge. But there her relief switched to panic. Thirty feet away, Maddy was facing the sky with her toes hanging over a smooth, stony lip. Her fists were clenched, her arms were shaking, and her knees looked ready to buckle. The slightest breath of wind might tip her over the edge. Phoebe didn't need to see Maddy's face to know what she was thinking. In a flash, everything became clear. Every muscle in her body tensed. Her heart pounded against her ribs and pumped fear into her arms and legs. Before she knew it, she was sprinting. With her breath tightly held, she raced across the sand at a speed driven by terror. She thought she cried out, but also felt herself suppressing a cry, in case it startled Maddy. Everything—not just Maddy's life, but maybe her own too—depended on the next few seconds. Every muscle, every nerve, every cell in her body focused on Maddy, and as she flew along, the rest of the world fell back and disappeared.

Two steps away, she pulled up, hooked her left arm around Maddy's waist, and drove her butt down into the ground.

Maddy hit with a grunt. She planted her palms in the sand and gawked at Phoebe, who was kneeling before her, trembling.

The sudden shock unhinged Phoebe. She hugged Maddy, sobbing, and clung to her fiercely. "Don't do it, Maddy, please don't. I know you're unhappy, but things will get better, I promise they will. Don't give up. It's not the answer, can't you see?"

"I'm not sure what I was doing," Maddy said, still dazed.

"Don't lie to me. I know what you were doing."

"I think I had, I don't know—some kind of blackout."

"You were thinking about it, weren't you?"

"Maybe for a second."

"You had me so scared. My heart is still pounding. I couldn't take it if I lost you, Maddy. It would kill me. Don't you know that?"

Maddy's lower lip trembled. "I'm sorry. I'm a horrible person. I ruined everyone's life—and now I'm ruining yours."

"What do you mean? You haven't ruined anyone's life."

Now it was Maddy who broke down. "Yes I have," she choked out between sobs. "You don't know the truth. It was me—I killed her. It was all my fault."

"Maddy, that's crazy."

"No, I made her unhappy. I told her I hated her. I said she was old and stupid. I told her so many cruel things, I can't even say them. I never did what she asked me to. I didn't care if she was sad or scared. All I thought about was myself."

"Sooner or later, most teenagers talk like that to their parents. It doesn't mean you killed her. Deep down, she always knew you loved her. And I know you did too."

"No, you don't get it. It really was my fault."

"How?"

"That night I was out with Davis. When I got home, it was three o'clock. I saw the bottle and the mess on the table, but I didn't get it. I thought, *how pathetic—drowning your sorrow in booze, just like Dad.* And then I went to bed. I went to bed, Phoebe, and I fell asleep thinking my mother was a loser—while she was sitting under a tree, a block away, dying."

Phoebe cradled her. "Don't blame yourself, Maddy. How could you know?"

"I should have come home when she told me to. I could have stopped her."

"I don't believe that. When people make up their minds to hurt themselves, it's hard to stop them. Your mother had this strong, stubborn side. Everybody thought she was so easygoing, but once she made up her mind, that was it. Nothing could make her change."

Maddy stopped crying. "What do you mean *strong?* She wasn't *strong.* She was weak."

Phoebe shook her head. "I wish you could have known her when she was young, before her life fell apart. You would have been amazed. I was always jealous of her."

"You? Why?"

"Everybody loved your mother. She was funny and smart, and she could charm a leopard out of its spots. People fought to be around her."

"That's hard for me to imagine."

"You never got to see her at her best. When she was young, her beauty took your breath away. I know she quit taking care of herself, but in college I never dared to bring home a date. They always fell in love with her."

"That must have been tough."

"It was, but your mother always shot them down."

"Good for her."

"You're so wrong about her. She wasn't weak. When she was young, she was fearless. She was always the leader between us. If she wanted something, she wouldn't quit until she got it. And if she thought something was right, she wouldn't bend. She stuck to her guns. I could never do that, Maddy. I was too afraid to fight the crowd. I owe her so much. Every chance I took, I took because of her."

"You did?"

"Yes. I was weak, not Zoe. If not for her, I would have spent my life in a library like a dusty old book. I wouldn't have made friends, gotten married, changed careers—I would have been a bitter, lonely woman. Zoe showed me how to take chances. When we were kids, she used to make me. Back then, I hated it, but now I'm glad she did. She taught me that everything in life is a gamble. You can't be afraid of getting hurt, because sitting back and doing nothing is the biggest gamble of all."

"I'm glad you told me that. It makes me feel less sad about her—but I'm jealous I never saw that."

"I'm sorry too. It's not fair."

"What happened to her?"

"She had some bad luck. She made a couple of mistakes. That was all it took. Life can be unforgiving. You don't always get a second chance."

"But to kill yourself because you got divorced and lost your job?"

Phoebe sighed. "She wasn't as strong as I thought she was. Maybe I put her on a pedestal. She had so much I was jealous of. But she was depressed, and depressed people can't think clearly. They can't see what they have, or what they might get back some day. They only see what they've lost. It's like a door that locks out the good things and locks in the bad. After a while, you think that's all there is. The Zoe I grew up with never would have taken those pills, but her depression destroyed that person. She wasn't herself when she took her life. You have to remember that."

"I always wanted her to leave me alone, and now all I want is to have her back."

"I know. I miss her so much, sometimes my whole body aches. I still can't believe she's gone."

"Me too. And then I hate myself. I don't deserve to have a mother."

"What a terrible thing to say, Maddy. Don't think that. What about the good times? Things were better when you were young, weren't they?"

"I guess."

Maddy's words struck a long-forgotten chord in Phoebe. "Did you know that when you were little, I was your favorite?"

"You were?"

"You even told our friends you had two mommies."

Maddy shook her head. "I don't remember that."

"I know I can't replace her, Maddy, but I'll never leave you, I promise. And I'll be your mother as much as you want me to."

She barely got out the words when Maddy buckled. She sobbed uncontrollably and fell into Phoebe's arms.

"I'll do whatever I can, Maddy, both Jake and I will. We'll do our best to make you happy. As far as I'm concerned, you're my daughter now, and I'll treat you that way the rest of my life."

Maddy kept crying.

"You have to look beyond the present. We'll be together for a very long time—college, marriage, and maybe someday, kids—and I'll be there for you through it all. Maybe I'm selfish, but when you're older, I hope that we can be close friends, the way Zoe and I were. Am I crazy, or do you think that could happen?"

Maddy was crying too hard to answer. She squeezed Phoebe so tightly her ribs almost cracked.

Although moved by Maddy's tears, Phoebe had the presence of mind to make good use of them. "But you absolutely *have* to follow our rules. It can't work any other way, Maddy. We're not asking that much—but you have to listen to us, and you have to come home every night."

She pulled away and nodded. "I know, I know it's not right. It doesn't matter anymore. Davis and I are through."

"When did that happen?"

"When I get home I'm dumping him. After Mom died, he treated me differently—no, that's not right. He treated me the same way—like nothing had changed. He wanted me to act like it, too, and if I didn't, he was a jerk. That's when I knew he didn't love me."

Phoebe hid her relief and fought off the urge to pile more dirt on Davis. "That's a lot for a 20-year old to handle."

"But he's supposed to be the mature one."

Phoebe smiled. "That explains the red bikini."

"Yeah, well, he turned out to be a jerk too."

"I'm sorry, Maddy. Some guys are. Not all. "

"You were lucky you found a good one."

Reminded, she glanced over the rocks. By now Jake and the boys would be looking for them. "What do you say, Maddy. Do you feel like going back?"

"I guess so. I think I'm better now."

92

Phoebe led the way down the steep path. Coming down proved harder than going up, and her sandals kept slipping on the fine sand. Every now and then she glanced over her shoulder to check on Maddy, who managed the path more easily in her bare feet.

When Phoebe touched down on the hidden beach, she stopped and gazed at the setting sun—so incandescently orange it could boil the sea. Its rays fanned the low, feathery clouds with fire, spreading across the sky as the sun fell. The wind had died off, and the sea was calm as a quiet lake. The water at the edge of the beach was clear as a mountain stream. Phoebe could make out the pebbles in crisp detail as they ran down the shoal, growing smaller and finally blending with a hundred shades of blue. How wrong, she thought, that Zoe couldn't be here now, admiring the clear blue water and the fiery orange sky, the way she'd always dreamed of doing.

She turned around to point out the sun to Maddy, but there in her place a ghost was climbing down the rocks. The dark chestnut hair, the high cheekbones, the curious brown eyes—they all belonged to Zoe. The illusion was so convincing that Phoebe froze and stared at Maddy, speechless.

Maddy stopped. "What's wrong?"

Phoebe glanced back at the sea, hoping that Maddy would notice. Then without warning, the feeling hit. Here it was—the perfect chance. Even if Maddy didn't go along, she couldn't let it pass. If she stopped to think about it for a second more, the moment would slip away and never return again.

She gave Maddy a bashful look. Maddy stared back at her, confused.

Without a word, she dropped her cover-up onto the sand, kicked off her sandals, and splashed into the water. When it rose to her waist, she pulled down the straps of her one-piece, and when it rose to her breasts, she yanked down her suit and freed her legs. Naked, she breaststroked into the cool, limpid water without looking back.

Maddy covered her mouth and stifled a cry. When Phoebe turned, their eyes met, and Phoebe knew she understood.

She swam further out. The cold water gave her goosebumps, but she didn't mind. It washed away the day's sweat, dirt, and cares, slipping over and soothing every inch of her skin.

While her back was turned, Maddy untied her top, wiggled out of her bottom, and splashed into the water behind her.

When she caught up to Phoebe, she gave her a smile that shone like the setting sun. It was a happy smile, awakened, Phoebe hoped, by some early, fond memory of her mother, and she did her best to smile it back in spite of the tears that were flowing down her cheeks.

Putting on their suits, they stared awkwardly into the sand, embarrassed, but neither one regretting their act. After dressing, they climbed up and over the rocky wall. When Phoebe held out her hand to help Maddy off the last boulder, Maddy not only took it but kept it clasped.

Soon Jake came striding into view, with Marty and Nate trailing behind. His face was tense, but as he got closer, it softened. "Everything okay?"

"We're fine, Jake."

"I can see. Why is your hair all wet?"

She and Maddy traded glances. "We took a swim."

He smiled. "Zoe would've liked that."

"I just wish she could have been there."

He gazed up at the fiery sky. "Maybe she was. Sometimes I swear she's watching us. Like she's in the air or these old rocks."

Phoebe nodded. Now she felt it herself, as if Zoe were looking down from the bluff and giving them her blessing. She let out a sob and buried her face in Jake's chest. As he embraced her, Maddy rushed to her side, laid her head on her shoulder, and stroked her back.

The outburst was short-lived. "I'm all right," Phoebe said. "That's it. No more tears. We've had far too many tears."

Finally, they walked back with Maddy between them. Phoebe held one of Maddy's hands, and Jake took the other. Marty and Nate, who were busy skipping rocks, quit their game and ran ahead, splashing through the shallow water. Phoebe smiled at their lanky arms and legs, windblown hair, and sunburned skin. Watching them, she felt at last they were no longer two separate families forced together by tragedy, but a single family bound together by love, and as they sauntered down the beach, she vowed to keep them happy and safe with all the strength of her grateful heart.

www.ingramcontent.com/pod-product-compliance
Lightning Source LLC
Chambersburg PA
CBHW032138270626
47172CB00008B/221